"A well-researched ....
questions of family loyalty and broader ethics. The nuanced
depiction of a seemingly 'good' young man torn asunder by
conflicting beliefs is where this novel really sings."

- Kirkus Reviews

"Graydon's haunting, thought-provoking narrative makes for
an immersive, memorable and cinematic read."

- Andi Reiss, award-winning filmmaker

"A family drama which plays out across continents during and
after World War Two. A novel with real honesty and depth, a
great debut."

**- Iain MacGregor, author of *Checkpoint Charlie*,
renowned historian, and publishing director at Head of
Zeus.**

"A moving family story which draws you in, leaving you
wanting more. Well-crafted and intriguing."

- Jenny Towey, Anglo-German Family History Society

"Oskar Bachmann searches for answers about his violent
father, his story taking us deep into the dark years of National
Socialism and the Second World War. A life, accompanied
by entanglements and guilt as well as a deep love for books,
excitingly told right up to its surprising conclusion."

**- Dr Doris Müller-Toovey, Head of New Conception at
the Military History Museum Berlin-Gatow Airfield**

"A heart-told story which kept me bound to it right until the
last page and well beyond. *Leaving Fatherland* is beautiful,
combining a grand scale story with an intimate portrayal of
our human frailty."

**- Philippa Forrester, author and former *Tomorrow's
World* and *Robot Wars* presenter**

LEAVING
FATHERLAND

MATT GRAYDON

CRANTHORPE
—MILLNER—
PUBLISHERS

First published by Cranthorpe Millner Publishers (2024)

ISBN 978-1-80378-209-6 (Paperback)

www.cranthorpemillner.com

Cranthorpe Millner Publishers

Printed and bound by CPI Group (UK) Ltd
Croydon, CR0 4YY

ABOUT THE AUTHOR

Matt Graydon has always written stories, first as a schoolboy, then as a journalist and PR. Now, in the culmination of his life's work, he has become a writer of striking historical fiction. He loves to explore offbeat perspectives, inspired by true stories, especially in his tales of life in wartime—*Leaving Fatherland*, his first novel, is a great example of this. In his spare time, Matt is a keen astronomer and astrophotographer and loves experiencing live music. He lives with his wife, two adult children and a mischievous cockapoo in Surrey, spending as much time as possible in the countryside he loves.

Dedicated to my beloved mother and father, and to all those who fought wars they did not want to.

ACKNOWLEDGEMENTS

I thank my German cousins for their kind assistance in researching the parts of this novel inspired by the life of their father, Werner Doehr; my wife and children for allowing me the inordinate amount of time spent researching, writing, and refining this novel; and all those who have helped me in my writing journey. Thanks also to Laura Hallett for creating 'The Map of Leaving Fatherland'.

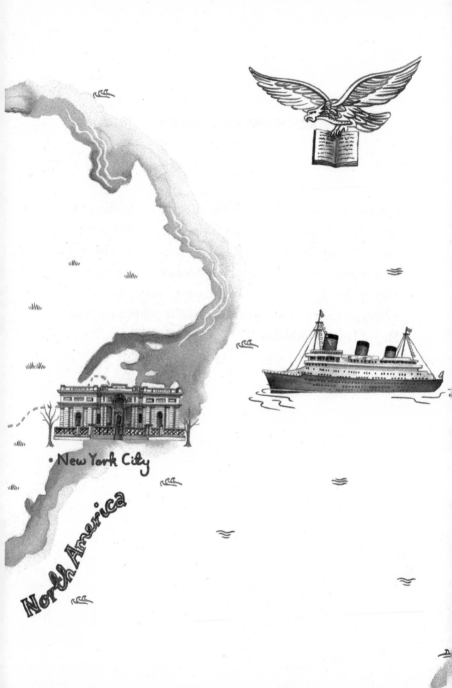

New York City

North America

1

CRUSHED

Ilse Valley, Germany
February 1928

Eating in front of Papa had always made me nervous. It often made him mad, so mad that he would curse out loud and slap me across the face. Sometimes it seemed he wanted to kill me. He hated the sound of it, you see. An often-congested nose meant I struggled to keep my mouth shut as I chewed. Despite my hunger, those salty pretzels Mama had packed for me would have to wait. Papa had beaten me for years. I had thought it was his way of showing me love. Punishment could be love, I'd thought, although I wasn't so sure now I was older.

Gazing up, we stood side by side watching Papa's pride and joy, a Stahlwerk Mark III model plane, soar across the cold, clear skies of the Harz. Glancing across at him, I noticed how big the bald spot on the back of his head had become. I matched him for height now. He did not like that either.

Flying model aeroplanes was the only time I connected with Papa. I loved aeroplanes, and so did he. Mostly, we had nothing in common. He seldom spoke to me, other than about politics and how Adolf Hitler would make the country great again, if only the Communists could be defeated. He often

1

quoted from Hitler's speech at the Nuremberg Rally. Papa thought Germany was too small for its population too. Gazing from the window of the Deutsche Reichsbahn-Gesellschaft passenger locomotive on our long journey here, it had seemed obvious to me there was more than enough space for everyone.

Papa often got angry about the smallest things, sometimes about nothing at all. I remembered reading to him once, in the early spring, when it was warm enough to wear knee pants. Mama had given me a newly published book, *Bambi, A Life in the Woods*, as a Christmas present. I sat on Papa's lap to read, the familiar smell on his breath hanging around my head. He fidgeted in the chair beneath me, muttering unfamiliar words. Then, as I whispered of Bambi snuggling up to the 'comforting presence' of his mother in the woods, the manly force of Papa's arms and legs threw me from my resting place. Ejected like a sick chick thrown from its nest, my baby teeth crashed into the stone hearth, leaving blood and enamel upon it.

Mama told me something happened to Papa during the Great War. He had never been the same since. I did not understand, as this version was the only father I had ever known. I still admired him though and thought there must have been some way I could change him. After all, he liked my brother Emil well enough.

I held my breath captive in my chest as the Stahlwerk's wings shaved through the canopy of a nearby Ilse Valley pine, sending needles raining down like miniature arrows. Papa glared at me, his thick eyebrows pulled down, nostrils flared. I trembled, praying no harm had come to the plane. He found reason to punish me every week. Something I had said, the way I had looked at him, or just because he felt like it. This time, I could release my steamy breath long and steady, as our 'knight of the sky' veered hard right, swooping back safely towards us in a seamless arc and landing on the makeshift runway.

We had flown in many locations around the Spreewald since he introduced me to our shared hobby. Strange he had brought me here, so far from our home in Halbe, just south of Berlin, but it felt like an honour. I worried though. Papa seldom had spare money, and the train tickets and our chalet must have cost many Marks.

The Ilse Valley had a deep carpet of frost, and icicles hung like swords from the trees, products of the coldest February in a decade. The river gurgled through the centre of a dense woodland that covered the primary valley, carrying frying pan-sized sheets of ice that bumped and ground together, accumulating like morning trams in Potsdamer Platz. We had passed an old derelict warehouse on our way here, part of an old copper mine, according to Papa.

Papa knew an ideal spot to fly, in a perfectly flat basin. After working for weeks on the Stahlwerk—a gift from Papa's old research partner—I prayed it flew well. We had twice launched it this afternoon, carefully monitoring its flight paths as it glided through the darkening sky. Papa strode towards it, eager to make use of the remaining time. Holding it aloft, he rotated it in his stubby fingers, examining every part.

"You're lucky. Any lower, that pine would've taken the wings clean off."

As he moved it back to the take-off position, I reached for my handkerchief and blew my nose clear. Cautiously crouching beside him, my legs twitched as he took a petrol canister and fuel pump from his rucksack.

"Take this."

Savouring the smell, I held the tiny pump and attached it to the canister. To save my own skin from punishment, I had long since mastered the technique. Disconnecting the fuel line from the engine and joining the tubes together, Papa turned the handle until the kerosene crept up the exhaust line. I watched him carefully adjust the ailerons and elevators, preparing for a high-elevation flight.

Papa stood quietly in thought for a moment, then looked me in the eye.

"Did you know I flew reconnaissance missions over Belgium in the Great War, in an Albatros C.VII?"

I bounced from one foot to the other, excited in the knowledge that Papa had been a real pilot, and even more thrilled he had told me first rather than my brother.

"That's incredible, Papa! The C.VII was an enormous improvement on the C.V. They did away with the Mercedes eight cylinder and refined the control surfaces. I read it—"

He cut me short, raising his voice to a boom.

"You sound so pretentious. Why do you always over-elaborate? Too much time with your head in books."

My heart shrank. I had read extensively about our Great War air fleet and could not help talking about it. I had to do *something* with my knowledge.

"Sorry, Papa. What was it like to fly?"

The corners of his mouth flickered upward for a moment before he returned his focus to the Stahlwerk.

"We should get this in the air while we can."

As the light of afternoon faded, Papa stooped to study the plane up close, examining wings and tail once more, before stepping away and turning to me. He smiled, a smile I had seen too many times, broad, lips tight at the corners, his eyes pointing at the stationary Stahlwerk.

"Always remember: lift, thrust, drag, and weight. Your turn."

He had told me many times about the four features of flight, as if they held some mystical importance for him. This time, his words carried more challenge than invitation. I could not let him down. My frozen hands gripped the tail, or empennage as I should call it, as Papa positioned the propellor at two o'clock and pushed down. The engine whizzed to life, lurching forward. I ran a few steps to help it on its way but pushed too hard, making it take off unevenly. It headed up steeply and to the left. I froze, holding my stomach tight, as it careered out of control, but it caught a breeze and corrected, sweeping back low across the grass. Rather than land, it swept across into the woods at the end of the valley and momentarily out of sight. I sensed, more than spotted, a murder of hooded crows sweeping across the sky and down into the trees. They showed me where the Stahlwerk sat, trapped high between tree trunk and branch or, worse, smashed to smithereens on the ground.

"I'm sure it came down near that tall tree, Papa. Where the crows are."

"I didn't see any crows. Run. Find it, boy. It will be dark soon."

I shook off my coat and removed my bow tie. I had worn one every day since Mama told me it made me look like Mark Twain, whose dusty books I borrowed from the community library near the Kaiser Bahnhof. Running breathlessly across the icy valley, I slipped on a hidden frozen pool, twisting my ankle. Letting out a shriek of pain, I slowed as I reached the trees, peering back towards Papa. From here, he appeared tiny, insignificant.

My first obstacle was the dense and entwined branches at the edge. They resisted me, withholding their secrets. Moving with a breaststroke motion, I made slow progress, trying to keep the weight off my left ankle. Peering up through the trees, I could see the first pinpricks of starlight dotted across the sky.

As I struggled into an open clearing, an elevated spruce beckoned from a hundred metres away. I knew our plane was nestled near its bottom. My thin arms were tiring from their battle with the dense undergrowth, and I considered defeat. But the thought of Papa's wrath at my giving up, and the rapidly descending cloak of dark, spurred me on.

I clenched my jaw down hard. My teeth ached, legs moving independently of my brain now, as I clambered over a maze of roots and rounded flint stones into clearer space. Startled by a shuffling movement in the trees ahead, I stopped again, landing in a deep, boggy pool, its freezing-cold water rising over my ankle-high boots and soaking my woollen socks. The spruce had disappeared. To my right, the open ground of the valley. Why was it not on my left? At the end of the deep basin, the sharp line of the hill eclipsed the sun, leaving a mean sliver of light to keep me illuminated. I had to find my father. Limping through a short avenue of trees, I was sure he would be standing there, waiting for me.

My heart pounded hard in my chest, meeting the whisper of the trees in my ears as the wind revealed its power.

"Papa! Papa! Where are you?"

My whimper was lost to nature. Gazing into the valley, the remaining rays of sunlight lit a nearby outcrop of rocks. Someone sat there, I was sure of it. Had Papa tired and looked for shelter from the wind? As I neared, my heart sank. A pair of stacked rocks and my imagination had created a human form. I shook uncontrollably. My chances of navigating a route back to our hut on my own were negligible. I could not even escape the woods.

Then a sound, a murmur of humanity. Quiet at first, steadily louder, fighting the wind. The voice, unmistakably Papa's, crept closer. I spun around, desperately scanning the valley. No sign. His voice rang out again. Louder still. I looked over to the woods and right, across the grass of the valley. Still nothing.

"Oskar! Behind you."

There, on top of the rocks, stood Papa, holding the Stahlwerk triumphantly above his head, his face as dark and unforgiving as the granite behind him. The crash had left its propellors bent out of shape, its right wing partly detached. He jumped to the ground, waiting. I felt weak, tears welling behind my eyelids, and staggered towards him, longing for his embrace. But he stood rigid, like Berolina, the iconic Alexanderplatz statue he had been furious they removed last year to build the U5 U-Bahn line in the capital.

"I'm sorry, Papa. I got lost in the woods."

"This was a test and you failed it, as you always do."

I hung my head, crushed, unsure how to reply.

"You must learn to navigate. Emil learned orienteering in the Hitler Youth. We'll speak to your mother about this."

I nodded, swallowing hard. Cheeks burning, fighting back my tears.

"Germany will have a great air force one day. When you're old enough, you'll fly real aeroplanes. Do you think you could do it?"

We stood in a vast open space, and yet I felt trapped, cornered. So, I just nodded and gave a half-hearted answer.

"I'll do my best, Papa."

He handed me my jacket and shook his head, tutting. Reaching into his worn leather rucksack, he pulled out a long silver torch, pressing the rubber button on its handle, shooting out a wide, powerful beam of light, like a limelight on a theatre stage. A startled crow, perched on the rocks, let out a screech and flew away towards the trees.

"Let's start back. When we get home to Halbe, you'll join the Jungvolk."

I nodded, desperately thinking of ways to avoid this fate. Papa, despite his short legs, moved at a pace that almost tipped me into a painful jog. Freezing air stung my eyes and throat. Having cleared the grassy stretch of the valley, we started up the hill, struggling to find firm footing on the rock-laden path.

"How's our plane, Papa? Is it ruined?"

He ignored my question, walking even faster. How could he not have seen my hurt ankle?

"Keep up. If we maintain this speed, we'll be there in under an hour. Take the plane. I need a spare hand."

He pushed the Stahlwerk in my hand for me to carry. Such was its length, I had to hold it with both hands at the base of the wings, to keep the tail from dragging on the ground. After a long climb, I fell at least thirty metres behind Papa. The path

8

before me darkened now as the moon and stars became cloaked in blue-grey clouds.

I reached the brow of the hill breathless, my legs weary. He had stopped on a narrow log bench, his head steaming a little as he took sips from his hip flask. I sat beside him just as he broke a hand-sized piece of gingerbread into an uneven two. He handed me the smaller piece and stared silently ahead into the distance, as if the hills and trees were visible through the darkness. Snowflakes landed on my eyelashes like comforting licks from Ralf, our Leonberger puppy. Papa switched his torch back on and shone it across the valley, illuminating the myriad of snowflakes, which seemed to collide and transform as they fell.

"Weather's coming in. We must hurry."

He huffed, flicking his snow-capped head upwards, covering his shoulders like dandruff, and marched away, swigging from his flask. Remembering the pretzels, I reached into my coat pocket. He could not hear me from here and eating them would distract me from the throb of my ankle. I delighted in pushing three or four at a time in my mouth, crunching down on them with abandon. I could hear Papa mutter criticisms of me and Mama out loud, so blocked out my feelings, focusing my attention on the half-moon above. Calling out loud the names of the visible lunar seas, craters and basins—"Mare Imbrium, Oceanus Procellarum and Mare Nubium"—I grinned as the half-eaten pretzel debris sprung from my mouth.

We reached our hut weary and frost nipped. The rustic cabin looked trapped and heavy, weighed down by a thick layer of snow. It reminded me of Mama's iced Christmas cake. I

9

reached up, knocking down a row of icicles hanging from the gutter near the front door and hurling icy javelins through the air, my hands red, raw and numb. Cupping them together, I blew warm breath inside as Papa found the door key, opening the lock with a single turn.

Stamping our feet in unison—the cold had seemed to numb my injury—we stepped inside. Papa struck a match, holding it to the wick of an old, rusty paraffin lamp. The steady flame illuminated old rowing oars, milk churns and climbing gear on the walls, creating dancing shadows as the warm light flooded around them.

While Papa spent time opening the door of each room and checking inside, I slouched down on the sofa, pulling a blanket across my legs, struggling to untie the laces of my boots with stiffened fingers. I hoped he might help, but he moved to load the wood burner with logs from the basket on the hearth and tidied the crocheted cushions on each chair. As the burner crackled and hissed to life, I set about assessing the damage to our plane and how I could fix it.

Papa sat on the chair opposite me, rubbing his thighs furiously.

"Don't just sit there. Make yourself useful. There's a metal jug out back with milk in it. Check if there's any cocoa in the kitchen. I need a warm drink."

Taking a candle from the small dresser and lighting it, I opened the door from the main living room and stepped into a small wooden-framed lean-to. Ice made patterns on the inside of the windows and the candle almost extinguished in the chill air. In the far right-hand corner, a rough wooden shelf hung from the ceiling joist on two thin pieces of rope. On it, a block

10

of butter on an old, chipped china plate and a blue and white metal jug full of milk. I wondered how Papa knew it would be there. We hadn't come into the cabin earlier, other than to drop a bag inside the front door.

Being careful not to spill any milk, I trudged back into the living room, where Papa was combing his hair in the mirror above the burner.

"I found the milk, Papa. I'll make the drinks now."

"Oskar. Come here."

I hesitated, checking his face for signs of anger, before balancing the milk on the dresser and turning to face him.

"Yes, sir?"

He sat rigid, brow lowered, his head down as he scoured a set of papers. Without looking up, he spoke.

"You know the research work I'm involved in is very important. Not just to me, but to Germany too."

I nodded, unsure of what he meant.

"Yes, Papa."

"In half an hour, a friend of mine will arrive. They're involved in similar research work at a nearby centre—the Borchers' factory in Goslar."

"Okay, Papa. I look forward to meeting him."

"It's her, Oskar. Best you get to bed when you've had your drink. You must be tired."

His sugary words deflated me. Rather than chat about our day in the mountains, he would entertain someone else. All at once, I felt like an outsider.

Hunched over the jug, I headed to the kitchen, trawling between old cans of tinned fish and soup to find a small tin of cocoa at the back of the cupboard. Warming the milk in a

11

pan on the tiny kitchen stove, I prised open the cocoa tin with a knife and peered inside: less than a spoonful. Filling the cups with warm milk, with no hesitation I tipped all of the cocoa into one of them.

Papa was warming his feet when I returned. I plonked the cup down beside him.

"Here you are."

He peered in, twisting his mouth.

"No cocoa?"

"None left. I'm going to bed. Goodnight."

My room was basic. Just a small iron bed. Putting on my pyjamas, I climbed onto it and under the covers. By its side was a table onto which I put my candle, reaching inside my rucksack and opening *Der Steppenwolf*, which I had borrowed from Mama. She encouraged me to read and learn at every opportunity. At this very moment, I missed her so. Fanning the pages, as I always did, the book released an old, deckled-edge photograph from its captivity.

Squinting in the flickering light, I held it close to my eyes, studying the faces in the image. Nine people—four men, five women—all well dressed, standing in what looked like a hotel lobby. The woman at the end of the group, although younger, was undoubtedly Mama. It fascinated me to see her so young and pretty. So happy, without Papa. I closed my eyes to think of her and drifted to sleep.

*

A fizzing female voice woke me. I pulled the sheets and itchy woollen blankets around my ears, simultaneously wanting and

12

not wanting to hear the detail of the conversation she began with Papa. I waited a while, so as not to appear an intrusion, and contemplated the right time to introduce myself. In the end, my bladder decided for me. Shuffling towards the thin, three-quarter door, I put my ear against it. Silence. Grabbing a blanket from the bed with one hand, I shaped the other to knock on the door, but that was ridiculous. Instead, I cleared my throat, slowly turning the door handle to find Papa and his friend sitting next to each other on the sofa.

Papa shuffled in his seat.

"Oskar, what are you doing?"

"I need to use the toilet."

He nodded, tipping his head in the direction of the bathroom, before glancing towards his companion.

"This is Maria. My colleague. Be quick. Get back to bed."

She leaned back on the couch, looking at me dismissively as I wrapped the blanket around my shoulders, her thin lips sealed. I had imagined, and dreaded, seeing someone glamorous. She would wear an elegant dress and city shoes, wavy hair swept off her face, all lipstick smiles and giggles. But this middle-aged woman was dour. Dark, straight hair, glasses. She wore flat shoes and what looked like a laboratory coat. Despite the dim light, the small swastika pin on her lapel was unmistakable.

I nodded, heading for the bathroom, cheeks hot, jaw clenched. Struggling to shut the door without pressing up against the little sink on the wall, I wondered how Papa, with his brandy barrel-sized torso, would fit in here. Tying a knot in the blanket so that it hung around my neck like a cloak, I undid my pyjama trousers and relieved myself.

I made my way back to bed and lay curled up like a baby, rocking forward and back, as I always did before sleep. Lying awake, I strained to hear the detail of Papa's conversation. Would she stay the night here? Who was she? Had Mama met her? Would Papa spend the day with me tomorrow or put me on the train home alone? As tiredness dulled my present mind, I fell into a sleep, dreaming of Mother.

The sound of a door shutting brought me back sharply to a breathless state of consciousness. I struggled to remember where I was, my eyes blearily searching every corner of the room for clues. The sudden scream of a lynx outside my window reminded me of my mountain location. Then, the sound of an automobile engine starting.

Gathering my blanket, I swung my legs off the bed, weak with shock and a lack of food. I paused, listening for a sign of Papa. The floor was freezing cold. I grabbed the thick, woollen socks from my bed, pulling them on before opening the door into the living room. It was eerily quiet and pitch black, other than a faint orange glow from the wood burner's embers. Papa's bedroom door was ajar. I peered inside, praying he was in there alone on the bed, but the room was empty, the bed perfectly made up. Blood pulsated in my ears as I flung myself down, burying my face in the musty covers, forgetting how to breathe.

"Papa!"

My feeble cry had no one to hear it. He had deserted me.

I stumbled towards the front door, wiping tears on my pyjama sleeve and spotting a piece of paper lying on a small heart-shaped table under the window. It had Papa's handwriting on it. Picking it up, my sleep-filled eyes danced over the words, scrawled in large and untidy inky capital letters:

GONE TO GOSLAR RESEARCH CENTRE IN FRAU DURCHDENWALD'S AUTOMOBILE TO CONDUCT URGENT WORK. BACK BEFORE DAWN. FATHER

Light-headed, I sagged against the door, consoling myself that at least he had written me a note.

2
FAMILY

Halbe
1930

I stood mesmerised, watching Papa from the top of the basement stairs. Above the workbench, his powerful frame twisted and turned like a factory machine. A half-empty bottle of vodka sat open on the side. My heart sank as he reached for it. I considered turning to leave, but rather than swig from it, he tipped its contents on a rag, using it to clean the exposed metal parts of a model aeroplane engine. As he buffed the carburettor cuff, forcing a thin edge between the cooling fins, I gazed on silently, fascinated. It had been almost two years since Papa told me he had flown a plane in the Great War. Despite several attempts, I could not get him to tell me any more.

Plucking up courage, I moved gradually down the stairs, not too loudly as to disturb his work, or too quietly to appear evasive. He turned as I reached the bottom step, a glaze of perspiration on his forehead.

"Do you need any help, Papa?"

Turning back to his work, he dismissed my offer.

"No. I'm nearly done here."

"Okay. My headteacher has asked for volunteers to give speeches at school. I thought it would be so good to talk about what you did in the war, as a pi—"

Without turning to face me, he interrupted.

"I do not think it would be good, Oskar. You will not make a good public speaker."

His voice was calm, even.

"If you would tell me a few things, I could work on that, Papa, do my own reading and research. I can practice my speech with Mother."

He cleared his throat loudly, rubbing the aeroplane fins ever faster.

"I've already read about the Fokker Eindecker, our first purpose-built fighter plane."

Suddenly, he pounded his fist on the bench, turning abruptly, pointing his fat finger straight at me, eyes bulging.

"You know your trouble, Oskar? You ask too many questions. How many times have you asked me about the war?"

"I don't know, Papa. I'm sorry. I won't ask again."

"Look at you. You're weak. Gangly, no muscle. You need physical training, not more reading. You must join the Hitler Youth, like your brother."

I wanted to say that Mother had told me I must never join. But it would put her at risk, so I remained silent and gave a half-hearted nod, before bowing my head.

He moved quickly towards me, pulling his arm back. I turned my head and ducked in defence, but his pumpernickel-heavy fist slammed into the base of my skull, briefly stopping blood flow to my brain, which seemed to vibrate for a few seconds before swelling to fill my skull.

I glanced at him through a flurry of stars blurring my vision. The usual sight of him fiddling with the silver signet ring on his left hand, as his temples bulged, emerged. He was shaping up to hit me again. Reaching for my face, it felt numb. I raised my hands, pleading with him.

"You've hurt me, Papa. Please st—"

His left fist buried itself so deep in my guts, punching a hole between my stomach and liver, I was sure it had touched my spine. I slouched, a high-pitched whine escaping my mouth as my lungs shrunk, forced upwards, making me struggle to suck in a mouthful of damp air. My mind searched for a provocation, any reason I had given him to hit me, but I could find none. Why did he beat me like this, but never my brother?

Despite his violence, I still wanted to rise and approach him, reason with him, understand what he was thinking, but all I could do was shake. He shoved me to the ground with both hands, the worn leather of his boot scuffing my head before flying off as he kicked at me on my way down.

Fury spent, he turned away, leaving me slumped in the corner of the basement. He re-lit a half-smoked cigarette with a quivering hand as a stilted sob left my lips. Behind him, candlelight from a rusty sconce illuminated the cloud of smoke, reminding me of a Spreewald lightning bug in the morning mist.

Pulling down the sleeves of his heavy-knit woollen shirt over his badly scarred wrists and knuckles, he whispered as he returned the boot to his foot, making the sign of the cross.

As it always did after a beating, Papa's tone lurched between that of a Sunday preacher and a boy petting his cat.

"You never learn. All you need to do is say, 'Yes, sir.' Is that too hard for you? I've tried so hard to make you understand. I'm going out."

He rose, climbing the creaking wooden staircase to the kitchen. Chin tucked into his fat chest, he glanced guiltily at me from rust-coloured eyes, then slammed the door shut.

I breathed steadily, motionless for a while, aware only of the pungent mix of mould, oil and tobacco smoke. It mixed with the faint smell of beeswax emanating from the leather razor strop hung a metre above me. He had used that many times to beat my backside before he began to use his fists. My body was present, aching from the beating, shivering against the cold and damp, as moisture from the walls seeped into my shirt. My mind detached, lost at sea, images of a floating Thermos flask and Ishtar's frozen ship flashing across my consciousness. Eyes still closed, I started a hopeful incantation under my breath.

Then, the sound of the door above me nudging open, scraping across the floor, brought me back to the present. Instinctively, I pulled my head in close to my knees. Quiet footsteps descended the stairs, shuffling across the basement floor towards me. I clenched every muscle in my body taut, my breathing speeding and deepening. Then a small, warm hand dug a space between my head and forearms and cupped my cheek. As I dared to peer up, Mama gently pushed strands of hair from my forehead.

"Oh, my dear boy."

Opening my eyes, I gazed up at the hazy outline of her face.

"Mama. I must have fallen, hit my head. It's a little dark down here."

She pulled me up from the ground, her wiry arms strong from housework.

"You should know, by now, not to lie to me. Your father was here, wasn't he? Are you hurt?"

She tilted my head this way and that, her warm, chocolate-brown eyes meticulously searching every centimetre of my head and face for signs of injury. Still, her brow wrinkled, her eyes focused on a stinging patch where my fair hair met my forehead at its roots. She kissed me there, a little spot of blood showing on her lip as she lifted my chin, so our eyes met.

"You've a nasty graze. Does it hurt anywhere else?"

I thought for a moment, messages from around my battered body travelling to my brain, which still worked despite the blows it had received. My guts ached, the back of my head and the bottom of my back, where I had fallen down. Mama had seen worse on many occasions, but I sensed she might cry.

"No, I'm fine."

She did not believe me.

"Tell me what happened."

I shook my head. Her face tightened, eyes peering down for a moment, moving slowly upwards, surveying my tall but still boyish frame from toe to head.

"He won't be able to do this to you much longer, Oskar."

I put my hands on Mama's shoulders, salty water like that of the sea filling my eyes.

"Mama, it scared me this time. He hit me so hard, I nearly blacked out."

"Ssshhhh. You're safe now. I will speak to him."

"No, please don't. It will anger him. I hate Halbe, Mama. When I'm old enough, I'm going to travel away from here to study. What do you call the study of the human mind?"

She appeared surprised by my question.

"Psychology. Why?"

"I think I would like to study it, when I'm older."

She raised her eyebrows and nodded. I would not tell her that I hoped to use this study to better understand my father. Moving away from her, I picked up Papa's model plane, noticing newly dried swastikas painted on its body and wings.

"Will the Nazis get into power, Mama? Perhaps I should join the Hitler Youth, it might stop Father beating me."

Mama shook her head vigorously, spitting out her words high and sharp.

"No, Oskar, you should not. The Nazis are bullies and thugs. We must never let them take control."

She threw her arms open and we embraced, her housework-heated body warming my icy limbs. Then she tipped her head towards the stairs.

"Come, he's gone out now. Change your trousers and I'll see to your head. We've stew for dinner."

Following her up the stairs, a sense of hope settled in my mind.

"I'm going to work hard, Mama. One day, I'll buy you a house in the Karkonosze Mountains, I promise. Near that waterfall you always talk about."

*

21

My brother Emil had left the back door ajar as he chopped birch logs in the yard. A chilled breeze carried the smell of chicken stew towards me. My stomach rumbled a strange sound. Papa's fist had made its mark.

The clock, hung crooked on the kitchen wall, let out a 'cuckoo' seven times. Mama, silent and steely eyed, moved to the sink to massage the leftover chicken meat left to soak. Slicing and laying thin strips on the table, she slammed down her cracked rolling pin, like a blacksmith livening molten iron. My head throbbed.

Papa's trip to market was now three hours long. I felt weak with hunger. Emil strode through the door, brow wet with sweat, biceps bulging through his shirt as he struggled with a full basket of logs.

"What's that mark on your head?"

Before I could react, Mama turned to us both, speaking her first words of the evening, quietly and calmly.

"Right. We won't wait any longer. Oskar, there's a loaf of bread in the tin. Cut six slices. Leave enough for the morning. Emil, lay the table."

Mama placed four of our Polish grandmother's old Boleslawiec soup bowls on the table, collecting the stewpot from the stove to fill our bowls with a ladle. As she turned back, I asked her a question.

"Mama, can we visit your mama and papa in Sieradz? I'd love to know them."

Her back stiffened as she turned to answer me. Stumbling, she let the laden pot slip from her shaking hands. In that moment, time stood still as it fell, hitting the hard floor and smashing into tiny pieces, swept to all corners of the floor by

22

the soupy tide. Our dog Ralf leaped up, wolfing down the stew nearest his bed as Mama stood frozen, staring at me. She shook a little and quietly wept. My brother wrapped his arms around her, snapping at me.

"Look what you've done. We'll clear up the mess, Mama. There's stew in our bowls. I'm sure Oskar will share his with Papa."

As we worked with brush, shovel, bucket and towels to clear the mess, we heard the sound of cartwheels skidding to a stop outside. Mama composed herself as a fist hammered the locked door.

"Aneta? Why have you locked me out? Let me in. Aneetaaa!"

Unmoved by the noise, she walked purposefully up the stairs to her bedroom.

*

Despite what he had done to me and his obvious inebriation, there followed an ordinary meal, with just Mama's seat empty. Papa, lucid, animated even, demonstrated a faux jollity.

"Great things are coming to Germany again, boys. I spoke with a banker from the city today. He told me the economy would rise, now the National Socialists are growing in power. We will one day be economically self-sufficient."

Emil grinned.

"I've my dare ceremony next week, Papa. Will you watch?"

"What is it you have to do?"

"I'll jump from the Buchholzerstrasse railway bridge to the ground below, watched by members of my troop. It will be a great honour for me."

23

Emil's attempt to impress Papa seemed illogical and just plain stupid.

"That bridge is fifteen metres high. Designed for trains not people. Gravity will pull you down, you'll be travelling sixty kilometres per hour by the time you hit the ground. Your legs will break, probably your back."

"Shut up, you pea counter. It's eight metres from where I'll jump and I'm not a coward like you. The leader of our *Fähnlein* will hand me the *Blut und Ehre* dagger if I'm successful, Papa."

Papa stared at me as my head drooped, eyes fixed on my stew.

"I'm going to the Harz Mountains again next week, Oskar. Do you want to come?"

I shrugged, stirring the stew slowly with my spoon before replying.

"The flat fields near Luckau would be a better option if we're flying."

His cheeks dropped, reddened eyes narrowing on me.

"I'm going to the Harz, boy. Come if you wish."

Papa and Emil cleared the dishes away, while I sat and watched, distracted by the sound of Mama clearing her throat outside the room. Having checked Papa's position, she made her way straight towards me, carrying an object surreptitiously under her arm.

Reaching the table, she put a leather-bound book in front of me, face down, title hidden. I ran my fingers over its back cover and looked up at her. She nodded, and I turned the book over to reveal, in tall, bold, black serif letters, its title: *All Quiet on the Western Front*. I swallowed hard. It felt as if she had given me a book of biblical, other-worldly significance.

I ran up the two flights of stairs in our *Kleinhaus* to my tiny top-floor bedroom, made smaller still by the steeply pitched roof on which I always bashed my head. Opening the old enamel bread bin Mama had given me to store my books, I tucked the Remarque tome safely away. Feeling stiff and sore, I flopped onto my bed, my mind replaying the beating Papa had given me and how easily his mood had changed. Rocking forward and back, I fell asleep.

*

I had tossed and turned all night, often waking, sure I was still in our damp basement. In every dream, Papa appeared as a giant, while I shrank ever smaller.

Making my way downstairs the following morning, I peered through the half-open living room door to see my parents sitting silently opposite each other, the fire already lit. On the table between them were an autumn-leaf patina Marianne Brandt teapot—the last surviving Bauhaus item following Papa's purge—and two small cups.

Squinting through the gap, I could make out the title of Mama's book, *Der Steppenwolf*. She held her arms out rigid in front of her to read it. Papa appeared irritated.

"Are you reading that page or merely staring at it? Why do you bother with that Hesse trash, anyway?"

Mama ignored his questions, her eyes unmoving, dwelling on one point on the page. A sudden wave of panic swept over me as I recalled my abandonment in the Harz Mountains. The photograph that had fallen from the book in the Bad Harzburg chalet must still be in there.

"Because it's enlightening, Karl, and goodness do I need that."

"What?"

"Never mind."

Papa rolled a cigarette between his fingertips for a few moments before placing it between his lips.

"Aneta, I need to tell you something."

Continuing in her distraction for a few more moments, she turned a page and lowered the book.

"Oh, really? What?"

"Hans Zinsser and Charles Nicolle, both notable bacteriologists, have invited me to attend a meeting next month. They're trying to build a body of support for greater typhus research, internationally."

"I see. Well, that's good news, I guess. But why would they choose you? You haven't worked in months and you're hardly an expert. Where's the meeting?"

"Guadalajara."

Mama slammed her book shut and glared at Papa.

"Where on earth is that?"

He shuffled in his seat, taking another draw on his cigarette.

"Mexico. I'll be away for some time, leaving in a fortnight."

Mama put down her book, gripping the arms of her chair.

"How much are you getting paid for this adventure? When will you return?"

"What I'm normally paid, plus expenses. The trip will last two months, maybe longer."

With her jaw clenched, head shaking a little, Mama rose from the chair, her voice flooded with emotion.

"What do I get from this, Karl? You've spent years away from us. Still, I work like a dog to make enough for us to eat. If you weren't so damned pig-headed, your father could have helped us."

There was a silent pause, a change of energy in the room, like the lull before the great storm that had grounded the aeroplanes at the Altenberg Fair last summer. I inched away slowly, but before I reached the bottom step of the stairs, Mama fired off a second round, this time calm and resolute.

"I know you beat Oskar again yesterday. Can you find no love in your heart for that poor boy? I wish you had never come back after the war."

As I climbed the stairs two at a time, a sound like an oar hitting still water echoed into the hallway. I flinched, hunching my shoulders up to my ears.

*

Staring at my face in my bedroom mirror, I examined every millimetre of the graze on my forehead. I was a quick healer. It had darkened, the scabbed-over wound transformed to deep red. Beneath it, a bright purple bruise. I had made many excuses before to the schoolteachers, ignoring the taunts from other children. My explanations ranged from 'fight with my brother' to 'trip in the dark' or 'bumping head on doorway'. I did not want to tell anyone my father had caused them. But over time, their frequency and severity drew concern and suspicion from one of my teachers in particular. A letter home from the school would only make Papa worse. I had to stop that at all costs.

Creeping down the steps, I turned left into the kitchen then down steps again into the basement. In its corner was a wall cupboard. Pulling it open, I found it full of old tins and rags. At the back sat a thin circular tin, with the word 'Leichner' on it. Stage make-up, used by Mama when she had attended a local dramatic group to rehearse plays by Toller and Brecht, before her glamorous appearance led to Papa accusing her of seeing another man. Mama decided never to attend the group again and so I hid her make-up away.

If Mama could not use it anymore, perhaps I could. Pushing the Leichner tin into my pocket, I made for the bathroom and locked the door. Opening the tin, I dipped my fingers into the greasy paste and dabbed it on my wound.

*

The following week, I lay in bed, my face aching in three different places. Papa had beaten me again, not as badly as last time. At least the graze below my eye would be faint by the time I had school again. I pondered if using Mama's make-up might be counterproductive. If Papa could not see the result of his actions, maybe he would be more inclined to continue. Dismissing the thought, I pulled the tin from my drawer and dabbed some of the make-up on my cheek. I preferred to avoid the stares and questions of others.

"Oskar! We leave in ten minutes, not a moment later."

Papa's voice echoed up the stairwell, full of stress. I dare not delay. We were to journey south by cart to the Saturday market at Oderin.

Mama remained distant and silent as we headed steadily towards Teurow, while Papa bristled with tension, frequently checking his watch. When we became stuck behind an overturned cart outside the town, he shouted and swore at the poor owners so hard that I was convinced he would have a heart attack.

We arrived to find the streets of Oderin teeming with locals on their way to find cheap foodstuffs, shoes, clothes and crafts. Papa tied our horse, Chefin, at the edge of the town square and hurriedly walked towards the other side, as Mama and I tried to keep pace. Suddenly, he stopped and turned to face us.

"Aneta, go and find what you can in the market for dinner. Oskar, you can stay with me for now."

Gazing at my mother's emotionless face, a blink of her eyes was enough for me to detect her hurt. She nodded curtly, squeezed my hand and walked slowly to the many rows of food stalls.

Wondering who Papa would meet, I followed as he headed towards the Wilhelmian town hall, its balconied tower overhanging four small oriel windows. As we neared, a middle-aged man burst through the dark oak double doors, wearing a brown shirt and round spectacles.

"Bachmann. About time."

His unusually bright, darting blue eyes made me nervous. I shuffled as he turned them on me, his lips pursed, cheeks raised.

"Is this your son?"

Papa nodded.

"The younger boy, yes."

Without hesitation, he strode across to me, gripping my shoulders and examining my face.

"I'm Ernst Naumann, veteran of the Great War. Assault troop leader with the SA. What's your name, boy?"

"It's Oskar, sir."

Without warning, he wiped the forefinger of his right hand across my face, sniffing it and holding it close to his eyes to examine it. I flinched in pain, looking to Papa, hoping he would say something. He remained passive, unwilling to challenge an SA officer.

"Are you wearing make-up, boy?"

Naumann had the kind of voice that brimmed with emotion, shifting to falsetto at the end of each sentence. Imagining the wound on my face now evident, my legs felt weak. Papa's eyes narrowed and he cleared his throat with open mouth, before sneering and finally saying something.

"His mother wears too much make-up, Herr Naumann. She kissed him as she headed to market."

He peered at me, clearly suspicious, moving his face close to mine until I could taste his coffee breath.

"Germany won't be saved by sissies. Be proud of your scars, boy. We need heroes and belligerents!"

I breathed again as Naumann switched his attention to Papa, whispering in his ear while his eyes stayed focused on me.

Suddenly embarrassed by my presence, Papa shoved both hands in his pockets and spoke to me through gritted teeth.

"Oskar, go find your mother in the market. Return here in an hour. I've some important people to meet."

*

On our way back from Teurow, Papa told us nothing of his meetings. He did tell us Naumann ran the Cafe del Mar, a small, rundown bar next to Lake Heidesee selling cheap beer and strong French-style coffee in tiny cups. He liked it there.

So, the next morning, I made my way to the cafe. Sitting on a stack of logs hidden by tall reeds overlooking it, I hoped Papa would appear. Mama had told me she was sure he often came here at this time of day.

While I waited, I studied a birdwatching book lent to me by Grandfather, making notes on a pair of stately great bustards just a couple of metres away, as they tore at an unlucky frog on the lakeside. The sound of heavy feet crunching down on the slate pebble path behind me disturbed the birds. They ran off fast as foxes into the bushes, a frog's leg each in their beaks. Peering through the gently swaying reeds, I saw Papa. He was hunched over, hands in pockets, his deep-set eyes glancing across in my direction, making my breath shorten, and heart pound. But he passed without noticing me and sat outside the cafe, lighting a cigarette.

Peering across through the reeds, I saw Naumann serve Papa a frothy beer, which he gulped at, spitting some out as Naumann landed a firm punch on the front of his shoulder. Naumann then pushed his face close to Papa's and mouthed something that I could not make out, before taking a paper from his jacket, which my father signed. The two men gave a Nazi salute to each other and the world around me shrank a little.

3
LIBRARY OF THE LAKE

Groß Köris
1930

The pages of the books I wrapped around my mind and soul like blankets brought distraction and great solace from the relentless strife of home life. I read on a wide range of topics, including literature, ornithology and psychology, which I had become more interested in as I tried to develop theories about Papa and his behaviour towards me. One topic helped me maintain a bridge to him: aviation. I carefully avoided asking him again about the war, but he would happily chat about model aeroplanes and comment on the articles in magazines I would bring home from school. This topic gave us no need to reveal anything of ourselves. I enjoyed this normality.

I was lucky at Heisenberg, my small gymnasium school in Groß Köris, ten kilometres north of where we lived. Despite a lack of friends (I preferred to keep myself to myself), I could spend any spare time in the school's well-stocked library, manned by its kindly, knowledgeable librarian, Herr Guntz. I had told him about my interest in aviation and he seemed to enjoy sourcing numerous books and magazines on the subject. This morning I would collect my latest batch.

As I pushed the library door open, Herr Guntz looked up from behind a pile of books on his desk. He stared at me, reaching into a drawer, his grin revealing a head full of tobacco-stained teeth as he produced a stuffed brown paper bag.

"Young Oskar. Presume you've come for these?"

I took the bag from him, peering inside and flicking through the titles: half a dozen copies of the American *Aviation* magazine, dated from January to June 1929.

"I'm grateful, sir. How did you manage to get these, if you don't mind my asking?"

"Haven't always been a librarian, you know. Now I must get on. See you soon, no doubt."

I gave him a grateful nod and walked away from the library towards the corner of the now busy school field, dodging an aggressively played football match on my way. With fifty minutes of lunchtime left, I could read through the relevant sections of the magazines and make a few notes for my talk tomorrow.

I was distracted by the lonely figure of a boy to my left, who was sitting and leaning against one of the apple-laden trees. Having often seen him reading alone, he fascinated me and, despite the pressure on my time, I decided to detour to greet him.

Engrossed in a book, he raised his head slowly as I approached, his saucer-like eyes, magnified by thick, circular spectacles, peering up at me. I held out a hand to shake his. In return, he flicked his head nonchalantly, eager to get back to his reading, the fringe of his unruly dark-brown mane bouncing up.

"I'm Oskar. What are you reading?"

He replied dismissively.

"I know who you are. I'm Timo Gumpert, halfway through *The Great Gatsby*, and keen to finish it. What's in the bag?"

He stared at my face for a moment, squinting.

"And what's that on your forehead?"

Embarrassed, I covered the wound with my hand.

"Oh, that's the trouble with my height. I bashed my head on a doorway."

He stared at me, unconvinced.

"And these are magazines, for research purposes."

"Well, what are you researching?"

I half-smiled, glad he was interested enough to ask.

"I'm giving a speech out here tomorrow, on aviation. Come and listen if you like."

Shrugging his shoulders, his eyes darted back to the pages of his book.

"Maybe."

*

Mine was the third talk in a series of five being held that week, designed to 'build ability in public speaking and expand knowledge in special-interest areas'. Our headteacher, Herr Blankenhorn, mentioned the subject of my speech—'The small aeroplanes and flying boats of the 1920s'—during school assembly that morning. As I walked towards the elevated platform at the back of the school field, my skin tingled, head dizzy, like when I was sad. There must have been two hundred boys gathered. I had few friends at school, but I noticed the crowd was silent, respectful.

As I stepped onto the small stage, my heartbeat seemed to make every organ in my body pulse. I whispered under my breath, "Lift, thrust, drag and weight," over and over, then began.

Stumbling on only the second word of my talk—saying Werville Air Coach, instead of Verville—I quickly recovered. My confidence grew as I looked out into the crowd to see the boys' eyes fixed on me, silent, concentrating, appreciating my knowledge.

"By far the largest flying boat was German, of course. The magnificent Dornier Do X, a semi-cantilever monoplane with all-Duralumin hull, wings composed of steel-reinforced Duralumin covered in heavy linen fabric and aluminium paint. It had a quite incredible twelve 524 horsepower Bristol Jupiter radial engines and a wingspan of fifty metres—three times the length of our school bus. Anyone want to hazard a guess at its top speed?"

At that moment, I spotted Blankenhorn at the rear of the crowd and, alongside him, Timo Gumpert, his hand raised.

"Yes, at the back."

Timo called back in a raspy voice.

"I'd say two hundred and eleven kilometres per hour."

Not just close—he was spot on. After fifteen minutes, my talk concluded to hearty applause, with many boys stopping behind to ask questions until interrupted by Blankenhorn.

"Boys, back to class now. Bachmann, I'd like to talk to you."

Leaving the platform, I strolled alongside our head, back towards the school buildings.

"That was quite a talk, although you should have referenced Siemens as having built the Do X engines. You've an innate ability to hold an audience, Bachmann. We should discuss your career options. Teaching, perhaps?"

"I love the topic, sir. But I'm not sure I'm cut out to be a teacher."

The combination of having spoken on a topic that would please Papa and this unusual praise from Blankenhorn made me feel ten feet tall. My euphoria heightened further as Timo met me at the edge of the field.

"Pretty good, Bachmann. Come to the library tomorrow lunchtime. I've something I want to talk to you about."

Over the next few weeks, I learned how truly obsessed Timo was with reading. We became close. His idea was that every week on Friday, we should exchange already-read books and swap notes. It became a ritual. Before each meeting, I fretted, believing he would consider my choices unremarkable, my commentary lacking insight, but he always appeared politely interested. Such was the pace of his reading, I soon fell behind, but never admitted it to him. I failed to finish many of his books before the time came to return them and escaped with often sketchy knowledge during our school break-time debates on literary themes and meanings. I quickly exhausted my collection of books, prompting me to borrow from Mama or Grandfather or recall themes from previously read tomes.

*

Three weeks later, school finished early. A fire broke out when Frau Sommer, our Korn-flushed cook, left a frying pan of oil on high heat. Flames soon curled out of the windows of the kitchen block, prompting panic and shouts as teachers ushered pupils away from potential danger. The kitchen staff quickly brought the fire under control, rendering the visit of shiny-helmeted firefighters unnecessary.

A furious Blankenhorn sent us all home. As the bus to Halbe arrived at the school gates, Günter Schmidt, a glowering bully boy, pushed my slender frame out of his way and marched to the front. As he tried to push past others bigger than me, a fight ensued. Instinctively, I stole away, heading west, down Berlinerstrasse, towards the lake. With Mama working, I did not want to go home this afternoon. Timo's house beckoned.

Within a few minutes, I was strolling along a narrow, tree-lined lane that circled the crystal-clear waters of Lake Zemminsee. During the summer, the lake teemed with eel, catfish and zander, making it a favourite spot for anglers, including my grandpa. The lane gave access to the handful of grand houses that backed onto the lake, each one gated and, according to Mama, who admired and despised wealth in equal part, for the most part held as second homes by well-to-do Berliners. Timo's perfect directions were imprinted on my brain, and as I turned a corner, now heading north, I recognised the house instantly. I stood for a while staring at its Romanesque columns, huge windows and manicured gardens and imagined Mama beside me. She would undoubtedly describe this mock-Renaissance villa as an 'ostentatious monstrosity'. Our modest west Halbe home, off Barutherstrasse, would easily fit inside it a dozen times.

There was no gate at the entrance to the Gumperts' house. Instead, two concrete pillars, bordered by high hedges, sat at the start of a long pebble path to the front door. One of the pillars held an indented brass plaque with the strange word

'Limmeridge' carved on it. I rubbed a fingerprint off the plaque before walking slowly along the path. Timo appeared at the far side of the house, toiling over a lawnmower and cutting the grass in a meticulous manner. He failed to see me at first, but as I began to walk towards him, he stopped to rub the back of his neck and turned to face me with pursed lips.

"Oskar. What are you doing here?"

"I missed the school bus. Can I stay for a while? There's another leaving from Christuskirche at four thirty. Did they let your year out earlier?"

He nodded, squinting at me through the thick lenses of his glasses.

"Your house is incredible."

He replied with such erudite confidence.

"My father's a banker. He bought it outright in 1922 with bonuses from successful railroad investments. Shrewd move, I guess. Best to have money in property these days."

He agreed to let me stay provided I helped him, and so I fetched a rake and bags from the small shed at the edge of the lawn.

"I've been wanting to show you something. Let's get this finished."

My mind dancing with ideas as to what Timo would reveal to me, I dragged the huge rake at pace behind him as he pushed the mower, cutting the lawn in perfectly straight strips. We worked together to bag the piles of mown grass left at the end of each section and tipped them on a large compost area to the right of the house. I took the opportunity to ask Timo about its name, noticing a wheeze in his breath as he replied.

"Why is your house called Limmeridge, Timo? It sounds English."

"It's a fictional house in a detective novel called *The Woman in White*, set in a place called Cumberland, where Mother's from. She was wearing white when Father met her in London and, well, the rest is history. Time for a drink. Come on."

The delicious cool hallway of the house was a sweet relief after our toil in the sun. I gazed at a disturbing brown and red oil painting on its wall depicting a hanged man and a bound woman, all the while listening to the soothing sound of humming drifting from the kitchen.

Timo's mother, Dorothy, stood at the sink washing dishes, perfectly attired in a long, dark-green dress, her hair in tight curls. I wondered why a woman of apparent wealth would need to do the dishes. She turned to me, a kind smile on her lips, soapsuds covering her arms.

"I heard you had a pleasant surprise today, Oskar. Shouldn't you have ridden the bus home though?"

Her lilting Northern English voice relaxed me, despite the interrogation.

"Yes, Frau Gumpert. Timo's helping me with schoolwork. I'll get a later bus."

My reply was plausible given Timo's intellect and seniority in age, but his mother raised her eyebrows and flicked her head upwards with a knowing smile.

"I've an idea where he might take you."

We gulped down our milk. I struggled to contain a giggle at the creamy coating left on Timo's rather pathetic attempt at a moustache. He frowned at me, wiping it away with the sleeve of his shirt.

Leaving the house, we strolled together between two long, perfectly manicured flower beds, full of bee-coated bright-blue cornflowers. We seemed to glide across the lawn, quickly reaching the lakeside. A mucky-white rowing boat, with *Red Night* hand-painted in blood-red paint on either side of its keel, sat on the pebble-strewn shore. We stood mesmerised by the view of the perfectly still lake, only distracted by a noisy group of velvet scoters that landed near us. The bright afternoon sun highlighted the myriad of leaves cloaking the well-established trees around the lake, causing them to reflect a beautiful rainbow of colours back off the water.

"It's wonderful, Timo."

Peering around the edges of the lake, a twenty-metre tower, about a third of the way round, out to the right, stole my attention. It seemed to hover on the water. Across to the left sat its symmetrical twin. Timo sensed my interest.

"They used to be at the end of concrete spits, but they're down below the water level now. I've only ever walked out to them on dry land once. Three years ago, when we had the drought. Do you remember it?"

I nodded. "What's inside them?"

"You'll see soon enough." He smiled, pointing to the tower on the right. "I'm going to let you see inside that one."

Glancing at the sun as a large, angel wing-shaped white cloud cloaked it, my stomach tightened. Strange. Nothing to be afraid of, I told myself. Pushing the rowboat to the water's edge, Timo jumped in, beckoning me to follow, handing me an oar. I had never rowed before, and it took us a minute or two to establish any kind of rhythm. But, once coordinated, we moved steadily towards our target through the flawless waters of the lake.

The tower loomed closer. It was circular, made of granite brick, with a tall, slated spire and Gothic windows. I imagined a woman in a white dress and long blonde hair might wait behind one of them. Timo tired.

"Oskar, can we stop for a break? It's my chest. I'm getting wheezy."

We paused in the water, Timo resting elbows on knees, gathering his breath. I put my oar in its rowlock and dropped my arm over the side, up to my elbow in the cool water, imagination running wild. Was the tower home to wild animals, too dangerous to keep in the house or garden? Jaguars, wolves, snakes or a chained bear? I wasn't fond of wild beasts and hoped not. Perhaps Timo's crazy aunties lived in there, sipping tea and inventing conspiracy theories? Or, more likely, it could be full of old ammunition and weaponry, a relic from the days when it acted as a defence for the government building that had once stood on the site of Timo's house.

"You rest, I'll row us the rest of the way."

As we reached the foot of the tower, he smiled knowingly.

"I can guarantee this place is not home to any of the things you've clearly been thinking about."

He explained that his father had given him the tower as a gift, to keep forever, even if someone else bought the house. I couldn't comprehend that Timo owned this building; it was as big as our house.

Roping the boat to the bottom of rusting iron steps on the tower's right-hand side, he climbed slowly up towards the door, stopping for breath halfway and calling back to me.

"Come on, I want to show you what I've been working on inside."

I gazed up. The tower appeared much, much taller up close. Stomach churning, I stepped out onto the lowest rung above the waterline. My arms felt weak. It was like stepping onto a biscuit. Water soaked up to my knee as my foot went through the rung. Thrust forward, I just about hung on, relieved that Timo, already inside the rotunda, had not seen my mishap.

As I reached the top of the ladder, Timo stuck out his head to explain how the previous owners had used the rotunda as a place to entertain guests, but then the army had requisitioned it as an arms store during the war.

"You're the first person from outside my family to see the inside."

I swallowed hard, stepping through the small door, letting out a gasp as the splendour of the rotunda's interior became visible. My legs trembled a little. One arm flew to my chest, the other held onto Timo's tiny, still-heaving shoulder as the scale and audacity of his project revealed itself to me. There stood before me a magnificent library, with book-laden shelf upon shelf perfectly filling almost every centimetre of wall, from floor to ceiling at least twenty metres above. I felt dazed and featherlight amidst the weight of knowledge in the room, wishing I could float upwards, soaring and circling like a Stahlwerk around the shelves to see every book up close.

"It's perfect, Timo."

He explained that roughly half the books were German language, the rest English, French or Latin, other than a few Yugoslav romantic poetry books, the complete works of

Dostoevsky, Tolstoy and Pasternak in Russian, a Japanese encyclopaedia and other miscellanea.

I felt immediately at home. A friend I could trust, surrounded by books. I put my shoulders back, standing squarely, chin raised, imagining a lectern in front of me, trying to breathe in the knowledge around me. Timo scrunched up his face quizzically.

"What are you doing?"

"Blankenhorn said I would make a good teacher... *Students, today we'll explore how observable behaviour has influenced the development of psychology...*"

Pretending to hold a book aloft, I pointed to it.

"*Open your books on page one hundred and twelve...*"

He sniggered.

"Is that the best you can do?"

I tried again. "*Today, we'll explore the evolution of the aviation industry. Albatros and Aviatik led an explosion of production. Our nation had a meagre eight aircraft in 1911. Our fleet had grown to eight squadrons by 1912. Albatros constructed one- and two-deck machines favoured by the military...*"

"Better, but too technical."

Satisfied with his judgement, I stopped and peered around the shelves.

"I've never seen anything like this. Where did they all come from?"

My straightforward question unsettled Timo. He seemed upset, a thin smear of steam on his glasses, his eyes watering behind them. He explained that most of the books had come from his grandfather, a learned academic. His mother had given him the English books, from visits home or posted to her by her family, and his father had collected others for him during visits to bookstores in Berlin.

I scanned the book titles as far as my eyes could read them, noticing some were not in perfect alphabetical order. Half of them I recognised. *A Farewell to Arms*, *Cheri*, *The Mysterious Affair at Styles*.

"How on earth did you get them all in here?"

Timo moved to gaze out of a window on the far side of the rotunda that faced west across the lake.

"Most boys do their homework when they get home, Oskar. Maybe play football, walk their dog. Do you know what I did for three months?"

I shook my head, sitting on a small brown stool by the wall.

He explained how for months he had rowed across the lake to meet his dying grandpa. They would sit together in his grandpa's motor car. He would tell Timo a different story each time. Some were his own, others from books he had read. Then he would give Timo another batch of books in a jute sack and he would row to the tower, sometimes taking hours to study them all and organise them on the library shelves.

"I often missed supper and worried my mother sick. Do you know, Grandpa wrote a paragraph of text in every single book he gave me?"

Each text had been neatly written in sharp pencil on the inside back cover.

"I reckon there's an entire tale spread across all those books. One day I'll pull them all together and tell the world my grandpa's wonderful story."

My friend sobbed, slumping to the floor under the window.

"He's gone now."

I moved from my stool, putting an arm around his shoulder.

"Will you show me around, Timo?"

He wiped away his tears, and we walked the circular route around the library floor.

"You obviously loved your grandpa, as I do mine. What about your father?"

"I don't have a close relationship with him, Oskar. He's a busy man, but a good one. I love him, if that's what you're asking. What about yours?"

I hesitated. Walking a few steps ahead of Timo, I turned to face him.

"Do you remember that wound on my head you asked me about in the school field?"

He nodded.

"My father did it."

He looked puzzled.

"What do you mean? Playing sport?"

I shook my head slowly, his expression turning to one of shock.

"He beats me, Timo. It's been happening for as long as I can remember."

Saying these words to someone outside of my family felt wrong.

"That's terrible."

"Thing is, I know Papa's not all bad. Something made him act the way he does sometimes. I want to study to find out what."

He pointed to the higher shelves, his serious face turning to a smile.

"A noble aim, Oskar. I have several books on psychology. They'll be up there somewhere, next to philosophy."

Opening a 'hidden' cupboard panel, Timo carefully pulled free a wooden ladder with inserted rubber grips that matched the heights of the shelves. He passed it to me, and I pushed it halfway around the rotunda wall and climbed, landing in the Agriculture, Fishing and Forestry section.

I descended, moved the ladder three metres to the right and clambered up again, this time right next to the psychology section. There were at least a dozen books: *Behaviourism* by John B Watson and *Conditioned Reflexes* by Ivan Pavlov in English; and *Psychologische Probleme* by Wolfgang Köhler in German.

Timo called up.

"My next project is to add signs that highlight topics from the floor, so I can be more precise. Bring a few down to read if you like."

"Thanks. What about aviation?"

"There's plenty, right over the other side. Only subject my father is interested in. He flew a plane in the Great War, you know."

"Really? So did mine!"

I quickly descended with my haul of books, slumping down next to Timo and burying my head in the illustrated *American Aircraft Yearbook 1920*. Sitting together in silence for a while, we turned pages, lost in a happy distraction.

After a while, he held his book close to his nose, sniffing the pages, then turned to me, grinning.

"Love the smell of books. I think they all have a slightly unique aroma, like fine wines."

I brought my book to my face and sniffed. It didn't smell of much.

"It's a bit musty, I guess."

"You've much to learn, Oskar. It's not mustiness. There are hints of other smells in there—vanilla, for example. Lignin, a plant polymer, is in all paper and it's closely related to vanillin. As books get old and degrade, they give off smells... a bit like old people."

He broke into an infectious giggle.

I peered down at the yearbook. Its deeply indented cover depicted a Marchetti MVT surrounded by a detailed garland. I ran my fingers over the surface, savouring the sensation. Inside, each page teemed with brilliant pictures: photographs of planes in the clouds, and landed on water, Zeppelins and aircraft carriers, all interspersed with maps and magnificent scenes of American mountains, valleys and cityscapes. I wanted to visit those places one day and closed my eyes, daydreaming for a moment, plotting how I might make it happen, before my thoughts returned to the present.

The library, books and conversation with my friend had blurred time. In a panic, I glanced at my wrist. The long, pale-blue hand of my black-faced Ruhla wristwatch was past the twelve, the small hand at four. My bus arrived in under half an hour.

After a breathless row back to the garden with Timo, whose wheeze had worsened, I made a dash for the bus, reaching it just as it pulled away from the church onto Seebadstrasse. I waved at the elderly driver to let me in. He braked hard and swore at me as I paid my fare. The drive back to Halbe took twice as long as usual, thanks to an overturned cart near Löpten-

Süd. Staring out of the window into the late afternoon sun, I felt nervous and rehearsed my lines for Papa. He would have seen other schoolchildren returning home and suspect me of mischief.

The bus dropped me a few doors from my house. I pushed our front door open nervously. There was no one downstairs. Then a loud slamming of a door, followed by the sound of heavy footsteps marching down the stairs. Papa stopped two steps from the floor, giving him added height as he tore into me.

"I know where you've been. Don't deny it. I prohibited you from seeing the Gumpert boy and you've disobeyed me."

His familiar temper and flushed cheeks were more obvious than an empty bottle. I wondered how he knew.

"There was a fire at the school, Papa. I wanted to make good use of my time. Look."

I pulled the aircraft compendium from my satchel, being careful to hide the psychology books. His face softened.

"Where did you get this from?"

"Timo's library. You wouldn't believe it, Papa. It's in a tower on Lake Zemminsee."

"You must never take favours, not from that boy."

He pointed to the backyard.

"Move the blocks of limestone away from the gate, onto the dug patch to the right of the outhouse. Do it quickly, before your mother gets home."

Already tired, I trudged wearily outside, stopping to gaze back through the glass in the door. I took a little comfort in seeing Father turn the pages of the compendium, a flicker of a smile crossing his lips.

4
THE SWASTIKA AND THE CROSS

Halbe
1930

The sound of Mama readying herself for work woke me. Every centimetre of my body ached from shifting that cursed limestone. Glancing at my Junghans alarm clock—a useless gift from my grandpa given its missing bell—I saw its misshapen long hand nudge five. If my afternoon at Timo's had been enlightening, Papa's banning of me seeing him again was both perplexing and depressing. As she kissed me goodnight, Mama whispered that there had been a long-running issue between Papa and Herr Gumpert, but she did not know its details. I would have to be careful.

Treading slowly to the bathroom, I noticed Mama and Papa's bedroom door open. Pausing on my way back, I peeped inside to see Papa lying on his back, letting out a snore so loud it made Ralf jump off the bed. Mama sat, deep in thought, at her dressing table, a sheet of writing paper in front of her. Picking up a pen, she moved her hand swiftly across it, my presence unnoticed.

I crept back undetected to my room, slipping into my still-warm bed, pulling the covers around my ears, asking myself questions as I drifted back to unconsciousness. What had been so important to communicate that Mama had rushed to write it before work? A shopping list? A final warning to Papa? Or a letter to her own father, asking if she could stay again, as she'd done for an awful month when I was thirteen?

I woke, for a second time, to find the top half of Mama's body hidden behind my bedroom curtains. Pushing them to one side, she appeared before me in her brimmed hat and lace pinafore, a broad smile on her face.

"It's going to be a beautiful day today, Oskar. Use it well."

Stretching my legs to rid them of pain, I moaned a little, prompting her to sit beside me. She leaned down, planting a kiss on my forehead as I sat up, awkwardly.

"Do you know, when we first courted, your father would sing me songs and bring me wildflowers. We could talk together for hours about history, science, music." She moved to the door, checking outside before pushing it shut. "He's going away for a long trip abroad."

Coughing repeatedly, I turned away from her, then acted surprised.

"Oh. How long for?"

She brought her hand to her chin, her finger and thumb pinching the still-taut skin on her neck.

"Three months. Maybe more."

I quickly accounted for the likely happiness that would derive from Papa's absence. No model aeroplanes (he would lock them away while he was gone), but Mama would be more settled. There would be no turmoil. Net positive.

"Okay, Mama. We'll help you run the house. I can tidy things for you. We could take up jobs at one of the farms. Can I ask you a question?"

She moved back to the window, distracted, then turned to nod.

"Of course."

I paused, unsure if I should ask the question that continually haunted me.

"Mama, why does Father beat me but never Emil?"

Pulling back the curtain, she stared out of the window, glancing at me sidewards before answering in a quiet, shaking voice.

"It's because you are different, Oskar. He doesn't like it, but I do."

Her answer told me nothing. All children were 'different', but I did not pursue the question. Walking back to me, she put her hand on my shoulder.

"I went to a good gymnasium as a girl. We'd a Prussian secondary school for girls as early as 1872. Did you know that?"

I shook my head.

"Prussian schools were very good. I excelled in literature and history."

She stopped for a moment, staring at the floorboards, on the verge of tears, but then looked up, eyes shining. I glanced at a bright-turquoise bar brooch pinned to her jacket. Unusual. I had never seen it before. She only ever wore jewellery to church. I pointed to it.

"That's pretty, Mama."

"Thank you. It was a gift. Did I ever tell you about my time in Berlin?"

Without waiting for an answer, she continued.

"I loved it. Had nice girls working with me at the house. The master and his wife were good to us. I remember taking a trip with my best friend to the farmers' market in Dahlem. We attracted a few admiring looks back then."

She giggled to herself, sitting on the end of the bed to smooth my crumpled clothes as I stretched, jaw hanging like a hungry baby to let out another yawn.

"The fighting was hundreds of miles away in Belgium and France, but newspaper headlines made folk panic about food shortages. The market sat in the grounds of a lovely old manor house. It overflowed with people when we arrived. Hundreds of Berliners working the aisles between stalls, grabbing fresh produce. Farmers brought it in from all over Brandenburg. Complete mayhem. Apples, leeks and onions all over the floor. There were even a few people dashed on the cobbled courtyard. I saw two plump women throwing lazy punches at each other over the last cup of salt!"

I yawned a third time.

"Why are you telling me this now, Mama? The sun's not even up."

She ignored me, staring ahead, eyes dancing like flames.

"We had to find enough to feed the master's lunch guests. Wasn't easy. Frau Kahlert wanted stew. We managed it, with twenty pfennigs to spare. I loved the freedom, away from the big old house we toiled in day after day. Can still smell that market. Freshly baked *Bauernbrot*, *Vollkornbrot* and *Roggenbrot*. Mustard from the fields of Gruiten and the sweet scent of Berlin basil. The stallholders didn't need to shout that day, but they still did."

As if acting out the scene, Mama leaped to her feet, pointing at me and adopting a terrible 'Mietskaserner' accent.

"*For you, young lady... wonderful porcini mushrooms, freshly picked in the forest, only hours ago.*"

I had never seen her animated like this. It was as if she was there, back in 1914, her feet on Berlin soil. My ears burned red with embarrassment, but I played along.

"Do you miss it, Mama?"

She ignored me, floating around my room with a hollow look in her eyes. Straightening curtains, pushing in a half-open drawer, throwing a pair of shoes in a cupboard. Arriving back at my bed, she pushed a hundred-pfennig coin into my hand.

"Buy yourself some books, Oskar. What about that novel Timo said you must read? The one about the toy rabbit. You must feed your mind."

She trotted purposefully down the stairs, leaving me staring at the coin in my palm. How many loaves would it buy at market? I went to the window, following Mama's steps as she strode away from the house in the shadowy dawn light using an umbrella as a walking stick.

Turning back towards my bed, I sensed a dreamlike figure ghosting across my view. I shook my head, blinking, and dashed back to the window to look again. Dragging up the stiff sash window, I stuck my head into the cool morning air. My eyes probed the dark beneath the oak tree at the edge of our property, darting in all directions, chasing any hints of movement. I ran downstairs, my bare feet slapping every other step, grabbing a worn broom on my way out as I rushed towards the hoary trunk of the tree.

"Who's there? Come out. Show your face."

53

All was still, silent. My chest heaved.

Hearing my shouts, Papa appeared, half-dressed, at the door behind me, his hair a towheaded mess.

"What in Jesus' name are you doing yelling at the tree? Come inside, boy."

"There's someone out here, Papa. I saw them from my window."

He gave a cursory glance around the yard. "Are you insane? There's no one there. Get inside. I'm going back to bed."

I peered around the bushes once more, before reluctantly following Papa back inside the house.

*

Every day since my sighting of the figure in our yard I woke early, thinking about who it might have been. Today was no different, and I could not contemplate getting up and readying myself for church. Emil and I would serve early mass today, as we did every other week, taking turns with the Zimmler brothers from Birkengrund. Papa always sang heartily in church, while Mama remained silent. As I pulled my white surplice over my head, my brother pushed into my room, leaning the door shut behind him.

I fell backwards on my bed when I saw what he was wearing. Instead of an altar-boy robe, he wore black corduroy shorts with a leather buckle belt and shoulder strap, brown military shirt with a '52' badge, and a black neckerchief and woggle. On his left arm, a swastika armband. His precious *Blut und Ehre*-inscribed dagger hung from his belt. He stood, shoulders back, chin in the air, staring down at me.

"Do you have spare socks?"

"Why are you dressed like a Nazi, Emil?"

"Don't be thick. Why do you think?"

"We're due at church this morning."

"Yes, and afterwards, I'll join my first parade. Our entire *Unterbann*, more than 600 of us, are marching to Teurow and back. Sister Maria will give us breakfast. You'll have to make your way back home alone or wait for me."

He rifled through my drawers, throwing neatly folded clothes to the floor behind him. I tried to fathom how he could pull this off.

"You can't ring the altar bells dressed like that. Father Eisengrein won't allow it. He hates the Nazis."

Emil kept searching, leaving the drawers looking as if a burglar had ransacked them.

"Stop fretting. I don't care what that old man thinks and, anyway, I'll wear my altar robe over the top to serve mass. Where are your bloody socks?"

"Bottom drawer. Does Mother know about this?"

He stopped and turned to stare at me, jaw clenched.

"Don't you dare mention this to Mother, not if you want to live. She's attending late mass with Papa. They won't need the cart. I'll be back at lunchtime."

Emil brought the cart to the rear of the house, out of view from our parents' bedroom. Clambering alongside onto the mounting step, I caught my boot in the hem of my robe, grazing my shin. A drop of blood stained the white cloth.

Chefin, now thirty years our servant, dragged us slowly towards the lane, as if he wanted no part of Emil's plan. Looking back towards the house, I spotted a battered old drum, edged with a red-triangle-teeth design, lying in the back of the cart.

"What's happened to your violin, Emil?"

"I still have it. The drum's more suited to marching. There are trumpets on parades too though. You'd be okay. I could ask our *Scharführer* if you could march with us. As long as you stayed away from me."

The part of me that yearned for acceptance felt attracted to this idea. Being one of the group, popular, anonymised. But Mama hated the Nazis. I would not betray her.

"No, thanks. I'll wait for you, look after the cart."

Emil slammed his palm down on the cart seat. Our sluggish horse refused to canter.

"Let me get down. I know how to make her move."

"Stay where you are. We don't have time."

Red-faced, he slapped Chefin's backside over and over with the driving whip until, suddenly, she lurched, her old muscles remembering their power and speeding through a canter to a full gallop down the lane. Thrown backwards sharply, Emil lost his grip on the reins. Two farmers, enjoying a smoke as they leaned on a field gate, let out roars of laughter as we hurtled past.

They shouted out, "*Gott wird dich retten!*" ("God will save you!")

Regaining control on the last corner before the main road, we broke into a nervous, hysterical laughter, relieved no harm had come to us or to Papa's beloved steed. It felt good. I hadn't laughed much with my brother lately.

"You know, Oskar, Papa knows I have to do certain things to make my way in life. You'll realise soon enough. We learn a lot in the Hitler Youth. Boating, shooting, Morse code, map reading. If you joined, maybe it would win you favour with him."

I hesitated, not wanting to lose this rare moment of camaraderie with my brother.

"I'll have a think about it."

Turning into the leafy lane to the church, we could see its small congregation already filtering through the doorway, welcomed by Father Eisengrein. Confused, I hoped an hour in God's presence would answer my questions. I would pray for Emil and hope no one spotted his hidden uniform.

Father Eisengrein stood, hands on hips and red-faced.

"You're late. Again. The cruets are ready, and I prepared all on the credence table. Light the candles as fast as you can."

We apologised profusely and moments later, my brother led us towards the altar. I followed on behind the priest with my giant candle, saying a silent prayer for Emil as we walked.

Please, God, help me understand how my brother carries a cross in his hand while a swastika adorns his arm.

*

After an hour waiting for Emil, I decided to risk his wrath. Spotting a neighbour and his wife boarding their cart, I asked for a lift. The ride home gave me time to think. Father Eisengrein's sermon taught us to follow Christ's example by seeking to understand others and to forgive them. I had listened intently. It made me realise I had never really understood my father, but Timo's books had helped me rationalise some of the things he had done to me.

57

Mama was laying the table for lunch when I arrived home, but only three places. Did she know Emil would not be home?

She turned and smiled as I walked into the kitchen.

"How was church this morning and where's your brother?"

Emil had not told me what excuse to give, so I thought on my feet.

"Oh, Father Eisengrein asked him to stay a few hours and help with some work at the church. He may not be back before you and Father head to mass."

Mama lowered her head to stare at me.

"He didn't say anything to me. Your father's unwell, we won't go to mass today."

She gathered up two of the sets of cutlery and plates and put them away.

I smiled. Papa and Emil's absence would give me a chance to run some of my book-inspired theories past Mama. Placing the vegetable broth and omelette she had prepared in front of me, she put her hand on my shoulder.

"We need to fatten you up, Oskar. You're too skinny."

Her mood was light and relaxed. Summoning courage to speak, I began, keeping my voice low, so only Mama could hear.

"The sermon this morning was all about understanding others, Mama. I've been doing a lot of reading—books about psychology, because I think they can help me understand Father better."

"Oh, really?"

"Yes, I've discovered that violence can either be viewed as a condition of human nature, almost as an instinct, or as a result of a damaged psyche."

Mama seemed distracted. She did not look at me as I spoke, choosing to gaze down at her meal. I continued.

"Apparently, abusive behaviour is a kind of coping mechanism. People can adopt habits to cover emotional wounds received early in life, from their own families. But Grandfather is such a wonderful man, unless Grandmother was horrible, but he never says anything about her..."

I looked up slowly, seeing first Mama's plate, her meal half-eaten, pushed to the centre of the table, and then up to her face, where a trail of tears now marked her cheeks. She said nothing.

"Mother, I'm sorry to upset you. I should not have brought this up."

"You're fifteen, Oskar. Please try and have some fun. It can take a lifetime to understand a human being. There are some things that are not as they appear, things you may never come to know or understand."

5
THE HEADLINE

Halbe
September 1932

I had never heard Timo's father swear, but as I stopped my furious pedalling and coasted towards him in the dim twilight, his words were full of expletives, as he struggled to push his son's oversized cases into the boot of his highly polished Wanderer. Breathlessly, I offered to help.

"Morning, Herr Gumpert. I'm a good organiser. Leave it to me."

I had arrived after a six-mile bike ride from Halbe to say farewell to my best friend. Today he was leaving me, departing to begin his university education at Oxford. I had readily agreed to his request that I look after the library in his absence and had already begun to plan my reading schedule. Resting his hands on his knees, Herr Gumpert smiled.

"Thanks, Oskar. I don't know why he needs to take all of this. Some of these cases are heavier than me."

Despite the chilly morning air, the light from an old storm lantern lit the beads of sweat on Herr Gumpert's face. I suggested he rest, while I removed all the cases and methodically rearranged them. He was right, the cases were heavy, no doubt full of books, but I managed to re-stack them—biggest, heaviest items at the bottom, small and flexible on top.

After thanking me, Herr Gumpert explained how he had planned all the logistics of the journey. After an hour's drive to Berlin-Lehrter Bahnhof, Timo would catch a fast train to Hamburg. His father had already arranged storage on the train and manpower at the station. Once in Hamburg, a taxi would take Timo to the port for the three o'clock ferry across the North Sea to Harwich. An English taxi would then take him to Oxford.

"So, dinner in his new accommodation, Herr Gumpert?"

Normally a stiff, stoical man, he smiled as I pushed the last remaining items into the car. His eyes glistened.

"You've been a great companion to Timo. You're a fine young man, Oskar."

He gazed at me for a while, as I shut the boot of the car, as if something troubled him.

"Are you okay, Herr Gumpert?"

He looked up, forcing a smile.

"There are fresh pancakes on the stove. Dorothy made them a few minutes ago. Timo's out the back, saying goodbye to his favourite things, hopefully not one by one."

Deciding not to ask the questions about he and Papa's disagreements, and ignoring my hunger, I went in search of my friend. From the side of the house, I could see Timo's figure in the rowing boat close to the shore and ran to meet him. Irritated at my timing, he continued to organise his books in the boat's hull.

"Good of you to come, but I must get these books over to the library. Arrived yesterday, would you believe it?"

Instinctively, I walked into the freezing-cold water until it was up to my waist, and I was alongside Timo. Being careful to keep the books dry, I flung my arms around him.

*

It was late April, and with Timo hundreds of miles away, the hours and days dragged. I had no close friends to turn to in Halbe. Most eighteen-year-olds I knew were graduating from the Hitler Youth and signing up for the armed forces. Papa's compromise to allow me to attend a Catholic youth group meant I had managed to avoid that fate.

Emil had left home. He saw university as a waste of time and, having joined the Nazi Party, worked as an apprentice engineer in Essen.

I spent most weekends with my grandpa. Despite living alone, he had no contact with Papa. Mama adored him though and encouraged me to see him. Every son grew up to challenge their father and take a different path, I reasoned. Our family was no different.

Today we had come to fish at the largest lake in the area, Oderin See, a few kilometres south of Halbe. We stood at its edge, master and pupil, on the fringe of a dense ash wood, having cast our jigs deep. I didn't enjoy fishing much. Pulling defenceless creatures out of their natural environment on the end of a hook seemed barbaric, but I suffered it to spend time with my opa, Albie.

He stood for a while, two metres from the water, legs apart. Turning to gaze at me, he squinted then frowned.

"Are you wearing make-up, Oskar?"

Embarrassed that he had spotted my now deep-seated habit, I felt a flush of heat.

"No, of course not."

Dropping the subject, he turned back to face out across the water.

"They've dismissed three of my old colleagues. Fine men, all of them. Helped organise the Franco-German school exchange for years. Parents and students loved it. But they're Jewish, according to the Nazis."

His stiff, gnarly hand landed on my shoulder like a rake, pulling me back from the water's edge as he reprimanded me with an angry whisper.

"You'll spook the fish. They know enough to spot danger. Keep yourself further back. Now those poor French children will be under the control of the Reich too. Learning German from the *Volkischer Beobachter*, being instructed to sing 'Horst Wessel'. It's tragic."

I stared across the still water. My grandpa's words lay heavy in my mind. I loved so many things about the Fatherland, but now there were beasts among us.

"Opa, should I become a teacher?"

He sighed, resting his rod on a stand, sunlight glinting off its polished brass DAM Effzett reel, and sat on his stool.

"If you're willing to toe the Nazi line, forego freedom of speech, become a vessel for hatred, you'll have a grand future as a teacher in this modern Germany, Oskar. If not, get out before the country goes to hell and drags Europe down with it."

"But I think it's what I want to do, Opa."

"Perhaps you'll find a way to teach *and* stay true to your principles. I hope so. You'll need to gain confidence too, Oskar. Teaching is performance as well as study. You must capture the imaginations of your students."

I thought about his words for a while, soaking up the decades of experience of dealing with the education system and the teachers within it.

Lightening the mood, he smiled, passing me a small leather-bound flask.

"It's getting chilly. Have some of this."

I had not acquired a taste for alcohol, like my brother, but wanted to impress Opa. Unscrewing the lid, I flopped back my head and sucked in its contents. The bittersweet taste was incredible, far better than the occasional sips I had taken of Papa's brandy.

"What is this, Opa?" I said, taking another swig.

"Hey, not too much. It's a cocktail, called a Manhattan. I used to drink them with colleagues in my teaching days."

He took another sip, resting his arms on his knees.

"You know, Oskar, my son was once a good man."

Raising the flask in his right hand, he continued.

"He became too fond of this stuff, and then something happened to him in the Great War. It changed him."

"What though, Opa? Mother says the same thing but has never explained."

"I really don't know."

"Mama is so sad. She hates seeing Emil in his Hitler Youth uniform. She's worried about the future."

Grandfather nodded slowly.

"She's a good, strong woman, Oskar. The best. Far more intelligent than your father, but she's never had a chance to use her brain. Come, sit down beside me a while."

Out of nowhere, there was a sucking sound and ripples spread across the water, where my line met it.

"Wait, Opa. I think I've got a bite."

Grandfather moved quicker than I had ever seen him move.

"Steady, boy. When you feel a tug, pull your line."

The line tightened, whatever was on the end pulling persistently.

"Strike your rod, Oskar. Like I showed you. Don't let that fish off the hook."

The excitement in his voice was contagious and, despite my ambivalence, I engaged, pulling the rod up in a sharp snap and reeling in, grabbing it halfway along as it bent and looked set to break in two.

"Keep striking, Ossy. It's a big fish."

Seeing me struggle, he waded up to his waist in the water, holding a large net in one hand and a hook in the other.

"Keep the line taut, boy."

After a minute, my tired arms drooped, but Opa hooked the fish and dragged him over to me, dropping him on the bank, where he lashed head and tail upwards, gasping for breath. Grandfather hugged me tightly, letting out a high-pitched cry.

"That thing is seven kilogrammes, at least! What a catch."

Opa deftly removed the hook from the fish's mouth and moved back into the water, cradling it for a few seconds before it swam away.

"Will it be okay, Opa?"

Grandfather nodded and smiled, and we sat down together, exhausted from our struggle. He opened the wicker basket containing our tea and passed me seeded bread, a small chunk of Emmentaler and an apple.

Chewing his food slowly and deliberately, he looked away to the water again, silent for a while as the wind picked up, blowing a dark-grey cloud across the sun and the sand across our picnic.

"Do you know what it means to be a German, Ossy?"

I shook my head, embarrassed at my inability to articulate an answer.

"Well, what about Roman history? Have you read it?"

Opa got to his feet.

"Not at school. Timo had some Roman philosophy books. *Letters from a Stoic*, I think."

He raised his arm with a pointed finger, voice rising.

"German literature is dying. No more Kafka or Remarque is allowed. No more free expression. The Nazis will stop at nothing to have complete control. They'll stamp on our writers, creating calamitous chaos before their new order appears."

He shook a little as he spoke.

"The Roman Empire appeared from chaos too and now Germany has its own 'divine Augustus'."

I nodded slowly, trying to appear as if I knew what he meant.

*

Heinz Jost was notorious at Groß Köris gymnasium. His angular features and blond hair, coupled with a legendary wit and charm, made him popular with the girls. After finishing school, he became a local news reporter. He longed to write 'proper' stories, like his heroes, who were covering the Nazis' election victory on *Der Angriff*, but was forced, instead, to cover tittle-tattle and tedium. When he arrived on our doorstep, my stomach sank.

"Jost? What are you doing here? Shouldn't you be chasing down Altheimer and his friends?"

He ignored my question, which related to his stories about the activities of SPD councillors, and smiled in the same supercilious way he had always done.

"Pleasure to see you again, Bachmann. Are you still friends with that odd character from school? The one who did nothing but read."

"Why do you ask?"

"I overheard two old women gossiping in a cafe about the 'strange boy' of Zemminsee. Apparently, he lives in a tower floating on water, full of old books. Sounds almost mythical, like some Hertha goddess legend, don't you think?"

I could tell he sensed a newspaper story. I had to dissuade him. Timo would be furious if his secret library was made public knowledge.

"Haven't seen Gumpert in a long time."

Realising immediately my error at referencing his name, I tried to make amends.

"He left the country and, anyway, the library was not impressive."

Jost gazed away at the trees for a moment, returning his focus to me with a smile.

"Bachmann, thank you. I'll be sure to pass on your best when I find him."

*

The article appeared in *The Spreewalder* a week later under the headline 'Library of the Lake'. A copy of the newspaper had been left on our front mat, I could only presume by Jost. Its cynical tone implied Timo was a friendless, introverted misfit who loved un-German books. Poor, unwitting Mrs Gumpert's quotes had been used against her own son. The mocking phrase *'kleine büchertürme'* ('small book towers') was used throughout by its author.

Shopkeepers across Halbe and Groß Köris stuck a copy in their windows, hoping the local notoriety might help trade. Local officials even displayed the story at the town hall in Teupitz. Timo's library was no longer a mystery.

*

Opa arrived at our house unannounced, one early evening in May. As I came downstairs into the kitchen, I sensed something was wrong. He sat at the table in silence, hands clasped over his bald head, fingertips feeling the lumps and bumps of a lifetime.

Mama, her hair colour transformed from deep brown to a dusky blonde, stood by him, hand on his shoulder. I stopped near the end of the table and glanced at her.

"Mama? What's wrong and why have you dyed your hair?"

68

Opa slowly raised his head, eyes full of tears, focused on mine.

"Opa, what is it? What happened?"

"The Nazis are building new libraries with one hand, destroying our literary heritage with the other. Thousands of precious books up in smoke."

He slowly raised his right hand up above his head as if in a Nazi salute before turning it into a fist, slamming it down on the table. Looking directly at me, a single tear slowly navigated the lines on his cheek.

Seeing Opa cry and Mama look so different felt cataclysmic.

"What's he talking about, Mama, and why is your hair blonde? It doesn't suit you at all."

"I'm sorry you don't like it, Oskar. But my hair's of no concern. The students in Berlin have burned many, many books. Now it's happening all over Germany. Gross stupidity."

My heart began to pound furiously. Timo's library! I hadn't visited since Jost's article appeared. A surge of adrenaline sent me flying towards the door.

"I have to go."

Riding my bicycle as fast as I could towards Limmeridge, I tried to keep visions of a burning tower from my mind. Reality struck home as I neared Timo's street in the dusk, hearing the sound of a baying mob grow ever louder.

As I turned the corner, I saw a rabble of maybe fifty people congregated around the Gumperts' front garden. Some wore the brown shirts of the SA and carried lanterns. There were boys in Hitler Youth uniforms and others in everyday clothing. They chanted as one, their faces etched with hate.

"Smash the tower, burn the books," louder and louder.

Hot and breathless, I pushed my way through the crowd, my eyes darting around to search out Timo's parents. Reaching the front door, an untidy swastika, painted in white, marked the battered woodwork. Peering past the jagged edges of smashed glass in its windowpanes, I saw inside a pair of Dobermans growling and baring their teeth but no sign of the Gumperts.

I gave chase to a cell of Hitler Youth breaking away in unison like a curling snake around the side of the house. As I jogged behind them, I peered down to the lake to see the *Red Night* ferrying half a dozen stormtroopers across to the library. I accelerated, sprinting as fast as I could past the group and down the garden, praying out loud through my panting breath.

A huge swastika lay in waiting, created with rocks from the Zen garden, sullying the lawn a few metres from the shore. Next to it were the smouldering embers of at least a hundred books, the charred page remnants of Timo's world fluttering in the breeze like fatally injured butterflies. I gagged on the smell, my eyes welling with tears, wondering why they had bothered to bring books back on land to burn.

Gazing across to the tower, I saw the first two men now at the top of the ladder disappearing inside the library, like rats scurrying into a hole, watched by a crowd on the bank. I had to stop them. Pushing through the bystanders determined to reach the water, I shouted as loud as I could.

"No! Stop. Why are you doing this?"

Two hefty beer-stinking men laughed and wrestled me to the ground. One of them sat his fat backside on my chest, delighting in telling me his cronies' mission.

"Stop your fretting, boy. They're carrying out Herr Goebbels' wishes. You cannot stop them."

Struggling to breathe, I turned my head to see the first flames licking at the windows and doors, the triumphant arsonists already rowing back to shore.

Released, I headed back to the house, hearing a sob in the darkness beneath a tree. Mrs Gumpert called out; her voice, made shrill by her ordeal, was almost unrecognisable.

"They're destroying Timo's life, Oskar. Why? Some of them are neighbours. People I've said hello to in the street."

She stood, her shoulders sloped, staring at the tower, the inferno of flames behind me dancing in her glasses, before opening her arms to hug me tightly.

"I let the dogs out at first, but one thug had a rifle and scared them off. I was terrified. All because I spilled the beans to that bloody reporter. He told me he was a history student."

I pulled away, lowering my gaze from her, my chin dipping.

"It's not your fault, Frau Gumpert. You could never have stopped them. Where's Herr Gumpert?"

"He's in Berlin. How am I going to tell Timo about this, Oskar? Please will you tell me."

I slowly shook my head, realising the explaining was mine to do.

*

For a week my dreams were plagued by the flames of Zemminsee, every conscious moment containing the weight of guilt at having let the library burn. Each night I crouched by my bed and prayed for my friend. Rather than talk to God,

71

I spoke to Timo directly, pleading his forgiveness, telling him how much he had to live for, how I would work all my days to rebuild his collection.

I didn't know Timo had even returned home from Oxford until the sound of a rumbling engine in our yard disturbed me from my chores. It was Herr Gumpert for sure. We did not know anyone else with an automobile. Gazing from my bedroom window, I saw Frau Gumpert approach our door while her husband sat, slouched and motionless, head down, in his car.

There was a brief conversation between Timo's mother and mine below me and then the sound of a quiet knock on my door. Mama came in, closing the door quietly behind her. Her face told me everything before she had said a word.

Taking my hands in hers, her kind eyes focused on mine.

"That was Timo's mother, Oscar. I'm afraid it's bad news. They found Timo's body in Lake Zemminsee, early this morning."

Her hands tightened on mine, knuckles white. I muttered to myself, tears falling freely.

"What? How? Timo couldn't swim. Why was he in the lake? It doesn't make sense."

"The local police diver found him near the burned-out tower, where the water is shallower. He had jumped from the tower and drowned. I'm so sorry, my boy."

A single tear rolled down my mother's cheek as she smiled.

"It might please you to know he was reading to the end. A copy of *The Picture of Dorian Gray* was inside his pocket. Here, this is for you."

She handed me an envelope, my name in Timo's handwriting on the front. The note inside read:

My dearest Oskar,

'The Devil never assails a man, except he finds him either void of knowledge or the fear of God'. The devils have left me destitute of spirit. I'm sorry to leave you alone among them. Feel no guilt and please don't forget me.

Timo

*

For a long time, my love of reading left me. Every book I picked up reminded me of my friend. My interest in the human mind remained, however, indeed intensified. Once I had passed my *Abitur*, I enrolled at the University of Leipzig, the birthplace of formal psychological studies, which, despite its association as a 'Jewish science', was receiving greater attention and funding under the Nazis.

6
FIRST STEPS

Berlin
July 1936

As we stepped onto the platform at Berlin's Lehrter Bahnhof, a little after midday, Mother seemed lost in thought. Eyes moist, she gazed at the swastika and Olympic flags adorning buildings around the station. A strong westerly breeze blew between them, making them dance and mingle. Gripping my hand tightly in hers, she spoke quietly in my ear.

"The lion is most handsome when looking for food, Oskar. Don't let what you see here colour your view of the Reich. Do you know what those rings stand for?"

I shook my head. The Olympics and sport generally held little interest for me.

"You need to find out. It's not something Hitler has any interest in."

"So why is he hosting the Olympics, Mama?"

"Because he's an egotist and the eyes of the world are watching."

Mother put her arm through mine as I carried our case out onto the Invalidenstrasse. She had decided to join me in Berlin for a few days before I started my training at the German

Institute for Psychological Research and Psychotherapy. We would stay with a friend of hers before she returned to Halbe.

Boarding a crammed double-decker bus, we stood near the luggage hold and journeyed through the streets of Berlin Mitte. Every shop, office, pavement and corner we passed seemed pristine, a sense of celebration bristling on the streets. Mother glanced at me constantly during the short trip, as if trying to sense what I was thinking.

The bus dropped us next to Hackesche Höfe, a bustling courtyard complex of cafes and shops. We located the street address down a narrow pebble-stone alley enclosed between crumbling walls, stopping before its unmarked door to knock. As we waited, I noticed the small leather-goods shop next door had its window smashed and boarded. The words 'Germans, defend yourselves! Do not buy from Jews!' had been daubed in white paint on its door. Mother stared at it, tutting.

"That's what those Olympic tourists really need to see."

A tall, dark-haired man edged open the door, sticking his head out to look nervously up the alleyway before beckoning us in. Once the door was shut, he embraced Mother, then held her shoulders with his large hands at arm's length.

"Aneta. Let me look at you. I'm glad to see you here safe. It's been so long."

He turned his kind eyes on me and smiled.

"This must be Oskar. The last time I saw you, you came up to your mother's knee."

They laughed together, the fondness between them evident.

"I'm Daniel. Daniel Brunner. Your mother and I worked together here in Berlin many years ago. She wrote to me and mentioned your love of books. We've many here in cases at the top of the stairs. Please, go have a look. You're welcome to take one to read but be careful which one."

"Thank you."

I turned to Mother.

"We should be going soon. If you want to see your old place of work this afternoon, I mean."

She nodded, her eyes pointing me upstairs. I climbed the narrow staircase, leaving them to renew their friendship. A brilliant, detailed pencil sketch of three children adorned the wall. Next to it was a beautiful painting of a green mountain, 'Kahlenberg' etched on a golden plaque beneath it. I opened the case at the top of the stairs and sifted through the stacked books inside, noticing immediately a copy of *The Oppermanns* by Lion Feuchtwanger. Timo had owned a copy, I remembered, now blown to the wind along with all the other books. Tucking it back in the pile, I pulled free a copy of *Before the Storm* by Fontane, sure it would not attract any unwanted attention from Nazi officials.

Mother and her friend were deep in animated conversation as I returned downstairs and interrupted. My question spoiled the mood.

"Did you draw your own children, Herr Brunner? Where are they now?"

He paused, his expression becoming serious before his answer finally emerged in a monotone.

"Yes. They're no longer in Berlin."

Mother quickly changed the subject.

"We must go. We'll return before it's dark, Daniel. I'll knock three times."

He nodded, kissed Mother on her cheek and took our bag away with him up the stairs. As we strolled back along the alley, where an old woman stood mopping the steps to her home, and on towards the main street, I blurted out what had been on my mind.

"Mother, why are we staying there? He's a Jew—it's too dangerous. Can we not stay in a hotel? There were plenty near the station."

She stopped, her face flushed.

"Please, keep your voice down, Oskar. I do not think of Daniel as a Jew, simply as an old friend, and that is enough. As for hotels, they are expensive and, as you may have noticed, there's an Olympics on."

*

We caught a tram south-west to Charlottenburg and walked a short distance along Schlosstrasse. Mother happily reminisced with lilting voice as she took in the sights.

"Berlin was an incredible place in 1914. Yes, there were mounted soldiers on the streets, but the war seemed like the culmination of years of progress. The Germans were sure they would win."

"I can believe it, Mother. You'll remember I loved Mark Twain as a boy. He called Berlin 'the Chicago of Europe'."

Mother raised her eyebrows.

"Sometimes, Oskar, I worry you think everything can be learned from a book. You need to live a little bit too."

Her comment wounded me. I dwelt on it a while. It was she, after all, who had turned me to the pages of books.

After a few silent minutes, strolling past huge houses with walled gardens and wardrobe-sized windows, we stopped before a large three-storey villa. Set back from the street, it was neoclassical in design with a vestibule surrounded by four grand Romanesque columns at its front. Its windows were tall, with arched tops, iron rails surrounding its many platforms and balconies.

Mother gazed at the house, her breathing accelerating, eyes dancing. Her mood visibly changed. I gently rested my hand on her shoulder.

"Why don't you knock, Mother? It would be good for you to go back inside. Perhaps there will still be records of the time you worked here."

She stared at the house a while longer, then turned her head sharply towards me.

"No. It was enough for me to see the outside. I've already told you about my time working here. There's no point dwelling on it. Come. Let's walk a while."

Remaining silent, deep in thought, Mother stopped at a metal-legged wooden bench with a slanted back beside a flower bed.

"Oskar, sit down. I want to tell you something."

We sat at either end, so we could turn and face each other, and then she spoke to me quietly, seriously.

"You must leave Germany as soon as you can. Go and study in America, just like you said you wanted to. I've got the money to pay for the crossing."

Her words seemed to drift into the blue skies above Berlin. I could not take them in. She paused, gazing at me, then spoke firmly and deliberately.

"I will say this only once. Never, ever ask me where the money came from, but know that your education is all I care about. Do you understand?"

*

The confidence I gained from Mother's presence with me in Berlin evaporated once I started at the newly opened Institute for Psychological Research and Psychotherapy in September. My basic, post-diploma training proved grossly inadequate in preparing me for the deluge of despair I encountered in my first few weeks. Situated halfway along a leafy lane behind Pankow-Heinersdorf station, in the sleepy north Berlin suburb of Heinersdorf, its external serenity masked the mayhem inside.

*

My first patient of the day, Dieter Vostell, a young SS officer from Treptow, arrived in consultation room three, screaming. He was not in uniform. Sinking to the floor before me, he pressed his fists into the side of his head, as if he wanted his brain to explode. I could not understand a word of his incoherent babble. It took a few minutes for me to calm him and get him into a chair, where he began to plead with me to cure his homosexuality, terrified his inability to give it up would lead to his execution.

"I'm nothing but a curse. The Fatherland can never forgive the way I am. Now the Reich has decided I cannot so much as glance at a pretty man. Please, please, is there some way you

79

can cure me? Make me like my brothers, married with glowing children, making the Führer proud."

There was not a centimetre of room for this sobbing man in Germany. He had no Fatherland. Although I despised the SS, Vostell was human, so I tried my best to comfort him, although this involved little more than telling him to flee and hide. His own morbid prophecy, so deeply rooted in his mind, could never be worked free. Vostell, either by his own hand or that of an SS executioner, was not long for this world.

*

Gripping a roll of papers in his hand, Bert Eidenschink, a middle-aged bank clerk from Prenzlauer Berg, entered the room silently. He glanced at me several times from behind large, gold-rimmed glasses then sat, his legs and shoulders tightly tucked in. Before I had a chance to speak, he asked me a question.

"Who do you work for?"

"We work on a cooperative basis. The Reich does not pay us. Please, speak freely."

Looking to the floor between us, he breathed heavily for a minute, before speaking again.

"I'm not a troublemaker. My wife and family live a quiet life. We've had the same family doctor for a decade. He's Jewish. A month ago, he disappeared. Then I hear the Reich has banned Jewish doctors. I want to know where he's gone. I've lived in Prenzlauer Berg my whole life. Do you know it?"

I shook my head.

"The Italians built their churches, brought their restaurants. They were forced out in the Great War. Slovaks went too. You know the Polish Jews learned our language. It made them better tolerated by us Germans. They weren't pious, maybe celebrating Rosh Hashanah, Yom Kippur, Hanukkah. Nothing else."

He went quiet again, putting his roll of papers to one side and glancing at the clock before bringing his hands back together.

"I had a friend. David. Our families regularly ate together, the children played games, helped each other with schoolwork. He ran a small grocery store on the edge of Wörther Platz. That was until last month when the Gestapo paid him a visit."

Eidenschink stared at me.

"I'm here because I can no longer stay silent when I see what is happening around me. Each day I wake and drink to numb myself. Please, tell me what else should I do?"

*

Mitte housewife Zelda Beck had money and, as it turned out, morals too. She arrived in the consultation room perfectly dressed in a flowing, turquoise silk-jacket dress with a shoulder-button jacket, a matching slouch hat and a thick pearl necklace. The deep hang of her hat cast a shadow across her eyes, the only evidence of her tears the handkerchief she brought to her face at regular intervals.

"How is it I can help you, Frau Beck?"

"I cannot find joy in anything anymore. It all started when she left."

"When who left?"

"Kresla. Our cleaner. I dismissed her."

Her tears intensified for a few moments before she regained her composure. I was curious as to why Frau Beck was quite so upset.

"She was more than a cleaner. Kresla had been a part of my family and my parents' family since before the Great War. Saw me grow up and my own children."

"Why did you dismiss her? I mean, given what you have told me—"

"Because she's Jewish. My husband insisted on it. His company has contracts with the Nazis. My mother would roll in her grave if she knew Kresla was gone. I've not slept in weeks. It feels as if I am carrying a heavy rock on my back..."

Frau Beck stayed a little over five minutes, expressing her feelings then leaving as the clock struck one. No more patients today and time for lunch. Gathering my notes, I headed down the wide concrete staircase, pondering the issues I had encountered this morning. All of them were caused by the sick society the Nazis had created. I had no answers, other than to listen and medicate. I prayed that, over time, my training at the institute would help me understand Father in a way my years of study at William Lundt's laboratory for psychological research had failed to do.

It was Opa who had told me about this place. He knew Leonhard Seif, an associate of Luftwaffe commander Marshal Hermann Goering's cousin, Matthias Heinrich Goering, who ran the institute. There was nowhere in Germany of any distinction where I could study without the influence of

Nazism, but Opa had said to me, "You might just find enough space there to maintain your values."

Arriving at the bottom step, I was met by fellow student Felix Bauer, an Austrian, whose grandfather had also worked in education.

"Oskar, you look tired. A late night, I hope?"

I shook my head.

"My patients all seem so disconnected, Felix. They've lost all control of their thoughts."

He smirked, raising his arms in a grand gesture.

"Perhaps they're not *real* Germans and have failed to be seized by Wotan."

He grinned at me. Jung's essay suggesting that the 'ancient god of storm and frenzy' had reignited the German spirit under the Nazis had attracted much debate here and in all psychology circles. Always philosophical, Felix had the ability to lighten my mood. His cynicism of the Nazis, love of English tea, which I had been introduced to by Timo's mother, and long, often technical conversations about the human mind endeared him to me even more. We strolled along the corridor together towards the canteen.

"Interesting you quote Jung, Felix. I thought your countryman, Freud, would have had something to say on the topic?"

"Ah, as you know, he's rather hidden away in the corners here. Have you visited the locked bookcase in the basement? His works are all there. I know who has a key."

We sat at one of the large round tables next to a window, decorated with a white tablecloth and napkins, fine china and silver cutlery. The Nazis were adept at psychological tricks, equipping lunchrooms well to keep workforces motivated. A bouquet of bright flowers at the centre of our table would not be enough to enhance my outlook.

"I'm not sure Freud has the answers I need. Understanding neurosis is not just about sexual conflict. There are other internal and external factors. Overcoming inferiority and striving for superiority are what drive us, Felix."

"Ah, individual psychology. You, my friend, have been reading Adler. Am I right?"

I nodded. "I find his ideas hopeful, Felix. They may even help me unravel my own family problems."

As Felix finished his meal, he smiled kindly, reaching into his jacket pocket.

"We must talk about that some time."

He passed me a worn-looking, printed leaflet across the table, an invitation to a talk by John Rittmeister entitled 'Psychotherapeutic duty and the new humanism'.

"I'm going. Will you come with me?" Felix whispered.

I did not know Rittmeister's work well and my friend's whisper made me suspicious.

"Why the secrecy?"

"He's a Jew and, most would say, a Marxist, not exactly flavour of the month in Berlin. He works in Zürich, but a few in this place are in contact."

I assessed the risk briefly, my desire for knowledge winning out over fear.

"I'll come."

"Good. Don't mention it to anyone. I've a list of approved invitees. The talk will be held in a disused ice factory next to the

84

Spree in Kreuzberg. We can get a lift with Jeismann. There's undercover Gestapo all over the U-Bahn."

*

Jeismann, a Freudian like Felix, maintained contact with many of the Jewish psychologists who had either left Berlin or wanted to. His driving was terrible. The tyres of his little Opel P4 hit the kerb numerous times while he and Felix chatted, weaving through the streets of Mitte and Prenzlauer Berg. I stayed silent. My nerves were making my stomach churn so badly I thought I would have to ask Jeismann to stop. This whole venture felt dangerous. Glancing through the rear window, I noticed that a large, black Mercedes had followed us at a distance of thirty metres all the way from Heinersdorf, but said nothing to the others.

Winding down the window to let in some air, I gagged at the sulphurous smell floating in off the river on the breeze. Jeismann turned the car into a gated courtyard beside the factory, parking it next to three others. He led us through a set of double doors into the main factory, a tide of warm evening sunlight flooding through its many windows.

We strode across the dusty chessboard floor towards a small crowd gathered around an imposing set of silenced iron wheels, pipes and pistons. On top of these, a slender, dark-haired man with round glasses stood head and shoulders above the crowd, his passionate voice already audible.

As we neared the last set of concrete pillars before Rittmeister's audience, all hell broke loose. Five black-uniformed henchmen, pocket pistols drawn, broke down a side door and stormed into the hall towards the group. Their plain-clothed leader, in a grey suit and long leather coat, paused, spotting our approach and calling one of his men back.

We headed in different directions, Jeismann back towards the double doors, Felix out of a side door, while I charged up a set of iron stairs towards the roof. Before I had cleared the first flight, my pursuer's hand gripped my left ankle tight, throwing me off balance. I groaned in pain as my right foot missed the step, my shin and face scraping down it, the sole of a boot on the back of my neck.

*

I had been bundled into a Citroën Traction Avant with another student, who I did not recognise. Nearing the Gestapo headquarters, my gaze drifted to Detlev-Rohwedder-Haus, the pristine, imposing home of the Reich Ministry of Aviation on Wilhelmstrasse. I would have liked to visit, had I not been captive in this French gangster car.

Turning on to Prinz-Albrecht-Strasse, the home of Nazi tyranny loomed large in the Avant's windscreen. The stories from Mother and Grandpa about what they did to Communists, Jews and gypsies in this place, tales of torture, ice-cold baths, electric shocks, rubber nightsticks and soldering irons, now flashed across my mind. My breath shortened and, like a nervous boy on his first day at school, my bladder leaked a little.

Marched through the doors into the main hall, I gazed around the Romanesque balustrade and high arches, light from the series of tall windows flooding the broad walkways, interrupted only by a steady stream of Nazis.

The Gestapo took me down steps to the right, along a dark corridor, pushing me into a small interview room. Inside, white, glazed, slatted brick walls surrounded me. An interrogator sat behind a cubby-hole desk, illuminated by the shafts of light emanating from the glass bricks above him.

Pushing his round glasses over the bridge of his nose with a single finger, he continued to make notes for a moment, before looking up and smirking as he spotted the obvious and embarrassing damp mark on my trousers.

"Sit, sit. You're not the first man to wet himself in this place. I've a few questions, that's all. You're Bachmann, correct?"

I gave a single nod, wondering how this man already knew my name. The temperature down here was much lower. I shivered a little as I fell back on the chair, a brushed-steel factory light flickering above me, making my eyeballs ache.

"Contrary to what you may think, we've no desire to harm you. The Fatherland needs people like you. Herr Goering will create a legion of great psychiatrists to deliver the Führer's aims. Why did you go to Rittmeister's talk?"

I had heard his mushy-mouthed Bavarian dialect before and tried to charm him.

"Sir, are you from Augsburg, perhaps?"

He stared at me, teeth grinding. Had I overstepped the mark? He was the questioner, after all. To my relief, he smiled.

"No, Singen. Almost a Swiss."

His smile disappeared.

"But definitely *not* a Swiss."

His eyes narrowed, the lines on his forehead deepening further.

"Answer the question."

"A fellow student suggested I go, to broaden my knowledge."

"Rittmeister is a Jew and a Marxist. Do you know where he is staying in Berlin?"

His question meant Rittmeister had escaped and, I hoped, Felix and Jeismann too.

I shook my head.

"Why have you not joined the National Socialists, and what do you know about Jeismann?"

"Very little. He just gave me a lift today."

"Bachmann, you've done enough for me to lock you up. Attending meetings organised by undesirables is banned. For now, continue your studies. We will watch you closely."

*

Relieved, I walked away free from Gestapo headquarters, acutely aware this was something not many people did. Heading south down Wilhelmstrasse, I reached the banks of the Spree and bought Bratwurst from a stallholder, wolfing it down as I collapsed on a wooden bench overlooking the river. Stomach growling and twinging with indigestion, I watched the salon ship *Marple* pass slowly by, wishing I could jump on-board and sail away from this place, back home to the Spreewald. For the first time, I realised my life was entwined with my nation's destiny. If I stayed in Germany, I could not escape the Nazis anymore.

7

AMERICAN DREAM

Port of Hamburg
Late July 1938

I had expected that Hitler's contravention of the Treaty of Versailles through the *Anschluss* in Austria would see the great port of Hamburg shunned by the international community. But as Mother and I strolled arm in arm to the overseas bridge, we passed American cargo vessels, whaling ships from Norway and two narrow Italian warships, a rare sight here, for Hamburg was not a naval port.

We stopped a while to watch passengers' cars dangled precariously above the hatches of the *Cap Arcona*, pride of Hamburg, before her journey to Buenos Aires. It seemed unfeasible they could be lowered bonnet-first this way.

As we reached the hull of the *New York*, Mother stopped very deliberately. I put down my case and gave her a long, lingering embrace.

The process of leaving the Fatherland had, it seemed, been straightforward. Much of this had been down to Mother. She had completed the paperwork for my student visa application to the US Consulate in Leipzig back in the summer of 1936, telling me she wanted me to focus on my studies. Somehow, she had found the money to buy me a tourist-class ticket across the ocean, so I could avoid the horrors of steerage. I had no idea where the money had come from and would never ask.

The gulf between my parents had grown wider. For a while, Father had seemed happy with me, even proud, as I completed military service and gained a Luftwaffe pilot's licence at Schönwalde, the new military airfield north-west of Berlin. Little did he know that, away from the Kranlich II training gliders, I had written to a contact at the University of New York, given to me by Mother, and gained a place there to further my psychology studies. Despite his distaste at the Nazis' treatment of the Jews, his belief in Hitler continued to grow, and he accepted a vaccine research post in Poland at Przemyśl. Mother quietly, and resolutely, resisted any show of support for the Nazis. Now I felt as if I was deserting her.

As we had said our goodbyes on the quayside, Mother held my arms and gazed long into my eyes, as she had done so many times when Father beat me or when she encouraged me to read. Somehow, this time was different. Her tear-filled eyes held a secret that her lips could not let go. I wondered if she and Father would separate for good. It would be no surprise. She had refused to join him in Poland, a land her own parents had left just decades before. I knew she would readily have sailed away with me if money had allowed.

Reaching into her jacket pocket, she placed a small package in my hand.

"This is for you, my son. Do not open it until you reach American soil. I love you."

*

New York City
Five days later

The relentless ocean waves that smashed into the hull of the *New York* felt normal, a physical extension of my helter-skelter life. But as we sailed slowly past Lady Liberty in pond-like summer waters, a sense of calm expectation came over me. An unseasonably cool breeze rushed around my ears and what felt like a colony of ants raced across my body, making it jolt stiff. Gazing up at this famous beacon of freedom, I thanked her for the chance to resurrect my dreams. The grand statue's sculptor, Bartholdi, based Liberty's face on his mother's, and so I thought of my own 'libertas' and saviour and thanked her too. Without dear Mother, I would not be here.

I recalled poring over Timo's books on this great nation, studying the hundreds of black and white landscape photographs in them: the Great Plains, the Mississippi Delta, the Rockies and the Sequoia Forest. Now I was determined to see them all in glorious colour. My real life was about to begin.

We sailed past Ellis Island, where thousands of my countrymen had filed through, full of hope and trepidation, to meet their destiny, and on into the *New York*'s vast namesake harbour. Passing a pair of tatty, overworked tugs on our starboard side, I gazed, fascinated, as the tiny workhorses pushed huge barges full of crushed rock across the bay, puffing white plumes of steam into the air. Behind us, a flock of gulls swept in, taking advantage of the fishy pickings left in our wake. The deckhands, waving their welcome across to us, teetered on their tugs' narrow ledges, surely a perilous activity.

91

Squinting, I could make out the name *Nieuw Amsterdam II* on a steamship ahead of us, docking at its pier head, ready to deposit thousands more new arrivals at the city gates.

Passing Ambrose Lighthouse an hour ago, the ship's foghorns had bellowed into the Atlantic air, the signal our journey was nearly complete. Excited passengers flocked to the decks, sharing binoculars to scan the horizon and spot the much-anticipated landmarks they'd longed to see, the assurance that America, and their futures, were now in reach.

The view of the Manhattan skyline, moving towards us like a slow-rolling wave, was magnificent. Although a country boy, I had been to big cities: Berlin, Frankfurt, Hamburg, even Paris and Madrid. Nothing compared to this. Deck crew handed us postcard guides to the Manhattan skyline. Now I could make out individual landmarks: 40 Wall Street, the Chrysler, Empire State and Woolworth buildings. Their scale took my breath away. Company names were everywhere, proudly displayed on harbour buildings: United States Lines, Cunard White Star, Grace Line and many more, all vying for business in this competition of capitalism.

A sea of smiling faces, representative of futures not yet realised, greeted us on the quayside. Some called out and waved as we approached our final resting place on the Hudson River. Nine days earlier I had left an emboldened homeland, now swelled with the Germanic people of Austria and the Sudetenland. Hitler's plan for world domination was still in its infancy. My relief at breathing 'free' American air was immense.

We docked at New York Harbour's Pier 88 an hour earlier than scheduled. The rumbling of the steamship's turbine engines was quiet for the first time in days, its furnaces and boilers cooling. As I collected my modest travel bag from the baggage room, I heard a familiar voice.

"We made it, Oskar! Let's meet for lunch."

Long-haired and softly spoken, Raymond, an artist from Belarus, had been my ship companion. He stood grinning behind me. We'd met on the third day of the voyage, when the *New York* had sailed straight into the jaws of a North Atlantic storm. She'd bucked and heeled in waves taller than the town hall tower in Hamburg, as my newly found friend and I clung to each other and a cold, grey steel leg, beneath a tourist-class dining room table. I told him about my two years' national service at Schönwalde. He recounted his years as a School of Paris artist, newly escaped from Polish oppression in his homeland. His dream was to open his own gallery in Manhattan. Our conversation helped distract us from the cacophony of shuddering, clicking, banging and bashing. At one point, the waves tipped the ship so high we could see the bow pointing towards the blackened clouds through the battered windows. I closed my eyes and prayed as the ship headed down and down into the cavernous deep below us. We broke into nervous laughter as a giant wave crashed through the ship, making it judder to its core as it came back up. The storm was thankfully short, but long enough to bond us.

"Sure, Raymond, look me up at the university. Best of luck with the gallery."

The queue to exit bubbled noisily with laughter and the excited chat of a multitude of tongues. My mind went into overdrive as I simultaneously translated conversations in Italian, Spanish and Polish.

A fashionably dressed father ahead of me turned to his children. One word he uttered seemed to echo in my mind. It sounded like *meh-shug-an-nay*, but I couldn't recall its origin or why I remembered it. After a few minutes, I was making my way down the gangplank, scanning faces in the noisy crowd. There was no one I knew, of course, but this place and these people seemed familiar, and my heart swelled with joy. I walked along the quayside, pulling the package from Mother from my pocket. I had kept my promise. Hurriedly, I opened it, pulling free a small, hammered, silver geometric box with the inscription: 'Once learned, knowledge can never be taken away.'

*

I felt a mixture of sadness and excitement as I squeezed into the crammed, tired-looking main hall of the New York Passenger Ship Terminal, desperate now for a quick transit and some space. A quick check of my consulate-stamped passport was enough to see me through the gates, but not everyone on-board *New York* made it as far as the terminal. Officials met rows of steerage-class passengers and pushed them into transport ferries, their next stop a dehumanising examination at Ellis Island. I wondered how many would get the chance to realise their dream.

Struggling with my bag, I clambered onto 12th Avenue, shocked by the incessant train of traffic heading along the road. Every kind of vehicle went past—trucks laden with food, building materials and cigarettes; motorcycles; American cars I could identify as Buicks, Cadillacs and Plymouths—but not the cab I had hoped to hail. After twenty-five minutes, with a warm sun and cool breeze enticing me, I cut my losses and hiked down the Avenue, soon forgetting the weight of my case as I absorbed the pleasant greenery of the west-side parks, a welcome change from endless ocean. Stopping at a roadside stall, I made my first American purchase, a copy of the *New York Post* and a candy bar called a Chick-O-Stick. Within half an hour, I reached Pier 66 and sat to read and enjoy my snack.

Almost immediately, a Negro cab driver wearing a smart tweed coat, tie and flat cap pulled over to drop off an overweight family. Jumping up, I ran towards him, calling out, "Hello. University, please?"

Grinning, he held the rear door open for me.

"Sure, sir. Get in. Which one?"

"New York University, please."

I studied the driver's features as we sped away, fascinated by his tightly curled, dense hair and broad, flat nose.

"Now, will you stop staring at me? It's making me uncomfortable. You never seen a black man before?"

I had only ever seen a couple of black people in Germany, both in Berlin and only from a distance.

The morning sun flooded the back of the cab with warm light. It turned out the driver's disposition was just as sunny, a friendly chuckle concluding almost every sentence he spoke.

"You're lucky to get a cab today. Most drivers are out on strike. I can't afford not to work."

"I'm glad. I remember a transport strike in Berlin a few years ago. Brought the entire city to a halt for days."

"Oh, so you're German? I'm terrible with accents."

I dropped my gaze from his rear-view mirror to watch the passers-by outside his window.

"Don't you worry, we've every nationality under the sun in New York. We all get along, most of the time. What are your plans?"

"I'm studying. But I hope to stay and make a living."

"That's great. We need all the brains we can get. You want a smoke?"

I nodded, and a packet of Camels landed instantly on the seat beside me. Taking my first American cigarette between my lips, I realised I had left my lighter on the ship.

"Excuse me, do you have fire?"

He threw back his head and chuckled, throwing over a tarnished brass lighter that, once lit, stayed alight despite the draught from the window. My confession of nationality had the driver study me with greater intensity.

"You seem a nice, polite guy. I'm guessing you're not one of those Nazis. We've seen a few here."

"No. Certainly not."

He nodded, satisfied.

"Sorry, had to ask. Fella named Kuhn leads the German American Bund. They're Nazis. I've read all about them. There's a whole bunch of them over on Long Island."

I pondered this for a while as we headed along the Hudson River, taking in a rather ordinary view of warehouses and factories, rather than high-rises. Why would Germans in the land of the free start a Nazi cult? It made no sense. The driver continued his commentary.

"There are two hundred and fifty slaughterhouses over there in the meatpacking district, producing the third largest number of meats in the entire country."

Perhaps making a connection in his head, he went on.

"I've read in the papers about the goings-on in your homeland. Hitler's a madman. Mind you, we've our own crazies here. Day before yesterday, a man attacked Mayor La Guardia on the steps of City Hall."

The driver seemed to lose his focus briefly. He shook his head and continued to shake it. Turning into Leroy Street, a yellow bus careered towards us, forcing my driver to swerve, skidding across a lane of traffic to the left, hitting the kerb and making me bash my head against the window frame.

"Douche bag! Son of a bitch!"

His pointless scream turned a few heads, but the bus had already sped away.

"New York drivers, huh? I'm sorry. Are you all right, sir?"

Rubbing an already emerging lump on the side of my head, I smiled through the familiar pain.

"I'm okay."

The Manhattan streets bustled outside my window. Laughing sailors carrying suitcases, a young woman pushing a perambulator with maternal pride, a businessman rushing out of a cab to a meeting, and a teenage boy and girl walking hand in hand. I found the normality of it all comforting.

Minutes later, the cab pulled slowly along the edge of a huge tree-lined park. I gazed across to a group of costumed actors performing a play beneath orange-leaved sugar maples that provided shade for the audience, who were arranged in a circle.

"That's Washington Square Park. Been a lot of debate about it lately. Commissioner Moses wants to re-route the traffic and take down a lot of trees. The Greenwich Village community doesn't like that idea too much. We'll see. Here you go. Main entrance to the university is across the road. Good luck, kid. You got a lotta shit wichoo, coming all this way to study. That's eighty-four cents, please."

I opened my wallet, pulling out the ten-dollar bill my father had given me years before.

"Are you kidding me? You have nothing smaller than a sawbuck?"

"No, I'm sorry. It's all I have. Take a dollar."

I strolled along the sidewalk, the cluttered background noise of the city reverberating, its sources both near and far. The chatter of nearby children, with their distinctive New York accents, vowels elongated and rounded. A church bell clanging in a fight for supremacy over the constant hum of automobiles and trains.

A colourful woman stumbled towards me in high-heeled shoes. She appeared young from a distance but close up, her wigged head and make-up-caked face belonged to a woman of forty or more.

"Fancy a date, kid? I give reductions to first-timers."

I felt repulsed as she winked at me, opening her coat to reveal her underwear. Father had once told me about an alleyway in Herbertstrasse where prostitutes still worked, despite the Nazi ban. He seemed to suggest I might use their services, concerned my lack of bragging about female conquests was evidence of virginity. I did not ask him how he knew about it.

As the university's reception loomed nearer, my mouth became dry, palms moist. Even though I had secured my place, I worried a bureaucratic obstacle might still stop me from enrolling. I imagined myself sweating on a downtown construction site or delivering parcels from a green Ford AA truck. I felt thoroughly unprepared.

Standing at the edge of the sidewalk, I tilted my head back, and back again as far as it would go, to gaze at the ten-storey building before me. White clouds passed behind the pointed roof, the light-brick and terracotta façade clean and new. It wouldn't have seemed out of place in thirteenth-century Cologne, its Gothic design impressive and stately.

Walking past the columns at the building's entrance, I pulled my bag up over the three deep steps and through the double doors. Here, in this vast foyer, I was, all at once, lost and insignificant. A group of young women in a huddle fifteen metres away peered across at me before giggling and returning to their conversation. To the left, across the highly polished floor tiles, sat the registration desk, manned by a retirement-aged receptionist in a blue uniform and tie. I rubbed my shoes up against the back of my legs, ran my hand through my hair a few times and made my way over.

Without looking up from his filing, the receptionist addressed me.

"Hello. Can I help you?"

"Yes, sir. My name's Oskar Bachmann. I'm from Germany, starting a postgraduate course in psychology."

"Very good. Your papers, please?"

Nodding, I hurriedly opened my overpacked bag, spilling socks, underwear and my copy of *Die Flammende Venus* onto the floor in full public view. I cursed, rummaging to find the papers folded and tucked in a pair of pleated trousers at its bottom. Two other new students had pushed in front of me in the queue. New York waited for no one. Back at the desk, the administrator quickly found my details, holding them close to his face to examine them at close quarters through thick glasses.

"Bachmann. Okay, I've all your term details here and there's a recent entry on file in regard to your accommodation."

"Oh?"

The receptionist's eyes widened.

"It appears you've an apartment at the Otto H. Kahn House in Carnegie Hill, on the Upper East Side."

I stared back at him, blankly.

"One of the most exclusive parts of Manhattan. Its former owner, Mr Kahn himself, was a German financier and philanthropist. They use it as a Catholic girls' school now, so I've no idea where you'll stay."

I felt immediately overwhelmed. Who arranged this? Surely not my parents?

"I see. Well, thank you. How's this being paid for, please?"

"It's all arranged. There's no name on the file, just a note that the landlord will find you in due course."

He handed me a set of keys, with an expensive-looking leather fob and an envelope containing ten dollars.

"Good luck with your studies. Just hail a cab from outside."

*

The Otto Kahn house may have been built in Italian renaissance style but, despite its grandeur, I felt a familiarity as

I arrived outside. Perhaps it was the fact it had been home to a German, but it somehow reminded me of Limmeridge, and my departed best friend.

I paused a while to take in the splendour of its French limestone façade and elegant second-floor pilasters, before making my way inside, immediately struck by the creamy yellow of the Caen stone stairs and hallway. Behind a desk sat a young nun, reading. She glanced at me, her expressive deep-green eyes telling me she would see to me when the chapter was finished. I approached slowly to give her time, noticing the thin paperback tucked inside the pages of her Bible, before clearing my throat.

"Yes, can I help you? The school is closed to further applications at the moment."

I found her acerbic tone attractive but told myself that falling for a nun was not a good idea.

"Oh, no. I've been told by New York University that I've accommodation here."

She gave me a puzzled, lingering look before leaving her desk for the office behind it. A moment later, she reappeared with an older nun next to her.

"I'm Mother Superior of the Convent of the Sacred Heart. You must be Mr Bachmann?"

I nodded.

"Follow me."

Smiling at the younger nun, I thanked her, hauling my bag behind Mother Superior up three flights of stairs and along a hallway to stop in front of the door at the end. Breathlessly, I thanked her, and she nodded curtly in return.

"The second floor is out of bounds, but you're welcome to use the restaurant on the ground and any of the facilities on this floor. Unless there's anything else, I'm leading afternoon prayer shortly."

"I do have a question. Who owns this apartment, Mother?"

"One of our benefactors. I'm not at liberty to reveal names."

She turned and left. My chest felt suddenly tight and short of breath, my head swimming as I pushed the key into the lock and turned it.

Inside was an apartment as big as my family's Halbe home, complete with a fully fitted kitchen, a marble-encased bathroom and a dining area with a huge window overlooking Central Park Reservoir.

Fully clothed, I flopped onto the walnut Emperor bed and fell into a deep, travel-weary sleep.

*

A week later

Despite the opulence of its setting, a sense of pious penance made depression-era staples a regular feature of the menu at the Convent of the Sacred Heart. That evening, I escaped the lecturing nuns and ate in my own personal dining area. Sat at the window table, picking over a Hoover Stew of macaroni, hotdogs, canned tomatoes and corn, I peered across at the reservoir, wondering how many times bigger than Zemminsee it must be.

Suddenly, I felt very small and a little lonely. Most of the students I had met on campus in my first week at NYU lived with other students in digs closer to the university. There was a serenity here, sure enough, which had its benefits when it came to studying and reading, but I felt alien in one of the most expensive apartments in Manhattan. Who was paying for this place and why? I had to find out. Staying in a convent school was not conducive to fun. I would have to find my own place.

I got changed and made my way down to the reception area. Seeing me descend the stairs, Mother Superior stepped into the office, reappearing to hand me an envelope.

"This is for you. Delivered by hand this afternoon."

"Thanks. Did you see the person who delivered it?"

"No, it was handed to one of the other nuns."

I tore open the letter and read the brief note inside. It simply said:

Hope you like the apartment. Meet at Sam's Bar and Grill, St. Mark's Place, 7:30.

Your landlord.

8

SCIENCE AND TREACHERY

Occupied Przemyśl
October 1939

Looking across at her middle-aged lover, all belly and misplaced hair, Agnieska Stanislaw felt nauseous. She glared as he leaned awkwardly from the bed to retrieve his last Eckstein from the pocket of his trousers which lay in a heap on the floor. Turning back towards her, Karl Bachmann grinned, cigarette hanging from his lips, in a pathetic attempt to look like a Hollywood movie star.

She had been seeing him for a while. Her father had failed to explain to her why this deception was necessary, but she owed him so much. It was not so bad. Karl was seldom capable of having sex.

"I hate you smoking. You must've seen how bad it is for you?"

Lighting up, he sucked in hard and blew a petulant billow of smoke towards her, making her splutter and turn away.

"If you mean the Reich posters, they don't seem to listen to their own advice, do they?"

She tutted, stomping to the bathroom, leaving the door open as she perched on the lavatory, figuring the distance might make him lose his guard.

Despite her previous efforts, he had told her little about himself. She knew he lived in a tiny flat in the old government building near Zasanie's communal cemetery, but that was of no use to her.

"Why don't you tell me about your family? It's not like I don't know you're married. What happened to your wife?"

He was silent for a moment.

"She's in Czechoslovakia, staying with a friend from her working days in Berlin. She's a dissenter. It's better that we're apart."

Agnieska pulled up her knickers and returned to the bedside, not wanting this opportunity to be wasted. Slipping her chilled limbs under the covers next to Karl, she pulled her manicured red nails across his chest.

"What about your sons? You told me one was in the Korps-Pionier-Battalion in the Saarland, but what about the other?"

Karl left the bed to gaze out the window into the courtyard below, as the twilight gradually left its corners.

"Why do you always ask so many questions, Aggie? He used to do the same. If you must know, he's at university in New York. I didn't want him to go. His duty was to the Fatherland, but he's never respected my wishes."

"Has he a name?"

Karl's eyes narrowed.

"Oskar. A mother's boy. I don't have time for him."

He collected the two white hotel robes from the back of the door, handing one to Aggie, before setting his short arms firmly on his hips.

"This war, and this place, will make me. I want my name in *Scientia Pharmaceutica*, maybe even the *Frankfurter Zeitung*. Never dreamed of working with Weigl, and yet, here I am."

As he spoke of his own ambitions, Aggie's mind drifted back to their first meeting at the Grand Cafe Stieber, one of few main-square buildings left standing after the Wehrmacht's bombardment. Thanks to an accurate description by her father, and an almost empty cafe, it had been easy to spot him sitting alone under a threadbare chandelier. She rehearsed her lines as she approached, surveying paintings by Boznańska and Mehoffer on the walls, noticing the many gaps left by the hasty removal of Jewish art.

"Aggie. Aggie!"

Irritated by her failure to listen to him, Karl demanded attention.

"Why don't we get back into bed? It's only six thirty."

Walking towards him, she held his hands and planted a kiss on his forehead.

"Karl, please, will you tell me about your work? I know it's something significant."

Enjoying his temporary sense of importance, he smiled.

"Much of what we do isn't pillow talk, Aggie. Quite the opposite."

"I'm not squeamish."

Raising his eyebrows, Karl sat back on the bed.

"Okay. We inject typhus into endless lice asses and clamp little matchbox-sized lice cages onto a poor bugger's leg and let them feed. After dissecting the satiated lice, we pull out their guts, grind them up and kill the typhus germs with chemicals."

Screwing up her face, she sat beside him.

"I preferred it when you told me you loved my feet."

"What if I told you we've perfected a vaccine for typhus? The basic trials worked."

Aggie felt a surge of excitement. This is what her father wanted to know.

"You're such a clever boy, Karl. That's incredible!" Leaning in, she forced herself to kiss his tobacco-tasting lips.

"What are you going to do next?"

"We don't know. You mustn't even mention what I've told you. Not to anyone. There needs to be much more testing. We have to produce the vaccine in quantity. We're going to need money, lots of it, and a distribution network."

"I won't say anything to anyone. You have my word."

Her job done for the day, she began to dress hurriedly, drawing suspicion from Karl.

"So the minute I tell you my secrets you're leaving?"

"I have to go, darling. It's Thursday, remember? I'm meeting a few of my girlfriends for a drink at the Klar Bar."

Pulling open the heavy Hotel Trojka door, she blew a kiss his way and made her way into the cool autumn night.

*

Curfew hour. The streets of Zasanie almost empty. Agnieszka navigated the shortest route to her father's office, avoiding any checkpoints. Striding through quiet, dimly lit streets and alleyways, she skipped over fallen masonry and timbers, thinking of her childhood. Her father had brought her many gifts from his business visits. Painted eggs from Hungary, garnet from Czechoslovakia, macarons from Paris. He went to New York City on numerous occasions and, despite his wealth, would find bargain items of jewellery in Manhattan pawn shops. All this was a tiny part of the generosity lavished on her as a child. She always believed there would be a time she could pay him back.

Her father's office fronted onto the far end of a small plaza. Since the invasion, he had hardly left it, his Polish heritage critical in IG Farben securing locally owned companies like Wola, Winnica and Boruta for the Reich. She knew he would still be working. Grabbing the knotted rope, she rang the heavy bell that hung to the right of the double, brass-knobbed doors. The loud clang echoed around the buildings of the square, prompting several heads to appear from top-floor windows.

Moments later, her father's head and torso appeared through a second-floor sash window, a cigar in one hand, a glass of red wine in the other. He arrived at the front door in a large-collared, fine-striped shirt, tie adrift, and beckoned Aggie inside. She headed quickly upstairs, arriving a dozen steps ahead of her puffing father.

They sat down together on a Bavarian antler settee, opposite Stanislaw's desk. Aggie gazed at the many framed business awards adorning the walls, sensing her father was tense, pensive.

"Well, this is a nice surprise. It's been, what, a month? Is this a social visit, or do you need some money?"

As he grinned, sarcastically, Aggie thought how much of a catch he must have been as a young man, before her mother had made him miserable.

"Don't be silly, Papa. It's me who has something for you."

He sat suddenly upright, jerking back and tilting his head towards her at the same time.

Enjoying seeing his anticipation, she sauntered slowly to the far end of the office, pouring herself a glass of whisky from her father's decanter.

"It's Bachmann. He told me that he and Weigl have cracked it. They've created the vaccine."

Letting the news sink in, Stanislaw's eyes danced, before a broad grin transformed his face.

"Well done, Aggie. That's incredible news. This war is going to be very good for IG Farben's business."

"Papa, can I ask you something? How did you even know that Karl Bachmann was working with Weigl?"

Stanislaw left the settee, fumbling in his desk to find another one of his Havana cigars, before turning back to his daughter.

"Aggie, I can't tell you that. Sometimes, things can be a little complex. Will you excuse me, I have to make a call."

*

Aggie watched the curfew crowd below rapidly thin out, scattering like disturbed ants down side streets, cloaked in the shadows of the onion-shaped dome of the Przemyśl Orthodox church, Our Lady of Sorrows. The shuttered window from where she stared and contemplated the evening ahead was the only one in her cosy apartment, a birthday gift from her moneyed father that stood in the church's precinct. Moments earlier, she had struggled into a black-lace corset, pinned her hair in tight curls and poured a red-silk chiffon dress over her body. He wouldn't be able to resist her, not that he could anyway. Tonight, she wanted to make sure. Slipping on her heels, she pulled the front door shut and marched confidently down Salezjańska.

A group of uniformed soldiers downing beer and chain-smoking outside a bar catcalled her as she passed, recoiling when she feistily chided them in German. Navigating the shortest route to avoid SS checkpoints, she soon arrived at the restaurant where she had agreed to meet Karl.

Brama Niedźwiedzia was a small, traditional place that stood close to the girls' institute, run by Basilian nuns. Diners could look out directly over the San while they ate. Peering through the door, Aggie immediately saw Karl, sat alone near the window, a bottle of Okocim before him. Rather than look towards the river, he gazed in the other direction, towards the layers of bomb-damaged, jagged brickwork in nearby buildings. The restaurant was quiet. Just one other couple sat near a small fireplace, a single glowing and hissing log keeping them warm.

Agnieszka brushed through the door, pursued by an icy draught. She had framed her immaculately made-up face with a fur wrap and could feel her cheeks glow as she waited for the petite waitress to guide her to Karl's table. She had not seen him in more than a month. Her father had advised her to lay low to give him more time to make arrangements. She smiled nervously at Karl as the waitress took her coat and wrap. As Karl rose from the table, she landed a brusque kiss on his cheek.

"You look stunning, Aggie."

"Thanks. It's a little chilly in here."

Overhearing her, the raw-boned restaurant owner hastily appeared, shuffling towards the fire to add another log. The corners of Aggie's mouth slid upwards.

"He obviously doesn't like the food in this place."

Karl ignored her attempt at wit, focusing instead on the typed menu in front of him.

"What will you drink, Aggie? It's been ages since I've seen you. I thought a young German boy had stolen you away."

"Vodka. Don't be silly. I've been busy. Working for my father."

Noticing Agnieszka's attire, the owner hovered again.

"We only have a bottle of Latvijas Balzams. It's been harder to source cheap vodka since the occupation."

Karl shuffled in his seat, reaching for his wallet and thumbing the few notes inside it.

Agnieszka stared at him for a moment, before ordering impatiently.

"We'll have it."

While the owner hurried away behind a strung-bead portière at the back of the restaurant, Karl gazed past Aggie, embarrassed, silently refusing to make eye contact.

"What's the matter?"

"It's not your place to pay for everything. Couldn't we have something less expensive?"

She laid her cool hand on his.

"Until you can afford to pay, it *is* my place. I want to make sure this is a good night, and I have a plan that could fix your finances."

The chilled vodka arrived quickly. Agnieszka circled the rim of her glass with a middle finger, gazing at Karl.

"You've had a few drinks already, haven't you? What's wrong?"

Karl stared at the words on the menu, reading them over and over.

"Hard day in the lab, that's all."

They ordered their meals and Agnieszka threw the vodka down her throat with abandon, filling her glass and Karl's. His eyes danced uncomfortably.

"Why don't you tell me about it?"

"Some abnormalities on the vaccine we need to work through. Scientific stuff. It would bore you."

She hid it well, but Karl's admission panicked Aggie.

"But you're still on track, aren't you?"

He laughed sarcastically through his reply, getting up and heading for the bathroom.

"Why are you so concerned? It's just my job after all."

With Karl gone, Aggie liberally covered her neck in perfume, the pleasant smell helping mask the stink of stale tobacco as Karl slumped back into his seat. As their meals arrived, she made her move.

"Darling, it's time you met my father."

Dropping the cutlery from his shaking hands, Karl spluttered, almost choking on the stew.

"What? Why on earth would you want me to meet your father? It's not like I'm ideal marriage material. No. Never. That's a bad idea."

"Listen. I've told him about us. He's aware of our situation."

Karl ignored her, wolfing down the stew, sending splatters onto his cheeks, his napkin and the tablecloth.

Slicing her potato pancakes into quarters, she tried another tack.

"You've things in common, you know."

He paused, holding his spoon in mid-air and fixing his gaze on her.

"Other than you, what exactly?"

"You're both in medicine."

"Oh. Well, I've no need of a doctor."

"He's not a physician, Karl. He's a businessman and works in the pharmaceutical industry, for IG Farben."

Dropping his spoon, Karl slumped back in his chair, his eyes lighting up. Resting one hand on his belly, he dangled the other to nod his forefinger in Aggie's direction.

"Now, that's interesting. It explains a few things too. Look at you. Elegant, eloquent, well read. I should have known you came from money, Aggie. I never understood what you were doing with me. Now, I get it."

There was a deep resentment in his voice.

"My father's in charge of the entire Polish business, Karl. He could help you."

"Look, even if I were to meet your father, these decisions are not up to me. Herr Weigl is not going to work with IG Farben." Looking away out of the window, his brow tightened.

"We can find a way, Karl. Just think of how wealthy you could be."

"I want to be a success, Aggie, but this isn't going to work."

She leaned in, her red lips sucking Karl's confusion away as their mouths briefly entwined.

"Shh, all this must be a shock. I'm so fond of you, Karl. Please. Just meet my father."

Aggie glanced through the window. Outside, leaf-sized flakes of snow blurred the night. Highlighted by the restaurant's glow, they seemed to fall in slow motion, each flake shining briefly before blending into the indistinct mass of white. She reached below the table, putting her hand on Karl's thigh as he sunk the last of the vodka.

Breathing heavily, Karl struggled from his seat. Grabbing her coat and wrap, Aggie skipped into the swirling white outside, pressing her lips to the window flirtatiously as Karl remonstrated with the owner, throwing a five-zloty note on the table.

She did not want to make this too easy for him. Hoping he would tire in the chase, she moved quickly away from the restaurant, the chill wind turning snowflakes into icy pins. Navigating the thin blanket of snow on the street, she headed down a bank to the riverside, being careful not to slip. Spotting a barge bobbing in the swelling San, she ran towards it, removing her Cuban heels and clambering beneath the roped-down tarpaulin to nestle alongside the building sand beneath it.

Outside, she heard the breathless, muffled sound of Karl shouting for her, moving ever closer.

Then she felt the wind again and giggled as Karl pulled back the tarpaulin and rolled awkwardly onto the bed of sand. A passing cargo ship sounded its horns as she pulled across their waxed-cotton blanket. In seconds, Karl was asleep.

*

Aggie stuck her head and arm out of the tarpaulin, the riverbank lighting illuminating her watch. It was 12:15 a.m. They had been here half an hour—long enough. Karl was comatose beside her, a strange whistling sound from his nose the only sign he was alive.

Taking off her knickers and coat, she shivered, pulling her dress down to reveal her corset. Carefully, she undid Karl's trouser button and fly and then gently shook his shoulder to wake him. As he stirred, she whispered in his ear.

"That was wonderful, darling. I'm so pleased you agreed to meet Father."

He sat up, suddenly alert.

"What? Where the hell are we?"

Putting her clothes straight, she smiled.

"Shall we go? I'm freezing."

9
THE SALE

Cafe Antek, Przemyśl
A few days later

Aggie pushed open the swing door of busy Cafe Antek, the breeze displacing a huge cloud of cigarette smoke. She had knowingly played along with her father's plan, but the prospect of seeing Karl realise his fate in the flesh made her sweat. He was almost sure to make a point about her father's wealth and create a scene. She just hoped her father got what he wanted.

Inside the cafe, uniformed Nazi officers sat interspersed with local civilians, laughing and shouting orders at anxious waiters. An SS sergeant and two privates sat at the table nearest the entrance eyed Aggie before tipping their hats to her.

She surveyed every blue and white chequered cloth-covered table in the cafe. No sign of him. Panicking, she felt her father's hand on her shoulder before he moved to whisper in a waiter's ear and then returned his attention to her.

"We'll wait for him in the room upstairs, Aggie. Waiter, bring coffee and cake."

*

Aggie sat in silence at the end of a table that ran almost the length of the bedroom. Her father read a local newspaper at the other. Made up with a plain white tablecloth and serviettes, at its centre sat a ringed babka cake dusted with sugar. She had tried not to stare at it for too long and resisted the urge to cut a slice before Karl arrived.

Her father cleared his throat, putting the paper to one side.

"Aggie, I've a confession to make to you. Please try to understand."

Aggie sat back, caught off guard by her father's comment. He was not one to open up and she presumed he would speak on the normal topic of finance.

He took off his glasses, gazing down at them as he rocked them up and down in his fingers, blinking rapidly.

"The thing is, I never really loved your mother, Aggie."

Aggie's face and neck flushed with heat, her eyes meeting her father's briefly then darting to the table. She remembered the silent dinners and frosty exchanges between her parents. They had never appeared to be in love.

"It's okay, Papa. I know that. It was obvious to us as children. You were good parents, that's all that matters—"

"I... Well, I loved someone else that whole time. Someone I shouldn't have, someone I still hold much affection for, even though I'll never see her again. I've never told your brother this. Can it remain our secret?"

There was a firm knock on the door. Aggie's father jumped to his feet and opened it, letting Bachmann inside. She looked up, distracted by her father's revelation, staring blankly at Bachmann and eventually forcing a smile.

"Herr Bachmann. You know my daughter. Please, sit down. Would you like some cake, coffee?"

Aggie could see that Karl was struggling with the niceties, so moved round the table to cut a slice from the babka cake, setting it alongside a cup of coffee in the spare place at the table.

Bachmann slumped down in his chair, arms folded like a belligerent child.

"Can we get to the point as soon as possible? Why am I here?"

Aggie's father ignored the remark and sat, putting on his glasses, opening his briefcase and reviewing a set of papers, finally putting them aside to address Karl.

"What has my daughter told you about me?"

"That you're some kind of answer to all the problems Herr Weigl and I face."

Aggie's father glanced sideways, his mouth lifting a millimetre at the edges.

"I'm a businessman first, Bachmann."

"And I'm a scientist."

An uncomfortable silence followed. A line drawn in the sand. Aggie's eyes bored into her father, willing him to soften. He did so in time-honoured fashion, pulling a half bottle of Asbach Uralt brandy (Aggie had told her father it was Karl's favourite) and a packet of cigarettes from his jacket. He pushed them towards Karl.

"Tell me about your inspiration, Bachmann."

"Why should I tell you anything? Things have not always been easy for me."

Karl poured a glass of brandy and downed it in one. Pouring himself another, he lit a cigarette. Aggie sensed an alcohol–nicotine calm coming over him.

"People like you have no idea what it's like to need money, to crave success. You're born with it already. Did you ever serve in the Great War?"

"No. My skills were needed on the home front. I managed a major vaccination programme for—"

"You did nothing if you didn't fight. If you had, your family would not have had to worry about money, like mine did. Do you know my wife had to work as a servant?"

"Where did she work, Bachmann?"

"In a big house in Berlin. I can't remember where or the name of the family. Aneta told me the lady of the house knew the Kempinskis, the family that own that big hotel by the Brandenburg Gate."

Aggie glanced at her father, noticing a gathering of his bushy eyebrows as his eyes squeezed shut, before replying.

"It must have been hard. But you had no children then?"

"We had a son. He stayed with his aunt until the war finished. Now he's an engineer in the army, posted to the Saarland."

Aggie's father stared intently at Karl.

"Do you have another child, Bachmann?"

Aggie peered at Karl as he nodded slowly.

"Yes, a boy studying in America. Why so many questions?"

He smiled and left for the bathroom. Aggie got up and rested her hand on Karl's shoulder.

"My father will get what he wants one way or another, Karl. Play nicely and this could work out well for us."

Returned, calm and focused, Aggie's father sat, bringing his hands together on the table in front of him.

"Family's precious, isn't it, Bachmann? I've always wanted to look after mine. First, I know you're having an affair with my daughter. Second, she gave me the details of the vaccine discovery. So, I'm going to make you an offer. I'm authorised to arrange for you to meet some very important people."

Aggie sensed Karl's unease and anger as he stared at her, scratching the back of his balding head vigorously.

"Well, who?"

"My company has links to the Reich. Herr Frank, leader in the Polish territories, will meet you. If it goes well, Herr Bachmann, you will lead a major distribution programme, vaccinating the army and civilians alike."

Aggie tensed, her fingertips gripping the edge of the table as Karl got to his feet.

"I... I can't do that. My allegiance has to be to Weigl."

"Think very carefully, Bachmann. Surely your first allegiance is to the Reich?"

Karl gazed at Aggie, thinking of their nights together, how much she knew about him. She sensed his weakness.

"Don't wait too long to decide, Karl. I thought I saw ambition in you. Cooperate with my papa. We could still have a future together."

*

IG Farben headquarters, Frankfurt
A month later

The scale of IG Farben's modernist headquarters felt overpowering to Aggie. As she arrived outside, weary and irritated, the pale, yellow globe of the sun hovered above them, not yet strong enough to burn through the shroud of thick, ghostly grey fog.

She had left Przemyśl in the early hours of the morning, her father arranging a private flight to take her to Krakow-Rakowice-Czyzyny military airfield for her onward journey to Frankfurt.

Despite the early hour, the main reception was a hive of activity. Apparently, there would be a board meeting today regarding plans to establish new plants for the production of Buna rubber. Aggie was directed to the pharmaceutical wing (Q1), a hundred-metre walk, where her father's office sat on the top (ninth) floor. As she walked, passing groups of industrialists in conversation, she could feel the power of this place seeping through the walls.

She was the only person left in the lift as it opened, and was met by a young blonde assistant, who took her coat and showed her to her father's office. He sat behind a large mahogany desk, meticulously studying a detailed map laid out on its leather top.

"Daughter. I thought you'd never arrive. Half the day is gone!"

"It's only eight thirty, Papa."

"You look tired. Some coffee, bread and jam?"

"Just coffee, please."

"When you've had your coffee, would you like me to show you around? You've never been here before, and the building is quite incredible."

"Perhaps. I've come a long way, Papa. What do you need from me?"

"You always were one to get to the point. Very well."

He signalled for Aggie to come to the other side of the desk.

"Do you see this place?"

"Grojec? Yes, why?"

"There's an old *dworek* about five kilometres north of there, which was once in the hands of the Polish nobility. I visited once, years ago. It's a beautiful place, sat in a sprawling apple orchard."

"Oh, and why are you telling me this?"

"There's going to be an important meeting there, whenever the right people are available. It could be months."

He explained to Aggie that Bachmann would meet Hans Frank, Governor-General of the Government of Poland, Ludwig Fischer, Governor of the Warsaw District, and Erich Traub, a scientist and virologist.

"I'm not sure how he'll cope with that, Papa."

Aggie's father shrugged.

"Once he's signed the papers, control of the situation will pass to Herr Frank directly. I'm not sure what they will do with Bachmann, although I have a fairly good idea. For now though, stay close to him."

*

Aggie knew the laboratory would be visited by Frank's henchmen today. Father had warned her. Last night had been the worst possible preparation. She had seen less of Bachmann lately but met him for a quiet drink in the Klar Bar. But their evening was hijacked by a drunken troop of off-duty soldiers singing 'Kampflied der Nationalsozialisten' over and over. Rather than try to beat them, they joined them, drinking cheap brandy until the early hours.

"Why don't you tell me what happened in Grojec? You hardly said anything about it last night."

Aggie followed as Karl strode to the back of the lab, reaching up to the shelves and pushing aside and knocking over empty reagent bottles before finding a small, full bottle with a typed label that read, 'Laudanum'.

"Stop asking questions, Aggie. My head is thumping. Help me find a cup, will you?"

She pointed to his desk. Picking up the chipped teacup and pouring in half the tincture, he crumbled in a sugar cube and grimaced as he downed the still-bitter brown mixture in one.

"I've signed a paper to say I'll work with Frank. They wanted vaccine samples this week. It's not ready for production. We haven't done enough testing."

Even as he spoke, Aggie could see the effect of the laudanum. Bachmann's face seemed to droop, his words spilling out at half-pace.

"What about your boss, Weigl? Where is he anyway?"

"He's in Austria. They told me he would be taken off the programme. I'd be in sole control, reporting directly to the Reichsleiter."

"That's great, isn't it? What you wanted?"

"Not really. Weigl is the expert."

Karl panicked as shouting and the *clack, clack* of marching boots filled the corridor outside. Pulling on a too-small, stained white coat, he moved steadily towards the door, Aggie just behind him.

"Bachmann?"

A slight, thin-lipped man in a grey suit stood in the doorway, the tip of a queue of terrified men and women standing two abreast in the corridor, flanked by SS platoon officers. Two of them pushed past a swaying Karl into the lab.

"Are you inebriated? At this time in the morning?"

Karl shook his head.

Aggie noticed that the Nazi officer, who had a Zeiss-Ikon camera hung around his neck, stared long and hard at Karl but paid no attention to her.

"I'm Kriminalkommissar Bergmann. My orders are to leave this subhuman group with you. Do with them what you will. My men will tag and return them to the ghetto when you're done."

Karl nodded and, hand shaking, accepted a file of papers from Bergmann, who then pointed towards the end of the lab.

"Stand over there. I need to take a picture of you for our records. At least try to look normal."

Aggie watched as the papers slipped from Karl's shaking hands to the floor, feeling a pang of sympathy for him. He stooped to gather them before moving to a table near the laboratory's far wall, leaning his backside against it to steady himself.

Bergmann pulled the bellows of the folding camera open, pursing his lips to blow away a layer of dust before flipping up the viewfinder to peer through it. Glancing up to estimate the distance to the table, he twiddled the focuser before cranking the camera handle, pushing down the shutter cock and pressing the release button. Slipping the camera in his pocket, Bergmann marched to the door and left.

Aggie smiled nervously at the SS men as she crossed the room to stand behind Karl, glancing down at the paperwork over his shoulder: '*Asthma, heart disease, diabetes, arthritis, lupus, cirrhosis.*' Every one of the Jews was over fifty and suffering from an existing health condition.

He hesitated but was sparked into action by the bark of an SS officer.

"What are you waiting for? Hurry up!"

Karl beckoned to the nearest Jewish woman. She stood hunched, scratching her arms, refusing to move. He took her hand, pushing her down in a chair and rolling up her sleeve, while Aggie spoke to her.

"What's your name?"

She screwed her eyes tight shut.

"Gelleh. Please be quick. I hate needles."

*

125

The sound of shattering glass and a heavy thud on Karl's bedroom floorboards woke Aggie, making her sit upright. She had stayed with him again overnight and they had made love, depite her knowing her job was nearly done. The burned-red clay brick lying at the end of Karl's bed was immediately visible, as was the jagged outline in the windowpane, showing through the parted curtains. A smell of diesel filled the room.

As his front door shuddered with the thump of a fist, Aggie pulled on her robe, skipping across the shards of broken glass to the top of the stairs. Below, the door shook once, and then again. How could Karl sleep through this?

His letterbox flapped open and a harsh *Hochdeutsch* voice echoed through the hallway.

"Open the door immediately or we'll break it down."

She hurried down the stairs, stumbling on the bottom step. Pulling the door open, a burly man in a long coat and boots, P-38 pistol drawn, barged past.

"Is Karl Bachmann in this house?"

The Gestapo ran past her, up the stairs. A moment later, their leader was at the top of them, looking down at her.

"Where is he? You're coming with us."

*

As the wheels of the black Mercedes spun, propelling Aggie and her captors towards the city centre, she struggled desperately to understand how Bachmann had got away, concluding that there must be an escape at the rear of his flat, or perhaps he had climbed out of the window.

"Officer, may I ask why you're trying to find Herr Bachmann?"

"The Jews he vaccinated are all dead or dying. Herr Frank doesn't mind dead Jews, but he hates failure and Bachmann has failed."

As the car sped around the corner onto the street leading to the Eiffel's railway bridge, it was flanked by four Waffen SS *Kradschutzen* determined to stop Bachmann reaching the Soviet sector across the San bridge.

The Gestapo leader spotted Bachmann crossing the road fifty metres ahead, headed for the half-dozen market stalls selling vegetables, cheese, meats and items of clothing.

Aggie heard the alternate thrum of motorbike engines slowing, changing gear and rumbling through the chattering, bartering crowd as their riders rode close to the edge of the kerb, trying to detect Bachmann. She spotted him grabbing a hat from the edge of the last market stall, putting it on his head at an angle and linking arms with a startled young woman. After another twenty metres, he mounted an unoccupied bicycle, his short legs pedalling relentlessly towards the bridge.

She knew this was the end for him but, against the odds, he reached the bridge unharmed and jettisoned the bike down the bank towards the river.

The car screeched to a halt, SS motorbikes alongside it, as Bachmann dived onto the wooden planks that bordered the railway tracks and ran along them, his movement now laboured.

Squinting, she could see huge banners depicting the sombre faces of Soviet leaders hanging from the façades of buildings overlooking the river. She heard SS assault rifle bullets pinging as they ricocheted off the bridge's cast-iron arches.

Bachmann slowed, his legs shuffling towards a pair of concrete gun emplacements sat across from the end of the bridge, about twenty metres apart. They had rusted rebars sticking out in all directions, the tallest on either side acting as flag poles for the hoisted Red Banners.

Another volley flew towards him. This time she watched him collapse like a rag doll, the weight of his torso still moving forwards as his legs collapsed beneath him. She shut her eyes tight, as a cry of, "*Pristreli yego!*" ("Shoot him!") went up from the Russian position.

10
A NEW FRIEND

Sam's Bar and Grill, Manhattan

I arrived at Sam's Bar and Grill a few minutes late. The transit journey from the Upper East Side took longer than expected. It was busy inside, the suited after-work crowd mobbing the bar, downing beers, laughing and smoking, but my eyes were immediately drawn to the walls. They were completely covered in brightly coloured advertisement posters. My favourite had joyful couples dressed in evening wear waltzing around a giant bottle of Budweiser, the background lit from a searchlight atop the Empire State Building.

Having surveyed the bar for anyone sitting alone, I ordered a beer from the quiet end and sat on a worn-looking stool to make a start on the book I had with me, one that I had pulled from Timo's shelves years before. Before I had even turned the first page, the barman shuffled away from the busy end of the bar towards me.

"What are you reading?"

"You won't have heard of it. *Behaviorism* by John B. Watson."

He nodded, placing a perfectly poured glass of Koch's Golden Anniversary on the mat in front of me and taking a lighter out of his black apron to light my cigarette.

"You're German, right? Nice to have someone in with a bit of intelligence."

I nodded, smiling back at him.

"You should feel right at home. You're in the heart of Kleindeutschland!"

"I didn't realise."

The barman polished the bar in front of him and continued.

"In reality, the German community headed to Brooklyn decades ago, but my father moved us here from Frankfurt in '32, to a place a block away from here. He's Jewish. Saw early what the Nazis were going to do to the country."

As the muffled volume of conversation increased around me, I sensed a looming presence on my shoulder and then a distinctly central European voice.

"Before you lecture this gentleman on political history, I'll have a whisky sour. Make it a double."

I turned to find a man wide as a door frame and just centimetres short of the bar's ceiling dragging a bar stool closer to mine with his foot.

He held out a swollen, ape-like hand in front of me.

"You must be Oskar. My name's Stanislaw, Aleksander Stanislaw. Call me Aleks. I'm your landlord." He grinned.

There was something strangely familiar in the resonance of his voice. Something that irritated me and made me feel comfortable at the same time. I examined his face for a clue to any past exchanges. As his warm hand enveloped mine, I felt what I can only describe as a sense of excitement. I already knew this man and I would become close, but I remained silent.

"You seem a little shocked."

"Umm, I expected an American, I guess. How did you know I'm your tenant?"

He sat, dropping his briefcase by his side, the buttons on his wide-lapelled, beige windowpane sport coat stretched to breaking point.

"Because no one ever reads a book in this bar. You seemed a studious type and I put two and two together. Sorry to disappoint. Born in Poland to German parents. I consider myself a German now."

"I too have some links to Poland. Whereabouts were you born?"

Pulling loose his silk tie with one hand, Stanislaw took a gulp of his sour.

"Przemyśl. Small city in the south-east, close to the Ukrainian border. My father still has an office there. It's always been important because of its location. I could bore you for hours on its history."

The walls of the bar seemed to shrink in towards me at that point, the world around them inconceivably small all of a sudden.

"I know exactly where it is. My father's in Zasanie as we speak."

In theatrical fashion, Stanislaw's hand flew to his chest, his head jerking back as a dazed look appeared on his face. I recognised myself in his gesture.

"My friend, that's astonishing. In the military?"

I shook my head, slowly sipping my beer, wary of revealing too much too soon, unsure of my instincts. I knew nothing about this man.

"Medical research."

Stanislaw rose to his feet, waving and flashing a smile at a young woman as she passed, before raising his glass in the air.

"To Przemyśl and to family."

I raised my glass half-heartedly.

"I've never been. My father only wrote once, before the invasion. I can't imagine it's much fun with the Schutzstaffel on every corner."

"Someone has to keep law and order, I suppose."

"Herr Stanislaw, please, I find it awkward to speak with you until I know the footing on which we stand. Do you understand?"

"Of course. My apologies. Come, shall we sit somewhere more comfortable?" He signalled to the barman then held out his hand towards an alcove in the bar's corner draped with a heavy velvet curtain.

Following Stanislaw into the alcove, I stopped as he threw down his briefcase on the seat and turned to leave for the bathroom. I glanced at the case, its contents now spilled across the blue upholstery, noticing a worn copy of the Nazi newspaper *Nowy Kurier Warszawski* lying on top of the scattered pile of academic papers.

The barman arrived with a bottle of Stork Club whiskey. Pouring a small glass, I thought about picking up the newspaper. Before I could, Stanislaw returned, his shirt unbuttoned, hair swept back with water, drops of which still dotted his forehead. He shuffled the papers back into his case, before expertly pouring himself a drink.

"You're quite naturally wondering why you are living in my apartment free of rent. I can assure you it's nothing sinister. I am the treasurer of the Bismarck Fund, set up by my father to help and support German students."

"I see. There must be hundreds of German students in New York. Why me?"

"I'm a lecturer at your university, Oskar. My father part-funded the development of the pharmacology department. If I'm honest, our selection procedure can be a little random sometimes. Bachmann is near the start of the alphabet. I hope you're enjoying the apartment."

A broad smile spread across Stanislaw's face. This information seemed a coincidence too far and yet it was plausible. I had heard the department recently received funding.

"Tell me about yourself, Oskar. It's a long way to come to study. Couldn't you have found a place in a German university?"

"It's been a long-held dream of mine to study in America. This new world is richer, is it not? In thought and outlook. America is now home to the best German psychologists, many of them Jewish of course."

He stared at me, suddenly quiet.

"I know nothing of psychology. I lecture in pharmacology, mainly focused on communicable diseases. We're talking shop!"

Stanislaw explained that the entire street in which Sam's Bar sat was crammed with German history, including the old headquarters of the Arion Society, which grew out of the idea that America needed more German civilisation. A singing and social club, it staged operettas and sponsored balls and once put on a big show at Madison Square Garden to celebrate the four-hundredth anniversary of Columbus discovering America.

I lit a cigarette.

"Well, that's the right way to spread German influence. Are they open to new members?"

Stanislaw leaned back on the seat.

"You're twenty years too late. Whole thing collapsed after the Great War. Everyone in New York hated us. Many still do, but I don't want to bias you. You look like a guy who loves his jazz. Am I right?"

How he could tell just by looking at me, I could not fathom.

"I'm meeting a couple of girls who used to work at the Onyx over at Cafe Rouge. Benny Goodman's band is playing. Luckily for you, the girls are German."

He winked at me, making me feel suddenly uncomfortable.

"Will you join me?"

I hesitated.

"I can't be out late."

Stanislaw laid a firm hand on my shoulder and gave me a huge smile.

"I can't promise you that, but I can promise you a good time."

*

Benny Goodman's orchestra tuned up a stone's throw away as I sat with a stratus of cigarette smoke swirling around my face under the beams and chandeliers of Cafe Rouge at Midtown's Hotel Pennsylvania. It seemed like a dream. Nearby, a young couple shot glances at each other, laughing and raising their glasses across a Florentine fountain in the centre of the room. He was square-jawed and wore a super-high-waisted, blue zoot suit. She was city-pretty and petite and had on a long, flowing, back- and sleeveless dress. There was something Shakespearian in the way they interacted.

Gazing around the room, I noted that each chair at every bottle-laden table had a nonchalant, flamboyantly dressed person sitting in it. I undid the top button on my shirt and leaned back on the table to see my landlord and now, so naturally, companion arrive back at the table with a woman on either side of him, each of them carrying a tumbler of dark-red liquid.

On his right, a vital, vivacious blonde, with an unruly tangle of hair hanging across her forehead, her expressive chilli-red lips pouting. To his left, a plainer woman. Lean and tall with short black hair, she smoked a cigarette and gazed at me through dark-rimmed oval glasses, inviting me to stare back.

The blonde wasted no time introducing herself, dangling her brightly painted fingernails in front of me.

"Hello, I'm Lena. Nice to meet you."

Noticing my interest, Stanislaw introduced me to her friend.

"Oskar, this is Sofie. Ladies, I met Mr Bachmann earlier this evening. He's staying at my place on the Upper East Side. We've got a lot in common."

As the three of us sat down, Lena next to Stanislaw, Sofie next to me, I thought how staged this all seemed. But I would enjoy it anyway. We toasted, and I blurted out a comment on the women's drinks.

"Why do you drink tomato juice?"

Lena giggled across to her friend.

"He's never seen a Bloody Mary, Sofie."

She turned back to me. Clearly an expert on alcohol, she delighted in putting me straight.

"It's more than tomato juice, Mr Bachmann. There's a big splash of vodka and a whole lot of spicy sauce in there too. Do you wanna try it?"

She held the lipstick-stained glass towards me, but the smell was enough to put me off.

"Ladies, why don't you tell Oskar about the Onyx?"

Lena started to talk but was quickly interrupted by Sofie.

"It was Joe Helbock's place, in a brownstone on 52nd Street."

She explained he was originally a bootlegger but ended up a self-appointed patron for jazz. The place was dingy on the way in but decorated with black and silver stripes with a huge black-marble bar at the back.

"Musicians used to leave their instruments with us for safe-keeping. I loved it there."

Sofie grinned as she reeled off the names of some of the performers she had seen there: Louis Prima, Jimmy and Tommy Dorsey, Maxine Sullivan and Art Tatum.

"Oh, and we saw this guy in there a lot."

She pointed to Benny Goodman, as the familiar opening guitar chords of 'Ain't Cha Glad?' relaxed me into my seat, and then the bandleader himself raised a clarinet to his lips. It was a tune Mother always hummed, especially when she was down. I wished she were here now, but I liked this girl. She had glanced at me a few times when she thought I would not notice. There seemed to be a depth to her that her companion lacked.

The next couple of hours passed quickly as the band played one familiar song after another. At first, the four of us exchanged snippets of conversation about our pasts, our surroundings, our plans for the future, but as we sank the everlasting supply of champagne and whisky arriving at our table, Stanislaw and Lena got friendly in an ongoing clinch, leaving Sofie and I to continue our conversation. I had recently read Mary Whiton Calking's work on dreams and was delighted Sofie took an interest. As the chilled clarinet sound of 'Indian Summer' concluded the set, an unexpected tear rolled down my cheek. Sofie put a gentle hand on my thigh.

"You're missing home, aren't you?"

I nodded and, without warning, she put her slender hands on my cheeks, giving me a long, lingering kiss on my lips. She gazed at me, pulling a handkerchief from underneath her dress strap and wiping her red lipstick from my mouth.

The four of us left the Pennsylvania arm in arm. Outside, my three companions chatted happily to other concert goers, while I stared across the street to Madison Square Garden, imagining what it must be like inside.

As we navigated the gridiron of Manhattan looking for another bar, we laughed and chatted like old friends. The other-worldly sight of steam rising from manholes and the constant drone of human activity convinced me of an industrious second population beneath the streets. Stopping in a doorway, full of the city's energy, a rainbow of bright neon danced before me in the black. As Stanislaw pushed Sofie and

I into a cab, shouting something indistinguishable to its driver, I knew this had already been one of the best nights of my life.

*

My fascination with Stanislaw and lack of any real friends in New York seemed enough reason to meet him again. I arrived at the shabby coffee bar on Christopher Street a few minutes early. Outside, a mess of steel girders, cranes and dust dominated the view. The air was thick with the shouts of the gang of workmen dismantling the Ninth Avenue El, apparently the oldest elevated railway in New York City. A pair of workers stood on a scaffold close to the cafe's thin window took turns to bring their mallets down on a pile. The sound of each thwack seemed ever closer.

As my blood pressure rose, Stanislaw arrived, all smiles, immediately handing me a book.

"Bachmann, good to see you again. Here, this is the book I promised you the other evening."

Our conversations at Cafe Rouge were a blur. I had no recollection of his promise. Staring down at the cover, illustrated in gold leaf with an Egyptian pyramid and the Pantheon in Rome, Twain's *Innocents Abroad* seemed too personal a gift.

"This is a first edition. I can't accept it."

Stanislaw held up his hand as he sat opposite me.

"Oh, come on. It's not valuable. Withdrawn from the NYU library. Worth getting your name added to their list, if you don't mind lodgings full of moth-eaten books."

"That's not the point. Why are you giving me this? I hardly know you."

Stanislaw shrugged, shuffling in his seat as the noise outside went up a notch.

"I'm sorry. I haven't been here before. Shall we go to another cafe?"

I shook my head.

"We're here now."

We sat in silence for a while, overcome by the noise outside, until the workmen stopped for a break.

"Oskar, we've a lot in common, maybe more than you think. I want us to get along."

I put the book away carefully in my bag.

"You could do with lightening up a bit. That book's funny. Do you have any friends, Oskar?"

His question hit a nerve.

"Sure, I've got friends, but I don't mind my own company. I spend a lot of time reading. I'm also in the German and chess clubs."

"Hmm, not exactly a bundle of laughs. I've an idea. Every other week, me and half a dozen of the more interesting Germans at NYU meet up in a room at the back of the White Horse Tavern in West Village. Landlord is a former native of Heidelberg. We drink, talk, play a game of cards or two. Next one is Friday. Will you come?"

I imagined Stanislaw might keep company with a louche crowd. The idea of joining a *Burschenschaft* (men's drinking club) really didn't appeal. It was the sort of place my father would enjoy. I shook my head.

"Okay, how about we meet once a week for a while? For a chat. I know the perfect place near the university. It's called the Minetta Tavern on MacDougal Street, south-west side of the park. We can eat there and it's cheap. You'll love the atmosphere."

11
SECRETS

Lower East Side, Manhattan
Early Spring 1940

Staring out of the thin, battered windowpanes of my apartment, I imagined the rain might shatter them. It had fallen steady and hard for two days without letting up. Despite the frustrations of leaking pipes and a neighbour who sang 'On the Mississippi' by Arthur Fields repeatedly and often late into the night, I had long ago settled into life at 11a Henry Street. The place was a massive fall from the luxury of those few weeks in the Otto Kahn house, but I felt less owned, despite the continuing deposits in my bank account.

Sitting back down on my unmade bed, strewn with open books and university papers, I gazed at the grey and green hexagonal wallpaper around me. Unmotivated, head foggy. The letter I held in my hands had arrived yesterday, but I didn't open it straight away. I examined it a while, running my fingers over its badly crumpled surface. It looked important, and that's why I hesitated. I had a university thesis due in tomorrow and I couldn't cope with any distraction. I returned to reading a B.F. Skinner essay on the behaviour of organisms, but couldn't help glancing at the envelope with its swastika-clasping Reichsadler postmark, typed address and postage stamp celebrating Hitler's fifty-first birthday.

Swinging my legs off the shaky iron-framed bed, I pulled an ivory-handled, initial-embossed letter opener, a gift from Mother, from the bedside drawer. Picking up the envelope, I hesitated again, before sliding the blade along its top. A childhood memory of Father and I, spotting birds in the Halbe Forest, flashed across my mind. I walked back to the window, taking advantage of the natural light, and gazed out on the sodden East Side synagogue, before pulling free the single piece of paper, a smudge of finger-printed blood on its folded edge.

Dear Oskar

I'm working these past few months on an important research project with Herr Weigl. All is going to plan. One day soon, I'll return to Germany.

I've not been good at keeping in touch, but now I've important reason to write to you. I fear for your future in America. Hostilities between our countries will intensify. Whatever your feelings about the Reich, you must return home immediately or face internment in New York.

You learned to fly. Now you've a grand chance to follow in my footsteps, join the Luftwaffe and help the Fatherland win this war quickly and decisively. I've often imagined you flying an ME-109. It would suit you, my son.

Your father, Karl.

I dwelt on every word in the letter. It felt odd to me. First, Father had never written to me before, other than that hastily scrawled note in the Harz lodge. Second, he knew I trained to be a reconnaissance pilot. Why would he mention a fighter plane? But he had resisted me coming to study here and would do what he could to tempt me back, I reasoned. Shoving the letter in the drawer, I straightened my bow tie in the cracked mirror, put on my homburg and Klepper raincoat and left for MacDougal Street.

*

My regular companion Aleksander stood on one leg, steadying himself with a shaking hand on the bar, as I pushed open the door of the packed Minetta Tavern. Embarrassed by his exhibitionism, I prayed he wouldn't look up and see me, my eyes immediately darting to focus on the beer-stained checkerboard floor tiles beneath me. Glancing up, I saw Aleks' other hand elevated, fingers pointing upwards. This learned lecturer was now a bar-room ballerina in fourth position. Using his balancing hand, he lifted a half-full glass of golden liquid to his mouth and gulped it down in one, wobbling a little before bursting into song.

"It's a lovely day today. So, whatever you've got to do, you've got a lovely day to do it in. That's true."

Lowering my dripping-wet homburg, I sat in the first free red booth I could find, the stench of new Naugahyde overpowering the smell of liquor and tobacco. Tonight, I finally felt as if I knew Aleks well enough to ask him the questions that had bothered me for so long.

A round of applause echoed around the bar room as a grinning Aleks spotted me and made his way over.

"Good evening, Oskar. What did you think of my rendition?"

I half-smiled, shifting in my seat.

"Another of your talents. Where's it from?"

"*Louisiana Purchase*. It's playing at the Imperial Theatre. Great show. I took lovely Lena to the first night. Do you remember her from those days when we were first acquainted?"

"Yes. I preferred her friend."

Aleks winked.

"Why didn't you say? We could have double dated. Drink?"

"Sure. I'll have a sour."

He returned to the bar, giving me a chance to take in the atmosphere, while thinking about how to ask him my questions. The place was full of swirling tobacco smoke and intoxicated laughter, but there were pockets of still and quiet and I focused on them. A young woman on the table to my right sat alone painting the chaotic scene at the bar using a mini-easel and watercolour palette. Lifting her nearly full burgundy glass, she turned to me, smiling.

"What do you think?"

Over in the far corner, an older man sat wearing a tasselled fez and red cummerbund. He possessed a tortured look around his thin moustache and repeatedly gazed ahead, furiously scribbling in his notepad, before staring ahead again.

"It's two for one for an hour. Here you go."

Aleks put a pair of sours down in front of me. We had been out together dozens of times now. I seldom paid for drinks.

"How's that dump you're living in on the Lower East Side? Still can't believe you voluntarily left the Kahn place." He grinned.

144

"It's not so bad. I won't be there forever. There's so many places in this great country I want to see for myself."

He shrugged, looking away to the bar.

"Up to you, I guess. I gave a lecture today on Alexander Fleming and his discovery of the *Penicillium* genus. Did you know that was thirteen years ago now?"

I shook my head, sipping my sour.

"Asked a few of the students to act out the interaction of *Penicillium notatum* with the colonies of *Staphylococcus* in the lecture theatre. It was fun. I should teach drama."

He laughed, but it didn't seem such a strange notion to me. I had crept in on a lecture Aleks had given on the dynamics of crowd infection last week.

"You received a standing ovation and wild applause from your students. How the hell do you manage it? That's my dream. Please will you explain."

Aleks chuckled.

"I can't, that's the point. I've a charm, some humour maybe. It strikes me, Oskar, that you take yourself too seriously."

He could see me deep in thought and angled his next question carefully.

"How's your father getting on with his research?"

"Funny you should ask. I received a letter from him yesterday. At least I think it was from him."

"Oh? Did he tell you anything about his work?"

"Not much. Said it was going well. He's going to return to Germany. Wants me to go back home too. Join the Luftwaffe. The same thing he's always wanted."

"Is it such a bad idea though?"

He grinned, but I knew he was serious as he continued.

"Can't you sense the Americans are turning against us? I feel hostility more often now. You've always said you love aeroplanes—doesn't it make sense?"

"I'd never go back, not unless forced, not while we're at war. Why would I give up my future and join the Luftwaffe? It would be suicide."

"Doesn't it make you sad though? You moan that you can't make your father proud and yet you've a chance to do just that."

I ground my teeth, looking away for a minute. Face hot, I turned back to Aleks.

"I've learned it's possible to hate what your father is and yet still yearn for his approval."

Putting a hand on my shoulder, Aleks grinned.

"Mine just pays my bills. I've no strong feelings for him. Maybe you'll meet him one day."

I downed my sour, staring at the crack in the base of the glass, while Aleks looked back towards the bar, dragging banana fingers through his lustrous hair.

"What about your family, Aleks?"

"Oh, Oskar. Must we? There are pretty girls here and plenty to drink. Can't you enjoy yourself, for once? I really don't want to talk about my family now. Why do they matter?"

"Isn't it normal for friends to talk about their families? I've told you about mine."

Stanislaw went quiet, turning his gaze away deliberately to scan the paintings on the walls of the bar. I had more to ask.

"Aleks, I hope you don't mind me asking you this, but it's troubled me ever since that first night we met in Sam's Bar."

His eyes locked on mine, his usual jovial mood suspended.

"Well, go on."

I paused suddenly, unsure if I should ask my question.

"Well, I noticed you had a copy of *Nowy Kurier Warszawski* in your case. It fell out on the seat. Why were you reading a Nazi newspaper?"

He sunk into his chair, lips pursed, eyes shifting.

"Are you a detective? Why does it bother you what I might have been reading that night? *Kurier Warszawski* has been around for years."

"*Nowy Kurier Warszawski* is *not* the same thing, Aleks."

"I've always tried to stay abreast of what's going on at home. My family still send it to me. Read nothing into it. One day soon, I'm going to teach you how to relax, Oskar."

His words irritated me. I sat silently for a while.

"There's something else. I finally got round to checking at the university student office. They had never heard of the Bismarck Fund. Why did you lie to me? Just tell me the real reason you let me stay in your apartment."

He seemed genuinely shocked by the fact that I had checked, his eyeballs bouncing as his brain decided what he should say in reply.

Moving towards a set of wall shelves next to the front door, he collected a deep wooden box and folded board and returned to the table.

"Look, I think my father might know your family in some way, from way back. I really know nothing more than that. Come on, let's play. Winner takes fifty cents from the loser. Okay?"

Mind full of questions, I reluctantly dropped the topic and agreed to play. Inside the box sat a hand-carved wooden chess set, sitting on a red-velvet lining. The heads of the four bishops were all missing. We set the board, Aleks white, me black, as usual. He moved his pawn from e2 to e4.

"Oskar, look. Perhaps the Kahn place was not right for you, but how about you stay for free in my spare room? Until the end of term. That way you could get your travel money together quicker."

I shuffled my brogues on the sawdust-covered floor, my breath catching in my chest.

"I'm really not a charity case, but thanks for the offer. I'll think about it."

"Check."

Aleks' queen, rooks and knight besieged my king. Castling was my only choice. As I took my hand off, he grinned, swiftly moving his bishop from a3 to take my rook. Defeat was surely imminent. At that same moment, a reveller who, with his friends, had surrounded our table, fell across it, scattering our board and pieces to the floor.

Aleks rose slowly, facing up to the group's leader, an unshaven man with deep-set eyes beneath a protruding forehead.

"What are you doing? Pick up the pieces."

The laughing group muscled up behind their leader, who was now eyeball to eyeball with Aleks.

"Asshole."

He spat out his insult, shoving an unsteady Aleks back towards me. Aleks pulled a small pistol from inside his jacket, holding his elbow close to his body. The group froze. Sensing trouble, the barman crept slowly towards the table.

"What the hell are you doing, Aleks?"

I ushered him towards the door.

"Come on, let's get out of here."

My heart pounded hard as we walked quickly along MacDougal Street, towards Prince Street. Checking over my shoulder, I saw the group of half a dozen men following at a distance of fifty metres.

"Next time you bring a gun into a bar, you damn well let me know. We could have been arrested. I can't afford to lose my place at the university."

Aleks put his hand on my shoulder as we walked.

"Calm down, Oskar. I've got a licence."

"What? Why do you have a licence? You've no need to carry a weapon."

"If you don't know already, my friend, in this place, it's a case of who you know, not what you know. I've a few friends in high places."

We quickly reached the corner of Prince Street, deciding to run and put distance between us and our followers. Turning right onto Sullivan Street, we hid behind trash cans in an alleyway where we could see the gang pass by.

"Stupid sons of bitches. Come on, we can take a detour."

We wove through a few alleys, eventually coming out halfway down Wooster Street and close to Aleks' place.

A grin as broad as Fifth Avenue spread across his face.

"I guess you're coming in for a drink?"

We laughed as Aleks pulled back the concertina opening of the Otis. He pressed the black button, with an imprinted white six on it, and I shut my eyes tight as we shuddered and lurched slowly upwards.

"Are you all right?"

"I'm fine. I just don't like being followed, okay, and neither do I like enclosed spaces. Don't talk to me until we're there."

It took an eternity to reach the sixth floor, where we stepped into the grey-marble-encased lobby, dimly lit by brass wall lanterns. There were only two doors on either side of us. Two apartments to an entire floor. Mine had eight. I ran my fingers across the cold, smooth surface of the walls and inhaled deeply, taking the strawberry scent from the vase of purple, pink and cream hyacinths on the side.

Stepping through his apartment door, it struck me how thick the walls were. I slipped off my boots and sank my feet into the reassuringly dense weave of his Persian rug before dropping back on a luxurious sofa full of cushions. Aleksander handed me an Armagnac, sitting down opposite me and resting his feet on a pouffe.

"Do you remember being here last time? You were a little intoxicated."

"Yes, I wasn't blotto. Anyway, I blame you. You're not a good influence."

I gazed around the apartment, enjoying its ambiance, imagining how my father would react. He always seemed to come into his own, bristling with charisma, whenever in the company of money.

"Aleks, that stunt you pulled in the bar, it really shocked me. I'd no idea you carried a gun."

"I know you love the city, but you must realise it's a dangerous place. Especially if you're German."

Sipping my brandy, I pondered Aleks' words.

"It sucks, doesn't it? I mean, being hated by others. I want to be a success here. It's tough. You can help me though, I'm sure. To find work in psychology."

Aleks' eyes scanned the wall above my head, where a series of art deco nudes looked down on us.

"Oskar, do you really think you're cut out to be some kind of psychiatrist? All that shock therapy and lobotomy sounds scary as hell."

Swinging my legs vertically and sitting up, a surge of blood went to my head.

"You know my reasons, Aleks. If it helps me understand my father better, I'll be happy and, anyway, psychiatry is all about the couch too."

He shrugged.

"I think you and I will go back to Europe before too long. There are more important matters than our careers to decide."

"You speak like someone who doesn't really need their job. Who pays for all of this, Aleks? What do you clear in a year? Three? Three and a half?"

"I obtain a little help from home. Everyone needs some help, right?"

I wondered if he knew that I was receiving payments. I'd always felt he knew more about me than he let on.

"You're working and you still receive help?"

I turned away from my friend, biting my lip, swallowing hard.

"Father doesn't earn much. He didn't want me to come to America anyway. But I am receiving some money. I don't know where it comes from."

Slouching, chin to chest, a tear gathered in my eye. I really didn't know for sure where the money came from. It had bothered me the whole time I was here. Aleks came to sit beside me, pouring me another drink.

"You'll see your mother again one day. Don't worry."

I turned to him, a gentle nod, wanting to believe him.

"What does your father do, Aleks? You never told me."

"He's a businessman. A very good one."

*

Two weeks later

I sat in silence, staring at the cracks on the badly plastered bathroom wall in front of me. They reminded me of the basement at home in Halbe, except those cracks were in brickwork. Weary eyes followed each line from its starting point, where a thick nail punctured the wall, down to the floor, up to the ceiling and out to the adjoining walls. I visualised the nail as Father's death, each line an explanation, leading nowhere. My tears had come in a burst, short-lived, violent, just like after the first few times he had beaten me. How dare he die. My heart felt empty, my head full of questions.

What happened to him in the Great War? Why did he hate Timo's father so? Why did he beat me? I still had no answers. I wondered whether the letter I had received from him a fortnight ago was really written by him.

The news of his death arrived via telegram. It simply read:

For attention: Oskar Bachmann.
3 April 1940

Karl Bachmann, German national (non-military), killed in Soviet-occupied Przemyśl.

Grenz Polizeikommissariat

For reasons I cannot explain, I sat, knees pressed against my chest, in the stuffy boiler cupboard outside my apartment using a cigarette lighter to illuminate the brief message. I read it over and over, trying to find a clue. Anything to help me understand what happened to my father. Was he murdered? What was he doing in the Soviet part of Przemyśl, anyway? Why had I received a telegram at all? How did the Grenz Polizeikommissariat find my address? What did all this mean?

I had not seen Aleks in weeks, but now I needed my only Manhattan friend. It seemed he knew. I heard someone knocking outside, and a familiar voice.

"Oskar. Oskar! Are you in there?"

I extended my leg to push the cupboard door open. Aleks turned, peering down at me in dismay.

"My dear friend. What on earth are you doing down there? Are you okay?"

"I'm sorry, Aleks. I've had some shocking news."

My friend took off his hat, dropped his head and stepped inside.

"What's happened?"

"It's my father. He's dead."

I stared blankly at Aleksander, gauging his reaction. He paced the floor, staring at the ceiling, before leaning on a sill and breaking into a theatrical sob. His eyes were dry as he turned to embrace me.

"I'm so sorry, Oskar."

I stepped back, gently pushing him away.

"How did he die?"

"I don't know. I received a telegram this morning from the Grenz Polizeikommissariat. It doesn't say. I only know he was killed in Soviet Przemyśl."

"But your father was working with Weigl, in the hospital lab? That's in Zasanie."

My mind went into overdrive, recalling conversations between the two of us.

"I don't remember ever telling you my father worked with Weigl, only that he was in research."

"Come, Oskar. You're forgetting things. You've told me everything about your father. I think there may be more to his story. I'm going to help you find out what happened to him."

I was not listening to Aleks, but instead, dwelling on my own feelings. Rather than sadness or relief, my primary feeling was emptiness. Part of my own identity had left with Papa, and answers I hoped he would one day give me would now never be told. My stomach felt empty too. For the first time I could remember in twenty years, I felt ravenously hungry.

"Will you take me out to lunch, Aleks? I want to eat the messiest, noisiest meal in all of Manhattan."

12

THE MOVIE

New York City
June 1940

It had been two months since news of Father's death arrived. Losing him and not knowing where Mother was, or how to contact her, became all-consuming. I spent many hours walking alone, wondering whether I should return to Europe to find Mother, how I might track her down and uncover the truth about my father's death. My unfinished business with him continued to haunt both my waking hours and my frequent dreams.

That morning, I took a longer route to the cafe, meandering through a warm and blustery Washington Square Park. I thought about whether Father had ever loved me at all. Whether behind his fists and cruelty there lay a sad, unfulfilled man, the punishment rained down on me simply because he wanted the best for me. Now, I would never know.

A downy woodpecker kept my focus for a while, followed by the morning song of a golden-crowned kinglet, singing in the park's famous Hangman's Elm. As I stopped to observe them, I sensed someone stopping behind me at a distance of a few metres, then following me as I continued walking. Every time I turned, the male figure behind me seemed to blend into the crowd, making it impossible to identify any individual. My heart raced as I sped up to evade him, but marching into a bustling Fifth Avenue, all sense of being followed disappeared, my attention stolen by a middle-aged woman who was tidying her greying hair and gazing longingly into the window of a shoe shop. For a moment, I was in my child's eye, staring up at Mother. This stranger looked, moved, even smelled like her. Time slowed as I walked, thinking of her. Mother's last correspondence had reached me in early March, a month before the Reich issued censorship regulations for foreign mail. It had a Czechoslovakian postage stamp. I spent hours reading the letter repeatedly, thinking about her and Father. She told me little about her circumstances, other than to say she was enjoying the goulash and uzené, a type of smoked meat, and trying to paint a little and read when she could. I thought too about Aleksander, concluding that, despite his peculiarities, he had been a good friend and great comfort to me.

Pushing open the door of Cafe Reggio, one of my favourite village haunts, I was met by a chaotic scene.

"Francesco, will you please shut down my precious machine before it explodes! It's like Cape Disappointment in here!"

Domenico Parisi, the Calabrian owner of downtown Cafe Reggio, sat charming an elegant customer, while berating his chief waiter, who frantically fiddled with the nickel-plated monster dominating the coffee shop, its spouts noisily jetting plumes of steam into the room. The vertical-boiler coffee machine, crowned with a mighty 'Aquila', could make nine espressos simultaneously and was Parisi's pride and joy.

Morning sun flooded through the cafe windows through gaps in the cloud, burning off the trails of condensation and warming my face. Outside, tourists stalled, holding onto their hats as the swirling wind kept the litter moving along the sidewalk. A familiar voice disturbed me, saying, 'Ciao' to every person in the cafe by name, before arriving with a grin at my table. His white shirt was crisp and smooth, trousers pressed, oxblood brogue shoes shining.

"Oskar, my friend, you're late this morning."

I noticed he wore a tie pin today, with the number twenty-five in the middle of an Italian flag. An anniversary badge, perhaps? I didn't bother to ask.

"What can I get you? Eggs?"

"No. How about a plate of pancakes? Not too brown, plenty of berries."

"Coming up, boss. You want coffee? I managed to fix the beast. It's always clogging with calcium."

Francesco spun around and headed for the kitchen door but, before he reached it, he picked up a newspaper from the front desk and headed back to my table, tucking it under my napkin.

Despite the glorious Greenwich Village weather and Francesco's effortless style, a sense of dread consumed me as I picked up the *New York Post*. Events in Europe over the last few weeks had been overwhelming. Germany had invaded Denmark, Norway, Holland, Belgium and Luxembourg. In London, King George VI appointed Winston Churchill as British Prime Minister. Churchill subsequently ordered the bombing of my beloved Berlin. Any chance of a quick war in Europe disappeared.

Detachment from my homeland shrunk whenever I picked up a newspaper. Turning the paper over and opening it flat, I read the headline, bold and black, 'Nazis Take Dunkerque'.

Below the lead story, a smaller article declared 'Allies Bomb Munich Plant'. I paused as this information sank in. Even though I had left it behind, my love of the Fatherland remained strong. As I read details of bombing raids on the great cities of Berlin and Munich, I worried that friends and family members could have died or been injured, their homes destroyed.

Francesco reappeared with a grin and flourish.

"Reading the news from Europe will send you crazy. Come, enjoy your pancakes. We're alive today in the greatest city in the world."

As he set down my espresso and a glass of water, the cafe's front door swung open, revealing an imposing figure in the doorway.

"Oskar. I'm glad I've found you here. How are you feeling?"

I got to my feet, genuinely happy to see Aleks.

"I'm fine. Please, sit down."

He lowered his enormous frame down on the chair across from me, beaming as it creaked.

"Don't you lecture on Tuesday mornings?"

"I'm on a special project today, and I need you to join me."

"What kind of project? I really need to get my focus back on my studies."

"It's important, Oskar. You'll find out. Surely you can miss one lecture?"

"Okay." I hurriedly mopped up the berry juice with the last of my pancakes. "But I wouldn't do this for anyone else."

We finished our coffees and left a couple of quarters on the table, saying our goodbyes to Francesco as we left.

Aleks hurriedly led the way, jumping into the driving seat of his black Plymouth Road King, discarded items of clothing and old newspapers strewn across the seats.

"Where are we going?"

Glancing in his rear-view mirror, he pushed his foot down hard on the accelerator and we glided away.

"We're taking a trip to hospital."

My mind raced. Hospital, why? Was a colleague ill? A research project Aleksander wanted me involved in, maybe? Perhaps a charitable venture?

The streets of Lower Manhattan seemed calm, compared to Midtown. Aleksander wolfed down a bag of Paczki doughnuts en route. As we pulled through the gates of the grand Bellevue Hospital in Kips Bay fifteen minutes later, I still didn't know why I was here.

The hospital walls were dark, impenetrable. It reminded me of an evening with my fellow students when this, the country's oldest public hospital, had become the topic of conversation. The place was notorious, and the local students eagerly volunteered tales of limbs removed without anaesthetic or lunatics crawling walls, trying to escape. But hospitals didn't bother me. Father spent time in them through his work and his descriptions made them feel somehow familiar.

We parked in the bays to the left of the public entrance and made our way up a spiral iron staircase on the north-facing wall of the main building. Four storeys up, Aleksander took his hand from his jacket pocket and made to knock on a door marked simply 'Research'. Before his hand hit the door, I grabbed his wrist.

"Hang on. Tell me why we're here. Why did you want me to come?"

"Your father didn't die in vain, Oskar."

I released his fist, desperate to understand what he meant. Did the people in this place know how and why Father died?

After a few moments, a young man in a white coat answered the door.

"Professor Stanislaw, please do come in."

"Thank you, Vincent. Where's Doctor Kaltz?"

"He'll be back any minute. He's checking results in the lab, I believe. Who's your friend?"

"Sorry, so rude. Should have introduced you. This is Oskar Bachmann, a student at NYU."

"Sir, pleased to meet you. What's your field of study?"

Aleksander interjected.

"Oskar, this is Vincent Mawcawny, a research scientist here at Bellevue. A real whizz-kid."

"I'm a psychologist."

"I see. I know a few people that need some help."

He laughed, turning his attention back to Aleksander. As he did so, another, older man, also dressed in a white coat, walked through the internal door.

"Lothar, at last! Good to see you."

Aleks held out his hand.

"I'd like you to meet Oskar Bachmann, son of Karl, and my good friend."

Kaltz held out a hand in my direction, staring me in the eye with intensity and focus.

160

"Bachmann. Delighted. Aleksander told me about your father's death. I'm so sorry."

I prickled at how familiar these strangers were with my grief and focused my gaze on Aleks.

"Perhaps you'll enlighten me now. Why am I here?"

"Of course. Lothar, shall we?"

Kaltz led the three of us through to a smaller room, where my head touched the ceiling. It contained a projector on a stand to the left and a screen covering the entire wall to the right. In between were two rows of red chairs, perfectly laid out. It seemed most odd to me that a research centre would have its own movie cinema.

Aleks rested a hand on my shoulder.

"Oskar, we're friends. Watch this film with an open mind. Don't judge things too quickly. Will you do that for me?"

I nodded, already uneasy.

A young woman in a bright-green dress handed us each a cup of coffee. I moved to sit in the front row, expecting Aleksander to join me. Instead, he sat behind me with Kaltz. The projector whirred.

The film was silent at first. Disturbing images of malnourished people in what looked like prison camps and ghettoes flickered across the screen, like extras in a horror movie. There were different locations, each labelled. From my rudimentary knowledge of central European geography, I recognised them as being in Poland, Czechoslovakia and Hungary.

The plight of the poor souls in the pictures was consistent in every location. Shirtless, hollowed eyes, sunken cheeks.

Many coughed or were bent over, vomiting, spots covering their stomachs, chests and backs.

I couldn't watch any more.

"When does this end? Why are you showing me this?"

Kaltz spoke calmly.

"Please. This isn't easy. Bear with us a little longer."

As he finished his sentence, the film flickered and the scene transformed, now with sound. It showed a large, old house, from a distance. A fountain was visible outside and a long entrance road, flanked by lawns covered in apple trees. The scene moved inside to a large room with a long table. On the other side of it, with their backs to the camera, stood six men, speaking in garbled German, gesticulating in front of a window overlooking the garden.

After a few seconds, the camera peeled around to the right, revealing the faces of three of the men, two in uniform and the other in civilian clothes, with only the side of his face visible. One was unmistakably the Führer, smiling, talking with the man side on, his identity obscured.

I strained to hear the dialogue on screen as a crackle like burning kindling filled the room. Through it I made out the words '*Impfstoff*' and '*Polen*' ('vaccine' and 'Poland').

In the next scene, the camera angle changed again. Now Hitler and the only other man not wearing a white coat were centre frame. The picture blurred momentarily before the face of the second man came into full view and as it did, the film, the surrounding room, and my companions paused in stasis. A muffled thump of my heart beating out of my chest returned me to a fully conscious state. The other man was my father,

Karl Bachmann, smiling awkwardly and shaking hands with the Führer.

Like technicians watching a squirming lab rat, Kaltz and Aleksander stared at me. As I turned my head slowly towards them, the last piece of film shot through the projector, leaving the screen black.

Aleks got to his feet.

"Oskar, are you okay? I'm sure this must be a great shock."

His words floated over me. I turned my head back to the screen.

No. That could not be my father. Yes, he thought the Nazis were good for Germany, but working directly for Hitler? How? Why? I sat silently, shoulders hunched, as my breathing quickened. Tears welled in my eyes. This made no sense.

"Whisky," Kaltz called to the woman in the green dress.

Aleks approached but stopped in his tracks as I turned to gaze at him from empty eyes, mumbling, 'lift, thrust, drag and weight' repeatedly. My mind scrambled, trying to process what I had seen. Explanations popped up like temporary scaffolding, as I tried to hold on to the last strands of goodness in my father's legacy. Each one quickly collapsed.

Kaltz held out a half-full crystal glass towards me. My left arm flew across it, sending the golden liquid contents in an arc, high across the room. The glass smashed against the wall on which we had viewed the film, sending shards of glass in every direction. I ran for the door and stumbled down the iron steps before sprinting across the hospital forecourt to flag a cab on First Avenue.

*

163

A week later, as I strode along the tree-lined mall towards the Corinthian-columned entrance of the Pantheon-parody Gould Library, I tried to convince myself that, perhaps, the events at Bellevue were a dream. They were a creation of my confused, grief-stricken mind as it tried to make sense of Papa's death. My rational mind reminded me that he had always been a Nazi; it was not such a stretch to imagine him further committed to Hitler's cause, especially if it would somehow make him 'famous'.

I must admit, I thought it strange to see this grand baroque building atop a hill in an area now filling with a poorer black and Hispanic community who would never see the inside of it. Pushing open the giant bronze doors of the library, my heart felt heavy. My reasons for coming here, personal and all-consuming. I suddenly felt guilty, my residency here so out of step with the lives of my family in Europe, but the stunning interior of the library brought my focus back. Stood in a small vestibule flanked by bronze standard lamps, I peered first at the stained-glass windows, then ahead across the black and white polished mosaic floor tiles to a steep staircase. I climbed it and entered the splendour of the main reading room. Its deeply coffered ceiling and splendid Connemara marble columns should have felt crushing for a Halbe boy like me, but peering around the drum of the main dome, I spotted the inscription, 'Where shall wisdom be found? Where is the place of understanding?' and together with the human scale of the bookcases, I found them comforting.

The newspaper section was vast. Heading to the foreign segment, I found Germany, then the year 1914, and located copies of *Vossische Zeitung*, a liberal Berlin newspaper that for generations had been the country's paper of record until the Nazis forced its closure. Starting in August, when Germany entered the war, I began to scan page after page, slowly at first, then speeding up as my eyes adjusted to the print size, attuned to any aeroplane references. I picked up the file holding the 8 November edition, its headline: 'Important Progress in the Argonne Forest.' Turning the page, I scanned the inside cover before my tiring eyes fixed on a small piece at the bottom of page three: 'Aeroplanes Deployed Over Enemy Positions.' It referred to reconnaissance missions over Belgium, then a brief line on a collision between two German planes in which a Berlin airman of note had been killed. Foolishly, I had thought there might be some reference to my father by name. There was not. I scribbled a few details in my notepad before packing my bag.

After wandering the aviation sector for a while, I descended the staircase back to the entrance hall. There was an office on either side of the staircase. As instructed, I headed to the one on the right. Glancing at my watch, I knocked on its shiny black door. A brief pause, then a deep, resonant voice like that of the stage actors I had heard on my visits to theatre shows with Aleks invited me inside.

Abram Kardiner, a New York psychoanalyst of great renown, sat in a leather armchair next to a chaise longue by the office window, holding a set of papers close to his face. He had an intense, presidential air about him, his sunlight-illuminated features instantly reminding me of Abraham Lincoln, whose bust sat with other famous Americans just metres away in the

Hall of Fame colonnade that circled this library. He smiled, rising from his chair to shake my hand.

"Oskar? Have a seat on my couch. I'm off duty."

His wry humour surprised me, putting me at ease.

"I'm so grateful for your time, Mr Kardiner."

"I've been up at the Bronx Veterans Hospital in West Fordham this morning. Only ten minutes in a cab. I don't have long, though. You're an NYU postgrad, right? Professor Greening said you wanted to talk to me?"

I nodded. He was right. Having read Kardiner's work, I had persuaded my senior lecturer, Greening, to write him a letter on the pretence I would like to interview him for my own studies.

"I would get you a drink, but they make you pay here. Please go ahead." He grinned. "No need to lie back."

"Thank you, Mr Kardiner. I understand you're researching links between neurosis in patients and trauma during their wartime experiences?"

"Not so much recently, other than this morning! I'm still in the process of writing up my studies on that topic from the last decade. Hope to publish maybe next year. Why?"

"Can I be honest, Mr Kardiner?"

"I'm a psychiatrist, you should be."

"I wanted to see you not in relation to my postgraduate studies but on a personal matter."

"Didn't I just say I was off duty?"

"It's not me, it's my father. I want to talk to you about his behaviour. You see, when I was younger there were episodes. They would always start the same. He would speak inappropriately loudly, his words would spill out much more

166

quickly, his tone hardened, the rhythm of words like a machine gun. I've developed theories about what might have caused his outbursts. I'm sure your more detailed—"

"You'll know from your own studies, I cannot give any diagnosis without a consul—"

"I know, I know. I just want your general thoughts, that's all. Please, Mr Kardiner."

Kardiner relaxed back into his chair, placing a still thumb and forefinger on his chin and nodding once. I had intended to give him a brief account, but he interrupted, asking questions as I explained my father's role in the war, how the beatings began, their frequency, how he would behave afterwards. I recounted it all feeling no emotion, then I told him Papa had been killed.

"How did you feel about his death?"

As Emil and I had attacked with glee a Spreewald beaver dam in our youth, letting the water flood over the banks, so Kardiner's question destroyed my own defences, leaving me a helpless, sobbing wreck for five minutes. He left me there, did not touch me or offer me anything until my tears subsided. As I looked up, he passed me a paper towel.

"I'm sorry, my feelings are still coming out."

"No need to apologise. Quite normal for grief to manifest in a huge wave. It's possible, Oskar, that your father suffered a trauma in the Great War and kept it with him for years, like a devil on a chain, only releasing it to abuse you, his son, but I can see no clear evidence from what you've told me. Sorry I can't be more conclusive."

Checking his watch, he stuffed his papers in a briefcase and got to his feet.

"I must go. If I can be of any use at NYU, do let me know. Look after yourself."

With that he got up, rushing away from me, the room and the library. I stayed a while longer processing my thoughts. My free counselling session had left me feeling lighter but also embarrassed that I had bared my soul to such a distinguished character for, apparently, no end.

*

Before going home, I returned to Washington Square Park by bus, stopping at the university office to check my pigeonhole. As anticipated, there was a message from Aleks inside it:

Please, Oskar, we must talk. I'll be at Cafe Reggio every morning at eight this week. I hope one day you'll join me. Your friend, Aleksander.

I screwed the message into a ball and threw it away, but by 7:45 the next morning, I was sitting in a secluded seat at Reggio's in the corner farthest away from the windows. I drank from an endless cup of coffee, rehearsing what I had to say to Aleksander. This cafe was like a home to me. I had experienced many enjoyable times here but, as the clock ticked closer to eight, I wanted to leave.

At three minutes past the hour, Aleksander walked in. He put his coat on the hook near the door and, without hesitation, sat with his back to me at a window seat on the far side of the cafe.

Francesco had the day off. The new waitress approached Aleksander and returned to the kitchen, leaving me hesitant. Should I leave money on the table and slip away? But Aleks took away any choice I had, pushing back from his table and striding towards the bathroom. Raising his head, he saw me, his stride slowing to a stop. He nodded, his usual grin absent.

"Oskar. I'm pleased you're here. Give me a moment. I'll be straight back."

As he disappeared into the bathroom, the waitress appeared, carrying a tray with a toast rack, holding four pieces of burned toast and a selection of jams and honey.

"Leave it here. Thanks," I said.

Aleksander returned and pulled out the spare chair, sitting and shuffling in it to get comfortable, before straightening his tie.

"Are you all right? I've been concerned. Haven't seen you around the university."

I stared, remaining silent, focusing on my reflection in a branded wall mirror ahead of me.

"Seeing the film last week must have been a shock, but I'd hoped to talk to you directly afterwards, to explain things. You need to know the truth."

I laughed a quiet, sarcastic laugh.

"I'm not sure I've *ever* heard that from you. Who was Karl Bachmann? I don't know any more. Expect you know more than me."

"I'm sorry you've had to deal with this, so soon after your father's death."

Aleksander put his hand on my arm. I pulled it away.

"I haven't been as open with you as I should have been, Oskar. There are things I know about your father that I need to tell you."

Beads of perspiration gathered on my forehead.

"Like what? What are you talking about?"

"Please, stay calm. Perhaps we should go to my apartment and talk there?"

"There is no one here other than us, Aleksander. Speak! Now!"

"Very well. Your father had been working with Rudolf Weigl for a while. Thanks to his work, a new typhus vaccine is ready. Your father was truly brilliant, Oskar."

"Get to the point."

"His work came to the attention of Hans Frank, our leader in Poland. Earlier this year, your father was persuaded to work with them."

I slumped in my seat.

"You saw the film, Oskar. Your father was there of his own accord. He knew it was the only way to distribute the vaccine out into the world. To help people. Hitler is trying to improve life for ordinary Germans. Your father knew this."

My eyes darted to Aleksander.

"You're a bloody Nazi, through and through. I should have known right from the start."

Timo's face appeared in my mind, then the baying mob at Zemminsee. My stomach churned.

"Oskar, please. Your father was a noble man, but pragmatic. Only the Nazis have the power to eliminate typhus in Europe. The League of Nations never managed it. Your father was smart, recognised his vision of providing vaccines to the poor and sick was possible but only by using the vast network of resources available and with Hans Frank's direct support."

I grabbed the lapel of Aleksander's sports jacket, pulling his face towards mine, my nose almost touching his.

"My father wasn't noble, and neither are you."

In turn, he grabbed my wrist, pulling it to my lap, looking me in the eye.

"Do you know how your father died, Oskar? It wasn't an accident. He crossed the River San for research purposes, and a Jewish gang hijacked him. Stabbed him to death as he tried to return to the bridge. There have been many of these attacks in recent months."

Aleks' explanation seemed unlikely. Why would a Jewish gang have reason to kill him? It made no sense.

"How do you know all of this, and why didn't you tell me before?"

"I've many friends in the city, Oskar, and my father still lives there. I received a letter from him only the day before last."

Aleksander moved his chair closer to mine and reached across the table to put his hand on my right shoulder.

"Oskar, I'm a Pole. The Germans have occupied my country, yet I understand what's happening in Europe. You shouldn't hate your homeland."

Pushing the table violently towards him, I jumped up. "I don't hate my homeland. I hate what's happened to it. Nothing is as dangerous as an ignorant friend, Stanislaw. Stay away from me."

13

THE ACCIDENT

The Morgan Library
Summer 1940

Meeting us in the Morgan foyer, our elderly guide simmered. Stiff, narrow shoulders, jutting chin revealing a turkey neck, greying hair tightly pinned back. She was a fearful sight. As our breathless Professor Tawnie made to apologise, she pursed her lips, poised to critique any excuses our lecturer might offer. He opted not to.

"You're lucky we're quiet today. Follow me."

The sweet, musty odour of old books hung heavy in the air as the dozen students in our group entered the magnificent East Room. I was careful to pick out individual scents, as taught by my best friend. Detecting a sharp, synchronous intake of breath as the room revealed itself to the students, I observed as one huddled group scanned the ceiling, pointing ten metres up at the ornately painted spandrels, trying to spot their zodiac signs. Another group marvelled at Avarice riding to victory in the English King Henry VIII's tapestry hanging above the imposing marble mantelpiece. I peered up at the tiers of books safely stowed in walnut bookshelves, my eyes moistening as Timo's teenage face appeared in my mind. He would have loved this place and would by now have already begun to navigate it.

My feeling of calm was transient, soon replaced by a suffocating tension as I realised the time to meet Stanislaw drew near. I moved slowly backwards as the guide gathered our group together near the fireplace. Her shrill voice brought my fellow students to attention.

"This was once a multi-millionaire's personal library."

Slipping away, I stopped twice, pretending to peruse books, steadily moving towards the grand rotunda and the cafe. I imagined no one would notice me gone for a few minutes.

Aleksander sat alone at the edge of the cafe. He crossed and uncrossed his legs continually, eyes darting in multiple directions. When he spotted my approach, he stood to welcome me.

"I'm glad you've come, Oskar."

He held out his hand and gave me an awkward smile. I ignored him and sat.

"How was the library?"

"Let's not waste time on chit-chat."

"Very well. I'll buy coffee."

As he walked towards the catering desk, I ran through exactly what I would say to him, changing my mind three times before he arrived back and took the initiative to speak before the tray of coffee was on the table.

"There are things I should have told you earlier, Oskar. Now, I've no reason to hide them. I'm a National Socialist. Have been the entire time I've known you."

His admission was no surprise, but somehow, I felt cheated and foolish.

"The Smith Bill will be law soon. All Germans will have to report to the authorities. The Americans won't want us around much longer. I've been receiving news from home on a weekly basis, Oskar. There's no going back now. We're going to take over the world, surely you want to be part of this great adventure."

"No. I do not. Why don't you shut up?"

Aleksander's head jerked back, his eyes widening.

"When I arrived in Manhattan, I'd a dream of learning, so I could use my knowledge to help people. Yes, to make the world a better place by understanding the frailties of the human mind. Hell, that might even stop a few wars. Aggression is the principal psychological cause of war and, guess what, I've known all about that since my childhood."

"The Reich needs people with your skills for the future, Oskar. First, we must win the war."

I glared at him.

"Be quiet. I haven't finished. A letter arrived this week from my grandpa. God knows how he got it to me."

I was lying. I knew exactly how. Cut to size, the letter's four pages were carefully inserted into an illustrated Westphalian recipe book. Opa had posted the parcel from a bookstore on the outskirts of Berlin to the newly opened corner bookshop at 102 Fourth Avenue in Manhattan. The owner of the store, a woman by the name of Eleanor Lowenstein, sent word to the university, and I collected it. On the front of the parcel was a stamp I didn't recognise (a black circle with a capital 'L' and small 'b' inside it).

"He founded free schools in Germany before he retired. Do you know what they stand for?"

He shook his head, avoiding my stare.

I stood, raising my right hand, forefinger extended, pointing to him as I slowly uttered the words.

"Respect for God. The same dignity for all humans. Tolerance of others' religion and ways of life. Renouncing violence and preserving nature.

"He wanted a quiet retirement. Tending his garden, fishing, reading the books he'd always meant to. But your Nazi friends paid him a visit, threatened him and burned his beloved books."

"The Gestapo are not my friends, Oskar. But I'm going back to Germany. You should too."

I sensed stares from nearby tables as I got up, a rushing like the Atlantic's waves sweeping up through my body into my ears.

"Bullshit. I didn't really like you when we first met, but, hey, you were my landlord and it seemed best to try to get along. I should have trusted my instincts. Understand something, Stanislaw: my future's right here."

"Wait. Oskar. My father instructed me to make contact with you. I need to explain why."

Ignoring him and his lies, I rushed towards the exit, turning back as I remembered something that had troubled me for weeks.

"The song you sang in the Minetta, a Jew wrote it. A genius Jew. Never, ever sing that song again."

Storming out of the front door and down the steps onto busy Madison Avenue, I ran as fast as I could, Aleksander's pleas ringing in my ears.

"Oskar, come back. You're angry. I understand."

I broke into a sweat, heading south-west across East 35th Street. Stanislaw's hoarse voice was still calling.

"I need to tell you something. It's important. Please stop."

I imagined his voice as Father's and ran even faster, trying to escape him and the Fatherland. Pushing people out of my way, I reached East 34th and turned right, looking over my shoulder every six strides. Stanislaw gained on me. My blood throbbed in my fingertips. The Empire State was only a hundred metres away. I would stop there, disappear into the crowd, gather myself.

"Oskar, pleeeease."

As I reached the busy pedestrian crossing, the tallest building in the world filled my view. I prayed for the light to turn green. Glancing sideways I saw Stanislaw careering through the crowd like an out-of-control truck just metres away from me. His heavy hand landed on my shoulder. Instinctively, I stooped down towards the street, his heavyweight body rolling over me, its momentum taking it onto the road and under the wheels of a speeding taxi.

A moment before Stanislaw hit the ground, he called out, "Oskar, I'm..." But the end of his sentence was lost to eternity, swallowed by the screech of tyres.

In seconds, strangers had surrounded his body, like vultures stalking a savanna corpse. An animated workman shoved me towards the taxi, shouting something unintelligible in my face.

I'm what, Aleks? echoed through my skull as I mumbled the words under my breath, over and over. Then the shouts and the blare of sirens drowned them out.

*

Inside Midtown South Precinct station, a procession of police officers and prisoners, mainly black or Hispanic, paced the aisles. Doors with a mesh of reinforced glass opened and slammed shut, phones rang repeatedly and the smell of alcohol, sweat and a herbal, diesel-like odour I didn't recognise hung in the air.

What was I doing here? I had never seen the inside of a police station before and fretted at how distraught Mother would be if she knew I were here. I couldn't even remember the journey here, or the faces of the officers who bundled me into the patrol car.

Handcuffs, fastened tight around my bony wrists, cut into my skin as the officers pushed me down on a seat in a tiny, dark interview room.

Aleksander loved the funny guys, Laurel and Hardy. A few months back, he'd dragged me along on a double date to see their new movie *The Flying Deuces* at Radio City Music Hall on Fifth Avenue. Stan and Ollie seemed to be sat here in front of me. The sergeant leaned in, his collar and shirt buttons stretched to breaking point. His sidekick's hat slid down over his eyes as his head tilted to take notes, his reddened, bent-back fingertips gripping a pencil.

"Name?"

"Did he die?"

"Yes, he died. Name?"

My mind churned, still enraged, unable to process what had happened. I offered a pitiful reply.

"He was my only real friend here, you know."

"Your name?"

"Oskar Bachmann."

"Age and address?"

"I'm twenty-five. Until recently, I lived with him."

"With who? The dead guy?" I nodded, slowly.

"Are you a faggot?"

"I'm sorry? I don't know this word."

"Are you a homosexual?"

"No. He was my friend."

"Where are you staying now?"

"Henry Street. 11a. It's on the Lower East Side."

"Where you from originally, Bachmann?"

"I'm German. From Halbe, south of Berlin."

The sergeant glanced at his junior, cocking his head with a smirk on his face.

"Well, Frankie, we have ourselves a Nazi. You all caused a lot of trouble at that shindig you held in Madison Square Garden last year."

"No, no. I'm not a Nazi. I'm a student here. At New York University."

The sergeant shrugged.

"We have four different witnesses who all say you deliberately threw that man in the road. What do you have to say to that?"

"It was instinctive. I mean, he was following me. I wanted to escape him."

"Do you admit you threw him on the road?"

"No. Well, yes. We'd argued, and he tried to stop me from crossing the street. It was an accident."

"The court will decide that. Book him, Frankie. Bachmann, you're headed for the Tombs."

178

"Hey, Bochemann. What's that you're reading?"

Amused at his ability to create a nickname for me, Harris pushed his grinning, toothless face against the bars. Eyeballing me, he hung his hairless, tattooed arms outside his shit-stinking cell.

Sat hunched and shaking on the edge of my desk-width bed, I stared harder at my book. A history of this Châteauesque hellhole, my latest loan from the Tombs' library. Reading helped me stave off the regular panics that cursed me.

"I'm trying to learn about this place. Maybe you should do the same."

"Can't read. Waste of time."

Harris moved to the far right of his cage, getting a better view of me.

"Why d'ya kill that fella, anyway?"

Lying back, I turned into the pitted concrete of my cell wall, breathing in the sheet's chemical odour as I scanned the words on the page up close.

"Shut up, Harris."

My fellow inmate's cuckoo laugh bounced down the walkway, meeting a squeak of shoes on the hard floor coming back the other way. There was a nearby jangle of keys. I jerked upright, instinctively swinging my legs off the bed, as the jailer unlocked my door.

"Get up, Bachmann. You're due in court."

*

The previous night I'd foolishly read about the history of Foley Square. It was once home to a native tribe and then, two hundred years ago, the site of the 'Bonfire of the Negroes', when thirteen black people were tied to stakes and burned alive by the English for insurrection. My limbs shook in my seat, heart racing.

"Stand up, please."

Judge Aarons addressed me in his cultured English accent. Removing his half-glasses, he massaged the dark, baggy flesh beneath his eyes, gazing around the wood-panelled walls, colossal round arches and fluted Ionic pilasters of courtroom five, before setting focus on me.

My mind raced as I stood. If Stanislaw had no chance against a taxi, I had none with this judge and jury. The moment I'd stepped into the courthouse three days earlier I had felt the heat of animosity in the room. My case that I'd accidentally killed Stanislaw relied solely on my word. A testimony of good character from my psychology lecturer at NYU did little to aid my cause. Half a dozen eyewitnesses queued up to tell a different story, a visiting Kentucky housewife who saw me 'chewing fire' in the Morgan cafeteria and a recently retired NYPD officer who claimed I 'rolled the guy better than Sammy Stein could' among them.

As the verdict was read, I already knew what was coming.

"Oskar Bachmann, the jury unanimously convicts you of the voluntary manslaughter of Aleksander Stanislaw, aged twenty-seven. He was your friend. You'd even lived with him in that capacity. On the day of Mr Stanislaw's death, it appears from the evidence, you'd had a furious argument and he'd followed you for over five minutes in an effort to catch you and smooth over your differences. When he caught up with you, rather than speak with him, you rolled him over your shoulder, straight under a fast-moving vehicle, as a wrestler might throw his opponent."

My eyes narrowed as I glanced at my lawyer beside me. Thumbing his large earlobe, he shuffled from one foot to another.

"Further, you stood staring, while strangers rushed to tend to what we now know were fatal injuries. You displayed a wicked recklessness as to whether he lived or died. Colleagues of Mr Stanislaw have confirmed he was a respected, popular lecturer who'd taken you 'under his wing'. He had his life in front of him. Your actions have deprived him of that and taken a loved son and brother away from his family."

Subdued chatter spread across the courtroom. Pausing, Judge Aarons brought his gavel down hard, silencing the room. Clearing his throat, he lowered his chin.

"Stand up, please."

I got to my feet, almost losing my balance as the judge pronounced sentence.

"You're a guest in this country and yet you've chosen to disregard that hospitality in the most heinous way. I see no reason to show you any leniency. Oskar Bachmann, I sentence you to eighteen years' imprisonment at the House of Detention for Men on Rikers Island. Dismissed."

*

As a single shaft of light shone through my tiny cell window, I stood on my bed and noisily struggled to open it. A finger width would do, enough to let in a little fresh air, clear the stink. It wouldn't budge. I tried to slow the pace of my breathing as I slumped down, sweating and naked except for my stained briefs and vest.

"You could ask the COs to complete a work order. I've seventeen outstanding."

A hushed voice from the shadows of the adjacent cell, both unfamiliar and un-American, spooked me. I went to the cell bars, pressing my face against them, momentarily enjoying the sensation of cold metal on my forehead. My hidden neighbour's breathing was steady, but I couldn't see his face.

He pushed his bent and stiffened hand out across the bars towards my cell. A friendly gesture, I thought.

"I wouldn't hold out much hope though. They put me in here late last night."

I stayed silent at first. Conversations with other inmates often led to trouble.

"Have you been in here long?"

"Five months, I think."

His voice became hurried, tinged with anger.

"I'm Naozumi, seen two snows through the windows of this place. This cell is my third. FBI said I was a danger to the community when they arrested me in the Public Library. Reading *Rashomon*, I was. They'd been informed I was a Yakuza. Ridiculous."

"We've that in common."

His voice lightened.

"Oh? I can't see you, but you don't sound like a Japanese gangster."

"I meant my innocence and a love of libraries, actually. No, I'm German."

He paused. It seemed I could hear him thinking through the walls.

"We're brothers now, in this great folly."

My turn to pause. What did he mean? I cursed myself for failing to keep up with the news.

"I'm sorry?"

"Ribbentrop and Kurusu have signed a pact with the Italians."

I left the bars and paced my tiny cell like a caged animal. This news and the finality of life in this maze of metal and concrete were now overcoming me.

His voice, louder now, called out.

"Would you join the fight? If you could?"

A meaningless, hypothetical question. He continued.

"I was long a soldier of the Empire. Defeated the Chinese, Taiwanese, Russians. That person is gone now. Dead, like many poor souls I fought with."

A small object skimmed across the floor, stopping in the centre of my cell door before me. I reached through the bars, dragging the palm-sized brocade bag towards me with my fingertips. I brought it close to my face to examine. It was two-tone, dark grey and white, like the old Rikers' uniforms I had seen in photographs. A doughnut button created a fastener at its top.

"What's this?"

"A *yakuyoke* charm. It will protect you, whatever your destiny."

The sound of chattering 'screws' grew steadily louder in the corridor, until I could clearly make out their words.

"Decade ago, this entire island was full of horseshit and garbage. It ain't changed that much."

Raucous laughter echoed down the passageway.

Tucking the gift under my bed, I peered across to the prison clock—too early for key turning. Two burly COs appeared at my door.

"Bachmann, I dunno what you've done, but the Deputy Commissioner wants to see you in his office straight away. Dress yourself."

Led from my cell, I glanced at Naozumi, giving him a grateful nod, as he watched me pass.

David 'Mickey' Marcus sat behind a giant desk in the warden's office, examining a folder of papers. The guards pushed me down in a chair before him. After a minute, Marcus looked up.

"You must have a friend in high places, Bachmann. I have an order here, directly from Bennett, the BOP Director."

I had never heard of him, but my mind switched to high alert, as I anticipated Marcus' next words.

"You know, Bachmann..."

He pushed his chair back from the desk, gripping the arms, before swinging his right leg over the left and looking me up and down derisively.

"My parents came here from Romania, fleeing persecution. I sure as hell don't want to give those Nazi bastards any advantage, but I'm to release you with a choice. You'll return to Germany and either see out your sentence at Tegel, which I understand is a lot better than Spandau, or enrol in the German Air Force. These are my orders. What will it be?"

Tegel would be no walk in the park, not since the Nazis had taken over. The Luftwaffe beckoned. I would pay a price for freedom in the skies above Europe, and God knew where else.

"Well, I've always liked aeroplanes, Mr Marcus, and it would have made my father proud."

He glanced at the COs and pointed to the door.

*

New York Harbour
February 1941

My heavy legs came to a stop midway along the gangplank where the prison guards had left me, hands cold and damp, a symptom of my shrinking heart. I turned and gazed back through the hazy dawn at the indistinct peaks and troughs of the Manhattan skyline. An entire continent, still unexplored, sat behind it. I did not mean my farewell to the land of the free to be like this, nor my future to be laid out as it now was. I wanted to learn and teach, not fight and kill.

Reaching into my pocket, I pulled out the small silver box I'd held tightly in my hand as I'd arrived in New York.

I looked at the inscription. It felt to me as if my knowledge was being taken away. Hesitating for a moment, I let the box slip slowly from my fingers. It fell with a quiet plop into the deep harbour water. Immediately, I felt regret.

185

My dream, like the box, had slipped away.

*

The captain had briefed his crew to treat me as a criminal until the ship was out of US waters, and so it was. They bundled me into an empty upper cargo hold, where I managed to slash my hand as I brushed away the many fragments of smashed glass bauble strewn across the floor. The *Karinas*, one of few merchant vessels now crossing the Atlantic from Germany, had left a ship full of Christmas decorations in New York Harbour yesterday. I wouldn't see them hang from that thirty-metre Rockefeller Center Norway spruce this year.

Sitting beneath the beam of light flooding through the tiny, barred window above me, I reached into my travel bag, remembering my companion Raymond from the ocean journey to New York. I had never got to have that lunch with him.

While we had waited for clearance to sail, they granted me a few minutes, under guard, to peruse a bookstore close to the harbour. The striking cover of Hemingway's new book, *For Whom the Bell Tolls*, with its black sleeve, bold red title print and mountain and church image, captivated me. I bought it using the few notes returned to me, along with wash kit, make-up and faded photographs, by the prison guards.

Wrapping my hand in a dirty sock to stem the flow of blood, I cast my eyes over its first chapter. The throb and whirr of the ship's engines and propellors began as we pulled into open waters, so I decided to compete, reading aloud to myself and enjoying the inclusion of many Spanish words in the text.

Shouting, "*Barracho! She called to him. Drunkard. Rotten drunkard!*" Hemingway's words echoed around the ship's iron walls, making a startled deckhand chuckle as he stepped through the door.

"Who are you talking to, Bachmann? You sound insane. Get up. Me and the boys want to hear your story."

14

TRAINING

Berlin-Gatow Air War School
March 1941

I bade fond farewell to the crew of the *Karinas* at the port of Hamburg, from where I had departed nearly three years before. An armed Luftwaffe corporal collected me and escorted me to a waiting military Mercedes. The driver said nothing as he pulled away, navigating the maze of roads around the port and heading east.

We stopped a while at Havelberg, near the Elbe, its ancient Gothic cathedral dominating the view from our windows. The driver pulled a flask from a side panel and poured himself a drink, reaching forward to turn on his Philips radio. I had never seen one in a car before. For just a moment, a few notes of British-sounding music and a German voice crackled through the speaker, unmistakably stating, "A total of 2662 Luftwaffe aircrew were killed during the Battle of Britain," before the driver quickly turned the tuning knob, glancing guiltily at me in the rear-view mirror.

I responded quickly with a false smile.

"I won't mention your fondness for the BBC to anyone. That's just British propaganda. I'm sure you know that."

In truth, the statistic was probably accurate, and my mind conjured nightmarish visions of RAF attacks, my plane crashing into land and sea. The driver's response revealed, without doubt, that he *was* a regular listener.

"The officer I carried to Hamburg wanted to listen. A lot of people do. Apparently, Erika Mann, daughter of the novelist Thomas Mann, has parodied the Führer on the BBC. It's disgraceful, of course."

I nodded slowly in faux agreement, deciding I did not trust the driver and would stay quiet.

Two hours later we arrived at the arched entrance to Gatow, its gates swinging open without question. The driver parked outside the main office, remaining silent. As a head appeared at my window, a sense of dread overcame me. I began to drag my damp palms down my thighs.

I was escorted to a small office behind the gates, where a junior officer asked my name before making a brief call on his telephone. A distinguished officer arrived, saluting me and eyeing me up and down before handing me the pilot's badge I had never received at Schönwalde.

"Gefreiter Bachmann, I'm Colonel Heinz Funke, Commanding Officer at Gatow. Welcome. We've been expecting you. How was your time in America?"

The car. The personal welcome. Funke's knowledge of my background. None of this made sense.

"Your uniform will be in your quarters. We've a special visitor arriving early in the morning. Get an early night."

*

189

I stared at my pilot's badge. Running a finger repeatedly around the wreath of half-laurel, half-oak leaf, blood dripped from my fingers. The giant, swooping eagle came to life, tearing the swastika from its perch, circling my head and dropping it in my pyjama pocket.

I awoke, breathless, my hands clasped to my chest. Klaus and Gustav, the two Hamburger Nazis with whom I now shared a ground-floor room in a tree-shaded barracks, stood laughing at the end of my bed.

"Your dream is over, Bachmann. We're due at the end of the branch line in ten minutes."

We stood shivering in long coats as a steady rain increased in intensity, while a chill wind circled around us, failing to shift the clouds from the dim dawn sky.

A steam whistle blasted out, scaring a murder of crows off the tracks. Looking to our right, the outline of a locomotive and clouds of steam appeared in the distance. Only at that point did Funke announce that we had the honour of a visit from *General der Flieger* Wilberg, a distinguished aerial reconnaissance expert and veteran of the Great War. Father had spoken of him reverently. I didn't understand why a man of his status arrived in the same way as day-to-day supplies.

"A security measure," I was told by a fellow reconnaissance cadet.

Wilberg stepped out of the carriage and was led by a *Flugführer* along the line of cadets. He inspected a couple of them and offered words of wisdom before stopping in front of me.

"Do your reconnaissance work well, Cadet, and you'll offer the biggest threat to our enemies. What's your name?"

"Bachmann, Herr General."

"Active service is not far away. Good luck."

My muscles trembled, a frog-like croak leaving my mouth. At this moment, I felt as if I knew absolutely nothing about flying. Wilberg climbed into a waiting car with Funke and sped away to meet the other senior officers.

I walked alone back to our barracks as the morning sun illuminated Berlin-Gatow, allowing me my first glimpse of its layout. I counted eleven aircraft hangars of various sizes, two enormous barracks and the extensive buildings of our air cadet college, either side of the main Kladow–Gatow road, to the south-east of the airfield.

Arriving at our room, I heard Gustav's rasping voice.

"During *Kristallnacht*, my brother and I led the attack on Bornplatz. We heard they'd been sacrificing human blood in there. Disgusting. I was proud to smash it up."

I cleared my throat, waiting until he finished his rant before opening the door. The two of them were sitting on the same bed in their vests, smoking cigarettes. They looked up at me through narrowing eyes, Gustav rubbing the back of his neck.

"It was an honour to meet *General der Flieger* Wilberg this morning. Don't you think?"

The two of them shrugged in unison, Klaus making his feelings known.

"I've heard rumours about him."

Gustav nodded his agreement.

"What rumours?"

"His mother's a Jew. That obese, drug-addled fool, Goering, declared him Aryan so he could use him."

"Wilberg is a hero. Haven't you read of his impact in the Great War?"

"I don't read. Anyway, we lost that war. Time to put those dinosaurs to death."

Gustav laughed.

"We're going out tonight, Bachmann. To drink and toast the Führer's success. Will you come?"

"No, thank you. I've some reading to do and letters I need to write."

*

An introductory briefing followed by a short training flight took up the first day there. As evening fell, I was suddenly alone, and shut my eyes to think of New York City.

Life here was so very different. In America, I had a routine but also complete freedom—to eat what I wanted, talk to whoever I wanted and go wherever I wanted. My biggest loss here, though, was the freedom to read whatever the hell I liked. The Nazis had banned scores of books by some of my favourite authors. It felt like a literary form of cold turkey that pained me, leaving my soul empty. But I managed to keep a few books stowed in my room. With my roommates gone, I lay half-naked upon my bed, reaching below it to pull out a copy of Henry Miller's *Tropic of Cancer*, an illicit purchase from Gotham Book Mart. There was not a single woman at this camp for weeks on end. I'm ashamed to say that my last sexual encounter had been in America, almost a year before. I pored over Miller's disgustingly beautiful prose for an hour, expecting to see my roommates back from the mess bar.

Instead, an SS *Scharführer* and his sidekick barged in without warning, standing bolt upright before me, right arms raised.

"*Heil Hitler. Flieger* Bachmann?"

I jumped to my feet, my book dropping to the floor as I half-heartedly saluted.

"Yes?"

"You'll address me properly. Put on your clothes."

"*Jawohl, Herr Scharführer.*"

I scrambled to put on my trousers, imbalanced, falling sideways. Buttoning my shirt, I stood instinctively to attention at the end of my bed.

"We've authority to search this room, having received a report of subversive activity."

My mind raced in unison with my heart. How? Who reported me?

"What were you reading?"

Before I answered, the young *Scharführer* grabbed my book from the floor, thumbing its pages while his *Schütze* flung books from my shelf to the bed, picking up and examining an old copy of Friedrich Hölderlin's *Hyperion*.

I knew these books, and many others I hid, were on Goebbels' blacklist, but I thought it best to act dumb.

"Please. What crime have I committed?"

The few days I had in Berlin before returning to Gatow had given me the opportunity to buy as many books as I could carry on the thriving black market. It was risky, but I knew I only had months to fill my mind before joining the Luftwaffe proper and succumbing to military life.

Throwing my precious books in a sack, the *Scharführer* delighted in threatening me. "We'll discipline you and burn these books if they are found to be improper."

As they left, I slumped back on my bed, shaken and furious at my loss, rocking myself to a premature sleep.

*

Our east-facing room was full of daylight from the rising sun as I woke the next morning. My drunken roommates had failed to close the thin curtains before collapsing into bed. I gazed out of the window. The wood's trees looked as if they would snap as they swayed wildly in the wind. It would be choppy in the air today.

For some naïve reason, I had expected life at Berlin-Gatow, only thirteen miles south of my old stomping ground, to be like that at the Schönwalde I had left to follow my American dream. That place had treated me well. I knew my way around the instrument panel of a Junkers W33, a Focke Wulf 58 and the now-obsolete Heinkel 51, and made good friends too, not one of them a Nazi, or so it had seemed. Some had written to me in New York, updating me on their lives. But things had changed, for them, for me and for Germany. Life here, a skip and a jump across the Havel from the Grunewald, was very different.

Now at war, the influence of the Third Reich increased at the same rate that my flying confidence declined. I noticed a tumour of terror that began at Schönwalde, whenever I climbed into an aeroplane, had grown larger. Now it was always with me. Not a fear of flying but of not being able to leave the cockpit.

Giving Klaus and Gustav a shake, I went to the brown-stained sink and shaved. They murmured and groaned, pulling the covers over their heads. I didn't wait for them and headed to a quiet mess hall to eat a breakfast of bread and strawberry jam, washed down with chicory coffee.

Gustav and Klaus joined me a while later and sat staring at their plates.

I attempted conversation. "How was your evening?"

Klaus looked up at me through bloodshot eyes.

"Beer, cards, cigarettes. Talking about women. The usual. Why didn't you come?"

"Sounds like fun, but I can't fly with even a hint of a hangover."

The two men smiled and looked at each other.

"Schleisser from across the hall told us you had some unwanted visitors."

"Yes. They didn't stay long."

"You need to be a little more careful, Bachmann. Your flying days could be over before they begin."

Sauer called me into his tiny, cluttered office the following morning to dress me down. The incident with the SS could have been enough for him to dismiss me, but Sauer loved literature and liked me as a result. We had already shared notes on several books. I knew he would not punish me.

"Be more careful, Bachmann. Can't you read something not banned by the Reich?"

I nodded, a smile flickering across his face as he looked down to review my flying record.

"Better get off to class. See me again tomorrow morning."

As I reached our teaching room, class began.

"Good morning, cadets. Today we'll learn how to calibrate air cameras. Once you think you know how to use one, we'll spend another week practising until you do. After that, you'll have the opportunity to identify targets from the air."

Being late to class, I was an easy target to be called to the front and soon stood over a Franke & Heidecke high-altitude camera. Our teacher addressed me.

"Bachmann, given your great experience, explain to the class the workings of the camera and how you operate it."

"It's an Rb 50/30 camera used on several of our aircraft for aerial reconnaissance, *Herr Flugführer*."

I peered around the room, eyes dropping as my classmates realised the teacher's attempts to humiliate me had failed.

"That means it takes images to build into three-dimensional reconstructions. It has motors and can work automatically."

We spent the rest of the lesson viewing images taken by various aerial cameras, identifying unusual features that might be hidden tanks or gun positions. At midday, I returned to my room for a break, falling to my bed to read the letter that had arrived from Mother that morning.

My dearest Oskar,

I hope you're keeping well at the air base and pray your training keeps you safe. Often, I sit and imagine you in an aeroplane, flying above me. I'm in good health, but lonely. I miss my boys terribly. One day soon, this war will be over, and we can return to Halbe. I am writing because there are some things I need to tell you now that your father's gone. I wish I could have done this with you face to face, but that may not be possible for some time.

You said in your last letter, you'd always wanted to please him, despite everything he'd done to you. You told me that, in the Harz, he'd told you he was a pilot in the Great War. It hurts me to say this to you, but his flying experience was very short. One day, I'll tell you more. Herr Gumpert served with him. When I stayed with him and his wife, he told me many things about your father's time in the military. They didn't surprise me.

The other thing you need to know is that your father did not come home to live with us until the spring of 1920, when he ran out of money and needed a meal. I'm sad he failed me, and you and Emil, in so many ways. For now, please take no extra risks. Eat well and stay safe.

I remain your devoted mother.

I read the letter again, before screwing it into a tight ball, fingernails digging into my palms. Turning my head into my pillow, I searched my memories for images of Papa from my pre-school years. I could find none, so I thought instead of our days staring together up to the blue skies above us as our model aeroplanes momentarily united our purpose.

*

Over the previous fortnight, we had spent almost all our time in the air, practising advanced manoeuvres, readying us for combat missions. That morning, I received a message to attend Sauer's office.

As I arrived, his door hung half-open. I stuck my head around it and he beckoned me inside.

"Shut the door, Bachmann."

As I sat, he examined a pile of papers, holding them close to his face to read, before pushing them in a drawer.

"You're now one of the most experienced pilots here. Despite what I would call a rather mixed flying record."

He stared at me.

"Thank you, *Herr Flugführer.*"

He explained that, under normal circumstances, I would have fifty to sixty hours' extra training in blind-flying, before moving on to a special reconnaissance pilot school. But the Luftwaffe did not have time for that. I would join a supplementary unit attached to Aufklärungsgruppe (Reconnaissance Group) 121 and learn the tactical methods required to serve the unit until required on the front line. That could be months or a week.

A frozen hand gripped my gullet. I swallowed hard.

"*Jawohl, Flugführer Sauer.*"

I remained statue-still.

"That's it. Pack your things, Bachmann. You'll be collected at 1800 hours. Good luck."

15

BREAKDOWN

Romania, Yugoslavia and Berlin
1941

Our '*Tante Ju*' swooped across a parked fleet of aircraft, skidding down to land on the bumpy grass runway at Focşani South airbase in driving rain. It was 6:05 p.m. on 29 March 1941. There had been plenty of chatter and laughter on-board, but I did not join in. Instead, I stared ahead, thinking of Mother as we flew over the country she now dwelled in, and on to Romania.

All of us were new airmen, the first to arrive in the region following Hitler's call for retribution on the Yugoslavs. Aufklärungsgruppe 121's latest recruits had arrived for duty, but I did not feel ready and could not be sure I ever would be. In my heart, I knew my personal mission was to survive, avoid killing anyone and restart my life. But my first real taste of war, and that of my Schönwalde roommates, was now hours away. I felt sick to my stomach as we emptied the bowels of the Ju 52 and headed for the shelter of the tin huts.

We had dinner in a badly lit, dowdy mess hall, its paintwork peeling and stained. The catering compensated. Baked pork chops, fried potatoes and eggs, with local elderflower juice, all served on linen cloth-covered tables with silver cutlery bearing the Luftwaffe eagle emblem. As the *Gugelhupf* dessert was wolfed down in an almost silent unison, we heard a loud commotion outside the main mess doors. Moments later, in stepped a highly decorated senior officer. All at once, the room stood to attention, the clang and clatter of fallen cutlery ringing out. Jaws dropped and stares darted around the room as a man with an uncanny resemblance to the Führer appeared before us.

After giving an old-fashioned military salute, he smiled and addressed the room in his relaxed Austrian dialect.

"Men, at ease. I hope you enjoyed your meal. The Luftwaffe does not believe in fighting on an empty stomach. I'm Lieutenant General Alexander Löhr, Commanding Officer of Luftflotte 4, overall commander of the mission you'll support. I'm here, briefly, because tonight marks a crucial step in our plan to avenge the Yugoslavs' treachery. For many of you, this will be your first experience of combat flying. Fortunately, you face a far inferior enemy. No match for the mighty Luftwaffe. Gaining detailed information on military installations around Belgrade is critical before we launch our main attack. Many German lives rest in your hands. Good luck and fly well."

The room rose as one, most airmen arrowing their arms in the air, with a shout of, "*Jawohl, mein Kommandant. Heil Hitler.*"

Löhr left as quickly as he had arrived. I would never again get away with failing to give the Hitler salute.

Klaus and Gustav, who had unfortunately been assigned to the same unit as me, sat a few places to my right and gave me withering looks. Our distrust was mutual. I knew they had informed the SS about my books. Now they sat with a group of young bomber pilots from Munich, who recounted tales of raids over London. The most confident was a tall blond fellow named Fischbeck. He spoke in animated fashion, as a father might tell stories to a young son or daughter.

"It was a Saturday-night raid in the heart of the city. I dropped low and landed a biggy on a railway station. At my altitude, I could literally see the bodies flung up in the air. I flew back across the green fields, without challenge, itching to drop a few more. Spotted a few dairy farms on the way back to the sea and blew a few barns to smithereens. Tried to miss the cows though."

The group roared its approval, except for one poker-faced flyer, who sat in the last seat of the table and hung his shaking head.

"You won't be laughing tonight, I can tell you. Night flying isn't funny. Never know where you are. If you're hit, you don't know what you're going to fall into."

Gustav laughed sarcastically.

"Don't be so dramatic."

The group left the table in sombre mood, heading for the strategic briefings in the main hangar. The dissenter continued, calling out after them.

"Once the fighters are in the air, you can't see them. They can hit you in the neck at any minute. I can't sleep for days after a night raid."

I liked this fellow. He spoke straight and true, free of the usual pilot's bravado.

"Thanks for the dose of reality. I needed to hear the truth, but now I'm terrified."

He smiled.

"I've learned already we all see this war in different ways. It's better to know the truth, so we can prepare for our destiny, don't you agree? I'm Usinger. Herbert Usinger."

I raised my eyebrows.

"Don't let the SS hear you say that. Bachmann, Oskar. My plan is to survive, unlike these dumb assholes."

Usinger grinned. He wasn't dour at all.

"It almost sounds as if you've something worth living for, Bachmann."

Despite the continued downpour, we walked slowly together towards Focșani South hangar and were the last to arrive in the basic, wooden building. I was glad of Usinger's experienced company and wise humour for a while.

The hangar, full of damp airmen awaiting instruction, buzzed with excited conversation and nervous laughter. Near the hangar doors, they had pinned a table plan to the wall, showing us where to report. I scanned the list, relieved not to see Gustav and Klaus' names in my group. Usinger shook my hand and left to join his team on the right of the hangar. After a few steps, he turned back to me.

"Bachmann, good luck. You'll come through this."

He smiled, nodded and walked away.

They split us into zones, each with an allocation of reconnaissance crews with light and heavy fighter accompaniment. Each group received its briefing via an officer, using maps and attack plans. I found my group in the far-left corner of the hangar, where a *Feldwebel* had already started his briefing.

"*Gefreiter*, hurry. You're late."

My group comprised twelve Ju 88D-1s, one of which I would pilot, four Messerschmitt Bf 109Es and four Messerschmitt Bf 110s, the type of plane piloted by Usinger. They ordered us to focus on capturing detailed photographs of the Ikarus plant and Zemun airfield to the north-west of Belgrade, south of the Danube, and some other industrial targets on the north side of the city.

The *Feldwebel* puffed out his chest, using his left hand to smooth down his service shirt.

"Yours is one of the more dangerous assignments. We've chosen you to fly it either due to your level of experience or because you excelled at flight school. Do your best."

We trudged towards the Junkers on heavy ground, his warning circling in my brain, as I learned the names of my observer, radio operator and lower gunner. I began to mutter, "Lift, thrust, drag and weight" repeatedly, before an intense wave of panic made me vomit. I looked up, sheepishly, swallowing repeatedly, wiping my sleeve across my face.

"Eggs don't agree with me. Does anyone have a cigarette?"

On the brink of a snigger, the three men looked at each other, shaking their heads.

"Smoking's banned in the Luftwaffe, *Gefreiter*. You must know that."

"What's your name, airman?"

"*Flieger* Lutz. Camera operator."

"Okay, Lutz. Listen to me. If we're going to get through this, we have to help each other."

A second airman, whose heavy-lidded eyes seemed knowing and somehow kind, reached into his pocket.

"Here, I'll light it for you."

As he reached the side of our plane, he pulled his jacket over his head to create a waterproof cave and lit the cigarette, signalling for me to join him.

"I'm *Flieger* Hans Meintner, your observer. And a fellow smoker. Please tell me you've flown a Junkers before, *Gefreiter*."

"Of course. A few times. At Gatow. The D-1s are excellent aircraft. Three hundred and thirty built last year. Jumo 211 engines, inverted V-12, it can top 1,000 horsepower. Robot Rb 70/30 and 20/30 cameras, heated from the gas exhaust system."

Each of the crew gazed at me as I reeled off my meaningless technical knowledge, knowing it would mean little as we took on our enemies.

"Okay. We've all flown before in combat. We'll help you through this. Take one of these."

Meintner put a small white tablet in my hand with a smile of reassurance.

"What is it?"

"It's pilot salt, officially known as Pervitin. We all take it, helps keep us alert up there."

I hesitated, staring at the pill in the palm of my hand, before swallowing it and mounting the ladder to climb aboard. For a few moments, I re-familiarised myself with the controls, flicking the many switches, fighting an urge to rock in the seat.

Complete focus, despite the hum of conversation around me. This would be my sixth flight in a Ju 88. Enough experience, I told myself. But this was no game anymore. Fiddling behind my seat (who designed this plane?), I located the fuel pump switches and pulled them forward. Radiators open. Magnetos to top. Throttle off the bottom, shift one and two, hit 'i'. The propellors spun. Damn. Moving forwards too soon. Throttle down a little.

Sensing Hans monitoring me, I turned, forcing a smile, giving a thumbs up. They had advised us to wait for a signal before taxiing in take-off formation, slightly left of the centre position on the runway, where the ground was less waterlogged. A beam of light from the small air traffic control tower to our right highlighted the raindrops that fell fast and furious at first, before slowing to a stop. Suddenly our orders rang out, like commands from God. I felt a sudden surge of energy, as the Pervitin reached my bloodstream, like a new life being born inside me.

"Taxi to runway. Line up and wait."

I engaged the throttle, following a Messerschmitt to the runway. We waited, my legs jittering while a flight engineer rushed across and adjusted the wing flaps on the Junkers in front. I glanced at my oil temperature gauge; the needle was creeping to the right. If it became too hot, we would have to abort, but the second command came just in time.

"Ready for take-off. Climb and maintain altitude."

Flaps to take-off position, fully extended. Outlet shutters open. Easing throttle to maximum. Rotate. The Junkers shook and clattered as we sped up fast to a hundred and seventy kilometres per hour over the uneven ground. As its nose lifted fifty metres up and over the lofty oak trees bordering the airfield, I felt I could reach out and touch the leaves with my fingertips. Retracting flaps and landing gear as we quickly gained altitude, take-off was now complete. My breathing returned to near normal as we cruised in battle formation. Peering above the clouds, I felt exhilarated, temporarily cocooned from any sense of fear.

We flew in silence for a while. I never wanted to fight or to kill anybody and would do all I could to avoid it. Closing my eyes for a few moments, I prayed we would complete our mission with no interception, no casualties.

Hans' voice filled my ears, disrupting my prayer.

"We're over Transylvania, Captain."

His reference to this place of childhood nightmares brought with it a thunderous storm that lit up the surrounding sky, Nosferatu's shadow bouncing from one black cloud to another. Now in 10/10 cloud, I could not see a thing through the aircraft windows. My neck tightened, beads of sweat running down my face. A loud *zum-zum-zum* rang out from the clouds. We had narrowly missed the tail of the Messerschmitt in front of us. I adjusted course to avoid the same fate, or worse, befalling the plane behind us.

An almighty flash lit up the sky, giving us a momentary glimpse of the tail of the southern Carpathians below. Two of our planes had collided. My mind froze, body rocking violently in my seat. *Lift, thrust, drag and weight.*

"Captain. Captain!"

Hans shook my arm to refocus me, pointing to the picture of my mother I had stuck above me in the Junkers' window.

"Should I take the controls, Captain?"

I shook my head as a luminous pink filtered through the cloud belly below us, the glow of Belgrade's city lights. My heart rate increased. Focus, focus. Eyes wide open, I extended the dive brakes, hurtling towards the ground in a sixty-degree descent that left my stomach in my mouth. Skirting the north of the city at five thousand metres, I peered down at rows of illuminated buildings, yellow arteries on the earth's surface, descending quickly to four thousand metres as our targets neared. Mission command assured us the Yugoslavs did not know we were coming. I wanted so badly to believe them.

"Capture images. Return without detection," they had said.

"Targets in sight, Captain, and..."

Hans paused, tension woven through his voice.

"Six enemy aircraft approaching. Fifteen hundred-metre altitude, from south-west."

The waxing crescent moon was no use to us, but the city light and the clearly visible exhaust flames of the enemy's IK-3s gave our fighters a target to aim at. They engaged, tracer fire zipping across the sky in both directions. Two IK-3s were hit and plunged earthwards, another two heading towards the last, trailing Junkers in our group.

As we decreased altitude, I could feel the blood pulse in my temples. The first volleys from the Yugoslavs' 20-mm guns shot across us. We had to hold out long enough to capture the images.

Lutz confirmed the pictures of the plant had been captured. I pulled us to port to sweep across the airfield, but two enemy Messers headed straight towards us. Grabbing the cold steel handle of the MG81, I closed my eyes and, with shaking hand, fired a thousand rounds in an arc across the sky, hoping the show of aggression would scare the enemy off without hitting them.

I was convinced a physical wave of hazy white smoke swept through my window panels, dancing around me in the cockpit. But there was no smell. Hans tried to grab the gun handle from me as two of our 109s swept in front, taking down the enemy aircraft. I stared at him, fixated, gripping the handle ever tighter.

"Let's g-g-get out of here," I stuttered.

The journey back to Focșani South went on forever. Hans relieved me of my duties mid-air, and I shifted to the observer's seat, the eyes of my crewmates burning holes in my skull. My father's face appeared in my mind over and over, berating my mistakes, my cowardice. As the Junkers bounced down on Romanian soil, rays of early morning sun pouring through the windows, I sobbed uncontrollably. My crew remained silent as they crawled out of the plane, too embarrassed to acknowledge me. Hans, though, put a hand on my shoulder.

"You'll be okay, Oskar. It's over now. Take some rest."

*

Hans' words of comfort took a long time to come to fruition. One of my crew had sent a report to my senior officer, stating that my mental condition during the Belgrade mission had put our plane and crew at risk. I could have assessed myself, but the camp doctor's diagnosis of stress-induced neurosis saw me sent to spend months in a 'quiet home' in the northern Berlin district of Frohnau. Part of me felt embarrassed to be there. There was a physical reason for most Luftwaffe medical leave: serious burns, burst eardrums or damage to internal organs. I was glad no one visited me, but another part of me was glad of the chance to be away from the conflict, able to read.

208

My days of recuperation gave me time to think about my fears and dwell again on why my father had beaten me and always favoured my big brother. I thought often about my fellow NYU student, Carl Thomas. He was trying to use available information to create a link between the experiences suffered by US servicemen in the Great War and the crime surge of the 1920s. I thought the whole topic fascinating.

That morning, after an intensive interview, I lay on an assessment table being probed by Krauss, a psychiatrist commissioned by the Nazis to assess mental patients. I cannot tell you how ashamed I felt by the whole experience. It was demeaning to be the subject of another psychiatrist's assessment when I had learned so much about the topic. But then, perhaps, I knew little of my own mind. Avoiding his stinking breath, I turned to gaze at the glum framed faces of surgeons staring back at me judgementally from the pictures on the yellowing wall. They had no doubt seen to the damaged soldiers from William II's Wahehe campaign.

Doctor Krauss used his hand to push my face towards him, shining an ophthalmoscope into my weary eyes again. I hoped he would find me unsuitable for military service and retire me but knew it unlikely. They needed every trained airman available.

Distracting myself from Krauss' probing, I thought of my brother. As my war began disastrously over Belgrade, his ended altogether. We had in fact been a part of the same offensive without knowing it. It was the first time we had been on the same side of anything.

I received the second of those damned telegrams days after the sortie that had sent me here. Slav guerrillas shot Emil dead in northern Yugoslavia as he repaired a road bridge for the 2nd Army's advance. I had nightmares about his death for weeks, seeing the sniper's bullet slicing into his skull, through his brain, and its messy escape. But now, in my waking hours, I felt little anger or sadness. I searched my mind for images of him. For some reason, I couldn't find many. Only a memory of us laughing hysterically after losing control of Chefin and our cart on the way to church. I would just hold on to that. My sympathy was for Mother, widowed and now without her first-born son. I knew she would struggle and prayed that she could find some happiness and that I would find her again one day.

Krauss straightened, looking disappointed.

"Sit up, Bachmann. I can't find anything physically wrong with you. Did you have any issues as a child?"

"My father..." I paused, shaking my head, a sense of futility stealing my words.

"Very well. My report will go back to your commanding officer. As far as I'm concerned, you are fit to return to duty soon. You can leave."

Strolling out of the hospital, I headed straight to the banks of my beloved River Spree. Pondering my future, I walked along it, off Schiffbauerdamm, then caught a bus to Cafe Buchwald, where father had taken Emil and me as children to enjoy *Baumkuchen* and orange juice.

Hitler's war had created carnage on many fronts, but as I looked out of the window of the bus, the streets of Berlin, control centre of so much destruction and chaos, felt and looked strangely normal. Crammed trams ferried Berliners across the city. Well-to-do women in smart hats walked their dogs. Men too old to fight struggled along with crate baskets on their bicycles.

Leaving the bus to stroll the last fifty metres on foot, I bought juice in the cafe and sat by its window, a comforting memory of a happy father filling my mind. I hung on to it until my attention passed to a carefree young woman walking by reading a book. Books, books! The bookstore Timo had mentioned to me so many times was right here in Berlin.

Raising my hand, I tried to attract the teenage waiter's attention.

"Excuse me, how far is Greta Schubert's *Bücherstube*?"

He paused in his delivery of cakes to a family on the next table, much to their annoyance.

"It's in Kreuzberg. Solmsstrasse, I think. About thirty minutes by bus."

Checking my watch, I had time. Pushing the change from my pocket into his hand, I rushed out the door and down the cafe steps, thinking of my old friend.

Dropped by the bus in light drizzle, I meandered through a large churchyard and cemetery south of the river, stopping occasionally when I spotted a gravestone of interest. Solmsstrasse was quiet. Only as the bookstore appeared in view was the peace shattered. Two men with contorted faces shouted aggressively at a cowering old man. I approached slowly, loitering outside the bookshop, as the man sobbed, his thin hands dropping the books he had held to land pathetic slaps on his assailants. One of them grabbed his arm, twisting it sharply behind his back with a snap.

"How dare an old Jewish pig like you presume to read books, hmmm?"

Instinctively, I moved to intervene but was pulled suddenly into the shop, the door slamming shut behind me.

"What the hell were you doing?"

A woman in her mid-thirties wearing a purple dress, dark hair pinned back, peered at me, as a mother might at her child if it was putting its hand in a fire.

"Don't you know who they were? That man's Jewish. He was in here earlier. They dragged him out."

"It's terrible. Every human has a right to read, just as they have a right to eat and to breathe air."

Her pretty eyes blinked rapidly, then turned to an open stare.

"Who are you?"

I held out my hand to her, smiling.

"Bachmann, Oskar Bachmann. I'm a Luftwaffe pilot. You're Frau Schubert, I presume?"

She said nothing, her eyes now looking me up and down.

"I was hoping to have a look around your shop."

"You're too late. The shop's closed."

Lips tight, I shrugged my shoulders, turning to leave, hoping she might pity me.

"Wait. There are plenty of bookshops in Berlin. Why did you come here?"

"Because I know about *this* shop, and you've had a big impact on my life."

Her sarcastic laugh echoed in the empty corridor.

"Oh really? And why is it you are not wearing a uniform?"

"Medical leave. If I had a choice, I would not return. My passion lies with books and learning. Perhaps we could sit somewhere?"

Her face remained still, ungiving. Reaching into my lapel pocket, I pulled out my Luftwaffe paybook, pushing it in front of her nose.

"Very well, Bachmann. You've ten minutes. Follow me."

We sat in a small office at the back of the shop, metres from the well-stocked bookcases I longed to explore.

"Frau Schubert, you knew someone from my youth. The father of someone very important to me who died."

"I know many people. What's his name?"

"Gumpert. He lived in a big house in Groß Köris, near Halbe, where I went to school. His son was my best friend. Here, I've a photograph."

Pulling a brass-handled magnifier from her drawer, she cracked every one of her knuckles. I had never seen a woman do this before. Bringing the tiny picture of me, Timo and his father with the library tower in the background close to her face, she examined it. Silent for a moment, she pursed her lips.

"Yes, I know him. He often visited the shop. I sent him books in the post too."

Her cheeks flickered a little, eyes glancing towards the door.

"Have you seen him since the war started?"

She hesitated.

"I never talk about my clients, and I know nothing about you."

"The books you sent to Timo's father, they inspired me."

Cutting me off, she threw her hands in the air and moved to the door.

"To do what, exactly? Join the Luftwaffe and bomb people?"

"No, let me explain."

213

As she sat back down, I told her of the many hours spent reading with Timo in the tower on the lake, my guilt at the destruction of his library and his taking his own life, my travails in America and how I wanted to continue to learn psychiatry and perhaps teach one day. She listened intently and when I had finished, pulled a small revolver from her drawer. I sat perfectly still, unsure of her intentions.

"I believe in instinct. It's always served me well."

Moving to the corner of her office, where a raincoat hung in a teak-inlaid recess, cupboards above and beneath it, she pulled a key from its pocket.

"But I may regret this."

Shifting a section of panelling aside, she pushed the key into the hidden lock, opening it into the blackness behind. The familiar smell of old books and mould filled the office.

"Well, are you coming?"

She switched on a dim light, its bulb continually buzzing as I followed her down a set of sturdy steps to the basement floor, five metres below. Ahead of us were scores of wooden, metal-edged boxes of varying sizes, stacked and numbered.

"May I look around?"

Giving a single nod, she held out her hand. I moved slowly towards the nearest pile, carefully opening one of the larger containers, anticipating the treasures inside, only to find tins of Ovomaltine. Open-mouthed, I turned back to Frau Schubert, now sat on a box watching me. She tilted her head.

"Your mind is a gold mine. Dig deep!"

I pushed my hand between the tins and found the familiar feel of a book cover. I pulled the book free: Brecht, *Life of*

Galileo. Digging deeper, Broch, *The Sleepwalkers*. Deeper still, Döblin, *The Three Leaps of Wang Lun*.

"How many books do you keep down here?"

"Last count, 2,372. They're all for sale to anyone brave enough to buy them."

"I'd have all of them if I could."

Warming to me, she smiled.

"One day, when we are all free, you can make me an offer."

Moving to my left, she lifted another lid and rummaged.

"Herr Gumpert wasn't only a customer."

Her comment did not surprise me. I knew there was more to their relationship.

"Oh, really? Do you mind me asking what you mean?"

"We've new stock here, from America, England, France, but it was Herr Gumpert who saved most of these books from the Nazi fires in 1933."

"It's strange. I'd always had the impression Timo's father didn't care for books."

"Oh, he cared for them. You know, we never hear about the quiet students who didn't want the books burned. But there were plenty of them. Herr Gumpert knew that. Look."

She handed me an open book, its Humboldt library stamp on the flyleaf dark, like new.

"He heard of the planned burnings weeks before, via his Jewish friends. Funded an operation to smuggle books out of the libraries, paying directly for them. He literally saved thousands of books. Many of them went to Kantorowicz's library, some here, others spread around."

I weaved between boxes to the end of the room, mounting one and sitting for a while in near darkness. It felt colder and damp at this end of the room, the crumbled mortar walls around me revealing solid granite blocks beneath, onto which I placed my hands. Closing my eyes, I saw Timo's face beneath water, not as a boy but now a man, smiling before struggling for breath and dropping into the murky depths.

"He spent many hours down there."

"I'm sorry. What? Who did, Frau Schubert?"

"Herr Gumpert, of course. The tall boxes, opposite you, are full of paintings. Grosz, Kirchner, Beckmann and others. He loved them too. I must get back upstairs. I'm going out and need to close up."

Cocooned in this haven of art and books, I could have stayed in the basement for hours, even days. Reluctantly, I followed her back up to the shop.

She eyed me fondly as I assured her I would buy some books from her when I could.

"Have a look now if you like. But be quick."

Not wanting to abuse her hospitality, I headed straight to the nearest section, H, and picked up *Winner Take Nothing*, a collection of Hemingway stories. Thumbing through, a story entitled 'Fathers and Sons' caught my eye and I decided to buy.

I handed the book to Frau Schubert. She opened it and scribbled her home address on the flyleaf, before handing it back to me.

"You can have it. Don't forget this place and never tell a soul what you saw here or what I told you about Herr Gumpert."

16

AFRICA

Derna, Libya
February 1942

My break from active service ended on Valentine's Day, 1942. I could conjure no love for the Luftwaffe as I returned. Months of ground-based duty and further flight training at Schönwalde, followed by rigorous examinations by a physician, convinced Luftwaffe seniors I was fit to rejoin Auf 21 as a pilot based at Derna, a port in eastern Libya. By early March I was back in a Junkers' cockpit, filled with dread about what awaited me but determined not to let it show.

Command had granted my special request to be reunited with my trusted navigator. For this small mercy, I felt grateful. Our unit was initially engaged in non-combat missions, flying over British stores and installations to shape a picture of the area around Tobruk. Our job today was to photograph Ta Qali airfield, two hours away across the deep-blue Mediterranean, in the heart of Malta. Home to No. 261 Squadron, RAF and scores of Mk II Hurricanes. It was without doubt our riskiest mission to date.

"I'm pleased you're back, Captain."

Hans put his heavy arm around my shoulder.

"If you feel any stresses, let me know straight away, okay?"

I nodded, giving my friend a confident smile.

"Don't fret, Hans. I'll be okay."

"You know the British airbase in Malta has taken delivery of the famous Spitfires? This will not be easy."

I pointed to a group of airmen twenty metres ahead. One of them was animated, laughing.

"They may have Spitfires, but do you know who we have with us today?"

Hans shook his head.

"The 'Star of Africa'. *Hauptmann* Hans-Joachim Marseille. We're in safe hands, so long as he wasn't out drinking last night."

He grinned. I felt happy to be back in his company.

"I'm also well stocked."

Opening my kitbag, I showed Hans the dozen Temmler-inscribed boxes inside, each one containing a vial of Pervitin.

A formidable fleet of Bf 109s and Ju 88s created a deafening whirr of turning propellors and engine noise ahead of us. A heat-shimmer fog of golden dust from the sand-coated airfield radiated around us.

Hans, myself and the rest of the crew put our hands on each other's shoulders, gathered in a close huddle. While the others shouted out, "For Führer and Fatherland," I chose, "Bravery and luck," for in my heart I did not fly for Hitler.

*

I could taste the dust as a train of convoy trucks, laden with victorious but exhausted desert-brown soldiers, passed by.

Today was a day I simply needed to reach the end of. It had been hell, and I worried my nerves would not survive the ordeal. The British put up heavy resistance and we had taken a battering in the skies from their 76-mm anti-aircraft battery, but Tobruk was now ours and our unit had only lost two of its planes and crew.

I sat at the entrance to the camp yard in the late afternoon sun, tired and battle-weary. I had not slept or eaten in days, relying on pilot salt to keep me awake. Now, I wanted to close my eyes and sleep, content another chapter of my own personal war was over. But the men around me were full of exuberance and celebration. The capture of this ancient city was a massive victory and bottles of Egyptian Stella, brought here by the British and recovered from a nearby warehouse, were being sunk with abandon. As the cool dusk fell, a pyramid of empty bottles fifteen wide and four storeys high stood tall in the yard.

The men broke open their cans of *Schmalzfleisch* (lard meat) or *Rinderbraten* (roast beef) or tipped their *Erbswurst* (pea flour and pork fat sausage) into pans of boiling water over campfires. My stomach rumbled with the cocktail of smells as I listened in on a nearby soldier's story.

"We were pursuing the trailing units of the Eighth Army, retreating from the Gazala Line, and came across a camp they'd deserted. They scarpered in such a hurry—the eggs were still boiling away over a fire. We had a feast!"

Schreiber, the most celebrated 'ace' in our unit, and a devout Nazi, was stood on top of an oil drum. He made no secret of his dislike for me. According to him, I was psychologically weak. He was right, of course, and never missed a chance to spread rumours about my background and reliability.

Thankfully, I had allies in the unit. The occasional insult from one of Schreiber's cronies didn't bother me. He had progressed straight from his *Flieger Gefolgschaft* and passed his Luftwaffe exams with flying colours. Ideologically and physically, he was a perfect fit for his Nazi purpose. I had seen and heard about terrible atrocities in the war, but an admission made by him one night, after a heavy drinking session, shocked me the most. He had boasted that, while a fighter pilot over Kiev, he had delighted in targeting women pushing prams and with young children.

"We'd a points system: ten for a mother, five for a walking child, three for a baby. It was fun. You won extra points for taking out a whole *Untermenschen* family. My maximum on one run was a hundred and three."

His admission had made me reflect that, to date, and so far as I could tell, I had killed no one while on active service. That is how I hoped it would stay.

Schreiber bellowed to his small, but noisy, audience.

"Men, the war in Africa will soon be over. Rommel will drive us to victory in Egypt. The whole continent will belong to the Reich!"

The main crowd had thinned out into smaller groups. Men continued to talk, laugh and drink across the yard, but not everyone celebrated. Strolling along the perimeter fence for a while, I noticed several men in the shadows who were not in a good way. Most just stared ahead, with blank faces. I had seen many patients like this at the institute in Berlin. One pilot, still in his headgear, surrounded by three of his mates, shook and twitched, reliving a near miss with a British shark-mouth Kittyhawk. I watched from a distance for a while. When he

220

began to lash out and I moved to help, I was challenged by one of his crewmates.

"Who are you?"

"*Gefreiter* Bachmann. I've done psychiatry. This man needs a barbiturate to calm him."

"Where the hell can we get that?"

"Try to keep him as still and calm as you can."

I began to run back towards the yard gates. I had seen at least one medic in the yard earlier, but there had to be more. Nearing the gate, I spotted the distinctive white armband of a medic crouched on the ground to my right, treating a badly wounded *Heer* private. I put my hand on his shoulder.

"Sani, I need your help."

"What is it? I'm kind of busy."

"Do you have any sodium thiopental? I can take care of the situation myself."

He turned to look at me through narrowed eyes, over his shoulder, his head flinching back.

"Oh, really? It's powerful stuff."

"I know. There's a pilot in a bad way. He's violent. Seems the battle has messed badly with his head. I'm a psychiatrist, trained at the institute in Berlin."

The medic got to his feet, reaching into a kitbag to produce two small phials of liquid and a syringe.

"Okay. I shouldn't do this, but here. Mix these two together and inject intravenously."

I nodded and thanked him, rushing back to the perimeter fence, where there were now five men trying to restrain the patient.

"Okay, make room. One of you roll up his sleeve."

221

Mixing the thiopental and sterile water in the syringe, I moved in next to the airman. His arm seemed devoid of a vein.

"*Flieger*, tear up your shirt."

He stared at me.

"Now. Tie it tightly around his bicep. Quickly."

Within seconds, a vein popped up, and I sunk the needle into it, pushing the plunger home hard and fast. The patient immediately relaxed and fell asleep.

"Okay. Get him into a medical tent. He needs rest."

As I wandered off in search of my only Luftwaffe friend, Meintner, I could not help but think about how that airman would end up. Would he see action again, as I did after my breakdown? How would the war finish for him? Would his mind be forever altered if he did survive?

I reached the point at which the compound bordered the main city hospital premises, now converted to a prison camp, with *Heer* machine-gunners at every point. A few metres in from the fence, Meintner sat alone, warming himself by a fire of wooden pallet slats.

"Mind if I join you?"

He smiled.

"Take a seat. Where have you been?"

"Came across a pilot in a bad way. I helped him out. You?"

He held a beer up towards me.

"Trying to find the answers in the bottom of one of these."

I lay down on the ground, weary now from the adrenaline of the last hour and the battle toil of the day. The sizzle, crack and roar of the fire were elemental, sounds that all humans were born familiar with, like running water. I closed my eyes. A childhood camping trip filled my mind, Papa assembling the tent, Emil and I laughing in the woods, Mother cooking on the stove. Ours had been a normal family sometimes. Huddled around the blue and yellow flames of the fire, I held on to this rare, good memory for a while before Hans' question came.

"Can you hear that?"

The soft, clear music of Lale Andersen's 'Unter der Laterne' filled the air. I turned to find out where it was coming from. The melodic accordion notes were floating towards us, a musical gift from our enemies across the fence. Many of our boys swayed in front of us, ardently singing the chorus: "*Wie einst Lilli Marleen.*"

As the song ended, there was a moment of magic I shall never forget. A small group of our crewmen, closest to the fence, turned the handle of a wind-up gramophone, sending 'It's a Long Way to Tipperary' back across the fence in a friendly act of solidarity.

I lit a cigarette, passing one to Meintner. We approached the high wire-mesh boundary fence, intertwined with barbed wire, together. The shadowy figures on the other side, barely visible in the dim light, were some of the many thousands of Allied troops taken prisoner that day. At least one accent was distinctly Irish, reminding me of several immigrant barmen I had met in the bars of Manhattan. We listened in, noticing one soldier leaning on the fence staring at us. He smiled.

"*Dia dhuit.* How are you boys doing over there?"

"You know Gaelic! Unusual, for a Jerry. We've had better days. Do you have any spare smokes?"

I nodded, handing him half a dozen through the fence. He carefully wrapped them in a piece of paper and put it in his pocket.

"Are you all from Ireland?"

"No. Most of this lot are South African. We're an endangered species now, proud remains of the Irish regiment. Your Panzers all but wiped us out in November at Sidi Rezegh."

"Ireland's a beautiful country, I've been told. I hope you see it soon."

"It is that. Come and visit when we've won the war."

He laughed, turning his back on me and rejoining his fellow soldiers.

Even from a distance, Schreiber's ranting rose above all the other noise. I looked over at Meintner; I knew he hated Schreiber too.

"Hans, how much have you had to drink?"

"A little, but I can make it appear like much more."

We smiled at each other instinctively as we strode towards him. A minute later, Schreiber was rolling on the ground, gripping his elbow in pain after an unfortunate collision with a blind-drunk navigator.

Our night in the compound ended with orders to return by foot to a requisitioned hotel near Fort Solaro, one of a few to avoid bomb damage. Within minutes of arrival in our room, Meintner and I were asleep.

*

I was beyond tired but, with encouragement from my effervescent friend, I made it out of bed and reported for duty. The large ground-floor area of the hotel, which would once have welcomed glamorous guests from around the world, buzzed with the sound of laughter and stories being told, as fighter crews from the three *Staffeln* of JG 27 mingled with our own boys and breakfast rolls were delivered. But this break from the business of war did not last long. After half an hour, a zealous young *Leutnant* (lieutenant) moved to the stairs, standing tall to address us.

"Men, the Panzerarmee has crushed the Eighth Army. The British cowards are retreating to oblivion in Egypt. We must seize this moment."

He explained that the Luftwaffe would provide aerial support to ground forces in pursuit, identifying and destroying any resistance Rommel's men might face.

"You'll receive your orders via your unit commander shortly. *Heil Hitler.*"

My war was to take me next to the site of a temple for Ramesses II. Our orders instructed us to head to Mersa Matruh, three hundred and twenty kilometres east along the coast, leaving at dawn the next day.

*

Our mission that day would help push home the German advantage in Africa. Rommel's Afrika Korps were moving at pace across the desert, pushing the British deeper back into Egypt, Mersa Matruh the next target. Fighter and reconnaissance units were in short supply, but we had been told that Luftwaffe reinforcements were on their way. We would head out over the Mediterranean, cutting inland south of Mersa Matruh to photograph British armoured units, and then return to base.

17

LIBERATION

Near Mersa Matruh, Libyan Plateau
June 1942

Metal. Taste of metal. A low, hollow, humming buzz. Radiating heat intensified. A gasp of hot air took my breath away. The nauseating smell of burning fuel filled my nostrils, followed by a dry, sweet odour. Like a New York sour, my favourite Manhattan cocktail. A bluster of desert wind made the sands sizzle through my thick eardrums, replacing the memory of whistling wings that accompanied our fatal descent from the skies.

My bloodied hand reached for the ripped chest pocket of my flying suit, unzipping it and slowly pulling out my lucky cotton *yakuyoke* charm. I rubbed it for a while, remembering Rikers prison. Never thought I would find myself in a place more hellish.

The pain, dull at first, sharpened. It grew from my trapped thin legs to my hips and spread across my pelvis. Sweat stung my eyes, dripping the long trip down my nose into a salty mouth. A dusty haze surrounded me. My eyes were wide open, but I could not see. Bright light but no form.

Images of Father gazing at the sky in a frosty valley, then down at me. A punishment. This crash, and the coming, inevitable transformation of my body to a dehydrated desert shell, the result of my capitulation to his will. But what choice did I have?

Pressure built in my legs, then chest. Heart pounding. A suffocating feeling climbed into my neck. Then a series of stabbing pains coursed through my body, making me spasm in agony. Turning to my right, I expected to see my co-pilot beside me.

Tearing open my heat-sealed lips, I tasted the blood on them as I croaked, "Hans, where are you?"

I remembered immediately that we had gone up in a Ju 88D-2 with a different cockpit arrangement. The reconnaissance camera had been poorer company. I hoped its battered condition might mean that Hans had fared better in the radio operator's position behind me.

"Crew, is anyone conscious? Crew!"

Silence.

Time passed in a daze before my eyes cleared and, with them, my mind. I strained to peer above the damaged fuselage of my stranded 'Three Fingers' Ju-88. Blinding sunlight streamed through the window, making me squint. Through my twitching eyes, the endless, desolate banks of sand were visible. I drifted again, imagining myself surrounded by a multitude of open books in the Gould Memorial Library, then felt Mother's hand on my shoulder. Comforted. No more war. Death or capture awaited me. But then tears came, washing the sweat away but just as salty. I felt completely lost. A survivor with no purpose.

I pieced together the events of the previous few hours. Vivid images came back to me in flashes. The dusty airfield in Derna, a dose of pilot salt, take-off over the mesmerising blue of the Mediterranean, an occasional smudge of cargo ship on its surface. Over land, we climbed high above the Egyptian desert, endless sand beneath us. A Bavarian bark from ground control, ordering descent to observation status.

A few moments of calm. Hans Meintner, my loyal friend, passing me a thumbnail-sized picture of his newborn daughter. I had commented on her full head of hair before a *ra-ta-ta-ta-ta* of machine-gun fire burst from the innocent cloud above us. Near miss. I dived hard, engaged the supercharger to increase engine power and reeled to port before a sharp turn and climb starboard. My head swivelled, searching for a sign of our attacker. The skies were clear. He must have been waiting in the layer of cloud above us.

A burst of red, strontium-hued tracer fire repeated every ten seconds from above. Like the synchronised firefly display I had seen with Timo over Lake Zemminsee. A volley of machine-gun fire rattled and ripped through the upper part of our starboard wing, between the fuselage and inner engine. A jolt as the rudder stuck, the cockpit filling with lung-clogging, coal-black smoke, the wing now a ball of fire near the fuel tank. We rapidly lost altitude, descending steeply at seventy degrees, my head filled with memories of struggles to keep model aeroplanes airborne under Father's watch, and of that near-fatal mission over Belgrade.

My crewmates watched, open-mouthed. I deployed flaps, landing gear and airbrake, pulling the throttle lever back, levelling our battle-weary Ju at fifteen degrees. The slender arm of our airspeed indicator shook violently as it nudged three hundred kilometres per hour. Wing vents open, fuel flooding out. Sand dunes, half-light, half-shadow, sat in wait a kilometre ahead.

"Brace for impact!"

Tilt to starboard to avoid tip of dune, now filling view. Blackout.

*

Aldo running towards me, jumping up, knocking me over. Laughter. Dog breath. Wet face. High clouds in blue sky, smell of jasmine. Father's face, looking down on me, tutting. Behind me, my brother Emil's boots striding down the path, while he laughed mockingly.

Adrenaline, or maybe the Pervitin, kicked in. My heart raced faster, changing gear, faster still. I put my hands together, trying to calm myself, praying out loud. Struggling to make the sign of the cross, my head slumped back onto the headrest.

A distinctive bird circled my clouded eye, as if hunting down fish in a pool. A common sandpiper, and a lifeline maybe. I recalled they only ever appear near water. Straining, I turned my head to focus on it. A drop of liquid trickled into my right eye, further blurring my sight. Reaching up to my head, I dipped my fingertips into a deep gash on my forehead, close to the small, ingrained lump, now a permanent feature from my New York taxi collision.

Crushing pain in my legs and pelvis. My body felt as if it was in two parts. I could still move my torso, arms and neck though, and think clearly. I had to stay positive. Reaching down with my right arm, I heaved at the control stick that held me captive. Impact with the ground had shifted the entire instrument panel backwards and left, knocking the stick out of position and down tight across my thighs. The energy-sapping efforts to move it almost sank me. Sweat poured from my shaking body. On my sixth attempt, I finally levered the stick off my legs, the release of pressure making them float. My torn trousers framed more bloody damage wreaked by the metal, but now, perhaps, with the strength I had left, I might manage to break free of the cockpit.

I grabbed the sides of my seat and, as if trying to fly away from it, thrust my damaged body upwards, crashing my head into the jammed canopy and blacking out. On waking, all was blurry again. A pulsing pain filled my brain next to the hum and roar of the sand dunes. The pain was worth it. My see-through prison was now open above me. Small comfort. The Junkers' tapered starboard wing delved deep into a high bank of sand, which also covered the nose and starboard engine. A thirty-degree tilt pointed the cockpit at the pulsing sun, raising the temperature inside to unbearable levels.

My eyes darted around the searing-hot cockpit, searching for something, anything, to eat. I reached into a panel to my left, hidden from the sun's rays, and pulled out two packets of dry crackers in wax paper and my badly dented canteen. Fumbling again, I felt the smooth surface of a circular metal object. Pulling it out, I saw the red-and-white-patterned tin. Scho-Ka-Kola, what a sweet find! Weakly pushing down the edge of the lid, I pulled out a ridged chunk of the coffee-infused dark chocolate. It was soft, like butter on a warm spring day, and I scooped it out with my finger. Putting it on my tongue, the bittersweet chocolate flooded around my missing canine tooth—knocked out by Father's punch—and settled on my gums, the sugar and caffeine reaching my muscles in seconds. I now had the strength to drag myself out of the cockpit, onto the short, nearside wing before the port engine. Behind the plane, a trail of jet-black oil ruined the smooth golden slopes, the only stain on the perfect rolling sands. The Junkers' tail end hung precariously, like an old man's nodding head, over the sand.

I reached back inside the cockpit to remove Hans' headgear. He sat motionless and bloodied. The enemy fighter's bullets had sliced down through his shoulder blades, out of his chest and into his thighs, killing him instantly. I held his hand for a moment, too weary for tears, before pulling his lids down over wide-open eyes.

Next, I dropped my shoulders and upper body over the edge of the wing to view the lower gunner's hatch. I gasped. Above sand, the escape doors hung open. Where was Jung? A surge of pain made me jerk and topple off the wing onto the steep bank below, my momentum taking me faster and faster down the sand. Rolling in agony to a plateau fifty metres below, I sank into the sandy platform, dazed and panting for breath, half-expecting to find my lower gunner. Beside me, instead, was a tiny rodent skeleton. The tumble embedded hot sand in my wounds. It stung like hell but stemmed the flow of blood. I tore off my shirt sleeves to create tourniquets and clumsily tied the sweaty strips at the top of my legs.

Scanning the surrounding area, I searched for cover and any sign of Jung. A tree, rocks, a deserted vehicle—anything to provide shade would do. But there was nothing other than

231

sand, the endless shimmer of heat and a deep-blue sky to meet it. My mind drifted, frazzled by the sun. I imagined myself the pirate in Pyle's painting *Marooned*, a copy of which had hung in the New York University entrance hall. My eyes panned three hundred and sixty degrees again, this time detecting a small dark spot on the sand two hundred metres away to my left. A human body, lying flat on the sand. Jung must have crawled across the desert and collapsed, exhausted in the heat.

"Jung! Juunngg!"

My desperate, rasping call was sucked from the air by the endless sand and outpitched by the call of the thirsty sandpiper, now landed a stone's throw from me.

In my heart, I wanted to rescue Jung, but my instincts told me that would be suicide. He was almost certainly dead, anyway. My only option was to return to the shade of the wing of my Junkers, stuck in the sand above me like a wafer in a Friendly's ice cream sundae. Clumsily, I rolled onto my knees and struggled to my feet. Kicking one foot after another, I slowly scaled the bank, howling in pain with every leaden step and stopping regularly to catch my breath. The sand fought against me, shifting down in huge wavelike swathes, leaving me thigh high in a hot, dry ocean.

Eventually, I neared the cockpit, as a raspy crackle came over the FuG 10 LW/SW radio.

"*Flieger* Meintner, do you read me?"

A click, then a pause.

"*Fleiger* Jung, are you there? *Gefreiter* Bachmann? Come in. Do. You. Read. Me?"

It was so good to hear a human voice. The radio had a range of fifteen hundred kilometres in clear weather. It could be base camp or perhaps a passing bomber relaying a message. I struggled the last couple of metres and hauled my body back onto the wing alongside the cockpit, desperate to hear the voice again. The radio was in reach over Hans' slumped shoulders.

"Hello. Hello. Do you hear me? This is *Gefreiter* Bachmann, over."

A crackle. Silence. I tried again. Nothing. The radio was dead, like my crewmates. I slumped, defeated and exhausted, my mind fogged with thoughts of my family, life in New York and Schönwalde.

Panic replaced sentimentality as I recalled explicit orders to destroy the Junkers' on-board cameras in the event of the plane being inoperable. Defying orders meant a court martial. The main cameras sat in the rear bomb bay. If I used a hand grenade to destroy them, I risked blowing the port wing clear off, leaving me no shade and certain death. To stay alive, I had to defy orders. What would it matter now, anyway?

An intolerable surge went through my body, like electricity, making it shake. From nowhere came complete panic. My life was only beginning. I could not let this deadly interruption of war stop me. Pulling my half-full canteen from its holder, I flopped, legs jerking, below the fuselage and lodged myself in the cooler, shady cover of the wing.

Closing my eyes, I tipped a dribble of water across my parched lips and whispered, "*Krasota spaset mir*" ("Beauty will save the world") under laboured breath, until my legs juddered still.

Waking from a deep slumber, my brain fooled me. Layers of my skin dripped from my body, leaving pools of pink flesh on my clothes. I had crawled into the cockpit to sleep as night had fallen the day before, not having enough strength to return to the shade of the wing.

Reaching for my canteen, I sucked in the last few drops of liquid and, with them, a stench hanging above my head. Struggling out of my seat, I turned to see Hans' youthful body transformed beyond recognition, flies swarming around him. I vomited what little liquid was in my stomach into my mouth.

Gazing at the horizon, to avoid the sight of Hans' corpse, I hauled my own battered body out of the plane. Losing my grip, I tumbled sideways but held on and gradually crawled under the wing, where I fell into another deep sleep.

Everyone, everyone is going home.
Everyone, everyone is going home.
Big people, little people,
Fat people, thin people,
Loud people, quiet people,
Everyone, everyone is going home.
Everyone, everyone is waving goodbye.
We say goodbye,
That was fun again today!
Everyone, everyone is waving goodbye.

*

"*Gefreiter*, wake up. Do you hear me? Wake up!"

At first, I thought the radio had come back to life, but the hand on my shoulder and the muttered profanities made me realise someone had found me. Whoever it was continued muttering.

234

"Why do I get these missions? I'm the specialist in lost causes."

I felt wonderful cool water on my lips and tried to move my tongue, but it was captive in my mouth, swollen like a tinned plum tomato, pushing against my cheeks and front lip. Seeing me stir, the soldier put his hand behind my neck, tilting my head, so a few drops of liquid rolled in. He continued his tirade.

"He's somewhere south of Mersa Matruh, they said. Should be straightforward, they said."

As my eyes cleared, I saw a soldier, wearing unfamiliar uniform, stood beside me, leaning on the wing of my plane. He frowned, biting the inside of his lip, while I struggled to speak.

"Wh-who are y-you? I've n-not seen your cap b-before?"

"You don't need to know my name. I'm special forces, a Brandenburger as we're known. Lucky for you my half-company has been holed up at Benghazi, after Tobruk, and I received orders to rescue you. Parachuted in a kilometre away."

My frazzled brain tried to process this information. Who would have our location? We had no radio contact. The Brandenburger tore me a piece of ersatz bread, handing it to me. I began to chew it but its dryness made me gag.

"You weren't supposed to be badly injured, airman."

He told me the plan had been to locate, feed and water survivors, stabilising our condition, before heading west on foot to a small communications centre.

"Given your state, the plan is dead in the water. Or sand. I should say sand. They'll have to pick us up from here. I've already relayed coordinates."

Seeing my struggle to eat, the Brandenburger broke a soup pellet into his tin mug and mixed it with water from his canteen, leaving it embedded in the sand and sun.

He smiled.

"That should be cooked in a few minutes, Bachmann."

"H-how d'you know my name?"

He did not have time to answer. Alert to any movements, he spun using his field binoculars to pick out a cloud of dust in the distance. A minute later, the sound of engines became audible.

"Shit. British patrol. Can you get up? We need to hide."

I shook my head. Without hesitation, he scooped me up, carrying me the agonising few steps to the cockpit and lowering me inside before clambering over me. We did our best to hide, my logical brain telling me it was a futile exercise. Within minutes, we heard voices below us. My rescuer peered from the floor of the cockpit.

"I can see two jeeps, an officer, half a dozen men. Can you use one of these?"

He passed me a Luger. It seemed ironic I had survived my Luftwaffe aerial encounters without killing anyone and yet here I was faced with the choice of kill or be killed on the desert ground.

"We should surrender. There's no chance of beating them."

"Very well. I'll fight them on my own. Our unit could be here soon."

Reaching into his kitbag, he pulled free an automatic machine gun. Shooting holes in the canopy, he pushed the gun barrel through and readied himself. I closed my eyes to say a short prayer, and as I opened them, I saw my countryman slouched, a single bullet wound in his temple. A sunburnt face, framed with a neatly trimmed beard, appeared above me, his whole body and firearm coming into view. He wore British khaki desert uniform, but his voice was more like an American's. Seeing my condition and the Luger lying on the floor, he spoke.

"I take it you'll be surrendering. You've been shot down behind our lines. We don't know how. There's no crab fat anywhere near here."

Stretchered down from the Junkers to a covered jeep, while our cameras and my crewmate's corpses were recovered, I was soon travelling across the desert, sand and a pungent smell of fuel flying across my face as the jeep sped back to camp. I checked my still-working wristwatch as we left and, again, as the jeep slowed on approach to the makeshift desert camp. I measured a journey of twenty-five minutes, meaning I had crashed twelve miles from wherever the British had taken me. To my right, an impressive column of American M3 Grant tanks joined an already large contingent of British tanks and 35-mm guns.

Jumping out of the jeep, my two escorts manhandled the stretcher, pulling me clear.

"Where am I?"

The soldier nearest my head answered.

"Miles from anywhere, Jerry. Guest of the 22nd Armoured Brigade."

The sergeant barked his orders. They took me to a quiet area in a white medical tent and left me, under guard, on a camp bed. The stench of dried blood and chemicals overwhelmed me, making me gag. Grabbing the thin sheet beneath me, I pulled it across my face but could not keep the smell, or the unbearable sound of human moans, out.

Despite the cacophony of pain around me, I fell into a deep sleep. In my waking slumber, I wondered first why command had called on a Brandenburger to rescue me. It seemed out of proportion. We were not serving a particularly strategic purpose, to my knowledge, nor were any of us that important.

I was puzzled by why this camp was even here, in the desert, and not further north nearer Mersa Matruh. Our job had been to assess the readiness of British positions between Cyrenaica and the major Egyptian cities before Rommel's final push. After the victories at Tobruk and Gazala, the Axis in Africa was unstoppable. But the Eighth Army was hardy and knew Egypt well. It wouldn't be easy.

An older man with white hair, matching the colour of his coat, approached and cleared his throat. He stood above me, examining my damaged legs over his half-rimmed glasses.

"*Guten Tag.* Hello? *Sprichst du Englisch?*"

"Yes."

He smiled.

"Good. Makes things easier for me. I'll assess you now and you'll get treatment before being transferred, under the command of Captain Buchan, who takes care of prisoners. Your name?"

"Bachmann."

He pushed a stethoscope onto my chest and held my wrist, with two fingers on my pulse.

"How do you feel?"

"Tired. A little breathless."

"Your heartbeat is through the roof. Have you peed recently?"

"No. I'm thirsty though."

The doctor pulled a pair of long-nosed scissors from his top pocket and moved them towards my loin. I flinched, turning my hips away from him.

"Stay still, man. I've done this myriad times."

Grabbing the rear band of my trousers, he pulled me towards him, slitting the band and sliding the scissors down their length. Trousers removed, I lay rigid, a flush creeping across my face. I covered my groin with my hands as a young female nurse approached at the doctor's request. Without warning, the doctor stuck a finger in both holes in my legs, making me screech in agony as he wiggled it around.

"Nurse, clean these wounds. Add sulfa powder and put him on IV plasma. I'll operate as soon as I can. Administer morphine if required. Bachmann, you've suffered severe heatstroke, dehydration and concussion. Both your quadriceps are badly damaged, and you've lost a lot of blood. The sand and tourniquets saved you."

Minutes later, the nurse fitted a mask over my nose and mouth, pulling the strap snugly over the back of my head. There was a hiss as the gas left the cylinder, travelling up the rubber tube and into the mask. Taste of summer strawberries. Nothing.

I awoke, disorientated, in a different part of the tent, floating like a magician's plaything. No patients, no movement. Bright white light surrounded me. I screwed my hands into balls and could sense their movement, but pinching them, felt nothing.

Then I heard male voices singing, loud and hearty. Could I be...? Surely not.

Through the haze, a female figure, dark-skinned with black hair and bright eyes, glided towards me.

"You've been in a deep sleep for twenty-four hours. The doctor is going to run tests on you while you're awake. If you're well enough, we'll move you from here."

Her soft, reassuring voice relieved me. I was alive.

"Nurse. What were those voices?"

"Oh, the choir. They sing to keep their spirits high. Prefer *Sa'idi* music myself."

She smiled, revealing her perfect teeth, eyes glistening. An angel of the desert.

*

The doctor's prognosis that I had recovered well enough to meet the chief interrogator, Colonel Buchan, was not entirely welcome. But after several attempts at extracting information from me on the intentions of the Luftwaffe, he realised I knew nothing of strategic use to the British. A few days of standing in agony at the sink in the canteen 'pot wash' followed before joining a group of around thirty other German and Italian prisoners boarding a transport plane to Cairo. Registered as 'departed' by the guards, we were pointed up a steep wooden ramp into the Dakota's rear fuselage. Last up the ramp, I made slow progress. The throbbing blood in my thighs brought a crushing pain. I paused, resting on my crutches. A wave of fear almost toppled me backwards as I contemplated what lay ahead. Looking, in turn, to the clear blue sky and the belly of the plane, now swollen with prisoners, my head swam. Leaning to the left, I vomited off the side of the ramp. *Lift, thrust, drag and weight.*

Landing at RAF Almaza, a little under four hours later, I was bundled into an open-sided military truck with a dozen other prisoners and taken on to Maadi, a leafy suburb of Cairo and home to an encampment of New Zealand soldiers, and a British interrogation camp. It seemed the British did want to continue their pursuit of information from me.

*

The oppressive heat at the surface above us had been unbearable. There was some physical relief at being underground, as I was led to the main interrogation room. But the golden words, 'Abandon all hope ye who enter here' painted on a black sign above its door soon ended it. I tried to pass it off as British humour.

The tiny door, which meant I had to spread my crutches wide and stoop through to enter, was flanked by two burly guards. Once inside, the heavy door slammed shut behind me, a guard pushing home the locking bolt.

I squinted, my eyes adapting to the lack of light in the room, and peered at the interrogator, whose face remained featureless in the shadows. My first sense of him was his voice. It was completely different to Buchan's. Less genteel, guttural, a different dialect.

"You think you're clever, don't you, Bachmann?"

I had not said a word. How could he make this assessment? And yet, he was right. I did think myself relatively intelligent.

241

"Your luck's out. Makes no difference how smart you are. In here, we always get the truth."

"Sir, I assure you, Colonel Buchan abandoned his efforts."

The interrogator gave a nod of his head.

"I have nothing to tell y—"

The guard beside me sunk his fist into my lower back before I had finished my sentence. I bent over, and a surge of familiar pain swelled from my kidney; it was nothing I had not felt before.

"We're not the most patient here, Bachmann. You were recovered by special forces, why? And what the hell were you doing near Mersa Matruh? There were no German units anywhere near where you were shot down."

I thought briefly about trying to throw him off track, to buy myself some time. But I was not afraid of a beating.

"It was a normal reconnaissance mission. I was simply carrying out my orders."

A long silence was broken by the sound of distant gunfire.

"Very well. I don't have time for this. Guards, take him outside."

One of the guards pushed open a door on the left of the room, while the other prodded me in the direction of a set of steps behind it. They dragged me up them to a sweltering ground level and through another door into a wire-fenced pen, its soil baked hard. I peered around the sweltering pen, where little piles of soil played host to short, protruding stakes. Moments later, a guard shoved a shovel in my hand.

*

Fortunately for me, hours after being told to dig my own grave, a more senior Luftwaffe commander was captured. No longer high priority, I was moved to another camp in central Cairo, overlooked by a Muslim temple. Within days, I was on a ship back across the Atlantic, this time bound for Canada.

18

ENGLISH ROSE

Lincolnshire, England
Five years later

I had a long time to think about the war and what it had done to me and my family. I was a prisoner of it, both physically and mentally. I never stopped feeling cheated that Papa had left this world with no explanations to me, no chance for me to understand him. A yearning for love from my father would never leave me, and Mama's disappearance left me with a hole in my heart that I would not stop trying to fill.

Opa had been my only family link through all my years of imprisonment, writing letters to me in Canada and now England. I will never forget the way he described the loss of so many family friends during the 1945 slaughter at the Battle of Halbe: 'If life a tree be, the Soviet frost has killed root, branch and leaf, leaving my soul an empty place.'

*

"It's not so bad here, is it? But the British can be brutal when they want to be. Did I ever tell you about that poor Muslim bugger in Cairo?"

Otto the submariner, my Pingley Camp compatriot, laid down his gardening tools and slumped down beside me exhausted, shaking his head.

"A British guard shot him out of a minaret window, pissed off with hearing the calls to morning prayer."

"Poor sod. I didn't even know you were in Cairo."

"Yes. I was the only survivor when my Junkers crashed in the desert. Strange that a Brandenburger parachuted in to rescue me, but the Canadians shot him. Got taken to a British desert camp, interrogated, and flown on to Cairo. I was glad to be out of the war, to be honest. Spent hours reading books donated by the International Red Cross while I was there. What happened to you?"

Otto smiled.

"Got taken to Norfolk, Virginia in America. They gave us books too and writing paper and cigarettes. Had my first taste of ice cream on-board.

"To be honest, I was pleased to be captured too. Never enjoyed sinking defenceless ships. Ended up in my own little piece of desert. Place called Papago Park in Arizona. They'd no military guards, only civilians. I still remember one of them. Guy called Jennings, who ran a petrol station. Always brought his nephew to watch films with us."

Otto looked towards the only cloud in the pale-blue Lincolnshire sky, which was now sitting in front of the sun.

"*How Green Was My Valley*. We used to sing 'Give My Regards to Broadway' together. One guard even tried to dance like Cagney."

A broad smile lit up Otto's normally stony face for a moment.

"What happened to you after Egypt?"

I told Otto how I was shipped back to New York, via the Suez Canal, Cape Horn and the coasts of many South American countries. Then we joined the Canadian Pacific Railway to Ozada, the 'canvas village' on the wide-open plains of the Alberta prairie.

"They had us logging for a while. I actually built some muscle for a change."

I was taken on to another vast camp at Lethbridge. It was like a town all of its own. They had incredible sports facilities—soccer, boxing, wrestling, gymnastics, tennis, skating—designed to keep the prisoners fit. They had great music facilities too.

"I set up a four-piece with three other Ju 88 guys, playing Louis Armstrong, Benny Goodman. They called us the 'Flying Fingers'."

I glanced across at the dozen bare-root English rose bushes set by Otto in neat rows in the loamy Lincolnshire soil. A veterinarian by profession, he served as a watch officer in a Kreigsmarine beneath the Atlantic before his capture by a US destroyer in '43.

"What happened to the runner beans?"

Otto scanned the area behind me, wiping his hand across his lips.

"Jackson wanted his precious rhododendrons planting first. Have you got anything to drink? I'm parched."

I handed my friend a cup of tea from the flask, and we moved to a bench sheltered from the warm May sun by the shadow of an accommodation hut to cool off.

Otto put down his tin mug and clasped my hand, giving it a firm shake.

"You know, Oskar, I always feel sorry that your father died and that your mother is lost. I might get to see my parents sooner than I expected."

I turned to look at Otto's smiling face.

"Oh?"

"Yes, and I've a favour to ask you."

*

Parking my dusty old BSA under the only tree in the garden, I disturbed a very active wasps' nest, nearly falling off my bike as I swung at them. The level of freedom I had now after my years as a prisoner in Canada felt good. It seemed to me that my life would restart.

Moving to a safe distance, I pulled off my filthy goggles, wiping dust across my moist forehead. Dismounting, I stamped my war-wounded legs on the ground. They always seized up after riding any distance.

Springfield Farm was off my usual route, which took me to the two post offices in Kirton Lindsey and, once a week, the RAF training centre south of the town. Today, I had a special delivery.

The four figures sat at a picnic table outside the house turned to stare at me, using their arms to shield the sunlight. Getting to his feet, the only man in the group bellowed at me.

"Who are you? This is my farm."

Hobbling towards them, my legs still numb, I stopped five metres short of the table.

"Hello, sir. Mr Procter?"

He gave a curt nod.

"I'm Bachmann, from Pingley. I have a message for your daughter."

The farmer stared at me, then across at the young woman sat opposite him at the table, his eyes narrowing to slits.

"Pingley? Margaret, what's he talking about?"

She cocked her head to one side, swiftly and confidently delivering her alibi.

"I've written a couple of letters to a prisoner there, Father. He's a vet. It's good secretarial practice for me. I asked his advice on our lamb troubles."

"Why the hell are you asking one of them? We've a perfectly good vet in Kirton."

She shuffled uncomfortably, unable to find an answer, prompting me to step in.

"The correspondence was initiated by the camp, sir. An effort to develop greater understanding with the local population."

Noticing a tin of rolling tobacco on the table, I reached into my pocket and held out my packet of Nazionali cigarettes towards my host. Procter's mood and heavy cheeks lifted a little.

"Don't mind if I do."

"They're Italian. From a Roman chap in the camp."

As I spoke, the second woman with her back to me rose from the table and turned towards me. Her cheeks glowed the colour of the strawberries she held in a basket.

"Would you like one?"

I froze, my voice stuck in my throat. It was the girl from the window. The one I thought would always remain a mystery, the reason I was frequently late back to camp. She was there, right in front of me, holding a punnet of fruit. Her bright-blue eyes held me in a gaze, golden curls of hair dipping across them. Her grin showcased flawless, cloud-white teeth, a matchstick-wide gap between the front top two.

"I'm Miriam. A friend of Margaret's. Has the cat got your tongue? I'm glad you avoided falling off your bike, by the way. That *would* have been a bad start."

"What did you say?", For a moment the cat *had* got my tongue. "Um, it was the wasps. I'm allergic."

Margaret rose to her feet, nudging my window girl out of the way.

"Excuse my friend, sir. You said you'd a message for me?"

I hurriedly searched my pockets, forgetting momentarily where I had put Otto's letter, before finding it in my breast pocket.

"Here it is."

Snatching the sweat-damp letter from my fingers, she sprinted into the house, tearing it open on her way. Her fretful mother followed and, after hurriedly stubbing out his half-smoked cigarette, the man of the house.

Miriam twirled a single lock of hair around her forefinger, a broad smile spreading across her face. A sudden flush of heat made me remove my jacket, revealing the embarrassing rings of sweat on my shirt.

"What's the view like from Moat House?"

She brought her palm up to her chest.

"I'm sorry? How do you know where I live?"

"I've ridden past on my delivery round. I've seen you in the upstairs window once or twice."

She laughed, tapping a finger on my lapel.

"You must have good eyesight. Did you like the view?"

Her forwardness was attractive but unnerving at the same time, and I was relieved to hear the front door of the farmhouse fly open behind us. We turned together to see Margaret stood in the doorway, howling with tears. Her mother laid hands on her shoulders, trying to console her. Miriam furrowed her brow and let out a long sigh.

"How have you made my friend so unhappy?"

"I'm just the messenger. Unfortunately, her boyfriend Otto is headed back to Germany. They need vets to help revive agriculture and the nation's economy."

Despite her friend's continued distress, Miriam held me in a fascinated gaze. I had never been confident with women, but knew enough to tell it was now or never.

"Perhaps one day they'll call for teachers too. In the meantime, would you like to meet?"

"You're going to land me into trouble. Fraternising is still illegal, you know." She grinned. "I ride my horse Wednesday evenings from six and Saturday mornings from nine at Clay Lane stables, opposite the farmhouse."

I nodded, looking up to see Procter heading towards me, grasping a hunting rifle. I sprinted to my bike, jumping on the starter pedal twice. As the engine roared to life, the first lead shot pinged off the chrome mudguard.

*

I had negotiated a late return to camp. It would give me thirty minutes with Miriam. Leaving Pingley, one of the guards, a former meteorological officer at Mildenhall, delighted in telling me that yesterday was the hottest June day on record. It wasn't much cooler today, and I was grateful for Otto's loan of medicated soap. Hopefully, she would notice.

Faces often faded from my memory, perhaps my mind's defence mechanism working. But, today, images of Miriam played constantly in my mind as I delivered and collected post, wishing away the minutes and hours.

Finally, five thirty came. I sped towards the stables, slowing only as I turned into the ditch- and divot-filled entrance to Clay Lane to avoid falling off. As the road flattened, I increased speed again, slowing as I spotted the stables to my right on the approach to the railway bridge.

I parked my bike, peering around the stable block, breath stuck in chest. All quiet. No sign of Miriam or any horses. Perhaps she had lied. Probably for the best. We could both be punished under fraternisation laws.

The sound of an approaching train grew louder as I straddled the bike, lifting my helmet over my head.

"Aren't you going to come and help, then?"

Her unmistakable voice, loud and clear, made my heart pound in rhythm with the fading thunder of the train. Looking over my shoulder, I saw her stride towards me, holding a pair of stallions by the reins. She wore a tight blouse and headscarf and stopped in front of the nearest stables to tie up the steaming horses.

Leaving my bike once more, I turned to face her, realising what a mistake I had been about to make in leaving. She

251

dragged the scarf away from her head, letting her hair fall free, and buried her hands elbow-deep in the forest-green riding pants she wore, a wide grin spreading across her face.

My German reserve only held me back for seconds before I ran to her, eyes focused, stopping a metre away to pull her body into mine. Our lips entwined, sweat, breath and longing forgiving six years of war.

She pushed me away, her cheeks as red as the strawberries at Procter's farm. Breathlessly, I responded to her question.

"How would you like me to help?"

*

We met secretly for months, always on a Wednesday or Saturday. I was sure the camp commander knew what was going on but turned a blind eye to my late returns. Then, just as the hot summer ended, my five years of imprisonment came to an end as the Pingley Camp authorities released me. My life had been paused. Now it could begin again.

Miriam wasted no time in asking her father if I could move into their house, which was undoubtedly a brave thing to do. But, despite being crippled with arthritis in the Great War and having plenty of reason to dislike Germans, George was agreeable on condition I slept in the spare room and contributed to household costs. I often wondered how he felt to have his son, Ralph, who had served on a Royal Navy minesweeper in the war, and now me sitting in a triangle with him at the dinner table.

*

Worlaby Pea Farm, where I found a job packing tins for the factory in Sheffield, had been hell that day. My body ached head to toe, reminding me of the time I took a beating from the Seissler boys in Halbe on account of being '*das Weichei*' ('the wimp').

Rose, Miriam's sympathetic mother, peered through the dining room window at a pair of blue tits in the hedge, before turning to welcome me to the table.

"I bet you're worn out, love. Let me plate you up some dinner."

Our shared interest in ornithology had bonded us quickly. George relaxed back in his chair.

"How was Worlaby? Did I tell you I insure the pea farm at favourable rates?"

"It was fine, thanks, George. More money in the bank."

I looked at Miriam and smiled, knowing she still found dinners with me and her family awkward.

"I'm capable of better if I get the chance."

Heading towards his drinks cabinet in the corner, George stopped to put a hand on my shoulder.

"You'll get the chance. Don't worry."

Rose filled our plates with slices of pork, roast potatoes, carrots, peas, gravy and apple sauce, which we all devoured in minutes.

"Would anyone be interested in learning a few German phrases?"

My question, which was really aimed at Miriam, who had shown little interest in anything German, was met with a mixed response.

Ralph pushed back his chair and stood.

"Will you excuse me, Mother, Father? I'm meeting Ernest for a pint at the Queen's Head."

George nodded.

"I learned all the German I need back in 1917, Oskar, but thank you for the offer. I need to sort out my tomato plants."

Rose butted in.

"Yes, Oskar, I'd love to. Don't you agree, Miriam?"

Her eyes lingered on me for several seconds, before she turned back to her mother.

"Maybe some other time. I saw some jobs in the newspaper I want to show Oskar."

"Very well. I'll clear up the dishes then."

I stayed at the table while Miriam collected *The Lincolnshire Echo*. She stood over me, pointing to a large advert in the vacancies section.

"Why don't you apply for this?"

Squinting, I read aloud, "University College Hull requires: shorthand typist, research associate in electrochemical energy, caretaker... I can do better, Miriam."

I didn't want to find a job there. She knew it.

"Keep reading down the page."

"Junior professor, Department of Psychology and Sociology. That does look interesting, darling, but you know how I feel. I always believed that one day I'd teach in a Germany free of Nazism. And..."

Miriam replied impatiently.

"And what?"

"I need to find out what happened to my mother."

Wrapping her arms around my head, she patted my back then wrapped her soft palms around my cheeks.

"Oskar, maybe it's best you don't know. You've a chance to move on now. Make a life here."

The previous weekend we had seen a British Pathé newsreel at the Grand in Brigg. Images of twisted rail lines, bombed-out cities and desperate Germans trying to find loved ones had cemented Miriam's view.

"I'm not going to Germany any time soon, Oskar. The entire country's still a disaster zone."

The same newsreel showed the mass graves of Halbe Forest, where many of my old friends lay buried. It had upset me beyond measure. For now, I could not disagree with Miriam. Finding out what happened to my mother would have to wait a while longer.

19

OPPORTUNITY

Kirton Lindsey
1947

If I had told my Luftwaffe crewmates that, a few years after fighting the RAF over Africa, I would be invited to give a talk to a group of British housewives, they would have handed me a parachute. The Women's Institute meeting came around fast. Mrs Millington, a kindly friend of Miriam's family and WI stalwart, had taken me in for tea after witnessing local men shout, "Sieg heil" at me across the street. She had persuaded me to give a talk. Despite my reservations, Miriam thought it a good public relations opportunity and so I spent hours preparing my notes, deciding to avoid references to my time in the Luftwaffe altogether.

Miriam bought me a new maroon and purple paisley-print bow tie from Burton's tailors in Grimsby. I didn't have the heart to tell her I hated it. It made me realise what good taste Mother had. Taking it from my shaking hands, she effortlessly tied it for me.

"It's perfect. So smart. Those women will fall for you before you've even said a word."

"Don't be silly. They'll be the hardest audience I've ever had. What should I say if they ask about the war? The last thing I need is more accusations of being a Nazi."

Miriam put her hands on my shoulders, gazing into my eyes. At times like this I relied on her fortitude.

"Be honest. Tell them what you told me on our first dates. You've nothing to hide. You're a good man."

Miriam kissed me on the lips and brushed my shoulders before handing me her dad's umbrella.

"Here, you'll need this. It's pouring. Do your best."

"Miri, I know I said I didn't want you to be there, but I've changed my mind. Will you come?"

She let out a long sigh.

"I've nothing ready to wear. What about my hair and make-up?"

"Please."

Raising her eyebrows, she shook her head before scurrying away upstairs, reappearing moments later dressed in a long skirt and blouse, her hair tied back, lipstick neatly applied.

"Wait here. I'll get my coat."

I picked up the old, brown-leather briefcase, another loan from George, and we left the house together arm in arm, shielding ourselves from the downpour under the umbrella. My heart beat hard in my chest as we walked. I was grateful for Miriam's company. I had done things many would consider scary: attending university in a foreign country, crossing oceans in compromised ships, even flying planes in combat, but they seemed trivial next to the prospect of addressing a room full of English housewives.

We arrived at the town hall fifteen minutes early. I was shocked to find it already full and buzzing with excited conversation. I must have seemed like a new boy on his first day at school as Mrs Millington made her way over to us with a broad smile on her lips.

"Evening, Oskar. Hello, Miriam. How's Mum and Dad? It seems word's spread. I'm glad you haven't reconsidered. We're all looking forward to your talk. Come on, I'd like you to meet someone."

She led us over to a petite, serious woman dressed in a long blue woollen skirt and button-up jacket, who was stood talking to the only other man present at the front of the hall.

"Oskar, Miriam, let me introduce you to Violet Harries, Chair of the Lincolnshire Humber Federation. She's come from Brigg, specially."

Cutting her conversation short, Mrs Harries turned, abruptly, to face me.

"Mr Bachmann. June told me all about you. The Luftwaffe sent my husband to his death in the English Channel in 1940. You'll excuse me if I reserve judgement on your character for now."

Miriam squeezed my arm tight.

"I'm sorry about your husband, Mrs Harries. I'm sure we're all glad the war's behind us now."

Mrs Harries smiled awkwardly, ushering us towards a seat in the front row, where I sat with her on one side, Miriam on the other. I peered over my shoulder, quickly scanning the room. Three quarters of the attendees were old enough to be my mother.

The large clock above the stage showed seven p.m. exactly. I stooped to retrieve my notes from the case as the room fell quiet, feverishly trying to release the catch. Moving it in all directions, I realised I needed the key to open it. Seeing my struggle, Miriam shrugged her shoulders, laying a reassuring hand on my thigh.

She whispered, "You'll be fine" in my ear.

A tall, thin, bookish woman stepped onto the wooden stage and stood behind the lectern.

"Good evening, ladies."

She peered over her half-glasses, scanning the room.

"I've never seen it so full in here. Especially given the weather. A few of you already know our speaker. Oskar Bachmann, once an inmate at Pingley Camp, is now an adopted resident of Kirton. His story is fascinating. We're delighted June Millington persuaded him to talk to us. Mr Bachmann."

A round of enthusiastic applause began. Taking a deep breath, I gathered myself and walked to the stage, hoping that, without notes, my talk would still make some kind of sense.

"Thank you. I'm honoured to be here tonight. It must feel strange for you to have a German on this stage so soon after the war."

A woman at the back made a sarcastic comment but, to my delight, was shushed into silence.

"I've no interest in dwelling on the war. My time in the Luftwaffe was an interruption to my life, not its finest moment. One good thing came out of it. My capture in North Africa led me to England, a place I now call home.

259

"Tonight, I'm going to tell you about my time in America, where I had once hoped to live out my dreams."

I paused and looked across the faces staring back at me from the front row. I could do this.

"My stay began in New York City in late summer 1938, following my journey across the Atlantic from Hamburg. It was my first time setting foot on a different continent. The start of an incredible personal journey."

For the next hour, my mind fired perfectly. I connected my experiences, the threads of my life, together, weaving a compelling tapestry. Occasionally I glanced at Miriam, who gazed back at me proudly as my words flowed, memories coming to my brain in a steady flow. Nearing the end of my talk, a potential stumbling block loomed. My reason for leaving America. I would avoid it.

"My destiny was in the Luftwaffe. After my journey back to Berlin, training for war began and the rest, as they say, is history. Thank you for listening to me."

I cleared the stumbling block, the hall erupting into sustained applause. An unexpected atmosphere of acceptance embraced me and my eyes became moist. These women's husbands, sons and brothers could easily have been targets for the Luftwaffe and yet they clapped, willing it seemed to forgive me.

Mrs Harries was quickly on her feet, looking around the room, unnerved, ready to take the wind out of my sails. She called out over the applause.

"Mr Bachmann, thank you. I'm sure no one in this hall has been to New York. It was fascinating to learn about the city.

We'd all like to know more, I'm sure, about why you left. What made you join the Nazi war effort?"

My brain went into overdrive, assessing the best possible answers, the levels of detail I should give.

"I did what all young German men had to do. I was never an agent of Nazism but had to support our country's war effort. We had no real choice."

I paused, staring out at the now silent audience, unconvinced by my answer.

"In truth, I wanted to please my father by becoming a Luftwaffe pilot. I'm sure you can understand this."

A surge of pain ran through my war-wounded legs, momentarily making me lose control of them and faltering on the stage. As Miriam moved towards me, Mrs Millington rose to her feet and addressed the crowd.

"Ladies, I'm sure you all found that a most interesting talk. For those able to stay, it's time for refreshments. There are tea, sandwiches and cake at the rear of the hall. Please drop your spare change into the collection tin."

I stumbled from the stage and back to my seat, helped by Miriam.

Mrs Millington approached us.

"Are you all right, dear?"

"Yes, just an old issue I have with my legs. I'm fine. Thanks again for the invitation."

"Would you like a cup of tea? I'm sure the ladies would love to ask you some questions."

I looked at Miriam, who turned to our host.

"No, thank you, Mrs Millington. We'd better go. Dad's expecting us back."

As we approached the door, the man who'd been speaking to Mrs Harries stepped away from his circle of conversation to greet us, spotting my limp as I neared.

"Old war injury? Enjoyed your talk. Ahh, Miriam, isn't it? Know your father well."

Immediately recognising his face, Miriam's flushed red as she dangled her hand before him.

"Mr Belton. Pleasure."

We shook hands. He was confident, well dressed and had a bellowing voice that seemed to echo around his enormous frame before leaving his mouth.

"Always wanted to visit New York City. Can't even imagine the scale of it. Your description of Times Square was wonderful. You've a great way with words, especially given English is not your first language. I'm Chair of Governors for the modern secondary school here in Kirton. Do you know it?"

"Yes, of course."

I turned to Miriam. "Didn't your little sister go there until recently?"

"Yes, she left the year before last. Went there instead of the grammar school, despite passing the eleven-plus. Didn't want to leave her friends."

Belton nodded.

"Yes. Well, good. I'd like to have a longer talk with you. How about you come for lunch on Saturday?"

I wasn't keen on the idea.

"Sorry, Mr Belton, I'm helping Miriam's father..."

Sensing an opportunity that I couldn't see, Miriam interrupted.

"We'd love to come. What time should we arrive, Mr Belton?"

"Good. Come for half past twelve. You know where we live, Miriam. The Priory on Queen Street."

Smiling broadly, Belton turned and re-engaged with his group.

We headed towards the door, waving at Mrs Millington on the way. Outside, the rain had stopped and a crescent moon shone brightly between clouds, lighting our way back home.

Reaching the oak tree on the corner of George Street, Miriam stopped, pulling me towards her for a long, lingering kiss.

"You were brilliant tonight, darling. They loved you. I do too."

"Thanks. Why were you so keen to have lunch with Mr errr...?"

"Belton. Jim Belton. You know, Oskar Bachmann, sometimes you're completely naïve."

I pulled away.

"What do you mean?"

"He's going to offer you a job. It's obvious! There are so many people here in Kirton who admire you. You should expect to have some luck come your way."

*

Jim Belton spent most of lunchtime telling uninspiring stories about rugby matches at his public school, Ampleforth, but his wife, a young German woman, was a delightful host.

Miriam's instincts had been right. Belton duly offered me a role as languages teacher at the secondary modern, 'subject to loose ends being tied up'. We left late afternoon, full of food and wine, with decisions to make. As we walked through St Andrew's churchyard, a thousand thoughts wrestled for attention in my brain.

I pulled Miriam down on a bench next to me, resting my elbows on my knees. She stared at me.

"Well, that went well, apart from your question about how they met! Are you happy?"

I tried my best to focus, sound excited.

"Yes. Yes, I think so."

In all my time in the Luftwaffe and as a POW, I had been cocooned, protected from decision-making. Suddenly, back in control of my life, it was terrifying. Squeezing my eyes shut, I let out a pathetic whimper.

"Oskar, what on earth's wrong with you?"

Nightmarish visions rushed across my mind. My hands clawing the wall in that dense, dark basement in Halbe, an old man covering and uncovering an oil lamp in front of me, black clouds, gunfire. A moment of clarity emerged.

"I have to go back to Germany, Miriam! Do you understand?"

"Why are you shouting at me? Please be quiet, people will hear."

*

I received a letter on the morning of our wedding day, the faint postmark on the envelope impossible to make out. Expecting a well-wisher's message, instead a photograph fell out into my cold, clammy hand, causing my legs to buckle. It was a slightly faded image of my father stood before a table clasping an untidy pile of papers in what looked like a scientific laboratory. Behind him, a set of out-of-focus test tubes. One thing was familiar: he looked inebriated. A rush of bad memories flooded my mind as I turned the picture over to reveal a note on its reverse, written in faint, spidery pencil: '*Du bist genau wie er. Voller furcht. Ruckkehr ins Vaterland.*' ('You are just like him. Full of fear. Return to the Fatherland.')

Struggling to fathom who had sent the photograph, and why on my wedding day, I drew on a decade's worth of strength, just as I had the very last time Father beat me. With shaking voice, I recited out loud one of my favourite book passages.

"Thought looks into the pit of hell and is not afraid... Thought is great and swift and free, the light of the world, and the chief glory of man.

"Thought looks into the pit of hell and is not afraid.

"Thought looks into the pit of hell."

*

Arriving at little St Andrews Church, our popularity, or perhaps novelty, in Kirton was evident. There wasn't an inch of space anywhere.

Reverend Willory told us our 'joyful day' marked the first marriage of a POW to a local girl, an act of greater significance than the joining of two souls. As I approached him and the altar, I imagined Mother looking over her shoulder at me, her kind eyes shining. I wished at least one of my family could have been here.

Leaving the church as Mr and Mrs Bachmann, a gusting wind blew a cloud across the sun and the veil across my bride's face. This girl, and her belief in me against all odds, had turned me into a pillar of Kirton society. Our wedding was now a route home, I hoped.

We arrived at the Kirton Town Hall reception to a small cheering crowd. The outside walls were resplendent with multicoloured bunting. An excited Mrs Millington was the first to greet us at the door.

"Congratulations to you both. You make a lovely couple. Come inside. I'd like to show you what the girls have done."

With a grinning face, she pointed to an enormous mural on the wall. My watery eyes were now fully in tears. It depicted a book-clasping parachutist floating down towards a ground covered in flowers, his sweetheart waiting there for him.

"That must've been hours of work, Mrs Millington. We can't thank you enough."

"About time you called me June. We'd a little help from the Brigg WI. Seems you've finally won Violet Harries over."

By seven p.m. the hall was swinging to the sound of the Brigg brass band playing Glenn Miller songs. My clumsy 'Moonlight Serenade' dance with Miriam over, I took her dear mother by the hand.

"She can be difficult, Oskar. Stubborn as a boot and a bit of a sergeant major. That will come in useful if you have children though."

I nodded as she tapped me on the shoulder affectionately and laughed.

George had been sitting next to the temporary bar, created from old beer barrels, for a while and pointed to the seat next to him as I approached.

"Do not get drunk on your wedding night, Oskar."

I chuckled. I had hardly drunk at all, while George had kept the bar very busy.

"You know, Oskar, I've never told you this before. I've fought Germans, and Ralph has too, but I already love you like you were my own. Good luck with Miriam."

I hoped for a few moments of quiet and sat supping a sweet Burton ale, staring at the picture of Father. Whoever had sent it must have been connected to either Weigl or the Nazis. Perhaps I would never find out. Within moments, my radiant bride approached.

"Oskar, there you are. Come and meet Sue and Gerry."

"Do you mind if I don't?"

She frowned, shrugging her shoulders.

"In Halbe, the bride and groom saw through a tree trunk together after the marriage ceremony. A first test of teamwork."

"Lincolnshire's one of the least-wooded counties in England, love, and can you really see me working up a sweat in my wedding dress? Come on."

*

1948

I had now taught at the secondary modern for over a year, acclimatising well at first and quickly learning the English way of teaching. Policies under the Butler Act made the school well-equipped and equitable. Opa would have liked it, I reasoned. Despite this, I had begun to struggle. Unable to get out of bed in the morning, each day started in a fog of indecision and tears, which I managed to hide from Miriam. She would not have reacted well. The tears spilled over into the daytime too, striking at the worst of times, once when I helped George pull out his cauliflowers and again as I read out loud from *Pygmalion*, which Rose was due to perform with her local theatre group.

My visions of home intensified. The voice inside my head telling me to return there never let up. Giving lessons to my pupils was challenging, given my moods, but most of them came from good homes and did not mock my occasional mind fogs or 'Bachmann blackouts' as they became known.

It was after a full school assembly, where our headteacher used his platform to talk about the continued challenges of building back Britain and the role of education in that aim, that I realised I had to go back to Germany. The Third Reich consigned to history, my country needed me, not this time to fight other nations but to help rebuild our own. Equally, I had to try again to find out what had befallen dear Mother. But first I had to convince Miriam.

*

Miriam's brother drove us to Hull in his green 1939 Vauxhall 12, its quiet but powerful little engine getting us there in just over an hour. Ralph, who was meeting a few of his old Navy mates in a pub near the Royal Infirmary, dropped us by the Royal Hotel on the Anlaby Road, waving goodbye out of the window as he sped away.

My wife had been quiet on the drive here, as Ralph and I had discussed our war experiences and smoked cigarettes. This was only the third time we had eaten out since our wedding. She clearly suspected something.

The restaurant was nearly empty as we arrived. Few people could afford to eat out. We requested a seat near the window and sat in the deep bucket seats, admiring the perfect white tablecloths and silver Sheffield cutlery. Our waiter showed us the menu on a blackboard. I ordered plaice and chips, Miriam steak and kidney pudding. With wine still absent around here, we settled for two bottles of pale ale. As soon as the waiter left us, Miriam put me on the spot.

"So, what do you want to ask me, Oskar? It must be something important to have come all the way here."

I had hoped to chat for a while, maybe encourage her to have a second beer, before I landed what I knew would be an unpopular proposition.

"Miri, the Marshall Plan is going to invigorate Germany. I know my countrymen will have our economy thriving soon. There are so many hard-workers."

"What's the Marshall Plan? I don't read newspapers, remember."

She sounded completely uninterested.

"Maybe you should, Miri. You'd see how things are improving in Germany. The plan is a major investment in Europe by the Americans. It's going to revitalise the major cities, Berlin included."

"Well, unless Hull is getting some money, how will this help us?"

Our meals arrived and the waiter poured our drinks. I wasted no time, raising my glass to toast 'us', then gulping down a few mouthfuls of pale ale and beginning to eat.

"Miri, I want to go home to Germany. I must. I'm not happy here anymore."

"Oh, I see. Did you really think a pie and beer were going to make me change my mind? The answer's still no, Oskar. You've a job here with prospects. Dad said we can stay another year at home. By then, we could save up for our own place."

My body felt heavy, my breath hitched as I replied.

"Miri, please. You must understand. I want to return to try to teach in Germany. They'll only accept applications once I'm back at home. I can get translating work to tide us through."

She didn't reply, looking out of the window and smiling as a group of children waved at her. We finished our meals in silence. Then, pulling her serviette from her waist to tap her mouth, she looked me in the eye.

"Okay."

"What do you mean, okay?"

"I agree. But on the condition you find us somewhere reasonable to live and have guaranteed work before we go. Oh, and I'll want a visit home every year. My parents aren't getting any younger. Okay, are you getting the bill?"

Her sharply delivered agreement was loaded, but it was agreement nonetheless.

20

SHADOWS

West Berlin
April 1949

My wife pushed a piece of dry bread and a hard-boiled egg on a cracked plate towards me, followed by a cup of black coffee. She knew I hated it. We had arrived back to a Germany splitting in two and it felt as if our marriage would go the same way.

"Do we have any milk?"

Throwing back her head, she laughed sarcastically.

"As a matter of fact, we've half a litre. Only because I traded the last of my mother's tea towels and tablecloths with our neighbour. I'm keeping it to make rice pudding."

I chewed hard on the bread, swallowing awkwardly. Life had been hard since our return and, in truth, there was no sign of it getting better.

"Things will improve, Miriam. The authorities have said there's much more work to do, translating documents for the French sector, and I'm still applying for lectureships. I know I will get one soon, once the universities receive extra funding."

This tiny basement flat in British-occupied Spandau was a fraction the size of her spacious house in Lincolnshire. I felt at home here though. We were a few kilometres from my old training base, Berlin-Gatow, in Wilhelmstadt, a dreary, half-derelict suburb of Berlin on the northern edge of the Havel.

I had no issue with a meagre diet. It had been my life for many years, until Father's death. But Miriam's family life in England had always been comfortable, even during wartime. George's farmer friends kept their larder well stocked with butter, cheese, choice cuts of meat and endless fresh vegetables. Following a crash at Gatow the previous year involving a British Vickers and a Russian fighter, political tensions had run high. The Soviets had blockaded West Berlin, stopping food getting in and almost starving us all.

Removing her apron, she stood, her face flushed red.

"You've been doing that for months. Things are going to change because I'll make them."

I stared at her, my eyes blinking rapidly.

"We're not staying here, Oskar. I've talked to a British woman I met at our club. Her name's Dorothy Jacobs. She showed me photographs of her beautiful house in Staaken. She has links to an Anglo-German family in Siegen, who own a major printing business and are doing well. They need a translator and will pay you twice what you earn here."

"But Siegen? There's no university there. Isn't that where the Americans found all the paintings in a copper mine?"

"I don't know, and I don't care. If you want to stay my husband, I suggest you give it some thought."

Grabbing her coat from the wall, she left the house, slamming the door behind her. Pouring myself another black coffee, I collected my writing pad and pen. I would try one more time.

University of Göttingen

I sat nervously in the Vice Chancellor's office, glancing to my left at the shelves of books, protected by the ornate mahogany and glass cupboards that surrounded them.

Herr Leichtenberg sat reading my lengthy application letter. It was the fifteenth I had submitted to universities for roles as assistant professor, junior professor and *Studienrat*. The University of Göttingen, the first to open in the British zone when the war ended, was also the first to offer me an interview.

Almost every teacher in Germany had belonged to the Nazi Party during the war years. I had never joined and now, with British and American efforts to de-Nazify German education, it seemed a good moment to seize my chance. The reality was different.

After five minutes he looked up, a grin spreading across his face. His first question caught me completely off guard.

"Where do you think our country should be in a decade, Bachmann?"

He kept his focus on me, twirling his pencil between fat finger and thumb. How to answer? The voice in my head said, 'On its way to economic recovery under a liberal, democratic government.' But that wasn't the answer he wanted.

"We all want to see Germany take its place as a strong, proud, independent nation again. It will take many years. We must be cautious. The role of academia will be critical in shaping our new ideas."

He gave me a long, withering stare from piercing, pale-blue eyes, searching for an assurance from me that I couldn't give. The resistance to de-Nazification here was strong.

Leichtenberg rose from his polished walnut desk and lit a cigarette, offering me one, which I politely refused. He stood over me, beginning his tirade.

"The cursed British have tried their best to turn this place into a bastion of socialist learning. Bringing in working-class students, ridding the university of the very things that made it successful. Thank goodness, since '47, we've had control back."

He sat down on the corner of the desk, half a metre from me, in a display of faux familiarity.

"You've an impressive CV, Bachmann, but why have you tried to hide your excellent Luftwaffe experience? I served in the Condor Legion in Spain and then flew 110s in Luftflotte 3. We bombed the hell out of the British heartland. How I miss those days. Now look at us. What are your greatest memories from your days with Aufklärungsgruppe 121?"

I paused, pointing at the packet of cigarettes he had left on his desk.

"Perhaps I'll have one, Herr Leichtenberg."

Lighting me up, he stared in anticipation, awaiting a great, patriotic story of valour that would bond us together irrevocably.

"I was only glad to escape alive. Thought my time was up when my Junkers was shot down in the hellish heat of the North African desert, making me the sole survivor. Facing certain death, all I could do was think about the life I wanted to live. That's why I'm sitting here today, Herr Leichtenberg.

Being a lecturer is that life. Perhaps you could ask me about my academic history?"

Distracted, he asked a couple of questions on my areas of academic speciality, before trying to lead me to the assurance he wanted one more time.

"Why Göttingen, Bachmann? This place still has many issues. Living conditions are poor and the teaching facilities inadequate. There are some advantages, of course."

Nazism was alive and well here, but I would not give this old Nazi the opportunity to talk about it. So, I gave a bland answer regarding the university's history. Disappointed, Leichtenberg showed me to the door, politely suggesting I might be better suited to other establishments.

*

I ambled back to the railway station in dejected mood. A door that had opened a little had now shut, of my own volition. Leichtenberg wanted me to swear allegiance to his university's stance and to fly in the face of the Allies' efforts to de-Nazify. I would have none of it, despite Göttingen being the only university to offer me an interview. Most replied with a simple rejection letter, while a few had stated they couldn't consider ex-servicemen and that there were other governmental schemes that could help me. I would have no choice but to agree to Miriam's plan.

Most of the Göttingen streets I walked along seemed in perfect condition. But as I approached the railway station, more and more buildings were missing altogether or badly pitted and scarred by debris from explosions, the casualties of

Allied bombing raids. Through the years-old destruction, Cafe Schöneberg's neatly painted sky-blue façade and magnificent window display of cakes drew me in. With an hour until my Berlin train, I couldn't resist. The smell of fresh baking and coffee and a warm, friendly atmosphere enveloped me inside. Collecting *Eierschecke* cake and coffee, I headed towards the far end of the room, where a middle-aged man sat reading a newspaper. Although now white-haired and overweight, I recognised him instantly and spluttered through my suspended breath.

"Herr Gumpert? Is that you?"

He remained silent, narrowing his downcast eyes to peer at me over half-rimmed glasses.

"I'm an old friend of Timo's, sir. Do you remember me?"

I hung my mouth, ready to apologise for interrupting him. But, at that moment, his face softened, a spark of memory lighting up his eyes.

"My goodness. I do remember you. It's Oskar, isn't it? No one's mentioned Timo's name to me in a very long time. Please, sit down."

The years had taken a toll on him. No longer the upright, business-like character I remembered, he sat with sloped shoulders, stooped over his table, a patchy beard half-covering a scar on his jaw.

"How's Frau Gumpert?"

"She left me long ago, before the war started. Went back to England. I couldn't blame her. We were never the same after Timo died. She locked herself away all day, crying, terrified the Nazis would throw her in prison or worse."

I nodded sympathetically.

"And Limmeridge? Do you still live there?"

"Oh, no. The Gestapo seized my home and assets long ago, in '36. Accused me of laundering Jewish money and locked me up. I was let go before the war began and found work handling financial accounts for friends, and friends of friends. Home now is Friedland, twelve kilometres south of here. Not a terrible place, other than the refugee camp. You?"

He glanced at my left hand.

"Married now, I see?"

Despite his sad story, it felt good to hear his familiar voice. A well of emotion swelled inside me and I almost reached across the table to hug him.

"We've many things in common, Herr Gumpert, and this too. I married an English woman. Met her while I was a POW over there."

The corners of his mouth lifted a little.

"Luftwaffe, wasn't it?"

I nodded, gazing at Herr Gumpert in shock as his nostrils flared and he let out a long, noisy exhalation.

"The bastard's puppet."

"I'm sorry?"

He stared at me a while, his eyes dancing, head jerking away, before fixing his sight back on me.

"I mean no insult to you, Oskar. I know your father died early in the war."

"Yes. How do you know that?"

"We've a shared past, connections from the Great War. I cannot lie to you. I hated him."

"I always knew, Herr Gumpert. But what was the issue between you? Father never explained."

He hesitated, drinking the last of his coffee, removing his glasses to rub his eyes.

"I swore a promise to Timo and his mother that I'd never tell you this story. But they're both gone now. My brother Helmut and I took flying lessons before the Great War. There was no air force back then. When we joined the *Heer* on the Western Front, they immediately drafted us to fly Fokker M.5s on reconnaissance missions over British and French positions."

I interrupted.

"It later became the Fokker E.1 fighter aircraft."

He peered at me, uninterested, continuing his story.

"A while later, your father joined our unit. He was full of bravado, managed to find drink all the time, but hid his alcoholism well, never once mentioning his lack of flying experience. On his first flight, in low cloud and strong winds over Verdun, he lost control. Crashed into Helmut's tail, sending his plane into a deadly spin. He told our superiors it was my brother's fault."

I closed my eyes for a moment, unable to look Herr Gumpert in the eye. Images of the Harz Mountains, the haze of Belgrade and the scorching sands of Mersa Matruh swirled in my mind, tormenting me.

"Albatros C.VII."

Herr Gumpert frowned.

"What?"

"Father told me he flew an Albatros. I remember those kinds of things. Perhaps it was a genuine accident?"

He brought his cup down hard on its saucer, a thick splinter of china falling to the tablecloth.

"Accident or not, your father wasn't fit to fly. If he'd confessed, maybe I could have forgiven him. He never once said sorry."

I pushed my half-eaten cake away, head dropping. Shocking as it was, his story did not surprise me.

"Mother said you knew all about Father's behaviour in the Great War. She told me in a letter she wrote to me at Gatow."

He paused, as if unsure what to say, closing his eyes for a few seconds.

"She wrote letters all the time, I remember that clearly. Is your mother still alive, Oskar?"

I slumped in my seat as a waitress cleared our cups and plates.

"She went to Czechoslovakia. I don't know what happened to her. I pray every day that I'll see her again."

His head dropped and with it, his haunted eyes, so full of loss, to gaze at the table. Then he looked me in the eye.

"Our lost loved ones cast a long shadow over our lives, Oskar. But they also give us wings to fly."

I looked to the ceiling, noting the perfection of its surface, my eyes now filling with tears.

"I miss her so much, Herr Gumpert, and Timo too. He was my best friend. I've thought about him so often, how things could have been different."

Reaching into the pocket of his shiny, frayed suit jacket, he pulled out a tiny notebook with a tartan cover and laid it on the table before me, putting his hand on top.

"I've kept it with me for a long time. My last real connection to Timo. He mentions me a few times, not always positively."

He pushed it towards me.

"It's best you have it."

I paused, unsure whether to read it in front of Timo's father, but he smiled and gently nodded in encouragement.

"You might not realise how highly he thought of you, Oskar."

I imagined the book might contain records of the library, perhaps a diary. But each and every page I read featured pencil-scribbled notes about me. Flicking through in date order, my eyes fixed on certain phrases: *This boy really believes he can be a lecturer, what a misguided notion*; *although lacking in technical knowledge, his passion for understanding the human mind is undeniable*; *he's my brother in books*; *now surrounded by centuries of knowledge and learning, I find myself missing the company of my friend.*

The final mention of my name brought all the youthful guilt of May 1933 flooding back: *I pray that Oskar is keeping my library safe.*

I gazed at the words a while and breathed in deeply before glancing up at Herr Gumpert and tucking the book away in my pocket.

"You couldn't have done anything to stop what happened to the library, Oskar. All of us have been swept along by the hand of history. Don't blame yourself."

I nodded. His words provided some comfort, if not an excuse. Checking the time on my watch, I rose from my seat to leave.

"Herr Gumpert, I must go. My train leaves in fifteen minutes. There's one more thing."

He got to his feet, moving to the other side of the table, brushing crumbs from his jacket.

"When on leave from the Luftwaffe back in '41, I met Frau Schubert in her Berlin shop. She told me what you did."

I put a hand on his shoulder.

"I've nothing but admiration for you."

His head bobbed downwards for a moment, before rising, his eyes fixed on mine.

"Still, I've no wife, no son," he said bitterly. "Please, go, you'll miss your train."

As I headed to the door, he called out after me.

"Keep flying, Oskar."

*

My surprise meeting with Herr Gumpert had given me hope. It was a reconnection to my past and to my purpose. I had wings to fly again but would have to keep them tucked away for now. I walked into our shabby Berlin home to find Miriam slicing kohlrabi in the tiny kitchen. I embraced her from behind and whispered in her ear.

"We'll make a good life together in Siegen. It's about time we started a family."

She turned, pushing me away from her, lips pressed together.

"What happened today, Oskar?"

"I realised how lucky I am, that's all. I survived the war, have a beautiful wife and a future ahead of me."

Smiling, she took off her apron, and pulled me close.

21

WINGS TO FLY

Tübingen
Summer 1958

Through all the wasted years in Siegen, I never gave up hope of lecturing. So, when finally offered an opportunity by former pharmaceutical executive, now University of Tübingen Vice Chancellor, Berndt Winter, I ignored my wife's wishes and leaped at the chance.

Stood at the lectern, a lecturer proper, scanning rows of students in raked seating before me in Tübingen's smallest, stifling hot, iodine-stinking lecture theatre, I wondered for a while if I had made the right choice. I saw apparitions from my past staring back at me. First, in the disinterested faces—of which there were many—I saw Father, mouthing his disdain. In the happier, more receptive faces, I saw Mother, Grandfather and Timo, smiling their encouragement. They quickly faded, my eyes focusing on the chatting students, using their lecture papers to fan themselves cool.

I peered around me, trying, through my nerves, to take in the detail, to embed this moment in my memory. *Lift, thrust, drag and weight. Lift, thrust, drag and weight. Lift, thrust, drag and weight.* A sink and mini-fume hood, for reaction demonstrations, to my left. Above me, a dramatic ceiling with satin chrome circular down lights, its once-open centre panels, filled in during the war, casting a claustrophobic shadow over the hall.

Winter, who had given me a chance to lecture here, against the Provost's advice, stood looking on from the side, clearing his throat to silence the lively hum of conversation. He approached, giving a single nod of his head before introducing me.

"Students, you'll know already how much I value resilience. Even more than talent. Your new lecturer is a lesson to all of us in the need for persistence. Having wanted to be a university lecturer since the days of the Weimar Republic, Herr Oskar Bachmann is to stand before you for the first time having finally achieved his aims. Please welcome him."

As a polite wave of applause swept around the theatre, I made a last-minute decision, one I could not resist. I had spent weeks typing up and rehearsing my lecture. There was nothing I didn't know about neobehaviourism. But I paused a moment, remembering my locked-away notes in Kirton, suddenly grateful to just be standing here.

Holding the lectern tight, I breathed in deeply.

"Hello, everyone. When I left the United States in the summer of 1940, most of you were babies. I'd no concept of what I was giving up. I knew the world was changing irrevocably, but I imagined I'd return to New York one day, complete my studies and take up a lecturing position. Perhaps I'd be able to afford a little place over on Long Beach, retire there and sit by the ocean, enjoying Blue Bell ice creams. Instead, the Führer took those years away from me and service in the Luftwaffe beckoned. The rest, as they say, is history. What I'm about to do may well end my career at Tübingen before it begins. Rather than give my scheduled lecture, I'm going to give one that's been a lifetime in the making. One that I must give. It's entitled, 'Leaving Fatherland'."

The Vice Chancellor, who was sat in the front row, got to his feet. About to reprimand me, he was silenced by a sharp round of applause from the students. Arrogant as it may have been, I spent the next hour telling them the story of my life.

The lecture theatre remained silent as I told of my struggles at home, my joyous but doomed trip to America and my failures in the Luftwaffe. One statement, laced with regret, but also hope, seemed to resonate more than any other with my students, prompting another wave of applause:

"Above all else, trust your instinct and believe in your purpose."

Winter, stiff lips pinched together throughout, got up again and waved his arms from the side to cut me short.

"Herr Bachmann, thank you. Students have other lectures."

This time, boos rang out around the auditorium. My head dropped a little, but calls of, "Finish" and, "More" spread across the room, becoming louder. I turned to the Vice Chancellor.

"I can have this done in a few minutes, Herr Winter."

There was no cheering or rapturous applause as my last words left my mouth, most students left in quiet conversation. I was certainly no Stanislaw, but the fact that a group of students approached to thank me and ask questions, well, that was enough.

One girl, small, with neat features and red hair, loitered alone for a while, ten metres away from the group. Younger than the others, she stared at me, approaching once or twice for a closer look. I beckoned to her to come over but, having been spotted, she threw her rucksack on her shoulder and rushed away.

When the last student left, I had to deal with Winter. Ever pragmatic, he'd seen the reaction of my audience and reluctantly agreed my lecture had fallen within the boundaries of acceptability. My job was secure.

I left campus in contented mood, strolling back home through the meticulously well-kept botanic gardens that separated our house from the university, my senses acutely alert to the flourishing lushness of the plants. The sweet smell of rhododendron, sunshine yellow of *Dionysia*, mass of purple and pink wild fuchsias and the orchestra of birdsong. For this moment, at least, I felt complete.

Our modest home, paid for by the university, was halfway along Stauffenbergstrasse, the street named after the famous Roman Catholic family. That pleased me. Colonel Schenk Graf von Stauffenberg was behind the failed attempt to execute the Führer in 1944. But Miriam was less enamoured with a home a fraction the size of our last.

As the front door closed behind me, there was an eardrum-piercing scream. I rushed to the garden, my calm contentment shattered. Carla stood there, angrily facing down her brother.

"Oww! Why did you hit me? I'm telling Mother."

"Shut up. You're always criticising our father. I hate you."

Carla ran past me without acknowledgement, sobbing and desperate for her mother's attention. Johann's shoulders slumped as he stormed away to lean against the pear tree.

"You must never hit your sister, Johann. Whatever she might say. You know she has problems. We'll take her to the doctor again."

Johann stared at his feet. My young children were already prodigies. Both were academically brilliant: Carla in history and music, Johann in mathematics. I had spent little time with them as they grew up, often missing birthdays and other special dates. Truth is, I found them an inconvenience as I tried desperately to fulfil my aims and always feared part of me was just like my own father.

"I get annoyed, Papa. Maybe if you told us more about your past, she'd stop accusing you. A letter came for you today. It had a foreign post stamp. Did you see it?"

I rarely received letters and felt strangely unnerved.

"No."

"I'll fetch it for you."

He ran inside, appearing moments later with the letter in his hand. Taking the envelope from him, I pushed it into my pocket, leaving Johann to make my way to the end of our long, narrow garden.

It banked right to the 'overlook', a raised terrace with views of the botanical gardens. Secluded, quiet and shaded by a mature weeping willow (I had regularly noticed my intolerance to direct sunlight, a side effect from my time stranded in the desert), it was my favourite feature here. My only irritation was that its ground-anchored cast-iron bench sat facing back towards the house and my family rather than towards the university.

Sitting down, I lit my pipe. I thought it sad that I wanted to take this moment of glory in, alone, without my family around me. I silently uttered a prayer, more an internal conversation of thanks to God and all those who had inspired me in life, before reaching for the letter in my pocket and examining it. The stamps were Spanish, depicting the Virgin Mary with baby Christ on her lap. It had a place called Reus on the date stamp, now more than three months old. I noticed our Siegen postal address had been crossed out, our new one added in bold typeface.

Tearing it open I saw it was brief and typed out in flawless German, signed in hand by an H. Zinger.

Herr Bachmann,

I pray this letter will reach you. I am a former Bf 109 pilot from Jagdgeschwader 27 and have carried a huge burden of guilt with me ever since I shot down your Junkers over the Libyan desert in the summer of 1942. I was attempting to take out your engines without causing mortal damage to the plane or, if possible, injuring its crew.

My heart beat faster as I was instantly transported back to that cockpit, my mind trying to make sense of his words, forensically checking my memory for anything that could confirm this story. If I'd caught sight of the plane that attacked us, I would have identified it, no problem. I knew the difference between a Messer and a Hurricane. The desert Bf 109s had yellow noses for Christ's sake. But the plane had ghosted out of the cloud above and then disappeared.

I saw the angle and speed of your descent and presumed you all dead. My mission failed. Years later, I met another pilot from Auf 21 at a Luftwaffe reunion. Poehler was his name. He talked about a Bachmann who survived being shot down in the desert that he roomed with at Pingley Camp in England. Said you read a lot of books and had fallen in love with an English woman. I knew it had to be you. I've spent years trying to track you down.

You must know, Bachmann, my attack on your plane was deliberate. But I had very specific orders to avoid killing the crew at all costs. I'm so sorry about your crew mates but I am pleased that you survived the war. My hope is that you can forgive me.

There was no further detail in his letter. No clue as to who gave the orders and why. The whole thing made no sense to me at all.

Glancing up, I saw Miriam striding down the garden towards me, a large kitchen knife in her hand. I shoved the letter back in my pocket as she stopped at the foot of the bank in front of me. She spat out her words brusquely.

"You look like you've seen a ghost. How did the lecture go? I hope you received a standing ovation. Did you not think to come and say hello?"

"The students applauded me. It was unexpected. I'm sorry, the children distracted me."

She raised her eyebrows, continuing to berate me.

"I've sent them to their rooms. Carla was bad-mouthing you again. Perhaps you could talk to her for a change? Answer some of her questions. She's a child, Oskar. She needs her father."

I didn't expect Miriam to be interested in my academic career. She never had been. But her inability to recognise a moment of significance for me with any sense of grace sparked a quiet fury inside me. It was further proof our marriage was dying. I stayed silent, gazing across the garden.

"There's nothing wrong with earning a good wage and keeping your family happy, Oskar. You'd a real career in Siegen and some money. Now you've dragged us here. Any novelty you represent to the students will wear off."

She was right. I had been taking private psychiatry bookings and had built a healthy list of clients in Siegen.

"Why don't you like Tübingen, Miriam? It's beautiful here."

She had already turned, marching back towards the kitchen, calling over her shoulder.

"Dinner in half an hour. *Schweinefleisch*!"

The scorching afternoon turned to balmy early evening. I studied the letter again. Who the hell gave this order and more importantly, why? Shooting a plane down without killing its crew is next to impossible. Thinking about it gave me a banging headache. Heading back inside the house, I took aspirin before joining the dinner table already occupied by Miriam, Carla and Johann. Ever eager to please, my son made his customary offer.

"Should I say grace, Father?"

I nodded, more concerned with the intent behind Miriam and Carla's stony faces. We ate in silence, with only Johann offering the occasional route to conversation.

"Did the students like your talk, Papa?"

"They did. I can't tell you how good it felt to give it, Johann. I wish you all could've been there."

Tutting, Miriam pushed her half-eaten plate of food in front of her. She got up, putting both hands on the back of her chair, furious eyes staring at me.

"I didn't mind coming to Germany. You convinced me the future was full of opportunity. I happily lived in that rat-infested tip in Berlin. If it weren't for me, we'd still be there. You've put me through things I won't mention in front of the children. Why couldn't you repay me with a normal, happy life? Money. Our own house. Why?"

"Miriam, please. Can we speak in private?"

Johann began to sob, while his sister jumped to her feet, putting her hands on her hips.

"Why, Father? Is it because you're a Nazi?"

Lurching from the table, I knocked over a glass of water, heart beating hard, perspiration appearing on my forehead. I didn't want to be with my family.

"It's been a long day, and I have a headache. I'm going to go to bed. Carla, go to your room immediately. Johann, help your mother with the dishes."

*

I lay awake for over an hour, my mind turning over a myriad of thoughts. Who was that student who had lingered in the lecture theatre? She wanted to speak to me but hadn't come forward. I pondered the letter again too, taking it from its envelope and straining to read it in the dim light of our bedroom. It made my head throb.

By morning, after a night of broken sleep and dreams, my head felt trapped in a gradually tightening vice. I reached out to my bedside table, finding the pethidine prescribed by the Siegen physician, who had repeatedly assured me nothing was seriously wrong. My headaches, he said, were a lingering side-effect from my desert crash and extreme dehydration. I never believed him. Putting the bullet-sized pill in my mouth, I glanced at the sleeping Miriam and the quarter-filled glass of water next to me, which was enough to wash it down my throat.

I snoozed for an hour, long enough to clear my head, and began some stretches at the bottom of our bed. Miriam stirred.

"Oskar, what are you doing?"

She frowned, eyes shut tight.

"Exercising. I want to take us out for lunch today."

Her eyes blinked open as she pushed herself upright in the bed. She regularly complained she was sick of having to cook. Her tone softened.

"Well, that would be nice. Can I choose where we go?"

I tucked my pyjamas under my pillows. Miriam's father had always treated his children to the best food and restaurants. She wouldn't be choosing anywhere cheap.

"Okay. But, please, a place we can take the children comfortably."

*

The Hofbräuhaus, one of the most exclusive restaurants in Tübingen, buzzed with conversation as we arrived. Well-dressed diners stared as we were shown to a table made up specially in a crowded corner under an arch. There was barely enough room on the table for us, but the menu was excellent.

Gulasch and *Spätzle*, *Nürnberger*, *Krakauer* and *Bratwurst*, *Haxe*. Swallowing hard as I looked at the price list, Johann immediately sensed my unease.

"Don't worry, Father. I can order from the starter menu."

A woman at an adjacent table looked over at us, contemptuously. Miriam bristled.

"Shh. Will you be quiet, Johann? We never come out to eat and will not be scrimping today."

I glared at Miriam but had no appetite to fight. Not in public. We ate again in near silence, over-attentive waiters seeming to hurry us along. Miriam and Carla swapped notes on their meals—the most expensive dishes on the menu.

Occasionally, I caught Miriam staring at me as I ate. With tables cleared, we allowed the children to explore the restaurant garden, ordering a digestif to finish. Miriam peered around the restaurant, returning polite smiles from nearby tables.

"Did you enjoy your meal?"

"It was reasonable. The most enjoyable thing was not having to cook myself. All the women I've met in Tübingen eat out at least twice a week."

"Can you please leave this topic alone, Miriam?"

"That's easy for you to say. It's me living a life I don't want to live. Not you. Perhaps you've forgotten. While I suffered pre-eclampsia, you were enjoying yourself, unreachable in Cologne. We nearly lost Carla."

"Not this again. I had a year's work after my meeting there. Do you not remember?"

Miriam stared, shaking her head. The waiter brought the bill on a silver platter, and I wrote the cheque. Before the ink was dry on it, Miriam coolly delivered her ultimatum.

"I want us to separate, Oskar. It's best for us to be apart for a while. I'm going back to England. The children will come with me."

Stunned, I didn't know how to respond, so I did not. She collected the children and paused by the table. The tension made Johann sob.

"It didn't have to be like this, Oskar. You can write to me in Kirton, if you wish. Goodbye."

22
THE COUCH

Three days later

The quiet tap on the door of my now nearly empty house could not have come at a worse time. As the afternoon light faded, I had been drinking whisky to numb my loneliness and the pain I felt as a result of my family leaving me. I could not work out exactly how I felt. Not angry; closer to empty.

Miriam and the children's departure must have been planned. No doubt her father had booked the flights. By now they would all be back in Kirton enjoying home-cooked meals. Miriam explaining why she had left me. I wondered if the children would miss me. Johann, perhaps. Yesterday a van had arrived to collect almost all the possessions we had gathered in eleven years of marriage. Miriam and I had fought over a few things. I had been left with a couch, table and two chairs, a bed and a wardrobe but, most importantly, my books.

Leaving the table, where I had pored over the few photographs I had of Johann and Carla, I walked slowly to the door, hesitating for a moment, focusing, in an attempt to appear sober. There on the doorstep stood the same small, red-haired girl who had loitered then scurried away after my

Tübingen lecture. I noticed that the skin of her face had a reddy-brown hue covering a multitude of freckles.

"Hello, Herr Bachmann. I hope I haven't caught you at a bad time?"

"Oh, good evening. You're a student, correct?"

She nodded and smiled knowingly in a way I first thought flirtatious, but I then realised it was simply that she could tell I had been drinking.

"Well, how can I help?"

"It's nothing to do with academic work."

"I see."

Her admission concerned me. Why would a student knock on my door if not to ask about their studies?

"You mentioned in the lecture you gave that you had practised psychiatry before becoming a lecturer. I wondered if you could help me."

"Well, I—"

"Please. I can pay and I know you could help me."

Opening her purse, she brazenly displayed a large wad of Deutsche Mark notes. It was perhaps bad judgement, especially given my state of partial drunkenness, but I opened the door fully to let her in.

"Please take a seat on the couch. I won't be a moment."

Making my way to the kitchen, I turned on the tap and gulped down three glasses of water one after the other. The leftovers of last night's meal lay on the side. Without hesitation, I lifted the plate to my mouth and shovelled in a few potatoes, cold gravy and a rind of fat. Anything to soak up the alcohol.

When I'd finished chewing, I stuck my head around the door and found my guest looking at the photos on the table.

"Would you like coffee? Sorry, I didn't catch your name."

Flushing red, she turned.

"I'm Faustyna, and yes, please."

After drinking her coffee, she got comfortable on the couch, while I placed my chair at a diagonal from where she lay.

"So, tell me how you decided to come here."

"I've been feeling very lost lately. I've partied a bit too hard. It's made me tired, anxious. I'm not sure if I should stay at university."

"Okay. Was there a specific time when you started to feel this way?"

"I've always felt lost to an extent. I think it's because I never knew my parents."

"Oh. What happened to them?"

"Mother died in the war. I never knew my father. When I was a little girl, Grandfather took me to live with him in Ecuador, just as the war ended. Place called Zamora, near the Andes. I hated it there. Stray dogs barking all day and, at night, noisy Italians arriving in their hordes.

"Grandfather drank heavily. Took tranquillisers too. When he was drunk, he talked about a woman he loved but couldn't be with. I know he felt guilty about some of the things he did during the war. His housemaid found him dead in bed last week."

"I'm sorry. Was your grandfather your only family?"

She nodded.

"I think so."

"You don't sound too sure."

"There were just some things that Grandfather said, mainly when he was drunk, that made me wonder. I meant what I said about being able to pay you. You see, Grandfather was a very wealthy man, and I'm getting a lot of his money. Should help with this."

Letting the coat she had kept on this whole time fall away, she revealed her pregnant belly and began to stroke it.

"Are those pictures on the table your children? Where are they?"

The last thing I wanted to do was to discuss my own family.

"Please, let's keep the focus on you. By the way, you should avoid being too open about your wealth."

Lowering her head, she broke eye contact with me for a moment. I started to sense this was more of a social visit from a lonely student.

"Is your pregnancy the reason you want to give up university? I might be able to find you some help. What happened to the father?"

"Just like Mother when pregnant with me, the father never knew he made me pregnant. It's amazing how we all turn out like our parents. Don't you think, Herr Bachmann?"

I felt winded by her comment. Part of me wanted to disagree, to say we were all a blank slate and had no excuses for repeating our parents' mistakes. But glancing back at the picture of my children, I realised I had alienated them just as my father did with me. Not through violence, but through ignoring their needs, distancing myself from them. I held my head in my hands for a while, wishing I could speak to them both. It was too late.

"Are *you* okay, Herr Bachmann?"

I looked up at her, quickly refocusing.

"If you don't mind me saying, Faustyna, you don't *seem* depressed, or anxious for that matter. I suggest you try some relaxation techniques. Wait a moment, I have some information."

Making my way up the stairs, I stopped in the half-landing bathroom to relieve myself, splashing my face with cold water after washing my hands. Pulling a sheet on breathing techniques from my case, I made my way back downstairs.

As I turned into the living room, I stopped in my tracks. The couch was empty. Moving to the table, I spotted that three twenty-Deutsche-Mark bills had been left there, next to a hastily scribbled note:

Thanks. Enjoyed talking to you. Feels like we have some things in common.

*

Mühlstraße, Tübingen
Christmas 1958

My Christmas tree, bought from a market trader in Tübingen, was much like the apartment I had recently moved into on the edge of the old town: tiny. The tree was a quarter the size of those I hauled into our Stauffenbergstrasse house from the spruce-tree plot in the botanic gardens. I decorated it with one trinket for every person I had lost from my life then sat alone, staring at the pathetic excuse for Christmas celebration, missing my family desperately. I had spent too little time with them over the past few years. Now they were gone. Pouring myself a brandy, I thought of Mother and Father, then Emil, wondering if we might have been together had things been different. Part of me held out hope that Mother was still alive, living out her days behind the Iron Curtain, hoping one day we could be reunited.

A colleague in the Economics Department had told me about a search agent in East Berlin who was trusted by the Stasi to deal with westerners using approved channels to locate missing persons in the Soviet Bloc. A file would be created that required approval by the authorities before any correspondence could be entered into.

I resolved, once more, to find her, and would start tonight. Pouring myself another brandy, I picked up the business card from the table and dialled the number. Given Khrushchev's threat to the west just weeks before that they should pull out of Berlin, the call alone felt like a risk.

After a brief delay there was a click, and then Herr Kurschat answered his phone.

"Hello, who's this?"

The line failed momentarily, then reconnected.

"Herr Kurschat, my name is Bachmann. I was given your name by my colleague, Herr Riedle. I need your help."

I explained to him, choosing my expressions carefully, how I had not seen Mother since early in the war. The line was persistently interrupted by delays and clicking sounds as the Stasi tape recorder broke down and restarted (I had heard this was common practice for calls to the east). We agreed that I would write to him with a detailed request and he would see what he could do. It was the best I could hope for.

*

Wuppertal
Spring 1959

Shifting on the spot outside busy Wuppertal station, I turned away at first, not wanting to hold Opa's gaze, as his wheeled chariot weaved through the crowd towards me. Pushed by Frau Schilling, the daughter of an old colleague, with whom he now lived, his skeletal frame perched like a hummingbird on an oak branch in the heavy-duty wheelchair. I didn't want him to sense my upset, but seeing his old skin, wrinkled like the dried fish he once hung in his kitchen at home, made my voice break as I waved and said my hello. As the chair stopped a metre before me, I could not help but get on my knees to embrace him, as I thought of wasted time. A sense of guilt came over me.

Frau Schilling, an unforgiving woman, whose lips were as thin as her personality, remained silent and stared as I rose to my feet, keeping hold of Opa's cold and twisted hand.

"Thank you for bringing him to meet me here. I can bring him back to your home if you'll leave me the address."

Shaking her head, she frowned, eyes narrowing.

"No, it's best we meet back here, at four, no later. The cold gets into his broken hip joints."

I wondered, briefly, why she insisted on meeting back at the station and not their shared home, given I had told her by letter that my overnight train would not leave until nine o'clock. But I did not press the point.

300

Hauling Opa's chair up onto a bus and parking him in the luggage area, I sat in the chair across from him. He had moved back to his birthplace, nearly three hundred miles from Tübingen, after his fall a couple of years earlier. Although I had written to him, often asking him for his own memories of my father, this was my first visit here.

I gazed across into Opa's grey-ringed, tired old eyes, those deep chambers into the past, knowing this would be the last time I would be with him. He was quiet now, not the animated, conversational man of my memories. I knew I had to use these precious hours wisely. As the bus approached a drop-off point, at the bottom of a hilly street, he spoke to me.

"We're going to collect something, Oskar."

Departing the bus, I peered up tree-lined Sadowastrasse. Gauging its steepness, I hoped I had the energy to push Opa up it. The irony of my now wheelchair-bound grandfather having chosen to move back to the city with the most precipitous streets in Germany was not lost on me. We passed several crossroads, the street seeming to get steeper at each of them. My war wounded thighs burned. After ten minutes I stopped, sweating and struggling for breath, while Opa nonchalantly tipped his head to greet a group of vibrant young women in colourful berets and head wraps. We moved on again and just as I reached the point of exhaustion, Opa said the words I had been waiting for.

"Stop here, Oskar."

Putting my feet beside the bicycle-sized rear wheels to stop the wheelchair rolling back, I leaned on its handles to compose myself, staring at my feet as he explained with weary voice where we were. Glancing to my left, I saw we were alongside a large white mansion house, on the corner of a converging street, its centrepiece a grand arched and columned window, with a combination bearded-man-and-foliage grotesque above it.

"That's where I was born, Oskar. Your father too. It's also the house in which your grandmother died giving birth to him."

I stared at the building a while, contemplating his words.

"You always told me Grandmother left you, Opa, when father was young."

"Well, that's not a lie, is it? I didn't want you to blame your father for killing your grandmother, but that's what happened."

I sensed bitterness in his words and felt sure he did not think this exchange of life worth it.

"I've been in correspondence with the people who own it now. They found something old in the basement. I thought you might be interested in having it, given you know so little about your father."

As I pushed Opa up the path to the front door, I speculated on what might be waiting for me behind it, deciding it most likely to be some form of family heirloom.

The grand door with its inlaid wrought ironwork opened to reveal a mother, happy but flustered, her three young children pushing their heads between her legs and arms and around her torso for attention.

"Good morning. Sorry about this. You must be Herr Bachmann."

"Hello. Yes. This is my grandson, Oskar."

She nodded and showed us inside, the excited children squealing as they ran off in all directions. Shutting the door, she pointed to a cardboard box, her children calling from different rooms.

"That's it. Please take it."

I acknowledged her goodwill and picked up the box, disappointed at its light weight. Slotting it on the shelf beneath Grandfather's wheelchair seat, I pushed the chair back out into the street.

As I struggled to keep control of the wheelchair as we moved back downhill, Opa's own knuckles white on its handles, he turned his head to the right.

"There are things in that box that I have not seen in the whole of your lifetime."

*

Grandfather held the lunch menu close to his face, reading the options out loud.

"*Schweinebauch*, *Maultaschen*, *Spinatsalad*. Nothing here takes my fancy, Oskar. There's no fish. I guess I'll have the chicken soup with herb dumplings."

After a thirty-minute walk, I had found a dowdy traditional restaurant next to the Wupper river. Grandfather knew I was itching to look inside the box and seemed to enjoy keeping me waiting.

"So, you haven't bothered seeing me in years. Is there something you need to ask me?"

"I'm sorry, Opa, really I am. I've been so busy with university work. There's no excuse though. I'm so pleased I'm here now."

He smiled.

"I'm pleased you got to teach in a free Germany, Oskar. I had my doubts it would ever happen, but you proved me wrong. What about your family?"

I paused, putting my fork repeatedly through the pile of Wurstsalat on my plate.

"Well?"

"They've gone, Opa. Back to England. I think I drove them away with my obsessions."

Grandfather lowered his head, bringing his serviette up to his mouth as he sank back into his chair.

"Oh, dear. I'm sorry."

"I've spent too long trying to understand Father and buried in books. I still don't know why he rejected me and beat me so badly. It's eaten at me my whole life, Opa. My studies failed to give me a real answer."

"Well, I never beat *him*, Oskar. There were times I felt like it. But I realised it was me wanting to take out my frustrations at being a single dad. He was a good boy, really. Not bright, but good."

"Opa, I remember once overhearing an argument between my parents. It stuck with me. Mama chided Papa for not accepting help from you. What did she mean? She wrote me a letter at pilot school claiming Papa did not come home after the war until 1920. Do you know anything about this?"

Putting down his spoon, Opa sighed and nodded slowly.

"Your mother was right on both counts. I offered him a job after the war, helping me on the schools' programme. We needed research done. I thought he might be able to help. He refused, didn't want anything to do with his 'socialist' father."

"And his coming home later?"

"Yes, that's true. But I can't be sure why. Your mother never spoke about it."

"Is there anything at all you can think of that made him the way he was, Opa? Anything?"

He sighed, looking down at the table mat in front of him before raising his head and looking me in the eye.

"Maybe it's time to open that box, Oskar."

I spent a few moments gazing at the old pictures of Opa and my father. There was one of them both on bicycles, grinning, another of them wearing rucksacks on the side of a mountain. There was a photograph of a woman in a black, corseted dress, hair swept back behind her head. She sat at an angle with a serious stare, her fingers pressed together in a triangle on her lap.

"That's your grandmother. She didn't normally look so serious."

I nodded and smiled. There were no pictures of her in our Halbe house. Now I understood why.

"They're nice pictures, but they tell me nothing, Opa."

"Keep digging."

I pushed my hand further down into the box. At the bottom I felt a pile of papers, which I carefully pulled free.

There was a school report, an old Bible and a letter from a doctor. But it was a 'Certificate of Discharge', dated November 1914, that brought a sharp and immediate intake of breath as

305

I saw it. My mind went into overdrive. Father had remained in the military for the duration of the war. I was sure of it. If this date was accurate, he could not have flown an Albatros over Belgium. Herr Gumpert must have been right.

My eyes darted across the 'Particulars' part of the form and then down to the medical certificate. Next to 'Disability with Description' were three words: *Alcoholism. Shell shock*. Next to 'Medical Category' were the words, *Permanently unfit for labour*. The paper had been signed by the medical officer.

I peered at Opa, my heart beating hard and fast. I wanted him to give me answers, but his once-sharp mind no longer worked as a well-tuned engine. As he gently pushed his half-full bowl towards me, he laid a bony hand on mine.

"Your father was a terrible pilot, and not a very good research scientist either. He knew you were bright, what you could do with the right opportunity. All he wanted was for you to right his wrongs, live the pilot dream he never realised."

A flicker of a smile travelled across Opa's lips and then his old head bobbed, eyelids drooping as he fell asleep.

LAST DAYS

St Marien-Krankenhaus Hospital, Berlin
September 1976

The dull, battleship-grey walls of St Marien-Krankenhaus, and the monotone voice of Berliner Rundfunk's presenter, broadcast from a small, crackling speaker above me, were strangely comforting as my eyelids flicked open. My entire body lay wet with sweat. I gasped for breath. My thirty-year-old dream had returned. I turned my head, now covered in hair as white as snow, to see delicate pink roses and a light mist filling the view from my window. The rolling sand dunes and shimmering sunlight of my dream faded as quickly as my breathing slowed. This was my resting place now, but I still had things to do.

It had been eighteen years since Miriam left me. She waited until I at least had some money before she divorced me though. The children spent their teenage years in England, before returning here as adults. The Germany of the mid-1970s offered slightly more opportunity than recession-hit Britain. It had been a struggle to resurrect any kind of relationship with them, for different reasons. Carla had become a Communist. She hated the fact I fought for Hitler and would never let me forget it. Johann, however, seemed to hold romantic views about me and my role in the war, which I found ridiculous. They had both visited me in this place, though, sensing my demise close. My quest to find Mother stalled completely when the Wall separated east from west in August 1961, the year after Opa died. I had not completely given up hope of finding her though.

Suddenly, my atrophied legs jerked stiff and straight, heels slamming against the wooden footboard of my bed, knocking my 'death notes' to the floor. The clatter spoiled the still morning quiet on Blütental Ward, prompting unconscious murmurs of protest from neighbouring beds. My nightmare was always the same. Paralysed, I lay on a sandy bank, face to face with a statue-still black cobra, my bone-dry mouth sucking in dust. The burning hot sand flowed, like a steady stream, endlessly downhill around the snake's body and over mine. A bayonet flashed past my left ear, plunging into the sand, centimetres from my sunburned nose. I turned to see Father looming above me.

The familiar sounds of thin rubber rolling over cracked tiles and of rattling metal brought me fully back to my present reality on the ward. The 'drug buggy' made its first visit of the day, pushed along by Nurse Edna. She parked the trolley, with its rusted bolts and dented shelves, close to my feet. They were now free of the tight, stiff bedsheets—a constant reminder of my days at Pingley Camp—that enveloped my deathbed-in-waiting.

When I arrived here, the doctors gave me months to live. They told me they would try to slow the progress of my disease. It was a neurodegenerative condition. I would only deteriorate until a point at which my muscles and breathing finally succumbed. Certain death. Not yet though. I needed to focus. The friendliest nurse on the ward could help me.

Edna let out a groan, her uniform stretched to breaking point as she stooped to gather my clipboard and scattered papers from the floor. She struggled to stand straight, clearing her throat before pushing her spectacles to the end of her nose to look over them, focusing on the notes. Humming, her eyes glanced lazily across the first and second sheets of paper as she soaked up the numbers and remarks, making sense of them.

"Herr Bachmann, how are you this morning?"

My days in this place had been the worst of my life. Captivity was familiar to me, but as a POW I always believed freedom was coming, my release possible. Now, my only escape would be into the darkness.

"The same as this morning, Nurse, and yesterday. And the day before. It's nice of you to ask though."

Thrusting a thermometer into my mouth, she proceeded to check pulse and blood pressure.

"Oh well, at least that's not worse."

She returned to the end of my bed, pulling a pen from her breast pocket and scribbling on my records.

"Sit up, please. I have your medication."

I had never been able to place Edna's accent. With the surname Horvat, was she perhaps a Yugoslav? I'm glad she didn't know of my past. She would have enough reason to hate me.

Reaching up to the red plastic triangle dangling above my chest, I hauled myself upright, while she pushed two pillows in behind my back.

"Nurse Edna. Will you do something for me?"

She stared at me briefly, then looked away out of the window, her mind drifting to the past.

"It depends on what. Do you know, today is exactly the eighth anniversary of me and my brother arriving in Berlin? Part of the labour agreement. I remember flying into East Berlin, scared stiff of the police with their snarling dogs and Kalashnikovs. We caught a bus to the west, ended up staying in a basement with some other girls looking to train as nurses."

Suddenly, her eyes darted back and focused on mine.

"Is it legal? Are you trying to smuggle something in? I don't want to be expelled."

"No, it's nothing like that. I want you to help me to hire a private investigator."

She raised her eyebrows as she put a set of differently coloured tablets down in front of me, alongside a glass of water and a little plastic cup full of a sticky bright-pink liquid.

"Why do you need a detective? If you don't mind me asking."

I paused, wondering if I should reveal my reasons, before deciding I trusted her.

"I'm trying to find out what happened to my mother. During the war."

Nurse Edna's head dropped for a moment, then rose slowly, her eyes glistening.

"I know how it feels to lose a parent, Herr Bachmann. I'm from Belgrade, lost both of mine in the Luftwaffe bombardment of '41. I was only fourteen."

Her words seemed to slow as she said them, as I remembered that awful night more than thirty years earlier. I consoled myself that I had never been a bomber, never killed a civilian on any flight I was involved in. I swallowed hard, changing the subject.

"What's this blue tablet, Nurse? It's not familiar."

"A new antipsychotic. Doctor Anders prescribed it for you. It will help stop your nightmares. Did you have one this morning? I noticed you woke with a start."

I nodded, tipping the pink gloop down my throat. It tasted like clove oil and stuck to my tongue and tonsils as I tried to swallow. Next, I threw the orange pill and one of the white ones into my mouth, gulping the lukewarm water from the glass to wash them down.

"Know all about antipsychotics, Nurse. Did I mention I studied psychiatry, and practised it for a while? I remember electroconvulsive therapy, hydrotherapy and insulin comas."

"I'm sorry, what?"

Edna, who had appeared lost in thought again, put her hand gently on my arm.

"I'll help you find an investigator, but only if you can get me another of those Heinrich Böll books."

I smiled and took another gulp of water as she moved on to deal with a fellow patient, and soon drifted back to sleep.

*

A steady morning breeze brushed across my face as I woke, the few remaining strands of hair on my scalp tickling my forehead. The tall double window at the end of the ward, its metal frame coated in chipped cream gloss paint, had been left ajar to cool the ward during the unusually warm, still night.

311

Beyond it, banks of green grass edged with pink, red and purple roses painted a pretty picture. I wondered why the outside of this place appeared so welcoming compared with its gloomy interior.

A distant shrill of children shouting and laughing brought me back to full consciousness. I gazed across at Davor, a forty-nine-year-old cancer patient, in the bed opposite as the nurses attended to him, marvelling at his ability to smile, despite his bleak prognosis and obvious pain. I had tried to help him, in my own way, by reading books in the library about herbal remedies and suggesting he might try bromelain and folic acid. He always smiled politely, knowing he was way past such treatment.

After a breakfast of cold porridge and ripe banana, my morning medication and a bed bath from an overly zealous nurse with a Viking helmet tattooed on his forearm, I picked up a copy of the *Berliner Morgenpost* left on my bed and secretly enjoyed reading about the machinations of this divided city of ours.

After an hour, my heavy eyes spotted a headline that made my heart beat a little faster: 'Independent Berlin Bookshop to Close at Year End'. The bookshop in question was Greta Schubert's Bücherstube. Frau Schubert had died, legally protecting the future use of the shop 'for the promotion of art, literature and freedom'. With no one having any interest in running the business this way, a successful legal challenge required the premises to be closed and redeveloped.

The shop had been one of the first to be granted a licence after the Allied occupation. I had been back half a dozen times since that first visit in 1941, spending hours thumbing through the books, chatting to the ebullient Frau Schubert. Herr Gumpert's legacy was entwined there too. I could not let it close.

*

What seemed like only moments later, my youngest child gently shook my shoulder.

"Father, Father. Wake up. It's Johann."

My leaden eyelids took time to lift. As if looking back in time, there stood a figure, smiling awkwardly, at the foot of the bed, holding a small parcel in his hand. In my mind's eye, I saw a young boy in a tweed short suit with long socks and bow tie, his hair combed to one side.

"Johann, sit."

I gestured wearily towards the chair beside my bed. Pushing his spectacles up his nose, he took a few steps towards me, pushing the parcel gently into my hands.

"I've brought you a gift, Father. Please, open it. I hope you like it."

"A gift? It's not my birthday until next month."

I shook the tightly wrapped package. It gave no clues. I pointed to my bedside drawer.

"Please open it and pass me the wooden case inside."

My son foraged around for a while, his face lighting up as he pulled the narrow mahogany case, edged in ivory, from the drawer.

"Is this it, Father?"

I nodded.

Johann passed me the box, upside down. I turned it over,

313

revealing the inlaid Luftwaffe insignia on top. The flying eagle was heavily scratched around the edges of her wings, the swastika almost gone.

The box had lain unopened in my drawer since my arrival at St Marien-Krankenhaus. Inside it was my last emblem of life in the Luftwaffe. I inspected it, noticing its curved edges, the small chips in the wood at one end. In Sicily, I had reluctantly accepted it from a second lieutenant, a veteran of the Great War and perhaps a comrade of my father's. I wondered how many hours Carla had dedicated to defacing it.

"Father?"

As Johann stared at me in anticipation, I recalled the times I had tried in vain to attract my own father's attention. I had not been much more attentive to my own children but had never beaten them. Mine was more of a long-term, casual lack of interest. Once, I had mistaken Carla for someone else's child at her own birthday party. She never forgot that.

Slowly, I opened the box, peering inside at the miniature dagger sat snugly in a purple velvet surround. Its red handle was wrapped in coiled wire, the pommel comprising a round circle with a gold swastika in the middle. The same design also sat across the tiny hand guard. On the blade, in tiny millimetre-tall letters, was the name Paul Weyersberg.

I looked across to Johann.

"I had a full-size one of these too. The Canadians took it from me in the desert. The Luftwaffe gave these miniature replicas as awards for service to Hitler. They only made a hundred of this model. It's an original, produced in 1934 and made of nickel. Much more valuable than the later aluminium versions."

314

My son stood, transfixed.

"It's fascinating, Father. Why have you never shown me it before?"

"I don't like to talk about the war, Johann. It causes trouble. The war was over a long time ago and I would rather it had never happened."

"But I want you to tell me about your wartime adventures."

Johann shifted his body weight from one foot to another, wringing his hands. He had always blamed Carla for stealing away the details of my life. I had sympathy for him, but not for his ridiculous naïvety. I pointed the end of the replica knife at Johann.

"My son, this will soon be yours."

"Not yet, Father. Please, tell me more about what happened to you in the past. What about your life in New York?"

As Johann spoke, I used the small knife to slice the tape on all four sides of the gift box. I opened it to find a small but beautiful green Ju 88 sat tilted on a brass stand, attached to a polished wooden base. Turning it over, I found the inscription: *For Papa. Love, your son, Johann. September 1976.*

Johann's sentiment was pure, well meant. It represented a moment of wholehearted love. My mind drifted back to childhood and my longing for an embrace from my unmoving father after I had gotten lost in those Harz woods. Just like my Papa, my heart was cold.

"Why have you bought this for me?"

He shuffled slowly to the other side of my bed, nearest my head, gazing down at me, before gently placing his hand on my shoulder.

"I'm proud of you, Papa. The bullies at school picked on

315

me because of my size and clumsiness. Knowing a little about your past made me strong. Their fathers were postmen or bakers. Mine was a Luftwaffe pilot. Not everyone in Germany is ashamed of the war. There are people who still believe—"

"Believe what, Johann? That the Reich will rise again? I pray that will never happen. Where on earth did you obtain this model?"

"I travelled to Mainz. My friend knew a shopkeeper there who kept undercover replicas of all our wartime planes and tanks. He obtained this one especially for me."

I shook my head.

"What about the rest of my career? Are you proud of that?"

The tension in my voice made him defensive.

"Of course, Father."

"It's a fine model. Please, put it away in the drawer."

Disappointed at me hiding his gift away, he attempted to embrace me before I could finish thanking him, holding tight, making me sweat. I pushed him away.

"Father, there's something else I wanted to mention."

He looked down at his lap, slowly rubbing his hands together.

"Well?"

"Papa, it's hard to describe. I'm sure someone's been following me. Not only recently, for a long time."

"Why did you not say something before? It could be delusional disorder."

"I didn't want you to worry about me, Father."

His revelation filled me with a sense of dread, but not surprise.

24

LOTTE

St Marien-Krankenhaus Hospital, Berlin
October 1976

"I mainly investigate adultery, sometimes dubious insurance claims."

Berchtwald Huber pinched out the end of his cigarette with a brown-tipped finger and thumb and slouched down in the seat beside my bed.

Keeping his raincoat buttoned to the top, he ran a hand through his dark, shoulder-length hair and grinned.

"I'm a former BKA officer, but don't worry, I'm no fascist."

He pushed his business card into my shaking hand.

"My rates are on the back of the card. What is it you want me to do?"

I paused. Having asked Edna to find me a detective, I now felt nervous revealing painful family details to this dubious stranger.

"Have you done any missing person investigations?"

"A few. Years back. Mainly lowlife: drug addicts, prostitutes, petty criminals. Used to be hundreds of them hanging around Club Unlimited in Genthinerstrasse before the authorities cleared it up."

Huber gave an exaggerated smirk, the thin line of stubbly hair on his top lip making the shape of a recoiling caterpillar under attack.

"Never found one of them. Probably because they were already in a wooden box before I began looking."

"I see. Perhaps I should find someone else..."

"Up to you. I've plenty to keep me busy."

Huber jumped up and, without asking, took a gulp of water from the glass on my bedside table.

"I'll see you around."

As he made his way to the door, I realised there might not be many investigators prepared to work for a dying man.

"Herr Huber. Wait. Come back."

He turned and walked slowly back to the end of my bed, a half-smile on his face.

"Please, sit down. Let me explain what I'd like you to do for me."

He sat, his eyes darting around my bed and table, before focusing on the opened packet of Bahlsen lying on the shelf.

"Go ahead if you're hungry."

He grabbed the packet, pulling out three biscuits, shoving them in his mouth whole, one after the other.

"I want you to find out what happened to my mother. She moved to Czechoslovakia from our home in Halbe early in the war. I never saw her again."

His mood changed as I spoke. He unbuttoned his coat and pulled out a small notebook and pencil, brushing away spat-out biscuit remnants as he spoke.

"Okay, I can help you with that. But I need to know everything about your mother. All you know and remember about her. The rest of your family too."

Huber sat and listened for an hour as I recalled every detail about my mother and what I knew of her life, until his notepad was filled, and he dug in his pocket for a spare.

"There's one other thing, Herr Huber. I've felt, on many occasions, as if someone has been following me. I'm a rational person and have tried to explain this away, but I've absolutely no doubt it's true. My son has experienced the same. Perhaps, in some way, this is related to Mother's disappearance?"

He got to his feet, eager, after such a long stay, to leave.

"Maybe. My primary investigation may throw something up to explain this. How will you be paying? My fee is six thousand Deutsche Marks. And a further four thousand on the successful conclusion of the case. I can start work with a two thousand deposit."

I swallowed hard. That amount would make a big dent in my savings, but time was short. I had to go ahead.

"What do you mean by 'successful conclusion'?"

"Written, irrefutable evidence as to the fate of your mother and, with luck, information on any party that may have been tracking you. I'll outline all of this in a contract."

"Very well. If you leave your details with Nurse Edna, I'll arrange payment."

Huber stepped forward and held out an arm. I shook his hand and nodded.

He left, turning back near the door to call out: "I'll keep you updated!"

*

A hot, moist, Kirschwasser-infused breath wrapped around my face and woke me. Besides the brandy, the smell of unwashed hair, laden with tobacco smoke and cooking odours, hung around my head, creating a pungent cavern. I opened my eyes to see my daughter glaring down at me, inches above my nose.

"Carla. Wh-what are you doing here? What time is it?"

She didn't reply, instead peering into my eyes without blinking. Gently, I tried to push her away to a comfortable distance. She held her position, steely eyed, unresponsive. Then, like a wolf caught in a snare trap, she let out a long, guttural scream laced with a primeval stress. Her saliva hit my face, her cries deafening me and echoing off the high ceiling and walls of the ward. Every conscious patient turned towards my bed, fearing another escapee from the psychiatric ward was on the loose. A young nurse appeared, put her hand on Carla's shoulder and gently pulled her away.

"Please, you must be quiet now. You're upsetting the other patients. Be calm, or you'll have to leave."

Slumping into the seat beside my bed, Carla's head dropped, her shoulders rising and falling. Her paranoia began as a child. I had diagnosed her myself but the doctors we had approached had been of little help. Her feelings towards me made it impossible for me to treat her.

The nurse's hand rested comfortingly on her for a while, but as my daughter cried quietly, the nurse nodded to acknowledge me and left. All the nurses had witnessed Carla's behaviour. She looked up and spoke through a stuttering sob.

"I'm here b-b-because I want to know why my own f-f-father is in-in-investigating me."

"What do you mean?"

"A man named Huber arrived at my door yesterday. He said he was investigating a case for you. Wanted to know if I had any grudges against you. Had the audacity to ask me outright if I had used anyone to follow you."

"Wait, Carla. I didn't ask Huber to investigate you. That shouldn't have happened. He's helping me find out what happened to Grandma. I so wish you could meet her."

Unconvinced, her sobbing intensified.

"You never came to my home to visit me, but now you send someone else. As if I'm a criminal."

Carla was right. She lived alone in a tiny Kreuzberg flat above a Turkish coffee shop, overlooking Landwehrkanal. Our past relationship meant I had only dared venture there once.

Her head tilted towards me and shook. Cold blue eyes, tinged with red, stared through a watery pool of tears. The elder of my two children by a couple of years, Carla looked ten years older than her brother. Her once-delicate features showed the signs of a life hard lived. A failed marriage, a lost baby and her rage. So much rage. Wiping tears on her sleeve, she reached into her bag, putting on a childish voice.

"I've brought you these."

She handed me a packet of cookies, slumping into the chair near my bed, eyes darting around the walls.

"My favourite. Thank you."

I put the Bahlsen biscuits in my bedside cupboard, next to the twelve packets already there, surrendering the slightest of smiles to her as she calmed.

"The irony of his question is that I've often felt like *I've* been followed in Berlin. On the U-Bahn, in the Tiergarten. I'm sure a man followed me here today from my DKP meeting. He stopped when I reached the hospital gates and turned to leave."

I nodded sympathetically, my mind split over whether she was relaying reality to me or describing the hallucinations that had so often come with her schizophrenia. But my own experiences and now Johann's admission made her story more believable.

For years, we could not be together in the same room. Like a dog with a bone, it became her obsession to extract information about my role in the war. I always remained silent on the topic. It wouldn't have helped to open the well and create more unhappy feelings for both of us. On occasion, my reticence irked her to violence and she would beat me with clenched fists.

"Have you taken your meds today?"

"No. I hate taking them. You know that. Why did you hire that crackpot Huber? Was he in the Gestapo? He looks old enough."

"Of course not. Hopefully, he'll find out what happened to Grandma. The part about being followed is true. I've felt it my whole life."

Carla stared at me a while, her hard features softening.

"I've always tried to love you, Father, but you never explained to me why you left America, or how many innocent people you killed in the Luftwaffe. I know you're dying, and it makes me sad. You talked to me so little as a child. I just want you to answer my questions."

She had berated me for years. Her Communist Party membership, a reaction to her mother's 'bourgeoisie materialism', just made things worse.

"We've been through all of this over and over, Carla. I had no choice."

"There's always choice, Father. ALWAYS!"

Her voice had risen, the way it always did before she flew into a rage. I put my hand to my forehead. It was damp, my heart beat hard in my chest. She was right: I had never revealed my true feelings to Carla or her brother.

"Please. We'll talk about this another day. I'm exhausted."

Her demeanour instantly transformed, anger replaced by a timid pity.

"I'm so sorry, Father. I didn't mean to upset you. Shall we play Skat?"

"Do you mind if I rest, Carla? Save it for next time."

I gave her a smile and she poured me a glass of water, handing it to me with a promise.

"I'll come again Tuesday. Enjoy your cookies."

*

Jan, the elderly orderly, cursed in his native Dutch as he bashed my wheelchair into the swing door, crushing his knuckles. Parking it in my favourite spot in the hospital social room, which I had sarcastically nicknamed *Regentenbau* after Prince Luitpold's baroque concert hall, he faced me with a pained expression on his face.

"You happy here, boss? I've other passengers waiting."

I nodded.

"Thanks, Jan. I hope your hand's okay. Will you collect me at lunchtime?"

"Sure thing. Enjoy your tunes."

I was the only patient here, as usual. Most in this part of the hospital were too sick to leave their beds.

At the far end, a large window overlooked the grounds, flooding the room with light from the changing sky outside. Four tall oak trees stood like guards around the pond below, their leaves whooshing as the wind curled around them. Light from the sun glistened on them as they vibrated. I saw the smiling faces that had greeted the *New York* on its arrival into the city.

The ever-present smell of tobacco flooded my brain with memories. How I would love a cigarette now. I wheeled my chair slowly around the room, viewing the paintings, drawings and photographs on the walls that hid the awful textured, yellow floral wallpaper beneath them. Most were portraits of past and present doctors at the hospital or of the industrialists who had subsidised it.

Arriving at the long white table against the wall, adjacent to the window, I smiled to myself. There sat a Hacker Centurion record player, flanked by two speakers and, to the right, a flip-top wooden box containing, at my last count, thirty-two long-playing records and a small vinyl-cleaning set. I began thumbing through the familiar collection just as a sudden downpour of rain battered the window.

There were plenty of popular LPs by George Harrison, Peter Maffay, Roy Black and The Monkees but, thankfully, some classical and jazz albums too. I fingered the worn, frayed covers, examining the pictures and tipping a few free to check their condition. My search stopped at Billie Holiday's 'Strange Fruit', a recording I had heard many times in Manhattan but only recently understood its meaning.

Pulling the vinyl free of its cover, middle finger at the centre of the record, thumb supporting the edge, I moved it towards the turntable, but one of my tremors shook it free of my grasp. Falling to the floor on its edge, it chipped. Still playable, I placed it on the record player and lifted the arm, its handle letting the stylus drop gently down, picking up the sound of many scratches. I shut my eyes, listening to the melancholic trumpet introduction, my mind drifting back to memories of Frau Schubert's bookstore.

I must have fallen asleep, just for a moment, because I woke to find a man in a dripping-wet mac standing before me.

"Didn't know you were a jazz fan, Bachmann. You surprise me."

Huber's appearance unnerved me. A sense of fear and anticipation stole my words.

"Are you okay? Should I call a nurse?"

"No, no, I'm fine. I was deep in thought."

The repeated sound of the stylus having reached the end of the record made me turn to scoop it away. I continued.

"My only moments of genuine joy in this place come while listening to jazz. My body is imprisoned in this waiting room for God, but with music my mind can still roam free."

Bored with my eulogy, he interrupted.

"Very poetic. Well, this isn't just a social visit. I've brought someone here to meet you."

"Oh? Who?" I scanned the room. "And where are they?"

He smiled, moving back to the door and opening it. A young woman, no older than twenty-five, stepped inside. They spoke for a moment before she left him at the door and walked purposefully towards me. She was slender, dressed in a baggy red Tangerine Dream T-shirt with a picture of a melted LP on its front, a long brown cardigan and flared blue jeans. Stopping two metres from my chair, she stood a while, fingering her aqua-blue necklace and staring at me through her fringe.

"Are you Herr Bachmann?"

"Yes. Who are you?"

She was awkward, intense, pausing as if to remind herself.

"Charlotte. Lotte, if you like. I'm a magazine journalist. Could I ask you a few questions?"

I shifted my body weight down and back, shuffling to a more upright position in my chair, glancing across to the door to see that Huber had already left. My only experience of journalists was that bastard from our gymnasium who ruined Timo's life with his fictional story.

"Who do you work for? What would you want from me?"

"The *Morgenpost* ran a piece initiated by Herr Huber last week. It mentioned you had been in the Luftwaffe. I work for *Der Prüfer*. We're running a feature with old servicemen looking back on their wartime experiences. Expressing how they now feel about the war. A chance to get things off your chest."

I maintained a sceptical stare, saying nothing, wondering how Huber thought any of this would help his mission. It all sounded suspicious.

"I've no desire to talk to you. People don't want to hear about the war now anyway."

Her body stiffened, fists clenched by her side. I was certain her eyes glistened.

"We've trawled the records already, Herr Bachmann. There are mentions of your service in Africa. A notation that you received an Iron Cross."

"Yes. I've two of those cursed things. Locked away, like my memories."

My defiance dented her confidence. Her head dropped. But after a few moments she looked up, eyes pinned on mine, and in them I saw a familiarity.

"Herr Bachmann, did you give a talk about your life at the University of Tübingen in the summer of 1958?"

Her forensic question stunned me. I was certain I had not mentioned my academic career to Huber. Perhaps there was some written record of my first lecture, but it seemed unlikely.

"How on earth do you know that?"

She did not answer, and at that moment, Huber reappeared through the door.

He strode towards us, trailed by Jan, calling out: "Charlotte. We must leave. Herr Bachmann is due back on his ward."

Our eyes remained locked on each other until Jan's hands clamped on the handles to my chair, and we began to move.

"Jan, wait."

I reached out and grabbed Lotte's wrist, looking up at her.

"Young lady, I don't know who you really are or how you know this precise detail of my life, but I must find out."

She gave a flicker of a smile, enough for me to know I would see her again.

*

A week later

Lotte sat bolt upright at the table in the hospital canteen, her notepad and pen in front of her.

"Good morning, Herr Bachmann."

She smiled as I was wheeled to the table, reaching into her coat pocket, pulling out a small, greaseproof paper-wrapped parcel.

"Here, I brought you these. Thought they might cheer you up."

Unfolding the warm paper, I found two freshly baked, sticky *Krullers* inside.

"My favourite. Would you like one?"

She nodded, reaching across the table. I noticed immediately the silver ring she wore on her middle finger. Its polished, square flat face, framed by the three supporting branches of the ring itself, bore an intaglio German eagle. Father wore the same design, as a signet ring, and for a moment his clenched fist loomed large in my face.

"Where did you get that ring?"

Lotte leaned back in her chair, her eyes widening.

"It was my grandmother's. I never met her. She died in the war. Mother wanted me to have something of hers. Why do you ask?"

"It looks familiar, that's all."

We gazed at each other across the table, a half-century between us. She had already written her first question at the top of the page and cleared her throat to begin. I interrupted.

"I know you want to ask me questions, but you'll have no answers before you tell me how you knew I lectured at Tübingen."

She peered down at her notepad, then glanced across to her right, anywhere but to look at me. Then I felt the table vibrate as she unconsciously jiggled her legs up and down before looking me directly in the eyes.

"I'm not a journalist, Herr Bachmann. We can leave that pretence behind. But I'd still like to know all about you."

"If you're not a journalist, who the hell are you?"

She stared at me again, unable to express the words that circled her brain. A single tear moved slowly down her cheek, and she ran out of the door.

25

THE VISITORS

St Marien-Krankenhaus Hospital, Berlin
November 1976

Through drug-hazed eyes, I glimpsed my reflection in the handprint-smeared mirror outside the treatment room. A frail, distorted shadow man, I appeared swollen out of shape by the knitting-needle jab to my shoulder.

The orderly marched me back to the ward, passing Davor's now empty, neatly made bed on the way. I stared at it, swallowing hard, knowing it would not be long before my bed lay vacant too.

I had thought about Lotte and my unanswered question all week. Helped to bed, my shaking left hand navigated nose and ears to land my reading glasses and lift a folded newspaper close. Before I had read a single story, I heard the sound of a woman clearing her throat and looked up to see Lotte shuffling slowly towards me.

Stopping at the end of my bed, she gazed at me through her long fringe.

"Herr Bachmann, I've some things to tell you. Given your health, I'm worried it may be too much."

I spoke softly to her.

"I'm okay. I don't want you to keep anything back. Please, sit down."

She nodded as she sat, her eyebrows drawn together, then paused, reading through some notes before laying them on the bed.

"Have you ever thought someone was watching or following you, Herr Bachmann? Like in the movies?"

I narrowed my eyes, memories and conversations flickering through my mind. The watcher in the yard at home in Halbe, shadowy figures in Washington Square Park and Berlin. My children too: Carla's 'madness', now Johann, sure he'd been followed.

She looked down, exhaling slowly and noisily. I wondered if she was simply replaying what I had told Huber.

"My mother has told me so much. Herr Bachmann, it's time for me to tell you who I really am."

I felt afraid to know, as if this young woman might unleash a past worse than the one I had tried to forget. My mind raced. Could she be working for the American authorities? Had they hunted me down now? I had no paperwork to prove they had released me from prison all those years ago. Or perhaps Aleks' mother had commissioned Lotte before her death? I replied calmly.

"Go ahead. It's about time you did."

She stared at the ground, deep in thought, before beginning in a voice that sounded like a mother reading to a child at bedtime.

"Do you remember a young woman visiting you at home in Tübingen? Shortly after your family left you. She told you all about her life growing up in Ecuador with her grandfather."

My brain went into overdrive. It was very hazy. I had drunk heavily for a time after Miriam and the children left. But I did remember. That girl had also been in my first lecture.

"Yes, I remember. She had red hair and was pregnant. It seemed odd she had visited me. Why?"

"That woman is my mother."

"So, the swollen belly she stroked on my couch is you?"

She nodded, smiling.

"The thing she did not tell you during that visit is that she is also your half-sister."

"What?"

"Please, let me explain. Mother told me that my grandmother, Agnieszka, lived in Przemyśl at the start of the war."

"Przemyśl? That's where my father worked for Herr Weigl."

She nodded, reaching into her bag and handing me an old photograph. Its subject was smiling, her elegant features, luminescent, burning through the grain.

"Your grandmother's beautiful."

"Was. She died in an American bombing raid near the end of the war. I knew nothing about Grandfather until last month. Mother wouldn't talk about him. But I kept pushing until one day she told me his name was Karl. Karl Bachmann. My mother always wanted to meet the only relative she had left."

I slowly shook my head, wishing I could leave my bed and pace the ward.

"That's my father, Lotte. You're making this up. He didn't have a daughter. Did Huber put you up to this? What do you want from me?"

"By the time Mother was born, your father was already dead. The SS killed him on the San bridge."

"The SS? I had been told a Jewish gang killed him. Why would the SS want him dead?"

"I'll tell you all about my great-grandfather Eryk later. He had letters from the Nazi leader, Herr Frank. Their plan had always been to take control of Weigl's work. Karl Bachmann never knew he had another child. If it hadn't been for Huber's article, Mother would never have found you."

Sinking into my pillow, I tried to process this information. Make sense of it. I had inherited a half-sister and a half-niece. After a while, Lotte got to her feet and moved towards me, slowly landing her hand on my arm.

I looked up at her. "Tell me more about your mother."

She closed her eyes for a moment, breathing hard, before beginning.

"My mother's name is Faustyna. She was a little girl when Great-Grandfather took her to Ecuador, as the war ended. He knew the Americans would execute him for his services to the Nazis if they ever found him."

Lotte told me how her mother had hated growing up there, with stray dogs wandering the streets, barking day and night, and noisy Italians arriving in hordes every week. Her great-grandfather had drunk heavily and paid her little attention. In the winter of 1956, his housemaid found him dead in his Zamora house, in the foothills of the Andes. Her mother became an orphan, but a rich one, inheriting two tonnes of gold from her grandfather's estate, and set about planning her return to Europe.

"She'd no close family left but wrote to friends back home. They helped her obtain a place at university in Germany. She started at Tübingen the same year as you."

"Why didn't she reveal who she was at the time?"

Lotte looked at her watch.

"Think about it. Would you have believed her?"

"This doesn't get me any closer to understanding why me and my children have been followed for so long?"

"There is more to my story, Uncle, much more. But I must go now. Get some rest."

*

I woke early and gazed into the majestic ash tree nearest the window. The diamond shapes in the bark reminded me of the wire perimeter fences at Pingley. Strangely, I thought about the regimented stability of life there for a while, perhaps a reaction to my mind's attempt at processing what Lotte had told me and the churn of questions I still had. At eight o'clock, Edna woke me with toast and a cup of milky coffee. She appeared flustered.

"Oskar, Huber's here already. I've told him visiting time starts at two, but he has an old woman with him who must leave Berlin this morning. I've spoken to Sister Keller. She will allow it. Sit up."

My heart began to pound in anticipation. Could Huber have found Mother and brought her here? I rehearsed what I might say to her, how I might make up for these decades apart. But as Edna moved away from my bed, Huber appeared, and with him a wave of disappointment. His companion was tall, her manly frame bent over, resting heavily on a stick, shoulder-length white hair brushed back and held in place by a thick purple band. It was not my mother.

As they arrived at the end of my bed, Huber's bloodshot eyes and lazy stagger gave away his hangover. I could not help thinking the old woman would have been better not to hang onto him. He raised a hand to greet me.

"Herr Bachmann. I've brought you someone I know you'll be pleased to meet."

The old woman released her grip of Huber's arm and steadied herself on the end of the bed. She raised her drooped head a little, high enough to fix a gaze on me through her thick glasses. A warm smile spread across her face, deepening its thick wrinkles and shrinking her eyes. And then she spoke, her voice as frail as her frame.

"Oskar?"

I nodded. Her stooped shoulders heaved and shook. Huber pulled a dark-pink handkerchief from the old woman's jacket pocket, reaching across to remove her glasses and dab her eyes for her. After a minute, she composed herself, slowly lifting her head again in defiance of her years. This time she spoke resolutely, as if giving evidence in a court of law.

"I'm Thelka. Thelka Zuzana Isternitz."

I looked at Huber and pointed to my bedside chair. He helped her sit down then made his exit.

She leaned forward slowly to lay her hand on mine. It was bony, misshapen, splattered with brown spots, but warm and steady.

"I'm so pleased that I can sit here now. I made a promise to your poor mother many years ago. I thought God would take me before I could honour it."

Resting on my left arm, I hauled myself up on the bed.

"Please, how did you know my mother?"

"Aneta was my closest friend. We met in Berlin before you were born."

Frau Isternitz's eyes dwelled on me, the same eyes that might have gazed upon Mother, listening to her woes all those years ago. They spoke to me without her needing to say a word. I examined every centimetre of Frau Isternitz's deeply lined face, waiting for her to speak her secrets to me.

"How did Herr Huber find you?"

She explained that Huber had tracked down Thomas Kahlert, the great grandson of her and Mother's Berlin employer, in the United States. He had kept possession of the family records, including details of previous employees, and was able to confirm Frau Isternitz had been in employment at the same time as Mother. Then it was a case of tracking her down in Czechoslovakia.

My eyes filled with tears as Frau Isternitz described how she and Mother had worked together as servants in the big house in Charlottenburg at the start of the Great War. The same house Mother and I had visited together at the time of the Berlin Olympic Games.

"I cannot stay very long, dear Oskar. I'm leaving for Prague later this morning. But I had to take this chance to see you. To tell you to your face how much your mother loved you. I know your childhood was a difficult one."

"Is my mother dead, Frau Isternitz?"

She buried her chin for a moment in the elephant-ear-lapelled jacket she wore, before looking up and nodding gently, her eyes glistening. A lump of phlegm caught in her throat, strangling her words as she began.

"She refused to leave the house early. We had to leave her behind. *SS-Hauptscharführer* Palitzsch sent patrols out every month, dragging undesirables off to camp. We received warning from an informer we knew. I had sons to protect, but she wanted to stick it out. I didn't understand her."

"Wait. Why were you undesirables?"

She explained how the SS had returned to the house the following day, kicking in the front door, smashing windows, ransacking every room. Not a drawer, cupboard or sideboard had been left untouched. Frau Isternitz had gone straight to her ground-floor bedroom, to a little silhouetted picture of a black apple tree, a bird in it, cat on the ground. Mother had given it to her as a gift.

"It was still on the wall. As I pulled it free..."

She fumbled in her pocket.

"This fell out. She always wore it."

Squinting, I could make out an eight-branched candlestick embedded in a small gold-coin pendant.

"I knew your mother might still be alive. It was a signal."

"I've never seen this before, but it can't be Mother's. It's a menorah, isn't it?"

Her eyes fixed on mine, she nodded.

"The truth is, I don't know exactly the moment your mother died."

I clasped my hand down on hers, holding it as hard as my tremors would allow. She leaned into me, gently, the smell on her clothes bringing back childhood memories. Her face, inches away from mine, shone with tears as I sobbed beside her like a lost little boy.

At that moment, Huber reappeared.

"Frau Isternitz, we must go now if you are to meet your friend and make the train home."

The old woman looked up, her present mind still trawling her memories.

"There's much more to tell you. I'm sorry I don't have more time."

Bowing her head, she pulled three envelopes from her handbag and laid them on the bed.

"These will tell you what you need to know. Your mother made friends with a guard who smuggled them out for her. She had a splendid memory. Read them in order. The dates are all visible. She had nothing to be ashamed of."

I had no time to ask what she meant. Frau Isternitz struggled to her feet, held onto Huber's arm and planted a long, warm kiss on my forehead.

"Your mother was always proud of you, Oskar."

*

An hour after she left, the envelopes sat exactly where Frau Isternitz had placed them on the bed. I had gazed at them, suspended in a place between inertia and motion, ignorance and enlightenment. I knew I must read my mother's hand, these memos from the past, but part of me was afraid to.

Eventually, I said a prayer under my breath and leaned slowly forward to gather them. Although only paper, they felt heavy in my hands. I examined the first letter, dated February 1943, putting the other two in my drawer. Holding it close to my nostrils, I hoped to sense even a hint of that comforting lemony scent of my mother. I squinted through my spectacles and peered through the scratched lens of the ward's magnifying glass but couldn't detect a location of posting.

Pulling the letter delicately from the envelope, I noticed it was slightly frayed along its folds, the handwriting inside it partially obscured. I would fill in the gaps.

My dearest Thelka,

The sight of Mother's handwriting brought back the sound of her voice in my head. I closed my eyes shut for a moment, then continued.

In my many hours alone in this place, I often think of our time working together for the Kahlerts in that big Berlin house. Do you remember the day they entertained Eryk Stanislaw?

A name from my past returning, but there must be thousands of Stanislaws. A film of my old friend in Manhattan played in my mind, breaking off with a vision of his flaccid body in the shadow of the Empire State.

I'll never forget. He knocked so loudly on the door I thought that old Berliner bear knocker would fall off. The day before had been the hottest of the year. We spent the afternoon in that enormous cellar, where the servants once lived, creating a catalogue of the Kahlerts' dusty wine collection. French Chenin

Blanc, Grenache and Pinot Noir, Spanish Tempranillo and Mazuelo and a mass of German Rieslings. I felt like a little girl as we explored every inch of the room by candlelight. There was all manner of curiosity in its dark corners. Do you remember being spooked as the flickering light illuminated the faces of those old, musty bisque dolls, black-spotted with damp, and having a mock battle with that collection of sabres and pistols?

Our special place was on the far left, up a steep set of wooden steps, through that tiny brick archway you became stuck in once. Oh, how I laughed. The platform up there was secluded, much warmer than the rest of the cellar. The old crates and beer and brandy barrels made excellent tables and chairs as we sat and talked, drinking our Schultheiss.

My eyes moved over the words quickly, searching for significance. The next sentence gave it, and I slowed, breath stuck in my chest, reading them over and over.

I told you I didn't want Emil's father to come home from the war.

The words were cold, brutal. For all their fights, I could not believe Mother would wish Father dead.

Removing my glasses to rub my eyes, I continued.

When Herr Stanislaw stepped into the hallway, he eyed the row of us young women paraded to greet him, like a slave-owner choosing his next chattel. I knew you liked him, Thelka. It was obvious. But he went straight to me, despite the thick gold band

340

on my finger, asking if I was Polish and if I would help him with his bags. You all watched, giggling, from the doorway as he boasted to me about his new car. I mean, it was pretty. That lustrous black paintwork, the seamless curve of the mudguards over the wheel tops, the polished chrome headlamps. I clearly remember the shape of the front radiator grill. It was the same as the mirror that hung in my quarters, and I saw my reflection staring back at me. I might have wanted to ride with Herr Stanislaw but when he asked, I pretended not to hear.

Herr Kahlert was in his element that night at the Deutsches Theater. I remember him chanting, "On the Rhine, on the Rhine, on the German Rhine, we all want to be guardians!" as the small band played 'Die Wacht am Rhein' in the foyer. People clapped. They were being polite, I think. We had tickets to see Immer Feste Druff! *It was the first time I'd visited a theatre. I only had the opportunity because we'd kept the Kahlerts' guests happy. I'd nothing suitable to wear. Frau Kahlert loaned me a silk hobble-skirted evening gown. It was a size too big and constantly slipped off my shoulders. I received plenty of lingering looks from the old men. As we moved into the theatre auditorium, Stanislaw set his eyes on me. He was charming and told me about his work for Bayer.*

I felt giddy and breathless on the balcony, dazzled by the theatre's chandeliers, its ornate golden boxes, the display of Berlin finery. A fish out of water and yet where I belonged all at the same time. Stanislaw sat me next to him. As the pianist shaped hands below me, moving them like a puppet as he played Walter Kollo's music, an intense, patriotic fervour swept through the audience. Stanislaw's eyes dwelled on me for too long. I felt uneasy and was glad to be outside as we all walked

341

south towards the Spree and the illuminated Brandenburg Gate.

The world Mother's evocative words created in my mind seemed alien. It was so far from how I knew her. I continued.

I showed you a photograph once, Thelka, of me in a crowd in the lobby of the Kempinski Hotel. It was taken on this night. As we arrived, Frau Kahlert fondly greeted the Kempinski family, old friends of her father's from the wine trade. The photograph, organised by the Kempinskis, was published in Die Woche, *to show the hotel was 'business as usual', despite the outbreak of war. There I was, next to Stanislaw, as the concertina camera, with its huge bell-shaped flash, snapped away. I wish you were in that picture. It reminds me of that time.*

The photograph! I could still remember it falling from my book in the Bad Harzburg cabin.

I have another big reminder, of course. After a salmon dinner, Herr Kahlert raised toast after toast to the Kaiser. I wasn't used to heavy drinking and Stanislaw had to help me to a waiting Schleissinger taxi.
Must go. Need to lie low. I'll post this and write more soon.
My love to you, Walter and the boys,
Aneta x

Why did Mother need to lie low? Where was she? Frau Isternitz had mentioned a camp. I looked up. Lotte had approached silently and now sat quietly in my chair.

"How long have you been there?"

She leaned in, resting an arm on the bed.

"A few minutes. You were totally absorbed. Are you okay?"

I tucked the letter back in its envelope.

"I really don't know. I'm utterly confused. Huber brought an old friend of my mother's to see me. She left some letters of hers."

Distracted, she nodded sympathetically, reaching into her bag to pull out a newspaper, opening the front page and folding it back.

"I wanted to show you this."

On page three was a picture of a group of young people stood outside Frau Schubert's bookstore with banners, under a headline that read, 'Campaign to Keep Beacon of Freedom Open'.

"What's this?"

"The people in the picture are my friends. We're not going to let the bookstore go without a fight."

I smiled and thanked her, thinking about the few real friends I had made over the course of my life. They had all died on me. This young woman might be the only friend who would not let me down. At that point, literally at the moment when I could see the determination to help in her eyes, I made a decision.

26

COMING HOME

St Marien-Krankenhaus Hospital, Berlin
December 1976

I woke early the next day, a little before six a.m., the ward unusually still, only the repeated cooing of a dove disturbing the silence. For once, as soon as my eyes blinked open, I felt alert. Trapped energy in my legs, with nowhere to escape to, made them twitch and shake. Lotte would visit again later. I had to read the second letter before she arrived. Reaching into my drawer, I pulled out the envelope, noting the posting date of March 1943. The letter inside had perished badly along its folded edges. Putting on my glasses, I rested it on the bed beside me, pushing the separated sides together, leaning as close to it as possible on my elbow.

Dear Thelka,

It's early morning here. The rhythms of this place mean I must write when I can and hope there are opportunities to smuggle my letters out. I prefer not to dwell on my predicament, other than to say I'm living in a small room with bunk beds, shared with a family from Šlapanice (the father worked at the sugar factory there) and another single woman called Anna

*Haas, who never stops talking. There is never much to eat and
I've lost a lot of weight. I noticed that my period has stopped.
I'm not sure if it's my age, as I know the same has happened to
younger women here.*

I slumped back on my pillow, letting the decades-old picture
described by Mother settle in my head. I blinked my eyes shut.
Opening them, the ward appeared a blur, a salty tear resting on
my lip. Mother had been in a camp. Wiping my face with my
pyjama sleeve, I carefully unfolded the letter and read on.

*Indulge me, my dear friend, let me finish reminiscing
about that day in Berlin. You found me sobbing the following
morning, on that sofa, below the huge painting of Johann
Kahlert III. You were kind, as always. But I didn't tell you the
truth of those tears. Now, while I can, I must.*

*It wasn't missing Emil's second birthday that upset me.
Stanislaw and I had flirted. We spoke many times in doorways,
in his room. He paid me much attention. I knew he liked me.
I liked him too. That evening after the theatre, he came to my
room in the night. He slipped into bed with me, and we made
love. When he got up to leave, I called out as he left my room.
I wanted him to stay with me. He rushed back, worried the
Kahlerts would wake up. That's when he spotted the menorah
pendant that had fallen to the floor when I pulled my clothes
off. I told him it wasn't mine and said I'd return it to its owner.*

*I remember the rumbling storm as I woke in the morning.
It felt like I was still in a dream, as I floated across the
carpet to the window. Gazing at the dramatic sky, a thick
bolt of lightning lit it up, hitting the ground on the horizon.*

A powerful, deep and rolling thunderclap followed, echoing across the atmosphere, seeming to penetrate deep into my fragile brain. I had a terrible vision as I looked into the mirror. I saw Karl dragging himself from a rain-soaked hole, torn to pieces by gunfire. It was my guilt getting the better of me. Little did I know that by that time he had been sent home. Over the next few days, Stanislaw expressed his feelings to me several times and gave me that opal bar brooch. You know what happened months later, Thelka. I'll never regret that. I hope he's safe wherever he is now.

It looks like they may move us out of this place in a couple of weeks. I'll try to let you know. Pray for me.

Aneta x

Turning to my pillow in silence, my body felt heavy now. I screwed the letter into a ball, keeping my fist compressed tightly around it. The sounds around me in the ward shrank into the background.

A man I had never met was my real father. The man I called Father was not. I was the product of a brief, illicit union.

The most wounding element of all of this was the life I had wasted trying to understand the complexities of what was, in fact, a very simple issue. Psychoanalysing Karl Bachmann's actions had been a futile exercise. He was an averagely intelligent, egocentric man, who cared little for anyone but himself. The reason he beat me, simple: he knew I was another man's child.

*

Breathless, Lotte sat down opposite me, dull light from the grubby windows illuminating a sheen of sweat on her forehead. The St Marien-Krankenhaus canteen was empty but for us. She seemed concerned, shocked at my condition, sat in a wheelchair, specially adapted with a support to stop my head drooping. She made sure I was comfortable.

"I read the second of Mother's letters, Lotte. It would seem your great-grandfather was my real father. Did you know this?"

She looked away, biting her lip.

"This is all such a web, Uncle, I didn't want to reveal too much all at once. I worried it might be too much. But, yes, I've known a long time. Mother has many letters, recovered from the house in Zamora."

"Why will your mother not come and see me?"

"She will when she feels she can. She suffers with depression."

"Maybe talking to me would help with that. I can't bring myself to read the third of Mother's letters yet."

"The right moment will come, Uncle."

She looked down, exhaling slowly and noisily.

"My great-grandfather watched you your whole life. And your children. He had connections, people working for him all over the place."

"Why was your great-grandfather so wealthy?"

"He was a businessman, lived much of his life in Poland."

"I knew a Stanislaw in New York. Surely a coincidence? He was a friend until I discovered his true nature. How many children did your great-grandfather have? Other than your grandmother?"

"Two children: my grandmother and a son. His name was Aleksander. He died in Manhattan. Under a taxi."

Her last sentence made me shake uncontrollably, a movie of Stanislaw's last moments playing in my mind, the smell of my New York City prison cell vivid. Lotte stood, resting a hand on me.

"I've read the newspaper articles over and over. Something never seemed right."

My eyes clouded with tears as the realisation of who Aleksander was struck home.

"I never meant to kill him, Lotte. It was an accident. I'll always remember. He tried to call something out to me as the taxi hit him."

"Perhaps it was, 'You're my brother', Uncle Oskar?"

I laughed through my sob.

"So, I lost a family member that day, but now I've gained two."

She sat back down, resting her hand on mine.

"I'm not proud of my side of the family, Uncle. But everything I've learned about you, when doing my research, made me want to meet you. There's more to my story."

She explained how Eryk Stanislaw had been a senior executive at IG Farben. His role in mass-producing the typhus vaccine, mainly for the Wehrmacht, had made him extremely wealthy. Then she produced a tattered piece of paper from her pocket.

"This is the remains of a letter from your mother to my great-grandfather, Uncle. My mother found it when she cleared belongings from Great-Grandfather's house."

Hands still shaking, I held the delicate piece of paper in my hand. It was clearly the second page of a letter and in my mother's hand.

I'm no longer the servant girl. The time has come, brave or stupid, for me to open my mouth and speak up.

That pendant you saw on the floor in my room, the one I denied, was mine. It belonged to me. I'm a Jew, even if necessity has meant obscuring my true identity to survive. On 17 May 1915, I gave birth to a baby boy. His name is Oskar, and he's now a fine young man. He's YOUR son, Herr Stanislaw. My husband knows this. He's taken out his anger on the boy repeatedly. It's possible for me to prove you're the father, with no shadow of doubt. As I write this, Oskar's spending the day fishing with his grandfather, blissfully unaware of his origins.

My offer to you is this. You'll support our son financially and use your position of power to open opportunities for him and my family. In return, I'll keep the fact of Oskar's parentage secret from those in the Nazi hierarchy, on who you rely for your wealth and who would take an interest. Now they have complete power, this is surely of more acute significance.

For the immediate future, you can write to me at this address:

Bei Herr Gumpert,
Seeschlösschen,
Berlinerstrasse 41,
15746 Groß Köris,
Brandenburg, Deutschland

Sincerely,
Aneta Bachmann

I suddenly felt an acute awareness of every sound, movement and smell on the ward. A sense of great shame came over me. Despite all the evidence, I had never connected the dots and come to terms with the fact that Mother was a Jew. Perhaps I had been afraid. The terrible possibility of what the Nazis would do to her too awful to bear, or perhaps I was just plain blind. But now it all made sense. The Polish grandparents we were not allowed to meet; Mother dyeing her hair blonde; her disappearance in Czechoslovakia. It made my father's sympathy for Nazism and cooperation with Frank appear even more unbearable. I felt anger, too, that Mother had kept so much from me, not only her heritage but my own, and the real reason my father had beaten me.

*

The doctors injected me in the morning; the effects would last all day. I felt alert, my synapses clicking quickly, bringing thoughts and memories together like a tapestry.

I had not seen Huber in weeks. An invoice had been received by Nurse Edna and, with most of his fee earned, I did not expect to see him again. I was surprised, therefore, when he arrived at the end of my bed in the afternoon with a man, dressed in suit and tie, of similar age to me for company.

"Hello, Herr Bachmann. You've not paid me yet, but I do not intend to charge you extra for finding this gentleman. I will ask Edna to arrange payment with you. Thanks for the assignment."

Huber nodded to me, shook the man's hand and left.

350

The man stared at me a while, saying nothing, before moving towards the seat by my bed.

"May I sit?"

I nodded. He sat, gazing at me again, then began.

"I'm Hermann Zinger. A former Luftwaffe pilot, just like you. I wrote you a letter twenty years ago. Do you remember it? I'm hoping you actually read it."

"Herr Zinger. Yes, I remember. I kept your letter, of course, but it left me with so many questions."

He nodded slowly.

"I'm here to say sorry once more."

His voice broke with emotion as he spoke. He bowed his head for a moment.

"The doctors told me you don't have long left."

I smiled across to him. "Please, strange things happen in war. I'm so pleased you've come. Are you still living in Reus, wasn't it?"

He smiled back.

"Well remembered. I'm still in Spain. We moved to the Bay of Biscay, San Sebastian. Incredible that Herr Huber tracked me down."

He paused, deep in thought.

"I didn't tell you the whole story in my letter because I didn't know it at the time. I know some more now."

"Please, go ahead, Herr Zinger."

"I was chosen for the mission due to my many awards for shooting accuracy. In theory, you can demobilise a plane in the desert without destroying it as long as you hit the right targets. The order to shoot your Junkers down came from Rommel himself."

I shook my head. Just as in the desert I had been baffled by my rescue by a Brandenburger, Zinger's revelation left a huge question.

"But why, Herr Zinger? And why, as you said in your letter, were you instructed to keep me alive?"

"I only know the request came from a powerful civilian to whom the Reich owed much. I do not have a name."

Zinger might not have had a name, but I did.

*

The disclosures of the previous few days, by letter and in person, came to me in a great deluge as my own time drew to a close. I felt washed up on a beach full of deceit and misery but knew there was one more huge wave to come; its source, the tatty paper envelope containing the third of Mother's letters to Frau Isternitz. The envelope itself was white, not brown, and its contents did not reach its edges. On the front was a handwritten date, November 1943, in blue ink.

I pulled the pale-brown folded letter from the envelope and opened it. My eyes darted over its surface. It was more a form than a letter, with printed boxes, text and lines written on it in a hand that was not my mother's. On the top left were the words, 'Konzentrationslager Theresienstadt'. The only sign of her was a straggly signature in the bottom right-hand corner, followed by a tiny 'v.c'. The Nazi guards had censored most of the text. Mother was almost anonymous, as if her soul had already departed her no doubt feeble body. The precious words left on the page spread a warmth through my body as I read them.

Thank you for your letter. It makes me happy to know normal life continues.

Please promise me you'll find my son one day. Tell him that I love him with all my heart. He should feel no guilt. I know he will achieve his ambitions and make me proud.

*

Strange, perhaps, but the realisation of why Papa beat me and Mama's loving farewell message from Theresienstadt provided me with some peace. The weight had lifted. That little black dot after the v.c (under duress) on her signature, her last act of defiance, ignored or missed by the ignorant SS, took on great meaning for me. I stared at it, the hairs on my neck erect, as Mother's spirit of kindness surrounded me. My mind played a film at double speed: her young face looking down on me; her soft, soothing voice; the sound of rushing water in the background; a warm, wet circle on my forehead from her kiss, cooled by the breeze; her straight back and jutting chin as she stood up to Father.

I cried quietly for a moment. Tears replaced by calm. My identity finally clear to me.

*

Over the next few days, when energy and spirit allowed, and I trusted my emotions to stay level, I read every word of Mother's letters again and processed what Lotte had told me. Realisation grew that Eryk Stanislaw, my father, had watched over me from a distance and, without me knowing it, controlled the highs and lows of my life. I questioned every key moment of my existence for signs of his hand. My journey to and expulsion from America, my early exit from the war, my friendships, even sweet Lotte. They all led back to him.

Knowing my life had been, in large part, controlled and influenced, made me desperate to achieve one thing during whatever time I had left. I must save the Frau Schubert Bücherstube.

*

Somewhere in the dark corners of my memory, I heard 'Durme, Durme', a Jewish lullaby. Appropriate now, for how I must sleep. Mother's voice, a tiny fragment to hold on to, repeating again and again. Through my eyelashes I saw a young doctor, one I had not seen before, reading my medical notes. An hour later, he returned with a nurse and told me they would try one last experimental treatment. He asked me to sign a waiver, which I did. Minutes later, they injected me. I felt alert, as if a young boy again, watching bees in a summer garden, but relaxed at the same time. My tremors subsided for the first time in days.

After morning coffee, Lotte arrived. Approaching my bed, she stopped mid-stride, eyes wide open, a broad smile spread across her face.

"Wow. You look so well today, Uncle. What did they put in your coffee?"

"They've given me some kind of miracle drug."

She lingered, pensively, at the foot of my bed.

"I've come to ask you something."

"There's nothing you can ask me or tell me now that would surprise me."

Swinging her bag off her shoulder, she nodded, hesitating for a moment, before sitting beside me.

"Do you still believe in God? I mean, now you've learned the truth of your life?"

"I'm not sure I do know the *truth* of my life. But, yes, I still believe in a god, just not the god of Karl Bachmann."

Lotte's blue-green eyes settled on me a while. We were flesh and blood. In family, there can be an unspoken understanding. I knew this now. All the words exchanged between me and Carla, the angst and division, the lack of understanding, had shrunk my soul. In Lotte's eyes, it seemed reborn. I thought of Mother in her Charlottenburg youth. Perhaps she had really loved Stanislaw.

"Lotte, do you know if Eryk Stanislaw ever mentioned my mother?"

It felt strange to me, but I hoped he had. I wished that my poor mother, who received no love from Karl Bachmann, had been thought of fondly by the man who fathered me. She shook her head.

"I don't know but I'll ask my mother."

"Thanks. Do you think she will ever come and visit me?"

"I've tried to persuade her, Uncle."

I smiled.

"What day is it today, Lotte?"

"Sunday. Why?"

"No. I meant, what date?"

"Seventeenth of November."

The initial 'buzz' from my injection seemed to wear off, and I dozed for a while, opening my eyes a few times to see Lotte intently reading a magazine. From my slumber, an old memory surfaced.

"Almonds."

She looked up from her copy of *Sybille* magazine and around the ward to see if a nurse was nearby.

"What? Are you okay?"

"I can still smell the almonds from the Pani Walewska cake she made for herself. Even though it was her day, Father moaned at her. 'Why don't you make Marmorkuchen?'"

Lotte sank in the chair.

"Umm, I'm sorry, Uncle. I don't know what you're talking about."

I turned to her.

"Today is Mother's birthday. This day in 1929, I gave her the first present I ever gave her. A French watercolour set in a wooden box. My gymnasium art teacher traded it to me in exchange for translating letters to his lover. I learned a few things from them."

Lotte grinned, putting her magazine down to listen more intently.

"That day was a Sunday too. I remember because we'd been to church that morning. Father berated Mother for failing to sing in church. She made her own music in the cart home though, humming 'Hey Falcons' as father stewed."

"What's that song? I've not heard it."

"A Polish folk song. Nice melody. Mother sang it often when Father wasn't around. Polish soldiers sang it in the Bolshevik War, but it's way older than that."

Reaching under my pillow, I brought out two envelopes. Inside one, a short message, which I had written then rewritten a dozen times. In the other, a banker's cheque. I handed them to Lotte one by one.

"I need you to help me. I want to commemorate my mother properly, make peace with myself. I can't do it alone. This one is for your mother."

I had not said the words out loud to her, but she knew how I wanted my life to end. She nodded solemnly and left.

*

The slowly spinning silvered-glass Christmas decoration, hung lopsidedly from the bedside lamp, captured my attention. It reminded me of those 'capped' Ju 88 bombs I'd often seen loaded at our Derna airbase.

Much of the previous few weeks had been a sedated blur, except for a few moments of lucidity where I had felt, more than seen, the quiet presence of Lotte by my side. Now a small crowd gathered around my bed. The departure lounge for Oskar Bachmann.

The miracle injections used to enliven me for a few hours took their toll. Those moments of clarity chipped away chunks of time, bringing death closer. But it was worth it.

My eyes cleared a little. I could see Johann and Miriam stood beside each other at the end of the bed. They seemed to give Lotte spiteful looks.

The doctor to my right tightened the cuff on my arm and pushed the five-centimetre needle into my vein one last time. These final minutes would be full of light. Lotte stood to my

357

left, squeezing my hand so tight, my fingers numbed. She continually glanced over her shoulder, finally becoming more relaxed as a stranger arrived before me. I did not know her and yet her face was somehow familiar. Lotte spoke slowly and quietly to me.

"Uncle. This is Faustyna. My mother. Your half-sister."

I saw a sadness in the woman's eyes but a faint smile on her face. She took my hand from Lotte and spoke, her eyes glistening.

"My brother, I am sorry it has taken me so long to come to you. I wanted you to know that, with your money and mine, I am buying the rights to the Frau Schubert Bücherstube. Lotte is going to help me run it. We'll call it Oskar's Bücherstube. I don't feel lost anymore."

She smiled.

Her words brought a last surge of happiness that raised the hairs on my neck. The spirits of my best friend and his father and my dear mother filled me. I knew my blood father's dirty money would help in the salvation of memory and knowledge.

I struggled to thank her but, just as in the desert nearly thirty-five years earlier, my tongue swelled, the words now forever trapped. She spoke gently to me again.

"Just before Grandfather Eryk died, he told of his lifelong affection for your mother. He tried, too late, to save her from the SS. She needn't have bribed him, Oskar. All the time he wanted you to succeed."

She let go of my hand as the bedside curtain opened again. A shaft of light was wrapped around the heads of the two people entering, who, at first, seemed joined together. As they slowly reached my bedside, I recognised one half as Frau Isternitz, the other a bearded stranger. The tasselled kittel draped across sloped shoulders revealed him to be a man of the Jewish faith. After Frau Isternitz left a final kiss on my forehead, he moved slowly to my side.

"I am Rabbi Schechter. Thank you for your letter. Be at peace now. The Almighty waits for you."

His cold hand laid on my scalp brought a moment of clarity. I had always imagined that the first time I stood in a lecture theatre to teach would be the defining moment of my life. It had been, but not in the way I expected. 'Leaving Fatherland' led me to Lotte. Her mother's presence in that Tübingen lecture room, then on my couch, was enough to connect me to my past, to my real destiny.

The rabbi stood back and the words of all the books I had ever read seemed to tumble from his lips as he held my letter before him, confessing my sins out loud. My failing eyes glanced around my bed one last time. There was no Carla, and my heart ached a little. This last goodbye might have given her some answers, some comfort.

But Mother was here with me. I could feel her presence now. I hadn't bought her that house in the Karkonosze Mountains, like I had promised. She forgave me though. I knew she did.

I rocked ever so gently in my bed. To and fro. A little less movement every time. Not, this time, to soothe my fear of Father, but to bring me nearer to Mother's love. And then, I moved no more.

A hush and a whisper. God is one.

AUTHOR'S NOTE

The story of my uncle Werner's crash in the North African desert, and his subsequent captivity as a prisoner of war in Lincolnshire, were familiar tales across the family dinner table as I grew up in Winchester in the 1970s and 80s. Hearing Mother recount childhood memories of her own dinner table in the 1940s was fascinating. They centred on her father, a former World War I gunner in the British Army, sharing conversation and Lincolnshire potatoes with his eldest daughter, twice imprisoned for being a conscientious objector; his Royal Navy son, an officer on the minesweeper, HMS *Rifleman*; and his daughter's boyfriend, a former reconnaissance crew member on a Luftwaffe Junkers 88.

That dinner table, and all its contradictions, struck a chord with me as did Mother's stories of her family hosting prisoners of war for Christmas dinner, and her mother gifting them sewing kits to send home to their own mothers. The scenes often played out in my mind, acting as an antidote to the jaded, polarised stories of war more familiar in comic books, novels and movies.

As I came to know my German family, and more of Werner's story, my urge grew to use it as inspiration to create my own novel. My research was extensive; life in Nazi Germany, the

Luftwaffe, the history of psychology and typhus vaccination, World War II in North Africa, et cetera. Over time, the story of *Leaving Fatherland* emerged and the book you hold in your hand arrived. In writing it, I believe I have matured as a writer, becoming more able to manage complexity in both character and storytelling.

View of North African desert, believed to be from the cockpit of writer's uncle's Ju-88, in summer 1942.

The chapters of this book set in Manhattan, Oskar's home as he studies in the hope of understanding why his father beat him, were inspired by my uncle's own pre-World War II studies in America. In real life, these took place 350 miles north of New York City, at the liberal Bates College in Lewiston, Maine. The most notable element in Werner's yearbook entry below is the way he refers to the Nazi regime: 'wild beasts'.

The Edmund S. Muskie Archives and Special Collections Library,
Bates College.

Other than events in Chapters Six, Seventeen, Eighteen and Nineteen—notably Oskar's visit to Berlin during the 1936 Olympic Games, his crash in the desert in a Ju-88, his capture and later imprisonment at Pingley Camp, falling in love with an 'English Rose' (my Aunty Roslyn), and the well-received speech at the Women's Institute, most of this story and its characters are fictional. The novel does, however, reference real events and places, and names of people who actually lived during the period.

CRANTHORPE
MILLNER
PUBLISHERS

Did you enjoy this book?

Why not leave a review, or email
digitalmarketing@cranthorpemillner.com to sign up to our
newsletter and receive advance copies of our upcoming titles.

www.cranthorpemillner.com